Mark,
Il enjoyed meeting you.
I hope you enjoy my novels.

Souther

Don Stanford

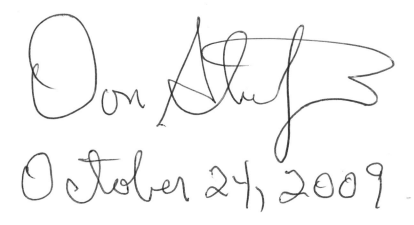

Don Stanford

October 24, 2009

Aberdeen Bay

Atlanta - Harbin - Beijing - Washington, D.C.

Aberdeen Bay
Published by Aberdeen Bay, an imprint of Champion Writers.
www.aberdeenbay.com

PUBLISHER'S NOTE

This is a book of fiction. Names, characters, places, and incidents are either the product of author's imagination or are used fictitiously. Any resemblance to actual persons, living or dead, business establishments, government agencies, events, or locales is entirely coincidental.

International Standard Book Number
ISBN-13: 978-1-60830-008-2
ISBN-10: 1-60830-008-0

Printed in the United States of America.

Foreword

As a native Louisianan, I love my state, but admit we have a mixed bag of citizens including those who are politicians. We are seen by many of the people in other states as being ignorant, corrupt, and backwards. While it is true that some of our citizens and too many of our politicians over the years have fit that description accurately, most of our people today are intelligent and moderately to well educated, and the bulk of our politicians are decent and forthright people.

In telling the story of Southern Kingdom, I have depicted only a segment of South Louisiana during the nineteenth century. There were two distinct societies living shoulder to shoulder in some respects, yet miles apart in others. Unfortunately, a man such as Adam Blythington could, during the time span this novel covers, commit crimes and live an immoral lifestyle without fear of word of these acts leaving the black community. The Ku Klux Klan played a large part in instilling fear among the black people, but other forces were at work as well.

In this book I have depicted several corrupt St. Landry Parish officials. To the best of my knowledge, St. Landry Parish had no corrupt judges, sheriffs nor candidates seeking those offices during the time span this book covers. Having had the privilege of meeting, and knowing personally, many of our elected officials - state, parish, and local - I can attest to their honesty and integrity.

There were landowners, such as Jacques Dupre', who treated their black employees fairly and decently. It is my hope that there were more men in South Louisiana during the period of time this book covers who shared the moral fiber of Monsieur Dupre'.

It is not my purpose to defend slavery (I have always found slavery to be an abhorrent institution) or to support the mistreatment of any human being regardless of race, color or creed. The reason I have written this book is to tell one of the stories that live somewhere inside of my brain and to entertain the reader. I have not set out to write an accurate history of the period of time following the Civil War. It is my desire that the reader finds this book both interesting and entertaining. If in some small way I enrich your life with my story, I am deeply gratified.

Lastly, I chose to write a book with a Louisiana setting and, more specifically, St. Landry Parish, because I have been told since I was a lad that one should always write about that with which one is most familiar. With the exception of my time spent in the United States Army and brief periods when my Father relocated the family because of his work, I have lived in St. Landry Parish, making my home near Opelousas, Louisiana.

Acknowledgements

I thank my Lord, Jesus Christ, for blessing me with whatever creative ability I possess, and for giving me this story. I thank my lovely wife, Carol, for believing in me, for encouraging me, for the countless hours she spent correcting my mistakes, and for acting as my secretary and one woman research department. I thank the countless friends and acquaintances who have been in prayer for me while I was writing this novel, and who continue to pray for me now. I thank my dear friend, Van (Jeep) Thompson for reading my manuscript and giving me positive feedback. I also thank my brother, Sherman Stanford who not only took the time to read my manuscript and reassure me that I had written a good story, but told me when I was only the tender age of twenty-six in words that got my attention, it was time to enroll in college or forget about higher education altogether.

As I look back on my life, thinking of the people who have been pivotal in my becoming a writer, certain individuals come to mind: My mother who made sure there were always books in our home and who imparted to me and my siblings her love of the written word; Miss Estelle Coco, my eighth grade teacher, who asked the class members to write a scarey story and chose mine as the winner; Mr. George Voinche, my tenth grade history teacher, who walked into the classroom one day, threw a piece of chalk my way to get my undivided attention, and then admonished me strongly for not using the intelligence God had given me; Mr. Sylvan Tassin, my English teacher throughout my highschool years, who kindly and patiently, but sternly, taught me his craft; Mr. Sidney Neck, my highschool principal, who was my "penpal" while I was serving in the army in Korea; and Mrs. Mary Dobie, the English Professor who helped me to believe I could be a writer. Last but certainly not least, I want to thank Aberdeen Bay for believing in me, and my novel, *Southern Kingdom*.

Southern Kingdom

Prologue

On a cold and overcast morning in early January of 1865, twenty-two year old Adam Blythington sat in his cramped London office. He looked around the office as though trying to identify familiar objects. His eyes settled on a black umbrella leaning near the office door. He had left the umbrella there to drip dry after walking the few blocks to his office in the rain; not rain really, more like moisture encapsulating his body. The umbrella had not kept the moisture off of his new suit. He breathed in the smell of damp wool. His body was still chilled from the damp cold. He picked up the copy of the *Times* he was reading earlier. Once again, he read the article about the American war between the states. The article predicted an end to the war within the next few months. The southern army had been routed in several battles and was in retreat.

Blythington's two older brothers were elated to learn that the war would soon end. Blythington Import and Export would soon be receiving bales of cotton that had been warehoused during the war. They envisioned the profits they would make once the blockades opened and ships began making their way to Britain with king cotton in their holds. The textile mills were hungry for the cotton they would turn into cloth.

Adam Blythington did not share in their joy. His father had left the bulk of the company to Edward, the eldest of the brothers. The middle brother, Timothy, had inherited a sufficient portion to ensure a life of fine living, provided the company continued to show a profit. Adam's share was a mere pittance in comparison. His income from the firm ensured that he would have to work for his brothers the remainder of his life to barely eke out a living. His brothers were able to gain membership in some of the finer men's clubs while he was only able to afford membership in a gentleman's club that catered to men of modest means.

He was unwilling to live out the rest of his life as an employee in his father's firm. It was an accident of fate that had made him the youngest of the three brothers. He felt he deserved to live as well as his older brothers.

The article in the *Times* might be the answer he had been seeking. The American President was determined that the south would be rebuilt and the union would be preserved. In the rebuilding, there should be opportunity for an intelligent young man with drive and ambition. He began to plan. His brothers should be willing to buy out his minor share in the firm. He had no hope of living comfortably from the sale of his share. If he could invest the money wisely in the rebuilding of the American south, there could be a fortune to gain.

Good sense dictated that it was best to consider his decision for a few days before approaching his brothers, but his impatience got the better of him. He walked to Edward's office and knocked on the door. Gershan Pottingham, Edward's assistant, ushered him into the anteroom where his small desk sat. It irritated Adam that he had to go through Pottingham in order to meet with his own brother. "I want to see Edward," Adam demanded. "The matter is urgent."

Pottingham looked at him as he would a street urchin. "Master Edward left instructions that he is not to be disturbed," Pottingham said. "You may return after two o'clock if you wish."

"I certainly do not wish to return later," declared Adam. "I want to see him now."

The door to Edward's office opened. "Pottingham, what is this all about? " he asked.

Adam strode to his brother. "I want to speak to you and Timothy about a private matter," he said. "I wish to speak to you now."

Edward looked at his younger brother. He had to admit he did not feel the fondness for Adam he felt for his brother, Timothy. Adam was entirely too volatile. "Could this not have waited?" he asked. "Timothy and I will be meeting in five minutes to discuss Blythington's strategy in regard to the cessation of hostilities in the colonies. We can see you after two o'clock."

Adam was irritated further. Why was he not asked to meet with his brothers on such an important matter? Timothy chose that moment to walk through the door. "Why the shouting?" he asked. "This certainly is not how gentlemen conduct business."

Adam did not want to be turned away, to be made to wait until the afternoon. "I have a proposal that should please everyone," he said. "Give me a few minutes of your time and I shall explain."

Edward shrugged. "Very well, but be brief."

The three brothers walked into Edward's office. Adam gazed around the office. There was no comparison between Edward's office and the tiny room they had given him to use. He wasted no time getting to the point. "I want to sell my share of the business," he said.

Timothy was the first to speak. "Adam, you know very well you cannot live the remainder of your life on the sale of your share," he responded. "We cannot have a destitute Blythington roaming the streets of London, can we? You have a secure position here that should see you comfortably through all of your years."

"Hmpf," replied Adam. "If the manner in which I live is so comfortable, you and Edward should try living the way I am forced to live. I am sure you would quickly change your minds." He feared he was making no headway with his brothers. "I do not intend to remain in London," he countered. "As a matter of fact, if you accept my offer, I will be leaving England. I plan to go to the American south."

"That is preposterous," Edward declared as he stared with incredulity at his youngest brother. "How would you earn a living?"

"I intend to invest my money shrewdly in the rebuilding of the south," Adam answered. "The opportunities are endless." He hoped his brothers would not discover that the idea had popped into his mind only minutes before he burst into Edward's office.

"What opportunities?" Timothy asked. "Have you thought this thing through?"

"I have given the idea a great deal of thought," Adam blustered. "I discussed the plan with several people who find it has great merit."

"I suppose it may have merit," Edward opined. "I want to make this clear to you, Adam. If we do agree to purchase your share, there will be no opportunity for you to return to us at a later date seeking additional funds. This 'deal' of yours will sever all ties between you and Timothy and me. You will have no part of Blythington Import and Export once the papers are signed."

"I accept your terms," Adam agreed.

Adam's share brought him more than he had anticipated. He was determined to guard his small fortune and use it wisely.

CHAPTER ONE

April 23, 1865 - May 20, 1865

On April 23, 1865, Adam Paul Blythington stood on the deck of the docked sailing ship HMS Morgan, which had brought him to America. He had never felt more alone or more exhilarated in his entire life. He gazed at his new homeland from the deck of the ship. London it was not, but it was far better than the pitching deck of the ship.

It had taken some time for Adam to develop sea legs. He passed the first week at sea in his small stateroom. He was able to spend a brief time on deck at the beginning of the second week. After another day or so, his stomach settled and he was able to tolerate the remainder of the voyage.

Although he had been impetuous in making his decision to seek his fortune in the American south, he had researched carefully before deciding which part of the south would be his destination. When he made inquiries, the state of Louisiana was said to be the best choice. The people he spoke to told him the citizenry of Louisiana were ignorant and gullible, two characteristics that would fit well with his plans.

Once he reached the conclusion to settle in Louisiana, he began the process of determining the area in the state that was most suitable for his plans. His research led him to St. Landry Parish, the largest parish in the state. The land was suitable for farming and raising cattle. Thousands upon thousands of arpents of woodland made the area even more desirable. Timber would be crucial for rebuilding the south.

Adam walked down the gangplank of the ship and inquired as to the location of the railroad depot. After being at sea for weeks, he wanted to rent a hotel room and rest for a while, but a hotel stay would deplete his funds and waste time. He decided to immediately begin the train trip across the country from New York City to Opelousas, Louisiana. There would be time for rest later.

*****

Rail travel to Louisiana proved to be a challenge. The railroads in the northern part of the country were well tended. Once he reached the deepsouth, there were many delays caused by the destruction and deterioration of the railway. Although he was fatigued down to the marrow of his bones as he traveled toward his destination, his dream of being a wealthy squire spurred him on.

He was chagrined to learn that the last leg of his journey was to be by stagecoach from Lafayette to Opelousas. When at last he arrived in Opelousas, Louisiana, on May 10, 1865, his eyes felt like they had been scorched by cinders and his body trembled with fatigue.

He inquired as to the location of the nearest suitable hotel and was directed to Hotel Bienvenu. After checking in, he walked up the stairs to his room where he directed the Negro man he had hired to secure his luggage to leave everything near the bed. He paid the man and then allowed his body to finally rest. He lay on the bed and, after only seconds, was fast asleep.

Adam awakened to find bright sunlight streaming through the hotel window. His mouth was very dry and his stomach was growling. He wondered how long he had slept. It could not have been very long because it was still daylight.

After removing his only clean clothes and his last change of undergarments from his luggage, he left his room and walked to the bathroom the clerk had assured him was down the hall. When he entered the room, he found an empty copper tub. He located a bellboy and asked to have water drawn for his bath.

The bellboy informed him that people usually didn't bathe around noontime, but he'd have someone fill the tub. The bellboy told him it would take about half an hour to heat the bath water.

Adam was astonished to learn it was noon. He had checked in at two o'clock in the afternoon. He had slept almost twenty-four hours. Small wonder his mouth felt dry and his stomach was empty.

After he had bathed and filled his stomach with steak and beans, he went outside and looked at the sights that surrounded him. In his opinion, for a parish seat, the small city was provincial. The tallest building was only three stories high.

He was not impressed by the people he observed walking the sidewalks of the city. Many of the men were either dressed in shabby gray uniforms or fresh blue uniforms. It wasn't difficult to surmise from this scene which group were the victors. There were a handful of men dressed in the wear of craftsmen or yeomen. Only a few men wore suits. Most of the women were dressed in threadbare garments.

Wagons of all sorts rolled up and down the streets. The war had been over only a few weeks and already rebuilding had begun. Compared with London, the area wasn't very impressive. Still, he did not regret his decision to relocate to the American south. Edward and Timothy could have England. Here, he would build his estate. His brothers would be green with envy once they learned how rich he had become. He would show them.

Adam walked in the direction the clerk had assured him would take him to the courthouse. He wanted to examine the tax records to ascertain what land was being forfeited for unpaid taxes. He located a sign that read, "Courthouse of Imperial St. Landry Parish." The building was more impressive than the other buildings in Opelousas, but paled in comparison to the buildings of London.

He entered the courthouse and followed signs directing patrons to the clerk's office. A short man in an ill-fitting suit approached him as he was studying the tax records. The man had light brown unruly hair, a medium build just going to fat, and dark piercing eyes. Adam's first impression was that he was a clerk.

"Do you have records specific to property that will be seized shortly or has recently been seized?" he asked the man.

The man looked at Adam and smiled. "I don't have legal records," he said, "but I know what's available. I think I can be of some help to you. Permit me to introduce myself. I'm James Fisk." He proffered his hand for Adam to shake.

He ignored Fisk's hand and studied him for a few moments. "How can you be of service to me?" he asked.

Fisk didn't take offense at Adam's refusal to shake his hand. "I mustered out of the army of the north a week after the war ended," he said. "I don't have the money a gentleman like you can get hold of, but I know how to make money. Land, that's where the money's gonna be. Whoever can buy up the most land is gonna have the most money. Land's cheap right now. I know how to go about getting the best land at the best prices. I'll help you, but I get a fee."

Adam came near dismissing Fisk. "Why would I want to do business with someone of his caliber?" he asked himself. He looked more closely at Fisk. There was something about the man's eyes. "This may be a man of low social standing, but there is a raw intelligence and shrewdness in his eyes." He decided to learn more about the man.

"How do I know I can trust you?" Adam asked.

"You don't," Fisk replied. "I don't know if I can trust you either. I have the knowledge but I don't have the money. You have the money but you don't know what I know. I can find out things you never could with your high breeding and fancy clothes. You need me and I need you. I can help you to get what you want and you can help me to get what I want."

Adam thought it over. The man did make sense. He would waste too much time trying to learn the things Fisk already knew. Fisk, with his low breeding, could travel in different circles where he would not evoke suspicion. Fisk could uncover information he would never be able to access. "I have a hotel room at the Bienvenu," he said. "Follow me and we will talk these things over."

Fisk shook his head. "I rented a small office on Market Street," he responded. "I'll give you directions. Meet me there in one hour. It wouldn't be good for people to see me at your hotel."

An hour later, Adam stood across the street from Fisk's office. He crossed the street and entered the office. He was not impressed by the exterior of Fisk's office and even less so by the interior. There were three mismatched chairs, a battered desk and a few wooden crates with papers hanging over the sides. Fisk pointed to one of the chairs. "Have a seat," he said. "I don't think I caught your name."

"Blythington," he responded. "Adam Blythington." He looked disdainfully at the chairs. "You said you have information about land I can purchase. Where is this information?"

Reaching into the crate nearest him, Fisk pulled out several sheets of paper. "I have it all written here," he said while holding up the sheets of paper. "Anywhere from whole plantations to small farms. I know how to get the land and how much you have to pay."

Adam looked at the man and thought of the words he had spoken. Fisk did not look like a man who could live up to his words. "I may be interested if you can back up your words with action," he responded.

"I can deliver," Fisk assured him. "If you have the money, you can buy thousands of arpents. I've got all the information." He smiled broadly.

Adam pulled one of the chairs to the front of Fisk's desk and sat down. Fisk went over his "records" with him. There would be a sheriff's sale the following Tuesday. Adam chose several pieces of prime land adjoining one another.

Fisk lifted a sheet of paper from his desk and waved it in the air. "This is the best one," he said as he continued to wave the paper in the air. "This one has a big antebellum plantation house. You'll need a headquarters. This will be perfect for you. There are barns and sheds on the property. You'll even get the animals and equipment. Great place to grow cotton." He handed the paper to Blythington.

Adam looked the paper over. If it was as Fisk described, he wanted the property. He and Fisk settled on four thousand, five hundred arpents of land for the transaction. The total amount he would have to pay, according to Fisk, was a little less than half of the money he had brought with him to America.

To become a plantation owner in less than two weeks after arriving in Louisiana was beyond what he had thought possible. He wondered if Fisk could deliver.

Fisk smiled. "I know what you're thinking," he said. "You're wondering if I can make good on my words. I can. It'll cost you, though. My fee is five hundred dollars. To show you that I'm not gonna crook you, I'll wait until after the papers are signed for my money."

"Five hundred dollars is a lot of money," Adam responded. "Perhaps I can do better with another land agent."

The smile was still on Fisk's face. "You can't," he said. "I know that for sure. I'm throwing in one of my services for free."

"What service is that?" Adam asked.

"It's only a small problem," Fisk replied. "The owner of that big plantation is trying to come up with the money to pay the taxes. I'll make sure he doesn't."

"How do you propose to do that?" Adam asked.

"I don't think you really want to know," Fisk replied. "Do we have a deal or don't we?"

Adam had not intended to take undue advantage of anyone to acquire his holdings. His intention was to purchase land legally and slowly build an estate. What Fisk suggested sounded as though something illegal might take place.

He thought about the large plantation with the antebellum mansion. If his brothers ever came to America, they would certainly be impressed. He did not want Fisk to give him the details of how the owner would be dissuaded from paying the taxes. His hands would be clean. "We have a deal," he said.

Fisk offered his hand once more and they shook hands to seal the deal. "I'll take care of everything," he said. "All you have to do is sign the papers at my lawyer's office and pay the money. The property will be yours by this time Friday."

*****

Fisk was true to his word. Adam handed the exact amount of cash for the land purchase to Alex Cortez, Fisk's lawyer, and signed the papers. Fisk was not present. After the papers were signed, Cortez said, "A mutual friend of ours is waiting in his office for you. I think you have some unfinished business."

Adam walked the few blocks to Fisk's office. Fisk was already celebrating. He handed Adam a glass and his bottle of rye whiskey. Adam poured about a quarter of an inch of the liquid into his glass.

"We need to toast our victory," Fisk said. He held up his glass. "To a long and successful association." Both men emptied their glasses.

Handing the five hundred dollar fee to Fisk, Adam said, "Thank you, Mr. Fisk. You spoke of a long association. Now that I have purchased my property, I do not see that there will be any need to do business in the future."

"You don't mean to tell me you're satisfied with that little bit of property?" Fisk asked. "This is just the beginning. Didn't you say you were building a kingdom? That kind of land might be a kingdom in England, but it's just a regular plantation over here."

CHAPTER TWO

May 21, 1865 - May 24, 1865

In the early afternoon of the following day, Adam rented a horse and buggy at the livery stable and drove out to inspect his new property. He followed the directions he was given by Fisk. After driving several miles, he entered the long live oak tree lined drive that he was told led to the main house.

At first glance, the mansion appeared to be impressive. It was a white threestory clapboard house with tall Corinthian columns in the front. A large gambrel roofed barn stood roughly one hundred yards west of the mansion. There were several smaller barns and outbuildings. Small frame houses lined both sides of a shaded lane far off to the northeast side of the barn. Cattle and horses grazed in the pastures.

As he drew near, he could see signs of neglect on the antebellum home. When he got nearer, he could see several Negro people sitting on the front porch of the main house or milling about in the yard. They watched as the buggy approached.

Adam brought the buggy to a halt beneath a large oak tree that shaded the front porch of the mansion. The Negro people watched as Adam walked toward them. "I am Mr. Adam Blythington," he said when he reached them. "I am the new owner."

A shapely, light complected, green-eyed female sauntered up to him and looked him over. Adam took her for a white woman until he heard her speak. He thought she was showing a great deal of insolence.

"I be Hannah," she said when she reached him. "I ran da house for Mr. Lance." She pointed to a Negro man in shabby clothes, "Henry, he da field han boss."

Adam looked at Henry. He was large, heavy muscled, and dark-complected. The man looked back at Adam contemptuously.

"These people have no respect," Adam thought to himself. "I shall change that in short order." He cleared his throat. "Those of you who want to work can stay," he said. "Anyone who does not want to work or is not fit for work will leave this property forthwith."

The Negro people studied Adam. No one moved.

Hannah smiled. "We's free people," she said. "Ain't nobody gonna run nobody off. We made dat plain ta Mr. Lance and we gone make dat plain ta you."

Adam fought to control his temper. He pointed to Henry. "Unhitch the buggy and feed the horse," he ordered.

Henry made no move to obey the order.

"If you do not obey my order by the count of three," Adam warned, " I will appoint another of the men to lead the field workers and you will be unemployed."

Anger registered on Henry's face.

Adam looked coldly into Henry's eyes and began, "One."

Henry averted his eyes, walked to the buggy, and set about unhitching the horse. The other Negro people became uneasy.

"I intend to make a profit on this plantation," Adam declared. "Anyone who does not work will be summarily dismissed."

The Negro people didn't understand all of his words but they understood the tone of authority in his voice.

Adam looked at Hannah. She appeared to be subdued. "Do you want to continue to be employed here?" he asked.

Hannah nodded.

Adam stared into her eyes. "I'm awaiting your answer," he said.

"Yassuh," Hannah replied.

"I expect you to do exactly as I say," Adam continued. "You may remain in my employ as long as you follow my orders. Is that clear?"

"Yassuh, Mr. Bliten, it clear," Hannah replied.

"The name is Blythington," he corrected in an irritated voice.

Hannah made another attempt at pronouncing the name. "Mr. Bliten," she repeated.

He recalled something Fisk had told him. It was customary for people to be addressed by their first names rather than their surnames. "You may call me Mr. Adam?" he said.

Hannah smiled. "Yassuh, Mr. Adam," she responded.

He turned back to Henry. "Why are the field hands not working in the fields?" he asked.

"We's taking da day off fo Mr. Lance's burying," Henry replied. He was not as self-assured. "Po Mr. Lance he falled offa his hoss and broked his neck. He gone be buried dis afahnoon."

Adam grew pale. He struggled for self-control. It would not do for his workers to see him lose control. He thought of Fisk's "small problem." Had Fisk murdered the man? Recovering his composure, he said, "There is work to be done. I am sure that Mr. Lance's family will do quite well without you. Henry, I want everyone at work immediately."

The Negro people mumbled, but everyone moved when Henry said, "Ya'll git back ta woik."

Hannah wasted no time getting the house servants back to performing their duties. Adam felt he had set the proper tone. He had shown them who was in authority.

Henry was walking off with the other field hands. "Henry," Adam called out, "I want you with me."

Henry walked back to his new employer.

"I want you to show me around this place," Adam said. "I want to know everything that goes on over here. Saddle two horses."

Henry left for the large barn. He returned a short time later with two saddled horses. Adam looked at the saddles. He was not a horseman, but he had used an English saddle for what riding he had done. He thought of purchasing an English saddle and then decided to keep the American saddle. He was now an American.

Adam was impressed with his new property. Crops were already planted. Henry told him the land was very rich. His brothers would be green with envy if they could see him now.

When they returned to the house, Adam told Henry, "I want you to take one of the workers and go into town in the morning and pick up my trunks. I was staying at Hotel Bienvenu. Tell the manager I will be in to settle with him. You can also return the horse and buggy. I shall stay here for the time being."

Adam entered his new home for the first time and was impressed by what he saw. The ceilings appeared to be at least twelve feet high and were covered with elaborate designs. Large crown molding ran around the walls where they met with the ceiling. The walls were wood paneled. The furniture appeared to be most satisfactory. It looked to him like a mixture of French and English furniture. There were thick drapes covering the large windows. The drapes looked like they needed to be cleaned. An air of neglect seemed to permeate the home. That would change starting tomorrow.

Hannah heard him enter and rushed to meet him. "We cooked fo you, Mr. Adam," she said. "I hope you lack da fricassee'."

Adam knew little of southern cooking but was willing to give it a try. Margaret, the cook, had prepared a chicken stew along with fresh tomatoes and cucumbers from the garden. Adam took a bite. He found the food to be delicious. He was going to enjoy his new life.

He looked around his new home. There would be changes made around the place. The house servants would give the mansion a proper cleaning. There would be no dirt found in his home. He would also speak with Henry to learn if there were any skilled workmen in his employ. The mansion would be repaired and repainted. The grounds would also be manicured and cared for properly.

He thought of one more thing. He had difficulty understanding his employees when they spoke. An English tutor would be hired to teach the house servants, Henry, and some of the field workers how to speak properly. How the servants conducted themselves was a direct reflection upon him. The property was presently called "Seven Oaks." Coming up the drive, he had seen several dozen oak trees. He decided to select a more appropriate title for the property. He thought of several names and dismissed them. Another name came to mind, "Southern Kingdom." It may sound ostentatious to some," he thought, "but this is my 'Southern Kingdom.'" He was pleased with himself as he thought of the name he had chosen. He would speak to Henry in the morning about having the title made up on a sign and hung at the opening of the driveway. The more he thought about the new name, the better it sounded to him.

*****

After eating and taking a bath, Adam retired to the bedroom Hannah had told him Mr. Lance LeBlanc had used as his own. It was a large room with heavy mahogany furniture. He took in the large four-poster bed covered with mosquito netting. It looked comfortable, but it was higher from the floor than the beds he had slept in previously.

As he looked around, he heard a soft knock on the door. "You may enter," he said.

Hannah walked into the room. "Is dare anyting you might be needin, Mr. Adam?" she asked. The dress she was wearing exposed more of her ample bosom than had the dress he had seen her wearing earlier. She had an expression on her face that puzzled him.

"I am preparing for bed," he replied. "I have everything I need."

Hannah continued to look at him with a strange expression. "Dere was tings I use ta do fo Mr. Lance when he ta his bed," she said as she stood seductively before him. "Might be you need some da same tings."

He suddenly understood what she was offering. His first impulse was to dismiss her and warn her never to approach him again in this manner. He stopped himself. It had been a trying day and he had been without a woman for several months. The news of the previous owner's death had been unsettling. A distraction might be what he needed to clear his mind.

He walked to the door and turned the key and then turned back to her. "This may be your attempt to ingratiate yourself with me or to gain the upper hand by having something you think you can use as leverage to control me," he said. "I will warn you one time only. What happens in this room will remain strictly between the two of us. If I hear that even a hint of what takes place in this room has left this room, you will be summarily dismissed."

Hannah understood the gist of what Mr. Adam was saying, although she didn't understand all of his words. She understood better the desire she saw in his eyes. "Dis gone be jus tween you an me," she said. "I gone make sho you took care of proper."

Later, Adam lay on his bed wondering where Hannah had learned her skills. When she left his room two hours after she had entered, he was completely drained.

Sleep began to come upon him as he lay on his back in the large bed. Another moment or two and he would be fast asleep. As he felt himself drifting off into a heavy slumber, the words Henry had spoken that afternoon came back to him, "Mr. Lance he falled offa his hoss and broked his neck."

He was sure that Fisk had a hand in LeBlanc's fall from the horse. He debated with himself whether he should go to the authorities and tell them of his conversation with Fisk or remain silent. He decided against going to the authorities. He might be implicated, or worse yet, there was the risk that this could lead to the loss of Southern Kingdom. It would be best to say nothing. He was innocent. If Fisk had murdered the man, it had nothing to do with him. His conscience was clear. Once again, he felt himself drifting off into a deep sleep.

*****

"Is you awoke?" Hannah asked him the next morning. Adam stirred and looked out the window. He could see daylight. He felt he was setting a bad example for his employees by staying in bed late.

"What time is it?" he asked.

"Bout six o'clock," Hannah answered. "Henry and Jeremiah, deys waiten to ax you some questins befo dey leaf."

He rolled out of bed. She looked at him and smiled and then she handed him the clothes he had worn the previous day. His suit was brushed and pressed and his shirt and undergarments smelled fresh. "Thank you," he said. "I can finish dressing on my own."

She smiled once more. "We got nutten ta hide tween da two eh us, Mr. Adam," she said. "I kin hep you ta dress."

"There is indeed nothing hidden between the two of us," he thought to himself. He felt a stirring in his loins as he recalled the previous night. Perhaps he should allow her to assist him. Wealthy Englishmen employed butlers for the chore, why should he not allow Hannah to act in that capacity? "Very well," he said.

Before he could say anything further, she picked up his trousers and smiled. He had to admit she was very efficient at all her tasks.

"Where are Henry and Jeremiah?" he asked after he was dressed.

"Deys waiten to da side doe," Hannah answered. "I tole dem dey was gonna wait til dey talk to you."

He went to the side door where he found Henry and Jeremiah waiting. "Henry, I need to know if any of our men have carpentry and gardening skills," he said as he stepped outside. "The house and grounds show signs of neglect. I intend to have that corrected in short order."

Henry scratched his head. "Gabral, Ephram and Danel, dey know sumpin bout billing," he responded. "Mosa da hands knows bout gardnin."

"I don't mean growing a vegetable garden," Adam stated. "I mean landscaping. Getting the grounds in order and keeping them up."

"I don tink nobody know nutten bout no lanscapin," Henry responded. "We knows how ta make tings grow. We kin plant, tend and harves, dats bout all."

Adam wanted a first-rate landscaper. Perhaps he could inquire with the neighbors and learn whom they would recommend. "Have Gabriel, Ephraim and Daniel report to me," he said. "I want to see them before I eat breakfast."

"Yassuh, Mr. Adam," Henry responded, "Deys bout to leaf fo da feel. I gone tell dem ta come ta talk ta you."

Adam thought for a moment. "It may be prudent for you to wait until after I have spoken to the carpenters before you go into town," he said. "Send them to me immediately."

Henry left and returned a short while later with three large Negro men in tow. "Dese da mens I tole you bout, Mr. Adam," Henry said.

Adam looked the men over. He hoped their carpentry skills were better than their appearance. "I want you men to look over this house and make a list of all materials you will need to complete the repairs," he said. "You will accompany Henry. Purchase whatever is needed and have it back here today. The repairs are to begin tomorrow morning."

"Yassah, Mr. Adam," Daniel responded. "We kin fix da house fo you."

As Adam waited for the men to complete their assessment, Hannah approached him. "Mr. Adam, deys sum tings we needs fo da kitchen and fo da cleanin," she said. "Margret, she writ dem down. She da only one know how ta write. Kin you giff da liss ta Henry sos he kin git dem when he go ta town?"

He looked at the list. There were several items written in a crisp, legible handwriting. He was nodding his approval until he came to an item on the list that confused him. "Why do you need all these yards of cloth?" he asked.

"We stawtin ta look po in da close wes got," Hannah answered. "We taut you might want da house servants ta look some bettah."

He recalled that the clothing of the house servants did look threadbare. It would not do to have his servants wearing rags. "I'll give the list to Henry," he responded.

A wide smile appeared on her face. "Tank you, Mr.

Adam," she said.

Henry returned some time later with Jeremiah and the carpenters. Adam was finishing with breakfast. Ruth walked to the table. She waited for Mr. Adam to look up at her. When he did, she said, "Henry say he waiten ta da doe fo you."

"Thank you, Ruth," he responded. As he started for the door, he called out to Hannah. She came out of the kitchen to meet him. "I've decided to go into town with the men," he said. "With all of the things we are needing, I must establish accounts with the merchants in Opelousas."

Hannah was disappointed. She had ordered Margaret to cook a delicious meal for Mr. Adam. She had in mind to continue to work into his good graces. She recognized that Mr. Adam would be a force in the parish. "Yassuh, Mr. Adam," she said. "I tole Margret to cook sumpin speshul fo you. I guess she kin do dat fo yo suppah."

"That would be nice," Adam responded. "If it is anything like the meal last night, it will give me cause to return poste haste."

"Dat man sho do talk funny," Hannah thought to herself.

Adam met with Henry and the other men. "Do you have a list of everything you need?" he asked.

"We ain't got no liss," Daniel replied, "but I gots da tings we needs in my haid."

"One more thing," Adam stated, "I want to change the name of this plantation. You will make up a new sign to replace the one at the front gate. It will read, 'Southern Kingdom.' Be sure to purchase everything needed for the new sign."

"Yassuh, Mr. Adam," Daniel responded. "We gone do dat."

Adam turned away from Daniel and turned his attention to Henry. "Henry, have one of the men saddle the best horse we have and bring it to me," he ordered. "I'll be going into the city."

Henry nodded at Jeremiah. Jeremiah jogged to the barn and returned a few minutes later leading a beautiful black stallion. The horse reared up and pawed the air with his hooves. "He a lil nerfus," Jeremiah said. "You bettah be caful, Mr.

Adam."
        Adam did not want the men to know how fearful he
was. The animal was beautiful. He put his foot in the stirrup and
swung his leg over the saddle. The horse began to jump. He held
on to the saddle horn to keep from falling.
        Jeremiah spoke softly to the horse and calmed him
down.
        Adam saw looks of disdain pass back and forth among
the men. He decided he would have to relegate himself to using
a buggy or become an accomplished horseman. It would not do
to have the men contemptuous of him. After the horse calmed
down, he started for town.

                                    *****

        Adam was walking toward the largest of the general
merchandise stores when he heard a familiar voice addressing
him. He turned in the direction of the voice.
        "Mr. Blythington, I was asking if everything was
satisfactory with your new home," James Fisk said. "You took a
look at the property, didn't you?"
        "I have," Adam replied. "Everything is satisfactory."
        "Where are you headed?" Fisk inquired.
        "I am opening accounts with several of the local
merchants," he replied with irritation in his voice. "I cannot
come to town each time something is needed at Southern
Kingdom." He liked the title even more as he spoke the name to
Fisk.
        "Southern Kingdom?" asked Fisk.
        "Yes," Adam replied. "I gave the plantation a more
fitting title."
        "I suppose you can do what you want with the name,"
Fisk agreed. "About the accounts: I told you that you still need
my services. That's exactly what a greenhorn would do. You
can buy the things you need today and pay cash, but I'll put
you in touch with some drummers who'll do business with you
directly at your plantation. You can set up a plantation store
so the darkies can start buying the things they need from you.

You can charge them more for the goods than they'd pay here in town. The smart thing to do is to let them charge at the store to the point where they're so deep in debt to you they won't ever be able to leave. You can control them better that way."

"Drummers?" Adam asked. "Who are these drummers?"

"Those are the men who work for the manufacturing companies," Fisk replied. "They come out here to sell their goods. You deal directly with them instead of stores here in town. You can buy cheaper and sell higher. Of course, there's a small fee for being the middle man between you and the drummers."

"How much for your services?" Adam inquired in a suspicious voice.

"Only fifty dollars," Fisk replied. "You'll make that back in no time."

"The fee seems reasonable enough," Adam responded. "It would not be in good form to cheat one's own employees. I admit that I came to the south to make a fortune, but my plans do not include cheating and taking advantage of people. Are there plantation stores on other plantations?"

"Cheating and taking advantage?" Fisk questioned in a hurt voice. "I wasn't suggesting any such thing. Having your own store would make it easier on your people. That way they wouldn't have to come to town and they wouldn't have to wait for their goods. The store is really good for your employees and for you. Most of the plantation owners have their own stores."

Adam contemplated the idea. It did sound as though it would be helpful to his employees. He did want to do what was best for them. "Mr. Fisk, you may contact your associates," he said. "I do want to do what is best for my people. Should I meet you in your office to pay your fee?"

"That's not really necessary," Fisk replied. "We can slip in there," he pointed to an alley, "and conduct our business."

Adam followed Fisk into the alley. He counted out the money and put the bills in Fisk's outstretched palm. He really did not like doing business in an alleyway.

"The drummers will be out to see you tomorrow morning," Fisk promised.

Adam returned to the lumberyard where he had left his carpenters. The wagons were loaded with the material needed for the repairs on the house. The three men appeared to know what they were doing.

"Mr. Adam, we got evating we come fo," Daniel said. "You need us ta stay heah or you want us ta go ta da house?"

"You may return to Southern Kingdom," Adam replied. "Get everything ready to begin work tomorrow morning." The men had a puzzled look until they recalled the new name of the plantation.

"Where is Henry?" Adam inquired.

"He ta da stow," Daniel answered, pointing to a store about a block away. "He say he gittin all da tings on yo liss."

Adam walked in the direction of the store. He wanted to pay for the goods and he also wanted to ensure Henry and Jeremiah did not leave before he was mounted safely on the stallion. The two Negro men were walking out of the store laden with bolts of brightly colored cloth when he reached them.

When Henry saw him he said, "Mr. Adam, I don tink I seen so much clot in my whole borned life."

Adam chuckled. "Have you found everything on your list?" he asked.

"Yassuh, Mr. Adam," Henry replied. "We gots evating."

"Meet me in front of the hotel," Adam ordered. "We will be leaving in short order."

He walked the two blocks to the hotel. He was relieved to see the stallion still tied to the hitching rail in front of the hotel. He entered the hotel and walked up to the desk.

The hotel clerk looked up from the newspaper he was reading when Adam entered. "Ah, Mr. Blythington," he said. "Is everything satisfactory with your accommodations?"

"Everything is splendid," he replied. "I am here to settle my bill."

"I hope we haven't lost your business," the clerk said nervously.

"Not at all," Adam responded. "I purchased Seven Oaks. I will be living there."

The clerk calculated the amount he owed. While he was

paying his bill, he heard a man speaking in an English accent. He turned toward the sound of the voice. A skinny man who stood almost a head taller than Adam was pleading with a man he presumed to be the manager. The Englishman had thinning red hair and a long hooked nose. The red-haired man was protesting his ejection from the hotel. He was begging the manager to at least allow him to keep his luggage.

He thought the red-haired man to be a most unusual creature. He listened more closely to his protests.

"I hope to be engaged very soon," argued the redheaded man. "Is it my fault the plantation owner reneged on my contract? With my background, my prospects are excellent."

"You owe for a week already," the manager responded. "When you get the money, you can have your luggage. Until then, it stays here."

"How can I hope to make a favorable impression in soiled clothing?" the skinny redheaded man asked.

"That's your problem, mister," the manager replied. "I have a hotel to run."

Adam interrupted the two men. "You spoke of a canceled contract," he said to the redhead. "What is your line of business?"

The redheaded man stood up straight. "Professor Havard J. Pennington at your service," he responded. "I am a professor of English, French, geography, history, mathematics and science. Many of my pupils have risen to excellence in their fields." He proffered a bony hand for Adam to shake.

He shook hands with the man and looked him over carefully. "I am in need of someone who can teach my Negro employees to speak proper English," he said.

The hotel manager and the clerk burst out laughing. "I don't think the professor can teach darkies to do anything but be darkies," the manager said. "I don't think folks around here would take kindly to darkies being educated."

Adam stared coldly at the manager. "I was speaking to the professor," he said in a clipped tone.

The manager and the clerk looked obliquely at Adam.

"Are you willing to teach Negro people to speak proper

English?" Adam asked as he returned his attention to the professor.

"I can teach them to speak proper English, French, German, Italian, Portugese, Russian and Spanish," the professor replied.

"I only need for them to speak proper English," Adam responded. "The position is yours."

"What is the amount of his bill?" he asked the manager. The manager gave him the amount and Adam paid the bill.

"Follow me," Adam told the professor as he strode out of the hotel.

Henry and Jeremiah were waiting in the wagon for him.

"Put your things in the wagon and climb in," he told the professor. "My hope is you can teach better than you do business."

Adam motioned to Jeremiah. Jeremiah jumped down from the wagon and untied the black stallion. He held the horse as Adam mounted. The animal was not as skittish as it had been in the morning. Adam settled in the saddle and set out at a canter toward home.

*****

The following day, which was a Friday, Adam could hear the sound of hammers as his crew of carpenters worked to repair the antebellum mansion. He had watched the workers for a while. He was no judge of carpentry, but to his untrained eye, the men were up to the task.

Hannah had awakened him at five o'clock, as he had ordered. In his mind, it would not do to have the employees at work while the master slept. It was now eight o'clock. He had breakfasted on eggs, bacon and biscuits. He was pleased with Margaret's cooking.

He had held Henry and Jeremiah from the fields. He intended to ride over the adjoining pieces of property that were part of his purchase. Henry gave instructions to Matthew, another of the field hands, for accomplishing the day's work.

Henry's expertise was needed to evaluate the condition of the adjoining arpents of land he had purchased. He wanted to learn if the arpents were presently planted with crops and how to proceed to make the best use of the land. He wanted to incorporate all of the land he had purchased into Southern Kingdom. He had not purchased the land to allow it to lie fallow. He intended to make a profit with his land.

Adam did not want anyone to learn why he wanted Jeremiah to come along. He intended to ride the black stallion again today. Truth was, he still feared the horse. Jeremiah had a soothing influence on the black. Adam was dead set on becoming an accomplished horseman, but he did not intend to die in the process.

The black stallion and two other horses were saddled and waiting. Henry and Jeremiah were helping Daniel and his crew while waiting for Mr. Adam to culminate his meeting with Professor Pennington.

Hannah was becoming indispensable to Adam. He had hired the professor on an impulse. There were no accommodations on the plantation for a school or any of the things that would be needed to furnish the school. He asked Hannah and she suggested a storage building that was not presently in use. According to her, there was lots of used furniture available in Opelousas as a result of the punitive taxes. A desk, chairs and whatever else would be needed, could be purchased cheaply. Books, pencils and writing paper were available in the general stores.

Professor Pennington and one of the field hands were ordered to take a couple of wagons into town and make the necessary purchases. Adam had given the professor sufficient funds to cover the purchases with instructions to be frugal in his dealings.

Hannah and the house servants would see to it that the schoolhouse was made ready. Hannah was especially pleased to be afforded the opportunity of obtaining an education. When Adam revealed to her that he had hired the professor and his plans for a school, she had responded, "I sho been wantin to get me some larnin."

He asked Hannah to let Henry and Jeremiah know it was time to leave. She sent Ruth, one of the maids, to fetch the two. Adam walked out to the hitching rail where the black stallion was tied. "He is a beautiful animal," he thought to himself. He looked at the stallion, "I will overcome my fear of you," he said under his breath.

Jeremiah untied the horse and prepared to hold his head while Adam mounted.

"That will not be necessary," Adam said. He wondered if he was being foolish. He was determined to have the respect of his men. He placed his left foot in the stirrup, lifted himself up and swung into the saddle.

The black began to jump as he had the previous day. Adam squeezed his legs tightly around the horse. He was not going to clutch the saddle horn as he had the previous morning. He spoke softly to the black and pulled back on the reins with a light even pressure. In a short time, the horse quieted down. There were no looks of disdain exchanged between the men this time. They looked at their employer with newfound respect.

The more he rode over the additional arpents of land, the more elated he became. Where there were fields, the land was growing crops of cotton and corn. Henry calculated he would need to hire an additional forty field hands to tend the crops. He was impressed with the forests of hardwood. He estimated he owned roughly one thousand, five hundred arpents of prime hardwood timber. Sawmills would pay thousands of dollars to purchase the rights to cut the timber.

All of the land he rode over was now Southern Kingdom. Only a few months before he was living, he felt, off of the largess of his brothers. Now, he owned an impressive plantation. He looked around at the land that was all his. He was in debt to no one. He would be looked up to by his peers. Peers? He would be peerless.

His holdings were impressive, but only mediocre, as Fisk had said. He would buy more land. He would not be satisfied with being one of the wealthy men; he would be the wealthiest man in St. Landry Parish. He would build Southern Kingdom into a plantation that would be the envy of all. He would no longer be the one who envied men such as Edward and Timothy. He would be a man other men admired and envied.

*****

When he returned to his home, he saw the work on the repairs to the antebellum home was progressing very well. He was well satisfied with the skill of Daniel and his men. He dismounted and handed the stallion's reins to Jeremiah.

Walking closer to the workers, he observed Gabriel and Ephraim tearing boards off of the side of the mansion. He walked up to where they were working. "What are you doing?" he asked. "I want the mansion repaired, not demolished."

Daniel quickly made his way to his employer's side. "Deys not tarin da house down," he said. "Da wood rat dere be rottun. I done check. Mos da house be cypris. Dems pine bods. Dey shudin be no pine on dis house. We got a few placis lak dat. Ifin we dawn pull out dem bods, dey gonna be big trubel."

"I see," Adam responded. "It would not do to leave rot on the house. Carry on, Daniel." He turned to Gabriel and Ephraim. "You may continue."

Hannah met him at the door as he was entering the mansion. "I got sum watah and a towul fo you ta clean up," she said. "Git dat duss offa you." She led him to a small room off of the dining room and then returned to her work. There was a washstand with a basin of clear water and a towel.

He cleaned up and then re-entered the dining room.

Hannah and Ruth were setting the table for supper.

Hannah looked up and smiled. "Mr. Adam," she said, "Margret done cook you sum rice and smuddered steak and sum tater salid. We sho hope you lak dat."

He had eaten steak but he had never tasted of any of the other foods she mentioned. One thing he knew for certain, he was growing fond of southern cooking. There were fresh vegetables from the garden to accompany the meal. Hannah served a plate of food and set it on the table before him.

"You kin have sum moik or sum tea ta go wit da food,

Mr. Adam," she said. " Whut evah you lak."

"Do you mean milk?" he asked.

"Yassuh, moik, dat's whut I sayed," Hannah replied.

"I'll take the milk," Adam responded. He took a bite. Once again, the food was delicious. Edward and Timothy did not have food such as this to eat. He wondered why he had ever envied his brothers.

After he had eaten, he asked Hannah to take him on a tour of the mansion. She smiled and said, "Folla me, Mr. Adam."

There were many bedrooms and bathing rooms. Each of the bathing rooms had an elongated copper tub, a chamber pot, a washstand on which stood a large pitcher and a basin. There was room in the mansion to entertain several guests at one time.

When he walked into the ballroom, he thought to himself that he had never seen such an exquisite room. The room was as large as Timothy's entire house. There were chairs and sofas placed tastefully throughout the room. Several large windows that opened to the verandah were covered by rich looking drapes. The massive chandelier was more elegant than any he had ever seen in England. He could find no words that were appropriate to describe the elegant room.

He thought of Edward and Timothy. They would be beyond themselves when they visited his home. "As soon as the repairs are complete and the gardens are made ready," he thought to himself, "I shall invite Edward and Timothy. I must see the look on their faces when they see all that I have." He was impressed with the large study and the parlor.

Hannah took him to the library. There was a large mahogany reading table and several comfortable stuffed chairs in the room. Bookshelves lined the walls. He stepped closer and looked at the leather bound volumes on the shelves. He had never seen so many books in his life, let alone all in one place. He decided he would read many of the books when he found the time.

Adam yawned. Although it was not very late, the day had been full and very tiring. "Hannah, have someone draw me a bath," he ordered.

"Yassuh, Mr. Adam." Hannah responded. "I gonna

make Fred heat da watuh and fill da tub. It gone be reddy in bout haf hour."

He drew one of the volumes from the bookshelf. "Send someone to get me when my bath is ready," he said.

"Yassuh, Mr. Adam," she responded.

She returned a little over half an hour later. "Da watuh be reddy," she said. "I gone sho you where da tub."

He set the book down on the table and followed her to one of the bathing rooms. The tub was filled with steaming water. He looked at her and she smiled.

"I gon hep you," she said.

She undressed him, helped him into the tub, lathered a cloth and began to bathe him. His skin tingled as she ran the cloth over his body. He felt desire for her growing as she expertly bathed his body. After she was satisfied that his body was clean, she dried him off and helped him into a thick robe. She opened a second door in the bathing room that led directly to his bedroom.

She led him into the bedroom and began to disrobe. He caught his breath as he gazed at the perfection of her body. "She is as beautiful as a goddess," he said to himself. Her lightly tanned skin was smooth and unblemished. She smiled at him as she stood beside the bed.

He wanted to wait and take in her beauty for a while longer, but desire for her grew to the point that he could no longer hold himself back. She drew him to her as the light draws a moth. He had no power to resist.

"Does you wan me to stay wif you fo a wile, Mr. Adam?" she asked.

He tried to speak but the beauty of her naked body froze his tongue. Somehow his body was moving closer to her. Suddenly she was in his arms. He picked her up and gently laid her in the large bed. He had no memory of removing his clothes when their naked flesh touched. "If she asks this moment," he thought, "she could have anything she wants." He was hopelessly lost to her beauty.

Later, when they were both sated, he lay on his back thinking of the power she held over him. He gazed down on her nude body as she lay sleeping quietly beside him. He could not afford to let her know how powerless he was to resist her, yet he could not stop himself from wanting her.

"She is a Negro servant and a member of a much lower class," he told himself. He could never take her as his wife. Not in the American south. Opposition to such a relationship would be formidable. He had a solution that he thought would work out very well. She would be his mistress. When he married, which he knew he would someday, she would remain his mistress. He would build a house for her on his land where he could visit her at will.

She awakened and searched his face with her eyes. "What you is tinkin bout, Mr. Adam?" she asked.

"I was solving a problem," he replied.

She smiled at him. "I kin sove anuddah problum fo you, ifin you want, Mr. Adam," she said. She began to run her fingers lightly along his body. His desire for her grew once again. He felt that he was bewitched by this beautiful goddess.

Roughly an hour later, she sat up in the bed, swung her feet to the floor and began to rise from the bed. He gently pulled her back down. "What is your last name?" he asked.

"LeBlanc," she answered. "We'se all LeBlancs. I wuz a Benit when I come heah. We tooked da masah's name."

"How long have you been living on this plantation?" he asked.

"Near as I kin figgah, I wuz tirteen when I come heah," she replied. "I figgah I be bout twenny now. Mr. Lance, he bought me cuz he seen me ta da slave aucshun and he want me in he bed. I did fo him whut I doz fo you."

He found himself becoming jealous of the deceased former owner. "Ridiculous," he said to himself. To Hannah he said, "You will never be with any other man ever again. You are mine now."

"Mr. Adam," Hannah said, "Da procmashun been sign. I be free. Long as you treat me right, I be heah. You dawn treat me right, I be gone."

He detected a veiled warning in her voice. He studied her face and tried to discern what she was thinking.

"I know the longing I caused in him," she thought to herself. Her plan was to control him by his desire for her. She was pleased with herself. Her plan seemed to be working more rapidly than she had anticipated.

"I want you to want to be with me," he said in a level voice. "I intend to treat you and all of my employees properly." His voice grew hard. "I do not want you to misunderstand what I am saying. I did not ask if you wanted to remain here as my mistress. I told you that you will remain here as my mistress. You will be well cared for as long as you remain useful to me. There will never be a time when our relationship will allow you to exercise control over me. I will not have you or anyone else toying with me. Do you clearly understand what I am saying to you?"

Fear gripped her as she considered his words. She had assumed he was under her control because she had read the depth of desire he had for her in his eyes. She knew what her nude body had done to him. She had used her knowledge of lovemaking to drain him and keep him wanting her, but he had drawn the line. His desire for her was real but he desired land, prestige and power even more. She would have to surrender to him for her own protection. She hadn't gained absolute control over him as she had thought.

"Yassuh, Mr. Adam," she said. "I unnerstan."

Adam looked at her. She was weeping. The hardness in his heart left him. "Are you all right?" he asked.

"Nossuh, Mr. Adam," she replied, "I not awright. I be verry not awright. I wan you so much an you talk ta me dat way. Whut I done did ta you?"

"I am sorry," he said contritely. "I must have misunderstood what you were saying to me earlier. I thought you had a plan to gain power over me by enticing me with sex. I see now I was mistaken."

"Oh, Mr. Adam," she said. "How you cuddah taught dat bout me? Dawn I pleeze you? Dawn I makes you happy?"

"Yes you do, Hannah," he replied. "I do not ever want to lose you. I value what we have. When you said that you would only stay as long as I treated you well, I took that as a threat.

Again, I am very sorry I hurt you. Please stop crying."
"Mr. Adam," she said, "I jus mint dat I diden wan ta be heah iffin you dawn wan me."
"I will always want you," he said to her with warmth and desire in his voice. "You are a beautiful and desirable woman."
He reached his right arm out and drew her to him. "Please lie down beside me," he said. "Stay a while longer. It would be horrible for you to be alone while you are still hurting."
She surrendered, lay beside him and curled up against him. He could feel her sensuous body next to his. Desire for her began to build, but he did not want to be indelicate and take her again while she was still hurting from the mean things he had said to her.
She pulled herself closer to him and moaned. "Mr. Adam," she said, "You sho doz stir me up."
He was pleased that she still desired him after the mean things he had said. They coupled once more.
About an hour later, she slipped out of the bed and dressed. She gazed at Mr. Adam as he lay sleeping. He was a man who had to be handled carefully. She would make sure to feed his desire and his ego. She had her ways. He wasn't like Mr. Lance, only wanting to satisfy himself. As long as she made sure his sexual needs were met, she could have her way. Mr. Adam never stopped until she was satisfied. He awakened fires in her she hadn't known existed. She would make sure that he always needed her in many ways. She shook her head. She had come close to making a grave mistake.

CHAPTER THREE

May 25, 1865 - May 29, 1865

When Adam awakened early Saturday morning, it was pitch dark in his bedroom. He walked to one of the windows and drew back one side of the heavy draperies that covered the window. By the faint light from the moon, he could make out sheds and barns. He could barely make out the row of trees that lined the lane where the workers lived. The scene appeared ethereal by the glow of the moon. Only a few months ago, he was relegated to a small office in London and now he was the owner of thousands of arpents of land, a mansion, horses, cattle and buildings and the employer of dozens of people in the deep south.

He was thinking of purchasing more land but he did not want to exhaust his funds. There were wages and expenses to pay between now and harvest time. He needed to guard his funds. There was a source of income he could tap into, however. He could sell the rights to harvest timber on his land. He could guess the value of the timber, but had no actual knowledge of its worth.

Perhaps Fisk would know. He hated to continue to do business with such a scoundrel. He could go directly to the Opelousas Sawmill and inquire, but he would not know if the price they would quote was the fair value of the timber. He decided to go into town and speak to Fisk.

He dressed and walked downstairs to the kitchen. Margaret had placed some pinecones and small pieces of wood on the embers in the large fireplace. Smoke was rising and a small fire was beginning to burn. Adam watched as she added more pieces of wood to the fire. Soon a fire was blazing.

"You taught you waz gonna stay sleeping," she said to the fire in the fireplace. "I knowed how ta tickle you and make you git awoke." She laughed to herself. She froze when she felt a presence in the room. "Who dare?" she called out. "It is I, Margaret," he answered. She turned to him. "Mr. Adam, you near done scairt da life outta me," she said.

"I did not mean to cause you alarm," he said, "I will be going into town this morning. I would like biscuits and coffee before I go."

"Yassuh, Mr. Adam," she responded. "I makes dem quick like."

Hannah walked into the kitchen. She looked clean and refreshed. Even in the long dress she wore, he could see her raw sensuality. He felt his loins stirring once again.

She looked directly into his eyes and smiled. She dropped her eyes down to his groin and lifted them again to look into his eyes. Still smiling, she said, "Mr. Adam, I see you is up erly dis monin."

He caught the meaning in her words. She had seen the effect she had on him. He studied her closely for signs she was attempting to manipulate him. She looked back at him frankly with desire in her eyes. He had completely misunderstood her last night. She wanted him in the same way he wanted her. He relaxed and smiled back at her. He was tempted to return to his room with her. There would be time later for what they had on their minds.

"Hannah, I will be going into town shortly on business," he said. "Please see to it that my horse is saddled and waiting. I will be away most of the day."

She knew she had made progress. This was the first time he had said "Please" to her. She left the room and returned after a few minutes. "I told dem ta make sho da hoss be brushed and curried," she said. "You wants ta look good when you goes ta town."

"She thinks of everything," he reckoned to himself. He wanted her as a mistress but he did not want to lose her other services. "Perhaps she can keep her room in this house and continue to run the household. This is a large house."

*****

"I have some people I can send to look at your timber, Mr. Blythington," Fisk answered in response to Adam's question about the worth of his timber. "Of course, you understand there'll be a fee."

"Always the fee," Adam said resignedly. "I understand. When can your people appraise the timber?"

Fisk pulled his gold watch from his vest pocket. "It's nine o'clock now," he said. "I think there's time for them to get started today. They could probably work through Monday and finish up sometime Tuesday. I should have the report Wednesday morning."

"Your people work on Sundays?" Adam asked.

"They work any time I tell them to," Fisk answered.

"We need to discuss your fee before I agree to your proposal," Adam said. "What figure do you have in mind?"

"You stand to make a lot of money on that timber," Fisk responded. "I'll make sure you get the best price possible for your timber. I get five percent of what the sawmill pays you for your trees."

"Five percent?" Adam choked out. "Is that not a rather high fee?"

"If you get ten thousand for the timber," Fisk responded, "I get only five hundred dollars. Of course, you could always sell your timber without my help. It'll cost you twice that amount in the long run." He waited a few moments for Blythington to consider the arrangement and then continued, "When I say a report, I mean we'll know the types, count and worth of the trees."

"Perhaps we should consider negotiating your fee," Adam stated in a matter of fact manner.

"If it weren't for me," Fisk responded as his eyes met Blythington's, "you wouldn't even own the timber. I got you that land for practically nothing. You can take or leave my deal."

43

"I accept your terms," Adam said reluctantly. "Once the timber rights are sold, I want to discuss the purchase of additional property."

"Ah," Fisk said with a grin, "I knew you'd come around. I can get you land that adjoins your present property or land anywhere in the parish, or other parishes for that matter. I can always make land become available."

"I prefer not to know the details," Adam said with drawn lips. "I want land that adjoins my property. I want all of the land the sale of the timber rights can purchase."

A predatory smile appeared on Fisk's face. "It looks like our association continues," he said.

Adam smiled at Fisk. "Yes, it appears we have remained associates," he said. "May our association bring us tremendous profits and success." He came close to adding power but stopped himself. He had no intention of sharing power with Fisk.

*****

Adam was up and dressed in his best attire early on Sunday morning. Although he was an Anglican, attending the St. Landry Church services would help to cultivate the persona he was hoping to build. He wanted to be accepted as a gentleman by the members of the upper class. He had attended the Anglican Church only when he had been forced by his father to attend. Religion didn't matter to him. One was as good as any other and none was of much value in his opinion. He had chosen the St. Landry Church because it was the church favored by most of the wealthy in the area.

He was impressed by the large brick structure of the church. The building was larger than he had expected. He removed his hat as he neared the front doors. He walked up the center aisle and sat in a pew on the right side of the aisle near the front. He wanted to be seen by the people of the area. If his plans were successful, he would have a place among the aristocracy. He also wanted to get a good look at the members of the congregation.

An organ began to play and the parson walked up to the altar. Adam looked around. One of the most beautiful women he had ever seen was sitting in a pew across the aisle from his. He could not see her as clearly as he wished. A silver haired gentleman was sitting to her right. He would have to arrange to be introduced to the beautiful creature.

He sat through the service with his mind on timber, land, expansion and many other things. He wanted the service to quickly end so he could meet the beautiful young lady. Custom demanded a formal introduction before he would be allowed to speak to her. The silver haired man appeared to be her father. Adam's plan was to introduce himself to the man. He tried to come up with a suitable excuse.

After the service ended, he made his way to the front of the church. He turned around and waited for the silver haired gentleman to reach the place where he was standing. He looked the silvery haired man over as he approached. The man stood about five feet, eleven inches tall; a very erect and distinguished looking man of about forty-five with only the very beginnings of a paunch.

When the gentleman reached him, Adam offered his hand. "Permit me to introduce myself," he said.

The gentleman nodded his head.

"I am Adam Blythington," he continued. "I recently purchased the plantation known locally as Seven Oaks. I am told we are neighbors." He had no idea who the gentleman was or where he lived. This was the best he could come up with on the spur of the moment. He had to meet the beautiful young lady.

The gentleman shook Adam's hand. "Indeed we are neighbors, Monsieur Blythington," he responded. "I am Jacques Dupre'. We live on Belle Bois Plantation." He turned to the young lady who was standing by his side, "This is my daughter, Annabelle. It's a pleasure to meet you, Monsieur."

"The pleasure is all mine," Adam returned. "If you have no other plans for dinner, I would like to extend the hospitality of Southern Kingdom to you and your daughter."

"Ah, but we do have plans, Monsieur Blythington," Jacques replied. "Perhaps you would like to join us." He squinted his eyes and cocked his head as though remembering something. "Monsieur Blythington, you spoke of a Southern Kingdom. I am confused."

"Please allow me to explain," Adam said. "When I first inspected my new home, I noticed dozens of oak trees as I drove up to the main house. I felt that Seven Oaks was no longer an appropriate name for the estate. As an Englishman, I felt Southern Kingdom might be a more appropriate name."

"Ah, I see," Jacques responded.

Adam wondered if Dupre' had accepted his explanation as logical or if he was mocking him. At any rate, in a short time he would have the respect of Dupre' and all of the gentry of the area. "I am happy to accept your invitation, Monsieur Dupre'," he said, "but only if you are sure that I am not intruding."

"How could a neighbor possibly be an intruder?" Jacques responded warmly. "You may join us in our carriage or, if you'd prefer, you may follow us in yours. Our carriage is on the south side of the church."

Jacques studied the young Englishman. He was not particularly fond of the English; as a matter of fact, he harbored deep animosity against the English. In truth, Monsieur Blythington was no longer an Englishman since he'd left his home to come to America. He was now a landowner and an American. He made up his mind to accept the young man as he would any neighbor.

Adam wondered again if he was being mocked. Perhaps Mr. Dupre' did not think he owned a fine carriage. He would show the Frenchie. Jeremiah was waiting for him in the carriage. "I will have my servant bring my carriage up, if you would please wait for me," he responded. He stepped to the front of the church and signaled for Jeremiah to come forth with the carriage.

He had ordered Henry to make sure the carriage was washed and polished and the matched carriage horses were curried and brushed. He swelled with pride as Jeremiah, who was dressed in royal blue livery, advanced with the carriage.

He watched out of the corner of his eye to measure the effect the horses and carriage would have on Dupre'. He could tell that Mr. Dupre' was impressed. "You may ride with me if you would like, and send your carriage on home," he said. "It would give me great pleasure to have a gentleman as distinguished as yourself and your lovely daughter accompany me."

Dupre' spoke to his daughter in French. Adam had no idea what was said, but Annabelle did not appear to be in favor of riding in his carriage.

After a few more moments, Jacques turned back to him. "We would be happy to accept your hospitality, Monsieur," he replied. He spoke in French to a servant standing near Annabelle. The servant answered in French and then left in the direction of Dupre's carriage.

"Where do you wish me to take you?" Adam asked.

"My son, Placide, and his lovely wife, Giselle, live on Bellevue Street," Jacques replied. "It's my plan to pick them up and return to Belle Bois. My servants have prepared a banquet to welcome Placide's return to St. Landry Parish."

"Please give the directions to his home to my servant," Adam requested.

Jacques gave directions to Jeremiah. Jeremiah nodded his head in comprehension. The passengers were seated and the carriage was soon underway.

Adam tried not to stare at Annabelle. Her hair was long and almost black. Her eyes were a lovely shade of green. He had never seen skin as pale and unblemished. He thought her bosom to be ample for a young lady as lithe as she. He could only see a hint of cleavage, but found what he saw most enticing. She spoke with a lovely French accent in a voice that sounded musical to him. Although she lacked the sensuousness of Hannah, he felt there was something smoldering beneath her genteel demeanor. He wanted to possess her, but he held himself back. He could not take her as he had Hannah. He would have to marry this one to bed her.

In only minutes, the carriage arrived at the home of Placide and Giselle Dupre'. Jacques stepped out of the carriage and walked to the front door. He soon returned with a dark headed man and a lovely woman. Adam thought the woman could easily pass as Annabelle's sister.

Adam stepped out as Dupre' neared the carriage.

"This is my son, Placide," Jacques said.

The man was about two inches taller than Adam and heavily built. He looked to be solid muscle. Adam felt his hand being crushed as Placide shook his hand.

"And this is my beautiful daughter-in-law, Giselle," Jacques said as he smiled brightly at the woman. "Please meet our new neighbor, Monsieur Blythington. He now resides at Seven Oaks. Mais, non," he corrected himself, "he resides at the Southern Kingdom."

Adam once more wondered if Dupre' was mocking him.

Adam listened as Monsieur Dupre' and his son discussed produce prices as they made their way to Belle Bois. After many miles, they finally arrived at the plantation.

Adam was awed by the sight of the giant oaks that lined both sides of the drive approaching Belle Bois.

Jacques noticed he was looking at the trees. "Those are live oaks, Monsieur Blythington," he said. "My grandfather was a young child when they were planted. Aren't they magnificent?"

"They are magnificent," Adam agreed. "They look old with their long gray beards."

"That's Spanish moss," Jacques commented. "It's not really part of the trees."

"Is the moss harmful to the trees?" Adam asked.

"Not at all," Jacques replied; "it only adds beauty."

A magnificent antebellum home with a stairway that curved up to the second story gallery and back down to the ground stood at the end of the drive. As much as he had been impressed with his own mansion, this one was even more impressive. "These people must be rich to have something this beautiful and still afford to pay the taxes," he thought to himself.

"Welcome to my home, Monsieur Blythington," Jacques said as they exited the carriage. "Please enjoy our hospitality."

Adam ran his eye over the grounds. Plants and flowers whose names were unknown to him were in abundance. Spring was showing its colors. "I have been meaning to hire a gardener," he said. "Your grounds are superb. Perhaps you could recommend someone to me."

"I am afraid our gardener's time is fully occupied with Belle Bois," Jacques replied. "You may ask him if he knows of someone he may recommend. There he is now." He nodded in the direction of a tall, thin, dark complected Negro man.

"Alex," Jacques called out. "Would you be so kind as to assist Monsieur Blythington?"

The Negro man known as Alex walked up to Jacques and Adam. He looked at Adam. "How may I be of help to you?" he asked.

"I find your work remarkable," Adam replied. "I am afraid our grounds are in disorder. Monsieur Dupre' said you may know someone you could recommend as a gardener."

"Perhaps I can help you, Monsieur," Alex responded. "My cousin, who works for me, desires to go out on his own. I recommend him highly."

"Please ask him to come and see me at Southern Kingdom," Adam said. He resented Dupre' for forcing him to speak directly to the Negro man as though he were an equal.

"Southern Kingdom?" Alex asked.

"Yes," Jacques answered. "Monsieur Blythington has given Seven Oaks a more appropriate name."

Once again Adam wondered if Dupre' was mocking him. It was not so much what he said, but the manner in which he said the words. Perhaps it was only Dupre's accent.

"Oh, I see," the Negro man said. He turned to Adam. "My cousin's name is Jules. I'll tell him to speak to you."

"Thank you," Adam said. "Tell him to ask for Hannah."

Jacques bid his family and guest to enter the home. "Marie must be on pins and needles," he said. "We have kept her waiting."

Jacques led the way to the dining room. To Adam, it more closely resembled a banquet room. The room was about half the size of his ballroom. In his estimation, the table could easily seat forty, or perhaps. even fifty people. The Dupre' family and their guest used only one end of the table.

After everyone was seated, servants began to carry serving dishes filled with savory food to the table. A middle-aged Negro woman seemed to be in charge.

"Mais, Marie, you've outdone yourself," Jacques said to the woman.

"Eat all you desire, Monsieur Blythington," he encouraged. "No one should leave my table while he remains hungry."

When everyone was served, Jacques bowed his head and led the family in a prayer of thanksgiving for their food. Once the prayer ended, everyone began to speak at once.

"There must be an interesting story to tell about your move to Louisiana," Jacques said.

"I hate to disappoint you," Adam responded. "The story is most uninteresting." He could not tell them he had come to Louisiana to take advantage of the distress of the southerners.

"Please tell us the story?" Giselle implored. "I'm sure you greatly underestimate yourself."

"There is little to tell," Adam maintained. "My family owns an import and export firm in London. My great grandfather started the business. Although the firm is very successful, it was not my cup of tea. I heard many favorable stories about the American south. The weather decided things for me. I wanted to get away from the dampness and the cold of London. I find the weather here much more favorable."

"You haven't suffered through one of our summers," Placide said. "You may change your mind and return to England."

"There is much more here to appreciate than the weather," Adam said with a twinkle in his eyes. "There are no ladies as striking as Mademoiselle Annabelle and Madam Giselle in England."

"Oooh, do you think so?" Giselle cooed. "Certainly you have met many beautiful women in England."

"None to match your beauty, Madam Giselle," Adam touted.

Giselle had lived in Louisiana all of her life. She was impressed with this foreigner who had such good taste and good manners. "Thank you very much, Monsieur Blythington," she said coyly. "You do flatter me."

"Only truth, Madam Giselle," he responded. "You and Mademoiselle Annabelle would turn heads in England. If you were to go to England, a woman of your beauty would be asked to have audience with the queen."

Placide had enough of the English dandy and his flattery. He was ready to change the subject. Giselle looked as though she were about to run off with the English fop. "Monsieur Blythington," he said, "your family must possess great wealth for you to come to St. Landry Parish and purchase one of the larger plantations."

Adam found Placide's remarks impertinent. Gentlemen did not pry into the personal matters of other gentlemen. At any rate, he would not reveal his dealings with Fisk. He had purchased the plantation and adjoining arpents for a fraction of their true value. "Suffice it to say we are solvent," he answered brusquely.

He was beginning to become anxious. Annabelle had not said a word to him. She did not seem to be impressed with him or with anything he said. He searched his mind for a means to draw her out. He could think of nothing.

The meal ended and Dupre' asked the men to retire with him to the drawing room. The women moved to the parlor. Adam felt he would not have an opportunity to court Annabelle. "Would you care for a cigar, Monsieur Blythington?" Jacques asked. "They're shipped from Havana. Placide is in the export import business."

Adam accepted one of the cigars. Placide struck a sulphur match and lit his cigar. "This is an excellent cigar," he said.

"Perhaps when Placide goes out again, he'll get a box for you," Jacques said.

Placide smiled. "I would be happy to get the cigars for you, Monsieur Blythington," he responded.

"Placide must have been a blockade runner and probably a smuggler," Adam thought to himself. "A very successful one from appearances. That explains how the taxes were paid on the property."

Giselle poked her head in the room. "Marie has made

lemonade," she said. "She's serving it on the verandah."

"Gentlemen," Jacques said, as he stood to lead the way to the verandah.

Annabelle continued to be aloof. Adam wondered what he had done to put her off. He drank his lemonade slowly while he searched his mind for an excuse to remain at the Dupre' home. Nothing came to mind. "I must be going," he said in resignation. "Thank you very much for your hospitality."

"Please come back and visit us," Jacques said warmly. "You're always welcome in our home."

"Thank you, Monsieur Dupre'," he responded. "You and your family are welcome to visit Southern Kingdom."

"That's most gracious of you, Monsieur." Jacques replied. "We'll find a time that's convenient."

Adam bowed stiffly to the ladies and shook hands with the men. He turned and walked to his waiting carriage. "Why has Annabelle proven to be so elusive?" he asked himself.

When Adam's carriage was out of sight, Annabelle said, "Why did you invite him, Pappa? He's a pretentious bore. Southern Kingdom? Does he fancy himself a king?"

"Annabelle," Jacques said sharply. "Manners. Remember you are a lady."

"He is pompous," insisted Annabelle.

"I thought he was very handsome and elegant," Giselle said wistfully. "He's obviously single. If I were in your shoes, I would pursue that one."

"You pursued him fairly well in your own shoes," Placide said coldly. "Perhaps I should call him out in a matter of honor."

"I did no such thing," Giselle protested loudly. "He's a gentleman. Annabelle is a fool for ignoring him."

"I would've been a fool not to ignore him," Annabelle responded. "No woman could love him as much as he loves himself."

"He is obviously wealthy," Jacques said to his family. "We would be wise to cultivate his friendship." To Annabelle, he said, "You have much to learn, mas cheiri. You could do worse than marry a man such as Blythington. A wise woman knows how to control her man."

"I would rather die," she responded.

*****

Annabelle claimed a headache after Adam left and went up to her room. She knew her father loved her but she was upset with him for hinting she should consider someone like Monsieur Blythington for marriage. He wasn't the kind of man she wished to marry.

She thought of her deceased mother and wished she could seek her advice. Her mind went back to the relationship between her mother and father and the love she knew they'd shared with one another. "If only I could meet a man like Pappa," she thought to herself.

She had turned eighteen in February. Several of the young men sought her hand, but she had found none who spoke to her heart. Robert Joubert, who was away studying medicine, had come the closest to winning her hand. She had very warm feelings for Robert but she didn't love him. Robert had moved on with his life and was now engaged to marry her friend, Angelina Granger. She was still fond of Robert but she knew Angelina loved him in a way that she never could have.

She thought of the young Englishman who had come to dinner. She had to admit that he was very handsome, but his arrogance greatly outweighed his good looks. Renaming Seven Oaks Southern Kingdom. How pompous. Did he expect he'd be royalty here in America?

She thought again of Robert. The quality she admired most in Robert was his kindness. Pappa had always been kind to Mamma. The man she'd choose as her husband would have to be kind. There would have to be kindness and warmth in her home. She pictured herself in her own home with her husband and children. The home would be filled with laughter. There would be love and warmth in her home. There would be many children. She loved Placide dearly but wished she had a sister. Giselle was sweet, but too scatter-brained to share the things she wanted to share with a sister.

Annabelle walked to one of the windows and gazed outside. She took in the beauty of the Belle Bois grounds. She appreciated all that her father provided for her, but her heart went out to the many people in the area, Negro and white, who were suffering.

The war had caused many hardships, but now that it was over, the recovery looked to be slow and painful. Many people were coming into the state to take away what little remained. The people didn't need a foot on their necks; they needed food and shelter. Tears rolled down her cheeks as she thought of the people who were desperate with nowhere to turn. She felt ashamed to have so much while others had nothing.

An idea entered her mind. She'd ask Pappa to ask all of the plantation owners to gather food for those who were hungry. She could even sell some of her jewelry to get money to buy clothing for the people. She'd do all she could to help those who had so little.

*****

Jacques Dupre' listened to his daughter as she poured out her ideas for helping the destitute. "Ah, my little one," he said when she finally stopped for breath, "you have your mother's heart. She would have given all she owned to keep anyone from going hungry."

"Pappa, we must do something," Annabelle cried out. "There are people who are starving. How can we sleep with our stomachs full while so many will starve?"

"Of course we'll help," Jacques responded. "We'll give food and I'll ask my friends to help. I'm sure there are many who will help."

Annabelle walked over to her father and hugged him tightly. "I knew you'd help," she said. "I'll collect my jewelry to sell to buy clothing."

"We'll help," Jacques stated emphatically, "but I won't have you selling your jewelry. Even Jesus said the poor would always be with us."

"But Pappa," she countered, "How could I keep such

things while so many are in need?"

"It's final," he answered sternly. "We'll do what we can to help, but we won't reduce ourselves to poverty."

Annabelle knew better than to argue further with her father. Perhaps she could sell a few things without him knowing. At least her father and his friends would help to feed the poor.

*****

The following Wednesday morning, Adam returned to Fisk's office.

"You've got a lot of good hardwood timber in your woods," Fisk said, as he went over the report with him. "My advice to you is to sell about half of what you have. With the price I can get you for your timber, you'll have all you need."

"Why only half?" Adam asked. "I want all the money I can get now."

"You'll have all you need for now with what you'll get from half the timber," Fisk replied. "You'd get enough if you would only sell a third. People would get suspicious if you moved too fast buying up the land."

"Perhaps you are right," Adam agreed as he stroked his chin. He made up his mind to sell only half of the timber.

"I can move on the sale of the timber rights now," Fisk said. "That is, if you want me to talk to the sawmill owner for you."

"I will speak with the sawmill owner myself," Adam said with an edge to his voice. "I prefer to keep our association private."

"Suit yourself," Fisk said with a shrug.

Adam and Fisk read through the report. The report seemed thorough to Adam. Fisk gave him instructions as to the maximum amount he could hope to receive and the minimum amount to accept. Adam felt that he was prepared to approach the sawmill owner.

"Robert Jacobson is a shrewd businessman," Fisk warned. "Don't let him talk you down any lower than that figure." He pointed to an amount written on the report. "He might try to talk you down, but he can afford to give you top price. With that new steam engine of his, he's cutting a lot of timber and making a bundle."

As Adam turned to walk out of the door, Fisk added, "Don't deal with his son, Luke. That boy doesn't know half of what his father does. You won't get what you would from his father."

*****

Adam arrived at the sawmill a short while later. He tied the black stallion to the rail that stood beside the side door of the sawmill. A sign to the right of the door said, "Office." He walked through the door and entered the sawmill. The noise of the mill assaulted his ears. "How can anyone hear himself think in this place?" he asked himself. He looked around. Unlike most businesses, the sawmill's office was located on the second floor. He climbed the stairs and knocked on the office door.

"May I help you?" asked a small man wearing a green visor.

"I wish to speak to Mr. Robert Jacobson," Adam responded. "I am Mr. Blythington." The small man ushered him into the office and knocked on another door.

"Come in," a voice called from the other side of the door.

The small man entered the office and returned in a short while. "Mr. Jacobson will see you now," he said.

Adam entered the office. A large man about six feet, four inches tall, who had to be Jacobson, stood behind the only desk in the office. "Mr. Blythington," he said as he offered his hand. "What can I do for you?"

Adam shook Jacobson's hand.

"Please have a seat," Jacobson said.

He sat in a chair across from Jacobson and looked around. He was not impressed with Jacobson's office. It reminded him of his small office in London. "I wish to speak to you about the sale of timber rights," he said.

"I know most of the timber land in this area," Jacobson said. "I'm not familiar with your holdings."

Adam was pleased he had Fisk's report in his possession. "I am the owner of what was Seven Oaks Plantation," he responded. "I also own several other parcels that adjoin that property. I have it all mapped out here." He handed Jacobson the portion of the report that mapped out the timberland Fisk had outlined for the sale.

Jacobson looked over the report. "Very thorough," he said. "May I ask you who put the report together?"

"The name of the firm is of no consequence," Adam replied. "I own the timber and I am here to negotiate the sale of the timber rights if you are interested."

"I'm interested," Jacobson responded. "If the timber on the property is as this report says, we'll have an excellent harvest of hardwood." He looked at the report once more. "Of course, I'll have to send my own people out to assess the timber before I give you a price."

"It is as the report states," Adam said boldly. "I do understand why you would want your own people to assess the timber." He rose from his chair. "I would like an answer by tomorrow at five p.m.. After that time, I shall offer the timber rights to another firm."

"That doesn't give my people much time," Jacobson responded, "but I'll see what we can do."

"My offer is firm," Adam stated bluntly

He was very pleased with himself. He recalled the details of the meeting as he rode the stallion to Fisk's office. The report had given him the nerve to demand a limited time frame. He felt sure Jacobson would find the timber to be acceptable.

*****

"I've already selected some sites for you," Fisk said as he cocked back in his chair. "The best piece is owned by Paul Breaux. Five hundred and twenty arpents. About two hundred arpents have good hardwood stands. About two hundred arpents planted in cotton. The rest is house, barns and pasture land."

"What is Breaux asking for his land?" Adam asked.

"Who said he wants to sell?" Fisk asked. "His land adjoins your property. It's really good land. The timber is like money in the bank and the cotton is already planted. Breaux may even agree to sharecrop the land."

"Why would he agree to sell and why would he agree to sharecrop his own land?" Adam asked with a puzzled look on his face.

"You said you didn't want to know the details," Fisk reminded him. "I can tell you if you really want to know."

Adam considered Fisk's statement. Something inside of him wanted no part of the deal. Something else told him this was only business. People get hurt in business and people get ahead in business. The better businessman wins. He was doing nothing underhanded. He was simply buying land through a land agent. "What else do you have in mind?" he asked.

"There are several other smaller pieces," Fisk replied with a smile. He had studied Blythington as he rationalized the land purchase in his mind. "If you put them all together, we come up with about nine hundred and thirty arpents. That should do us for now."

Adam did not like to think of himself and Fisk as "us." He said nothing, however. "How much will the land cost?" he asked.

"If you get what I think you'll get for the sale of the timber rights," Fisk replied, "even after you pay my fee, you'll have more than half of the money left. In another month or so, we can start thinking about adding to your holdings."

"What is the amount of your fee?" he asked.

"I figure with the sale of the timber rights and the land transactions, oh, about a thousand dollars," Fisk answered.

"A thousand dollars," Adam choked out.

"That's only if you get what I think you will for the timber," Fisk responded.

"I do believe I am making you rich," Adam said with a hint of sarcasm in his voice.

"Don't forget who's making you rich," Fisk responded boldly. "This is a mutual association. I told you when we met at the courthouse we'd be good for each other."

"Yes, you did tell me that," Adam agreed.

*****

Adam walked up the stairs to Robert Jacobson's office. It was five minutes before five o'clock. He knocked on the door. It was opened only moments later by Mr. Jacobson.

"Come on in, Mr. Blythington," Jacobson said. "We've been expecting you."

Adam entered the office. There was a young man in the office he had not seen before. "This is my son, Luke," Jacobson said. "I'd like for him to be in on the meeting, if you don't mind. He's learning the business."

"I have no objection," Adam responded.

"Come on in my office," Jacobson said.

Jacobson sat at his desk. Luke sat to the right side of his father. Adam took the same chair he had sat in during the previous visit.

"We've gone over your timber," the elder Jacobson said. "That is, as well as we could in the time you allotted us. It's pretty much as your report said. We're prepared to make you an offer."

"I hope you will keep in mind I already know the value of the timber," Adam stated. "As I said, I am prepared to go elsewhere to sell the rights to my timber."

"I understand that," Robert Jacobson said. "I don't think there'll be a need for that. We're offering fair market value."

"Go on," Adam said.

Robert Jacobson's offer was well above the minimum price Fisk had outlined. Adam was determined to receive the maximum amount Fisk had told him he could expect. "Your offer is below what I am willing to accept," he said as he began to rise from his chair.

The elder Jacobson looked at Adam with dismay in his eyes. The younger Jacobson had a look of contempt on his face. This was the one Fisk had warned him about. He wished he had objected to the presence of the son in the meeting. It was too late.

"Hold on now," the elder Jacobson said. "No need

to rush off. We're still talking. What number did you have in mind?"

"As you know," Adam replied, "I took the time to have a survey conducted of my timber holdings. I know the timber you are buying and its worth."

"We're in a buyer's market right now," Luke Jacobson said. "We have many other offers to consider. We can buy timber for less than the price we already quoted to you. What makes you think your timber is worth more than that of the other land owners?"

"It is not what I think, young man," Adam responded caustically. "It is what I know." He quoted the price he wanted to receive from Jacobson. "Either accept my offer, or I go elsewhere."

The younger Jacobson tightened his jaw. Anger registered on his face.

"We'll give you your price," the elder Jacobson said.

The son turned to his father in dismay. He looked back at Adam. He looked as though he were going to speak but remained silent.

"There's one stipulation," Robert Jacobson said. "I want right of first refusal on the remainder of your timber holdings and any other timber you might acquire. If I get the yield I'm hoping for, I might want the rest of it."

"Agreed," Adam responded. "It is a pleasure doing business with you."

He shook Robert Jacobson's hand and then offered his hand to Luke Jacobson. Luke looked at the hand and then at his father. He reluctantly reached his own hand out and shook Adam's hand.

*****

Adam felt as though he were walking on air when he entered Fisk's office. He had run a fantastic bluff and had won.

Fisk looked up from his desk when Blythington walked in. "What's making you so happy?" he asked.

"I received the maximum amount for the timber," Adam

answered. "I am prepared to continue. Have you made any headway with the purchases?"

"I was waiting on the money is all," Fisk answered. "Breaux is willing to sharecrop if you'd like or you can put someone else on his land. We're ready to move."

He started to ask Fisk how Breaux was persuaded but decided not to ask the question. "How is Breaux as a farmer?" he asked.

"He's a good farmer," Fisk answered, "but he likes his spirits too much. If he can leave the bottle alone, he's very good."

"How can we be sure he will remain sober?" Adam asked.

"We can't for sure," Fisk replied, "but we can use some heavy persuasion. If I explain it to him correctly, I think he'll give up drinking. He has too many children to want to take that kind of a risk."

"How many people does Breaux employ?" he asked.

"He has about twenty darkies working for him," Fisk answered. "Ain't none of um capable of running the place. Breaux would be your best bet. Maybe you could get another white man out there to run the place."

"I thought the north had fought a war to free the Negro people," Adam said. "You surely do speak ill of the people you risked your life to free."

"I put the uniform on because I had no choice," Fisk replied. "I really don't care what happens to that bunch. I fought hard to save my own skin."

"We will leave Breaux on the property for now," Adam said, "Should he show signs that he is not dependable, we will replace him." He rubbed his chin. "What about the other property?"

"We're ready on that too," Fisk replied. He had noticed that Blythington used "we" when he spoke of decisions that were to be made. His association with Blythington was growing stronger. "We had a few snags to work out. Nothing major."

Fisk quoted the price of the land and reiterated his fee. He asked Adam what he had received in payment for the timber rights. Adam realized his hard stand with Jacobson

had increased Fisk's fee. Fisk smiled as Adam counted out the money.
"I'll take my fee in advance this time," Fisk said. "You know you can trust me and I know I can trust you. You can go to Cortez's office tomorrow and sign the papers."

*****

Adam handed the stallion's reins to Fred and walked into the house. Hannah was waiting for him.
"There's a servant from the Dupre' place waiting to see you," she said slowly and carefully. She smiled when she saw that Adam had noticed the difference in her speech.
"Please bring him to me," he responded. He was amazed at the difference Professor Pennington's tutelage had made in her speech in such a short while.
She returned with a young Negro man who had a remarkable resemblance to Belle Bois' gardener.
"May I help you?" Adam asked. He knew why the young man was there to see him but he was not going to make it easier for the man.
"Monsieur Blythington, I'm Jules Dupre'," the man said. "My cousin, Alex, told me you spoke to him about the position of head gardener for your plantation."
Adam had not thought in terms of a head gardener. It would take several workmen to get the grounds in order and maintain them. "I did speak with your cousin," he replied. "I assume you are up to the task?"
"Yes, Monsieur," Jules answered. "I've been working with Alex. I took the liberty of walking over the area surrounding your home. It will be very beautiful when I've carried out my ideas."
"Excellent," Adam responded. "You may speak with Hannah about your salary and housing."
Hannah signaled for Jules to follow her. Jules stopped and turned back to Adam. "I almost forgot in my excitement," he said. "I have a letter for you from Monsieur Dupre'." He handed the letter to Adam and followed Hannah.

Adam read the letter. He was pleased with the contents. He reread the letter more slowly. It read:

Dear Monsieur Blythington,

My family and I enjoyed meeting you on Sunday past. It is good to get to know one's neighbors. It is my hope that my humble home and hospitality were acceptable to you.
Entertaining is difficult with the deprivations put upon us by the war.
As you were preparing to depart, you extended an invitation to myself and my daughter, Annabelle. We would like to accept your invitation. It is my hope that Sunday coming following services is convenient for you. Please pen a response and send it to me via Jules.

Yours respectfully,

Jacques L. Dupre', Esquire

He wasted no time penning a response. Annabelle was coming to his plantation. He wished he had more time for Jules to get the grounds ready. Thank goodness Hannah and the household servants had gotten the house in order. Everything was cleaned and polished.

Repairs were ongoing to the exterior of the house. That could not be helped. The repairs were advancing but it would take some time before they were complete. At least the Dupre's would know he was not leaving the mansion in disrepair.

"Hannah!" he called out.

She came running. "Yassuh, Mr. Adam," she said breathlessly. She caught herself. She was forgetting all that the professor had taught her. "Is anything wrong?" she continued.

"We will have very important people as guests Sunday," he responded. "Please ask Margaret to prepare a feast worthy of a king. We want to impress these people."

Hannah had never seen Adam so excited. "Who are these people?" she asked. "The Dupre's," he replied. "Mr. Jacques Dupre' and his daughter."

She wondered if the reason for his excitement was the daughter. She would wait and watch.

She assured Adam that all would be in order for the Sunday visit. She would make sure he was impressed with her resourcefulness.

CHAPTER FOUR

May 30, 1865 - June 3, 1865

There was a flurry of activity at Southern Kingdom. Adam harried the servants to be meticulous in making sure everything was perfect. In his excitement, he had less need for Hannah in his bed.

Adam needing her favors less left Hannah with feelings of insecurity. She was sure the Dupre' girl was the cause of her problems. She smoldered in her hatred for the woman who was stealing Adam from her.

Hannah couldn't afford to do anything that would anger Adam. Her position was too tenuous to demand his attention. She had tried to flex her muscles once only to find herself in a precarious position. She'd take no chances, but there would be a way if she waited.

In the meantime, she continued to work diligently as Professor Pennington taught her the proper pronunciation of words and was broadening her world by teaching her to read and write. Speaking properly would help her greatly, whether she stayed at Southern Kingdom or cast her lot elsewhere. In the back of her mind she hoped she could become a proper lady in hopes that Adam would consider marrying her.

She took a trip into town Saturday afternoon. Although there was now a plantation store run by Teddy Dunbar, a man Adam had hired in town, she wanted to make sure everything was as fresh as possible for the Sunday meal. She had the other house servants pick fresh vegetables from the garden early Sunday morning.

Margaret had all the help she needed, perhaps even more, as she prepared the meal for the Dupre's. Hannah had even drafted the professor to help with the place settings. She wanted to ensure everything was set out properly. Adam would suffer no embarrassment.

*****

Adam set out early in the morning with Jeremiah driving his carriage. He had arranged to pick the Dupre's up and take them to church services. The Dupre's would return with him after services.

Later that Sunday morning, Hannah watched as the carriage drew up to the mansion. She wanted to have a good look at her adversary. She watched as the Dupre' woman descended from the carriage. She was a very pretty young lady; just the kind who would turn a white man's head. Hannah smiled as she sized up her foe.

Her fears left immediately. She was certain that she was going to win the battle. "This young woman doesn't have what Adam needs; the fire he can't live without; the fire that I set to burning; the fire that I'll keep smoldering; the fire that only I can keep under control," she said to herself. "Adam's desire will always send him back to me.

"He'll be happy with that white woman for a while and then he'll come back to me. He needs passion. He needs someone who can match him. This little thing can't hope to satisfy him that way. She can only keep him happy for a little while." Hannah breathed a sigh of relief. It was only a matter of time. She could wait. The young thing was more an object of pity than of anger.

Hannah continued to smile as she saw to the seating of Adam's guests. She checked the dining room table once more. The professor's help was invaluable. China, silverware and crystal were placed for each of the guests. Everything was perfect. Mary, Ruth and Fred began serving the delicacies Margaret had prepared. She could tell by the looks on everyone's faces that the meal was a success. She was satisfied that she hadn't let Adam down.

Jacques Dupre' patted his stomach as he rose from the

table. "I'm afraid I've eaten too much," he said. "The food was so delicious, I couldn't stop myself. If you don't mind, I'll sit in one of the rockers on your verandah and rest. You two young people can occupy yourselves with a stroll about the plantation while I rest."

Annabelle frowned at her father. Her last wish was to be alone with their host. She would express her unhappiness with her father later. She was forced to walk with Monsieur Blythington. Her father left her with no choice.

Adam offered her his arm. "I would be happy to show you around," he said. "I realize my holdings pale in comparison to Belle Bois."

She held her parasol in her left hand and took his arm with her right hand. The weather was perfect for a walk. The sun shone brightly in a cloudless cobalt blue sky. Although there was abundant sunshine, the day was mild. She looked at Monsieur Blythington. She would have preferred another companion for such a beautiful day.

Adam said nothing as he walked along with Annabelle. He was not good at small talk and could think of nothing of any significance to say to her. They arrived at a pecan orchard. The leaves on the pecan trees were beginning to cover the tops of the trees. He stopped to admire the trees. He looked down at Annabelle. Her beauty took his breath away.

"What really brought you to our parish, Monsieur Blythington?" Annabelle asked.

He gazed at the beauty that surrounded him. He saw things differently when he was with her. He turned to Annabelle. "My mother died when I was only nine years old," he replied. "My father sent me away to school. I was only home for holidays. My father died when I was eighteen. He left almost everything to my two older brothers. I realized I would be forever in their shadows if I did not strike out on my own. I wanted to amount to something." He looked away from her and gazed again at their surroundings.

Once again he turned and focused his attention on the beautiful young lady who had agreed to walk with him. "I now own this estate," he continued as he extended his arm toward the fields. "I still amount to nothing. The education I received was excellent, but I was never taught how to be a person. My mother provided what little training I have before her death, but with her passing, that part of me failed to grow."

He stepped away from her and walked several feet and turned his back to her. "I do not expect you to understand," he said. He turned around and faced her. "Not that I think you would not try. You have a close family. I was a nuisance to my older brothers. Someone they hoped would not embarrass them." He stopped once again and looked at her. He had made a fool of himself once more.

"I misjudged you, Monsieur Blythington," she said as she walked up to him. "I mistook your efforts to compensate for the loss of your mother when you were yet a child and the pain you suffered because of the terrible treatment you received from your brothers for something else. I'm very sorry."

"A miracle," Adam thought to himself. "I would not have guessed in a million years that this was the way to soften her heart."

"I try too hard to compensate," he said. "The truth is, I have had very little experience with ladies. Eaton is an all male school. I apologize for my blunders."

"It must have been difficult growing up without a mother, Monsieur Blythington," Annabelle said. "I'm fortunate to have had my mother with me until only a short time ago." Tears welled up in her eyes. "She grew weak last winter and perished." A sob escaped her lips.

"I am very sorry," Adam said as compassionately as was possible for him. "I know the loss you are suffering. I remember how dreadful the loss of my mother was to me. I lost a very important part of my life." He gazed around again and then looked back at her. "May I ask a favor of you?"

"You may," she responded.

"Please call me Adam," he said. "Monsieur Blythington sounds so formal."

She smiled. "Certainly, Adam," she said, "but only if you'll call me Annabelle."

"That pleases me very much," he responded.

The couple commenced walking once more. Annabelle seemed content to be with him. Adam looked at Southern Kingdom with new eyes. He was elated to show this beautiful young lady his property.

"This is remarkable for a man as young as yourself," she said as she swept her hand to encompass his plantation. "I want to ask another question of you. Tell me truthfully why you decided to name your plantation Southern Kingdom?"

"It does sound rather pompous," he responded. "I finally had something that was my own. I wanted it to be something my brothers would admire when they came to visit me." He shook his head. "That is, if they ever think I am important enough to visit. I did not stop to think how the name would sound to the people who live in this area. Perhaps I should change the name."

"No," she said, "I think it's an appropriate name. I wish your brothers were here to see what you're building. They'd reconsider their opinion of their younger brother."

"I am pleased that you think so," he responded. "I should get past wanting to impress them."

"I can understand how you feel after all you've been through," she said. "A poor young boy alone in the world. I wish I had known you then. I would've embraced you and tried to take all your pain away."

"You are so kind," he responded. "I no longer feel as empty and alone. It certainly is wonderful to have someone who understands me."

On impulse, Annabelle threw her arms around him, rose on tiptoe and kissed his lips. "I'm sorry," she said when she pulled away from him. "You must think I'm very forward."

"No," he responded. "I think you are very kind." He smiled. "I am twenty-two years old and that was my very first kiss."

"Then it makes a first for both of us, Adam," she said. "I'm eighteen and that was my first kiss." She was happy for his sake that she had only allowed her beaus to kiss her cheek.

"I am happy to be the first man you ever kissed," he responded as he smiled brightly. "I hope in the future we will have many other firsts."

Annabelle smiled. "Perhaps," she said. "One can never tell."

Adam and Annabelle walked hand-in-hand as they returned to the house. "May I take the liberty of calling on you?" he asked.

"I'd be very pleased to have you call on me," she replied. They continued their walk toward the house in silence. Annabelle assumed Adam was deep in thought. Adam's thoughts would not have pleased her. He had decided she was going to be the woman who would bear his children. He was wondering how she would be in bed. He was pleased that she had not interrupted his thoughts.

When they neared the house, Jacques called out, "Ah, I'm glad to see you haven't lost your way. Did you enjoy your walk?" He looked at his daughter. She was smiling as she returned his gaze. To his dismay, he saw that she was actually holding Blythington's hand. There was certainly magic in the air of Southern Kingdom.

*****

Annabelle sat in the Belle Bois library trying to concentrate on her book. Her thoughts continued to flow back to the previous afternoon when she had walked with Adam Blythington. She couldn't believe how badly she had misjudged the man. What she'd taken for arrogance was a broken man's struggle to overcome his painful shyness and his low opinion of himself. The hapless young man had suffered emotionally by losing his mother at an early age. Making matters worse was a father who took little interest in him, and two older brothers who did all they could to make him feel worthless. Even though he and his brothers were an ocean apart, he was still trying to prove his worth to them.

Her heart raced as she recalled the brief moment when she'd been moved by sorrow to kiss him. He'd seemed so sad and vulnerable. She had never allowed any man, except her father, to kiss her lips and then that was back when she was a young girl.

She wondered what it was about Adam that had drawn her to him? She recalled how he'd reluctantly revealed the suffering he'd endured as he grew up in England. She had seen the pain in his eyes as he traveled back in his mind over those troubled years. She had longed for a man who would touch her heart. Perhaps he was the one to whom her heart would surrender.

Pappa had looked at her strangely on the carriage ride back home. He had finally asked her what had changed her mind about Adam. She wanted to tell him all she had learned about him but something held her back. Adam was too sensitive for other people to know how much he had suffered. He had trusted her with his painful memories. This was something only between herself and Adam. She had searched for an answer that would satisfy Pappa and protect Adam. "Perhaps I was too hasty in judging him," she had finally replied. "He seems to be a nice man." Her father had smiled and then turned to gaze out of the carriage window.

She picked up her book once again, but after reading only a few sentences, she set it down again. She found herself missing Adam and wanting to see him once more. He was different from the other young men who'd tried to court her. He was a man of ambition who wanted to make something of himself, yet he had a soft and gentle side. She was sure his childhood experiences had turned him into a deeply caring man. He was the kind of man who would share her aspiration for taking care of the downtrodden.

It surprised her when she realized she couldn't wait for him to come calling. Now that she knew him better, she understood why he seemed to be arrogant; it was only his way of disguising his vulnerability. She'd draw him out after they were married. She laughed out loud at herself. How foolish of her to already be thinking of marriage. Still, the thought of marrying Adam and helping him to become the man she knew he really was deep down inside, intrigued her.

CHAPTER FIVE

June 4, 1865

The following Tuesday evening, Hannah came to him. "Mr. Adam" she said, "there's a Negro man talking to the field hands. He wants us to organize. He says we need to come to you and ask for more money. His name's Alfred Clark."

"Thank you for coming to me," Adam responded. "Please fetch Henry and return to me." Hannah nodded her head and left to get Henry.

Adam's first reaction was to go to Fisk with the problem. He stopped and gave the problem further consideration. If he asked Fisk to solve the problem, another agitator would take Clark's place. He had to make a statement the employees would long remember. He pulled one of the two federal issue handguns he owned from his desk drawer. Fisk had insisted that he purchase the handguns for protection as he traveled back and forth from town. He sat at his desk with the handgun in his lap.

Hannah walked in with Henry. Adam saw a look on Henry's face he did not like. Henry had the same look as the day Adam arrived at the plantation. Whatever Clark was saying was stirring up the people.

"Henry," Adam said, "Please hitch a wagon and place it near the steps of the side porch. Please put a shovel and several burlap sacks into the wagon."

Henry gave him a look of contempt but set out to do as he had been ordered.

Adam turned to Hannah. "When Henry returns," he said, "please have Mr. Clark come to my office to discuss the plight of our employees. Use the front door when you bring Mr. Clark into the house. I would like for you and Henry to remain as witnesses to our discussion."

Henry returned about twenty minutes later.

"Please remain in my office, Henry," Adam said. "I would like for you and Hannah to be witnesses to my discussion with Mr. Clark."

Henry sat in a chair in the corner of the office.

While Adam waited for Hannah to return, he questioned himself as to whether or not he had the nerve to carry out what he had concluded was necessary to preserve Southern Kingdom. James Fisk had killed and had ordered the killing of several men. Fisk did not seem to be guilt-ridden; in fact, he appeared at ease with what he termed, "solving business problems."

Adam held no personal animosity toward Clark. "You might say this is self defense," he reasoned to himself. "If Clark lives, Southern Kingdom dies."

Hannah returned with Clark. He had dark eyes, short black hair and was of medium height and build. He wore glasses and was light complected.

"Please be seated, Mr. Clark," Adam said.

Clark seated himself directly across from Adam. Hannah and Henry sat in the back corners of the room opposite from one another.

"I understand you are concerned about my employees," Adam said to Clark.

"Slavery has ended, Mr. Blythington," Clark said. "It's time for you southerners to pay decent wages to your employees."

"I am now a southerner, Mr. Clark," Adam responded. "I arrived here shortly after the war. I am originally from England, but I digress. Please continue, Mr. Clark."

"I, and others like me, are organizing people of color," Clark continued. "We're demanding fair treatment and equal wages for our people."

"Very noble, Mr. Clark," Adam responded. "It is your opinion that my employees are underpaid."

"It isn't my opinion," Clark stated. "I've talked to your employees and others on my journey here. I'm aware of what you and your kind are doing."

"My kind?" Adam asked. "Would you please explain what you mean by that."

"I mean people such as you who exploit people," Clark said. "What are the wages you pay your employees?"

"You would have to ask that of Mr. Dunbar, who operates our plantation store," Adam replied. "He keeps track of the employees' hours. Our employees charge goods at our plantation store. Mr. Dunbar pays the employees for the hours they work after he deducts the amount the employee charges at the plantation store from that employee's wages."

"That's the problem," Clark said. "There's nothing left after the plantation store deducts for the goods they've purchased on credit."

"Why do you blame me or Mr. Dunbar for that?" Adam asked. "It is not we who charge the goods."

"You have it set up so the people of color become virtual slaves," Dunbar replied heatedly. "The emancipation proclamation means nothing to you."

"My employees are free to come and go as they please," Adam countered. "There is nothing to keep them from leaving Southern Kingdom. Of course, they do have to pay what they owe at the plantation store."

"How are they expected to pay?" asked Clark becoming even more heated.

"The same way anyone would pay," Adam replied, "with their wages, of course. By the way, I pay white and Negro field hands the same amount."

"Do you employ any white field hands?" Clark asked.

Adam waved his left hand in the air. "Mr. Clark, I have listened to your concerns," he said. "I have answered all of your questions, yet you are not satisfied with my answers. We could go on with this discussion all night." He leaned slightly forward in his chair. "I want to make you an offer." There was a note of intimacy in his voice.

"What kind of offer?" Clark asked.

"I will give you five hundred dollars to leave this plantation and never return," Adam replied.

"I can't be bought off," Clark responded with contempt.

"I will raise the amount to one thousand dollars," Adam offered.

Clark blinked his eyes. One thousand dollars was a lot of money. He shook his head. "I said I can't be bought." Adam contemplated the reaction of the Negro man sitting before him. "I will raise the amount to two thousand dollars," he continued. "What do you say to that?"

Clark was amazed. He had never seen that much money. He believed in his cause, but two thousand dollars was a lot of money. Reluctantly he shook his head. "Mr. Blythington," he said. "What would I be if I sold out to you?"

"Rich," Adam countered. "You would be rich." He watched Clark as he considered the offer. He could sense that the man was reaching his breaking point.

"If you make it five thousand dollars," Clark said as he leaned toward Adam, "I promise to leave and never come back."

Adam smiled coldly. He had found the agitator's price. "I understood you to say you believed in your cause," he said. He turned to Henry. "What do you think of your hero now?"

Henry shook his head in dismay. He looked down at the floor.

"I hope you learned something today," Adam said. He raised the handgun from his lap. "I know you will never return to bother me, Mr. Clark." He leveled the gun and pulled the trigger. The handgun barked. Clark fell from the chair and lay dead with a bullet hole between his eyes.

"Mr. Adam," Henry said. "You done kilt him."

"Yes I have, Henry," Adam responded coldly. "I will allow no one to take Southern Kingdom from me. Do you understand me, Henry?"

Henry shook in fear. Mr. Adam had taught him a lesson by making him unhitch the buggy horse. He had learned another more important lesson today. He looked at Mr. Adam in abject fear. He'd make sure he never crossed Mr. Adam again.

"Henry, pick him up and put him in the wagon," Adam ordered. "Cover him with those burlap sacks and take him to the plantation graveyard. Dig his grave and bury him. I want a wooden marker on his grave. There is to be nothing written on

the marker. Everyone will forget his name but not my warning."
"Yessuh, Mr. Adam." Henry responded.
"Henry," Adam said once more.
"Yessuh, Mr. Adam," Henry answered in a shaky voice.
"Remember, I shot Mr. Clark without hesitation," he said. "If word of this ever reaches the authorities, I will do the same to you."
"Ain't nobody gone tell no owtority," Henry responded. He wasted no time picking Clark up and carrying him out.

Word would get out among the Negro people. They would not be so willing to listen to the next agitator.

Adam thought about what he had done. It was not as difficult as he had anticipated. He felt no regret. He had killed in self defense. Clark would still be alive had he not threatened Southern Kingdom.

He turned to Hannah. "You do not look upset or surprised," he said.

"Mr. Adam," she responded, " I knew when you told Henry to hitch the wagon and load a shovel and some burlap sacks Clark wouldn't live through the night. I knew exactly what you had planned."

"Yet you did nothing to stop me or warn him," he responded. He was astounded.

"This is my home, too, Mr. Blythington," Hannah responded. "I want to see Southern Kingdom succeed. I would like to share your dream of making this the largest plantation in the parish."

Adam studied her face. She had pronounced his last name without hesitation and without error. She was an enigma. She had allowed him to kill a man in cold blood to protect Southern Kingdom. "I am tired," he said. "Would you like to come to bed with me?"

She smiled at him. "I'd like that very much," she replied.

The lovemaking was better than before. When he awoke, Hannah was lying in his arms. She felt him stir and opened her eyes. "It must be almost time to get up," he said.

She turned her head and looked toward the window. "It must be close to five o'clock," she said. She rolled over and began to leave the bed.

"One moment," Adam said.

She turned her head toward him. "I will more than likely marry Annabelle," he said. "That will not alter our relationship. I learned something last night."

"What's that?" she asked.

"You are more valuable to me than all the Annabelles in the world," he replied. "My feelings are stronger for you than they will ever be for her. You and I are soul mates."

She turned around and embraced him. "I love you, Adam," she said. "I'll always be yours." She left the bed and walked out of the room.

He was stunned by her confession of love. He thought about his feelings for Hannah. They were as close to love as anything he had ever known.

CHAPTER SIX

July 1865 - October 1865

"Five thousand, four hunderd and forty arpents of land is a substantial sized plantation, but it is not nearly large enough," Adam thought to himself as he sat in the plantation office waiting for Paul Breaux to keep his appointment. His original plan was to purchase a nice home and enough land to guarantee himself the life of a squire. He wanted the power and prestige that would come with such a life. His plans had changed. He now owned thousands of arpents of land and a mansion and still wanted more.

He had the power that came from controlling such a vast estate, but what he had assumed would satisfy him when he had decided to leave England was not enough. He wanted more power and more land. The plantation had to be even larger. As Fisk said, "This is only the beginning. There are plantations larger than Southern Kingdom."

He had sent word for Paul Breaux to meet him at noon. He grew more and more impatient as he waited for Breaux to arrive. Breaux was already an hour late. The office walls seemed to close in on him as the minutes ticked off and his mood worsened.

He stepped out of his office and went outside to the garden. "Punctuality," he thought to himself; "a man should always be punctual." Breaux would learn to be punctual or he would be replaced.

He heard the sound of horse's hooves in the distance. The sound grew louder as he listened. As the horse drew nearer, he could make out a disheveled man on a brown horse. About a week's growth of beard was on the rider's face. He wore a straw hat pulled down over his ears. The hat was pulled so low that Adam could not see the man's eyes.

The man pulled on the reins, stopped the horse and dismounted. The dismount looked almost like the man had fallen from the horse.

Adam looked at the man more closely as he swayed drunkenly before him. His hair was black with some gray mixed in and his beard stubble was about half black and half gray. The man was about five feet, ten inches tall. He was not a large man but he was powerfully built.

"You Blitinton?" the man asked as he eyed Adam. "You da man I come to see. I'm Paul Breaux."

Breaux smelled like he hadn't been near soap and water in weeks and liquor fumes assailed Adam's nose when the man spoke.

Adam was not impressed with the appearance of Paul Breaux. "I am Mr. Blythington," he answered. He pulled his watch from his pocket and held it up for Breaux to see. "You are over an hour late."

"Yah," Breaux said, "I was playin cards. I guess I loss track of da time."

"Playing cards?" Adam asked with incredulity in his voice. "You are late for a meeting with me because you were playing cards?"

"Yah, dats what I said," agreed Breaux. "It rained yestidy and we coulden do nuttin in da feel. Me an some a da hans was playin cards."

"Henry is working with the Southern Kingdom field hands at this moment," he thought to himself. "The rain is not what is keeping Breaux from working. He has chosen not to work." "Mr. Breaux," Adam said sternly, "I now own the land you farm. If you intend to remain on my land, there are certain things you will have to understand."

"I already understan, Mr. Blitinton," Breaux said angrily. "You and you buncha teeves stole my lan. Now you tink you kin give me orders. I wanna tell you someting, Blitinton, we been in dis place longer den you. You ain't gon tell me nuttin. I'm gonna farm de lan cause I got to feed my chirdren." Breaux shook his head in frustration. "I wish you could talk in French; I'd really tell you how I feel."

Adam was angry with Breaux because of his lack of respect. He was giving Breaux the opportunity to continue to farm the land and this was how Breaux thanked him. "I have a mind to run you off and replace you," he said. "My associate assured me you are a most capable farmer. That is the only reason you continue to reside on my land."

"Let me tell you someting, boy," Breaux said as he wagged his finger in Adam's face. "Dat lan was my Daddy's and his Daddy's befoe him. It's gonna be my lan agin. In da meantime, I'll farm da lan. Jus don tink you can tell me what to do. Da klan gonna teach you a lessin if you try to go too far."

"The clan," Adam responded. "I hope you are not staking your future on the benevolence of that organization. You would do well to end your insolence and do as I instruct you." He had heard about the clan or klan as the locals spelled the name of the organization. He made up his mind to visit Fisk early in the morning and ask him about the clan. Meanwhile, he had to do something about Breaux.

"Walk this way," he said as he turned and made his way to the office. Breaux followed behind him.

Hannah was in the hallway as Adam and Breaux entered the mansion. He signaled for her to wait for him in the hallway. After Breaux was seated in the office, he excused himself and went out into the hallway to meet with her.

"Hannah," he said in a hushed voice, "send Fred to get Henry. When Henry arrives, I want him to show Breaux to his quarters. He is to have the empty employee house."

"I understand," she answered in a hushed tone.

"I want you to have someone take Breaux's horse to the barn and unsaddle him," he continued. She left the room in search of Henry.

Breaux was not leaving Southern Kingdom until Adam determined whether or not his threat of contacting the clan had any merit. If Breaux had made an empty threat, he would be dealt with for his insolence. That sort of behavior would not be tolerated from any Southern Kingdom employee.

Henry returned from the field at a run. Two of the field hands followed after him. Hannah knocked on the office door and Adam opened the door.

"Henry's having problems with one of the field hands" she said. "He says he needs to speak to you."

Adam asked Breaux to excuse him so he could speak with Henry. He was impressed with Hannah's ingenuity.

Adam met with Henry in the hallway. "Yassuh, Mr. Adam," Henry said when Adam stood before him. He waited obediently for instructions from his employer. He would do exactly as Adam said, no matter what he was asked to do.

"Henry, " Adam said. "Paul Breaux is in my office. I want you to escort Mr. Breaux to the empty employee house. He is to be under guard until I give orders to the contrary. Under no circumstances is he to leave that house until I order his release. Is that understood?"

"Yessuh, Mr. Adam," Henry said.

Henry followed Adam into the office. The only man in the office besides himself and Mr. Adam was a white man. He was perplexed. Mr. Adam was ordering him to make a white man go where he might not want to go. The orders were strange, but he would do as he was told. He walked over to Breaux. "Mr. Breaux," Henry said, "You gotsta come wif me."

"I ain't gotta go nowhere," Breaux said. "Especially wit a Negro. You bettah not touch me, boy."

Henry caught Breaux's arm and began to pull him. Breaux tried to resist but he was no match for Henry. Henry threw Breaux over his right shoulder and walked out of the house heading toward the row of employee houses.

Adam pulled out his pocket watch. It was only a little after two o'clock. He had time to ride into town and return before dusk. He walked up to one of the field hands who had come in from the fields with Henry. "Saddle my horse, Matthew," he said. "Be quick about it."

"Yassuh," Matthew said. He returned a short time later leading the black stallion.

Adam mounted the Black and took off for Opelousas at a gallop.

*****

"I guess I was wrong when I recommend that you let Breaux stay on the land," Fisk said. "He's a hard worker. I didn't figure he'd talk back to you like that."

"What about his threat to involve the clan?" Adam asked.

"I'm not worried about that," Fisk replied. "Several of my men are Klan members. Now that he's shown his insolence, I don't think we can keep him around." He noticed Blythington hadn't protested his use of "we" as he spoke of what needed to be done for Southern Kingdom.

Fisk's words did not shock Adam. He had killed a man to protect Southern Kingdom. If Fisk thought it best to eliminate Breaux, then he would be eliminated. No man would be allowed to talk to him the way Breaux had spoken to him.

"Where is Breaux now?" Fisk asked.

Adam explained the action he had taken to keep Breaux from leaving Southern Kingdom. "Too bad he didn't work out," Fisk said. "You can head on home, Mr. Blythington. Wait about an hour after you get there and then send Breaux on home. Tell him you'll meet with him another time. My men will take care of everything."

"What do you intend to do with him?" Adam asked.

"Do you really want to know?" Fisk asked.

"Yes, I do," he replied. "I want to be assured I will have no further problems with Breaux."

Fisk thought of the changes Blythington had undergone since their first meeting. "He'll have an accident on his way home," he said. "You won't have any more problems with him. You can do whatever you want to with his family."

"They can stay on the land if they can work," Adam responded, "otherwise, your men can escort them off of my property."

"He has three boys who are hard workers," Fisk said. "They're a lot like their Pappa, though. You may have trouble with them later."

"Tell your men I want the Breaux family off of my

property before the end of the week," he responded.

*****

Adam returned to Southern Kingdom, waited an hour and then walked to the house where Breaux was being held. Henry saw him coming and walked out to meet him.
"You may release Breaux," he said to Henry.
"Is you sho, Mr. Adam?" Henry asked in a shaky voice. "Dat man is powerful mad."
"I am sure, Henry," Adam replied.
"You dawn unnerstan, Mr. Adam," Henry said in a stress filled voice as he tried to convey his fear to his employer. "Dats a white man. I made a white man do whut he din wanna do."
"I understand that, Henry," Adam responded.
"No, you dawn unnerstan," Henry said in a voice of dread. "Dat man gonna tell da klan whut I done. Dey gonna come heah and git me an hang me up from a oak tree."
"You have nothing to worry about," Adam responded. "Mr. Breaux will be joining Mr. Clark tonight."
Henry opened his eyes wide and drew in a deep breath. "Oh, I sees, Mr. Adam," he said. "I guess you nos whuts bess." Henry looked very relieved. It sure wasn't wise to cross Mr. Adam.

*****

The cotton harvest was going well. Paul Breaux was replaced by Anton Deville. Deville was a harsh taskmaster, but the results he produced were those Adam demanded. According to him, running a farm was never intended as a way to gain popularity.
Henry had shared his pleasure with the Southern Kingdom cotton harvest with Adam. He said he had never seen a finer harvest in all his years of farming. The pickers had gathered many bales. The cotton bolls were continuing to open. Many more bales were yet to be picked.

The buyers from the north and from England were paying top prices for the cotton. After several years of embargo, the textile mills were begging for cotton. Adam wondered how much of his cotton was going through Blythington Import and Export. It tickled him to think of his brothers clamoring to purchase his cotton.

Fisk had picked up nine hundred and forty more arpents of land for Southern Kingdom shortly before the harvest began. The unfortunate landowner had fallen out of his wagon. The poor man had fallen in such a way that the rear wheels of the wagon had crushed his chest killing him instantly. The bereaved widow was in such a hurry to dispose of the property that she sold the land at a reduced price. She was able to have a modest savings and purchase a small house in the city where she could continue to raise her children. It was sad that such a fate had befallen the poor woman.

Adam now owned six thousand, three hundred seventy arpents of land. Still, this was only the beginning. With the money from the harvest, he hoped to double the plantation's size by the summer of 1866. Other landowners were reaping in profits, but other owners did not have James Fisk. Fisk would ensure his holdings grew while other plantations diminished in size.

Repairs on the plantation house were concluded with excellent results. The antebellum mansion had regained its splendor. Adam gave Daniel and his crew new assignments. The houses along Shady Lane, as he now called the lane where the employees' houses sat, had fallen into disrepair prior to his purchase of the property. All of the houses would be repaired and painted. Following the work on the houses, the barns and sheds were to be repaired and painted. Everything would be in top condition. No one would look down on Southern Kingdom.

Jules Dupre' had done wonders with the gardens. There were flowerbeds of various sizes and shapes. Flowers of almost every color grew in the beds. The bushes were once again shaped and new ones had been planted to replace those that had died or were diseased. Plush grass grew on the lawn. The trees were pruned and looking splendid. Adam loved to stroll about the gardens with Annabelle while she exclaimed at the miracles Jules had rendered.

Adam thought of inviting his brothers to share Christmas with him at Southern Kingdom. He decided to wait until after his marriage to Annabelle. She would impress them as she hosted his parties. The perfect time to have them over would be in the spring of the year when the gardens would be in full bloom and the heat of summer had not begun. He looked forward to seeing the envy in his brothers' eyes.

On the twenty-third of July, Adam had turned twenty-three. How many twenty-three year olds could boast they owned so vast an estate? With his marriage to Annabelle, he would be accepted completely by the upper strata of St. Landry society. Things were going better than he had planned.

CHAPTER SEVEN

November 1865

"That was a delicious meal," Adam said as he pushed his chair away from the table. "Marie outdid herself this time."

"She's a wonderful cook," Jacque Dupre' agreed. "I think I may have eaten too many of Marie's delicious meals. I may have to begin walking longer distances."

"You still look fit," Adam said.

"Pappa, you'll always be young and fit," Annabelle remarked. "I see the way the ladies look at you."

"If only that were true," Jacques responded. "I'm growing old. I had hoped for grandchildren to dote upon in my old age. Alas, Placide and Giselle have disappointed me."

"Placide isn't your only child, Pappa," Annabelle said. "I'll marry some day and have children. They'll love you just as I do."

"Ah, mas cheiri," Jacques said as he smiled lovingly at his daughter. "You'll never disappoint me. You're so much like my dear Adelaide. I regret that she'll never hear the laughter of les petite enfants." A tear slid down his face as he remembered his departed wife.

"It's almost a year since the passing of Mamma," Annabelle said. "You're too young to remain single. I know she wouldn't want you to be alone."

"That was a terrible day," Jacques responded. "So seldom do we get cold days as we did last December. A week of freezing temperatures was inconceivable. Poor Adelaide. The cold was too much for her in her condition." His face registered sadness. "Non, mas Cheiri, I don't think I'll ever find another like my Adelaide."

Annabelle had hoped the eleven months that passed since her mother's death had helped her father to put some of the sorrow behind, but he still grieved for Mamma almost as he had at the time of her passing. Theirs had been a great love. She was beginning to love Adam more deeply. She hoped his love for her would be as deep as Pappa's love for Mamma.

She looked at Adam. He was tall and handsome. He wasn't adept at making conversation, but she understood this was the result of his painful childhood. She was happy now that she understood him better. She'd give him the love and nurturing he'd missed during his childhood. She was convinced Adam would open up to her in time. In her heart she hoped their lives would be filled with tender moments like those her mother and father had shared. She looked up at Adam and smiled.

Adam returned her smile. He had been courting Annabelle for over six months. She had warmed up to him, but she had not allowed him to get further than kisses. When he had confessed his deep love for her and told her how great was his desire for her, he had expected her to surrender to him. Instead she had said, "Non, you know we must wait. That is for the marriage bed only." He could get no further. He let his eyes take in her luscious body as she smiled at him. He wanted to complete himself with her, but was resigned to wait until the marriage bed.

"What are you thinking?" Annabelle asked.

"You were speaking of grandchildren," he replied. "I was picturing you with a baby in your arms."

"Describe the child to me," she asked with a dreamy look on her face.

Adam thought quickly. "You were holding a little boy," he replied. "He had dark hair and green eyes. He looked very much like you."

"Did he also look like you?" she asked with a smile.

"Yes, he did," he replied. "His coloring and the shape of his face were more like mine."

She smiled. "He was a very handsome child then," she said.

"Very handsome," he responded.

Adam and Annabelle had forgotten Jacques was still present until he said, "All this talk of a grandchild. Is the time never going to come when I hold my grandchild in my arms?"

"The time will come, Pappa," she responded as she gazed into Adam's eyes.

"She practically said she is going to have a child with me," he said to himself. "She is letting me know she would marry me if I asked." He grew excited as he thought of having his way with her. She would produce his heir.

He tried to reconcile himself to the remaining five and a half months of courting. It upset him that custom demanded a courtship of one year for genteel people. Thank goodness Hannah would relieve him when he returned to Southern Kingdom.

*****

Darkness was beginning to settle over Southern Kingdom when he returned to his home. He found Hannah in the kitchen. It was earlier than his usual bedtime, but he felt an urgency to be with her to relieve the lust that had been generated by his visit with Annabelle.

He walked behind her as she stood at a table polishing silver. "I need to meet with you if there is nothing that compels you to remain here," he said.

She turned to look at her lover and recognized the desire in his eyes. She knew that the desire had been sparked by Annabelle. "That girl has no idea that her refusal to couple with Adam is the only reason he still wants her," she thought to herself. She was more than willing to allow herself to be used to quench Adam's desire. He would know soon enough how little Annabelle could do for him.

She looked around to make sure none of the other servants could overhear. "I have nothing here that has to be done now, Adam," she replied. She called him Adam only when they were alone. She thought it best she address him as Mr. Adam when others were present.

He had noticed that none of the other servants were

present. He was tempted to take her in the kitchen. That would be unwise, though. Any of the servants could walk in on them. "Come with me," he said in a husky voice.

She followed obediently behind Adam. She had something to tell him, but her news would be better received after his passion was released.

After they reached his bedroom and the doors were secured, she undressed slowly. She watched him as his desire for her heightened. No matter how many times he saw her nude body, he always gawked as though this was the first time he had seen a naked woman. She turned away from him and lay on the bed.

He was amazed at what her nude body continued to do to him. It was as though each time was the first. He thought of her body at other times, but the picture in his mind's eye could never compare to the reality of her body. To him, her body was perfect. He wanted her to give him pleasure, but he did not allow himself to take pleasure selfishly. He drove himself to give her as much pleasure as he received. He moved over to the bed, lay beside Hannah and pulled her to him.

Her desire for Adam was great, but she wanted the lovemaking to come slowly. "You're the first man I've really given myself to," she said as he kissed her body. Although he was driving her mad with passion, she felt the need to communicate the depth of her feelings. "I gave in to Lance LeBlanc because he was my master. If I gave him pleasure, my place on the plantation remained secure. Those days when he was especially satisfied, he gave me gifts.

"My mother was the mistress of a plantation owner as were her mother and her mother's mother. Giving myself to the master was all I knew. I never questioned why the master used me for his pleasure." She found it hard to continue as the craving took her breath away. "I tolerated Lance. I gave my body to him but he never had my heart or my mind. Adam, everything that I am is yours. I love you."

"I love you, too," he responded huskily. He was doing all he could to hold himself back until she was ready to receive him. He had allowed himself to tell her many times that he loved her. He was convinced that he did love her and that she would never use that love against him.

He was curious about her background. She was only thirteen when LeBlanc purchased her. He wondered if Lance LeBlanc was her first. He tried to find a way to ask her without causing her to think he was only acting out of curiosity. He could find no way to ask other than with a direct question. "Was Lance LeBlanc your first?" he asked.

Her body became rigid and she closed her eyes. He could see pain etched on her face.

"No," she replied in a voice filled with anguish. She was silent for a few moments. When she finally continued, anger flashed in her eyes. "My father was the first. He decided to sell me when my momma found out what he was doing."

He was dumbstruck. Using your own daughter that way. Selling your own child. That was below anything he had ever imagined. How could a father lower himself to doing that to his own daughter?

"Who is he?" Adam demanded when he found his voice. "I want to make sure he suffers for what he did to you."

"No," she replied firmly. "I don't even want to think of that time. I have a new life now. I thought I was going to die when it happened, but I didn't. I adapted. Being used by a white man became my life. If I could please him, I was treated well.

"Before I was sold, my momma taught me everything she knew about pleasing a man. She told me, with my light skin, green eyes and good hair, white men would want me. It's not the life she chose for me. It's the life she knew I'd have. Her father was a white man. She wanted to prepare me for the inevitable."

He knew how to uncover her father's name. Sales of slaves were recorded. Fisk would find the information for him. Her father would pay for what he had done to her. The price would be steep. Death would be too good for him. He would be humiliated. He would be ruined. Adam decided he was going to speak with Fisk in the morning.

"I'm sorry for all the terrible things that happened to you," he said. "I want to protect you and make sure you never suffer again."

"You've already made my life much better," she responded as she kissed his cheek and nestled her body against his. "You've given me pleasure. I had no idea that making love could be so satisfying until you made love to me. I'm thankful you opened my heart and taught me to love."

He did not feel threatened by her, in fact, he felt a protective tenderness for her. He could tell by the way she looked at him and held him that she loved him deeply. He needed her love. It gave him a contentment he had never known before.

She moved herself more closely and gave her body to him. He was carried on wings of fire as she touched and kissed his body. He felt that she was making herself one with him. They were one; she was closer than any other woman could ever be to him.

Later, after they were both spent, they lay in one another's arms. He felt a sense of inviolate peace as he lay back with Hannah at his side. She held him closely as they rested. He no longer felt the urgency of passion, but enjoyed the feeling of her body as it pressed against his. There were two things he would fight to the death to keep; Southern Kingdom and Hannah LeBlanc. She was the only real wife he would ever know.

"Adam," she said softly as she lightly traced her fingers up and down his chest."

"Yes, my love," he responded.

"Adam, I'm pregnant," she said.

Panic coursed through his body. A child of mixed race? That could be nothing but trouble. He settled down. He trusted her and respected her counsel. He waited for her to continue.

"Did you hear what I said, Adam?" she asked.

"Yes, I did," he replied.

"What do you think we should do?" she asked.

"Hannah, I have no idea what to say," he replied. "I love you and I know you will tell me the best thing to do."

She smiled. Only a few months ago he would have accused her of getting pregnant to hold on to him. Now, he was waiting for her to suggest the course to take. "I told you my father was a plantation owner," she said. "He refused to acknowledge me. I was raised as a common slave. My mother taught me the only skills she knew. I don't want that for our child."

"Slavery has been abolished," he said.

"I know slavery's been abolished," she responded. "I don't want our child raised as a field hand or a house servant."

"What do you suggest?" he asked.

"During the slavery days, most of the plantation owners sent their children of mixed color off to boarding school and then on to universities in Europe," she responded. "They didn't acknowledge their children, but they made sure their children were educated and became people of substance. That's what I want for our child."

"I hardly think we could hide your pregnancy," he said. "Do you propose to claim that one of the field hands is the father of the child."

"Would you want that?" she asked.

He was silent for a while. "No, I would not want that for my child," he replied.

She was beside herself in happiness. Adam had called the baby she carried his child. "I've thought about that," she said. "I may not show for a while yet. I'd like for you to build a house on your property that's far enough away from this house so that I could have privacy. I can have the child there and then we can hire a wet nurse. Everyone here will know that he's our child but no one will ever speak that aloud. When the child's old enough, we'll send him to boarding school."

"Would you not want to raise the child yourself?" he asked.

"No," she replied. "I have a place on this plantation and a place in your life. I refuse to give up either."

He turned to her and smiled.

"Why are you smiling?" she asked.

"I was picturing you big and pregnant," he replied. His mood became pensive.

"Now, what are you thinking?" she asked.

He was no longer surprised when she read his moods.

She knew practically everything about him. "I am going to miss seeing the body of a goddess," he replied, "such a perfect body." "My mother taught me exercises," she responded. "I always do them when I'm alone in my room. My mother kept her body beautiful even after the birth of four children." Her voice took on an angry note. "She was a good breeder for the master. She gave him three good male slaves and a daughter who he sold."

"I have no idea how many children we will have," he said, "but I promise you all of them will be educated and they will have every advantage." He pulled Hannah closer to him. "I find it peculiar that you did not propose marriage as a solution."

"How could I?" she asked. "We live in the south. Marriage between the races is illegal. Marrying me would ruin you and, probably, would bring about my death. The only way we could marry is for you to sell everything here and move up north, but your destiny lies here."

"How can you take the prejudice of the south so calmly?" he asked.

"Calmly!" she cried out. "I'm having a baby for the man I love and I have to stand by while he marries another woman. That has nothing to do with being calm. My heart aches every time I know you're with her. I've cried myself to sleep too many nights thinking about Annabelle becoming your wife.

"Because I won't see your dreams destroyed doesn't mean I'm calm. What allows me to accept all of this is that I know you'll never love her as you love me. I know she can't satisfy you like I do. I know when you lie with her you'll think of me. That's the only way I can accept what I must."

He held her closely. He had not thought of the sacrifice Hannah was making. His heart opened to her. "I love you," he said. "I will never love another woman as I love you. Nothing will ever come between us."

She gave herself to him once more. He made love to her with gentleness and tenderness. She knew he wasn't only quenching his desire. He was giving himself to her.

They lay in each other's arms later. Neither spoke for a while. She lay her head on his chest and began to weep.

"Why are you crying?" he asked and then thought how stupid his question must sound to her. "How shallow of me; with all of the things that have been forced upon you, I should have already known the answer."

"I don't think you know why I'm crying," she responded. "I've never been happier in all of my life."

"How can that be?" he asked, "with all you are going through."

"Because you love me and you're treating me like someone who has worth," she replied. "You didn't turn you back on our child. I feel like I have a part in building Southern Kingdom. I'm not worried about anyone taking my place in your heart."

He thought about what she had said. She had made a special place for herself in his heart. No one could ever take her place. For the first time in his life, he resented social hierarchy. He hated the system that prevented him from taking her as his wife. She was right, though, they were building Southern Kingdom together. Although her contribution could never be openly acknowledged, she had given her heart to him and to Southern Kingdom. She was willing to give herself to him unselfishly. Everything he had done before his love for her was to satisfy his own desires.

He began to weep from the heaviness he felt in his heart. She held his head against her breast as he wept. When he lifted his head, she kissed his tears away. "Why do you feel so sad?" she asked.

"Everything I have ever done until now has been for my own gratification," he replied. "I do not care what happens to me; I want you to be happy. All of my life I have looked down on people who are of a lower social class than I, and I have sought to elevate myself to a higher social level so no one could ever look down on me. I hate the very thing I worshiped because of the injustice it does to you. I do love you. Your social position means nothing to me. I am saddened because we cannot be husband and wife. We should think of moving up north."

Hannah's heart leapt with joy. She was convinced that he really did love her, but she wouldn't let his love for her destroy him and take away his aspiration.

"In my heart we are husband and wife," she said softly. "I hope you feel that way, too."

He nodded his head.

"No matter what happens, we'll always know that in our hearts. Annabelle is going to be your wife in name only." She hesitated at the next words she knew she had to say. "You need a legitimate heir. She can give you a legitimate heir. Your marriage to her will give you acceptance that you need to build Southern Kingdom. Southern Kingdom is your dream, not hers. You can have your dream and we can have each other. I'll always be by your side."

"Would you marry me if I asked you?" he asked.

"No, Adam," she replied as she hugged him tightly. "There's only one way we can be happy. We'd both regret our marriage because it had meant giving up Southern Kingdom. I believe in your dream for Southern Kingdom. I'd like for your dream to be our dream. You're mine in the only way that matters to me, in my heart. The only way I'd marry you is if we could have our dream, and we both know that's impossible. All I ask is that you never stop loving me."

"You told me you are a LeBlanc, because you took on your master's name," he said. "Would you take on my name as you did his?"

"Hannah Blythington," she said speculatively. She liked the way it sounded. "Hannah Blythington." She smiled brightly. "Yes Adam, I'll take your name. I love the way it sounds."

They held each other and thought of what could have been, but would never be.

*****

Hannah Blythington thought of her night with Adam as she gave the servants their duties for the day. There was no doubt in her mind that he loved her. When he learned she was going to have his child, he wanted to marry her. She thought of how differently she saw him now than when he first arrived at the plantation. He had been only one more white man she'd have to learn to please so she could survive. She had tried to learn his weaknesses to use them for her own protection. She had been very fearful of him.

Slowly, she'd found herself falling in love with him. He had made the way for her to learn to speak correctly. Professor Pennington was opening the world up for her. She was reading books and learning about places that were beyond her imagination. She had learned words that helped her to express what she was thinking. She felt like a sponge soaking in knowledge. Adam had given her a new life and he shared his dream with her.

She was no longer only a toy to be used and disposed of when it no longer gave pleasure. Lance LeBlanc had laid his fat body on her and huffed and puffed until he was satisfied. She always felt dirty with him. It was different with Adam. He was so handsome. She loved the feel of his body as they made love. He gave her more than he asked of her.

She loved Adam with all her heart and he loved her, too. They would always be one. Their child wouldn't be a wedge between them. Their child was bringing them closer together.

Hannah thought of how it would be if she really were Mrs. Blythington. She would host all of Adam's parties and wear the finest dresses from Paris. Southern Kingdom would attract all of the important people. She and Adam could travel abroad. All of those things would never be hers. Annabelle would be his wife. She would host his parties and she would give him his heir.

But, Annabelle would never have Adam the way she did. She could be his wife, but she would never have his heart.

Adam wasn't like other men. There was a ruthless and dangerous side to him. She didn't fear that side of him any longer. She understood him when he took action against those who opposed him. He would never have to protect himself against her. She would stand with him as he struck down those who stood in the way of his dream.

*****

Adam watched Hannah as she worked with the other house servants. The more he watched, the more he recognized the changes in her. She was no longer haughty, but carried herself with grace and dignity. While the new dresses she had made were certainly not Paris originals, they were pretty and tasteful. He wondered where she had developed the ability to design and sew a wardrobe. She no longer wore her hair tied up in a kerchief. She wore her long silky brown hair down over her shoulders. Her smooth light tan skin glowed.

Hannah's green eyes sparkled as she looked back at her lover. "Why are you staring?" she asked.

He cast his eyes around the room. The other servants were out of the room momentarily. "You are so lovely," he replied. "You have changed so dramatically since I first arrived."

She swelled with pride. "I'm glad you've noticed," she said. "I feel like a different person."

"She is a different person," he thought to himself. "To someone who doesn't know her background, she could pass for a Caucasian." Her skin was slightly darker than most Caucasians, but her features would not belie her identity as a white person. Her speech had improved to the point that she very seldom made a grammatical mistake. He could take her to another area in the country and marry her if she wished.

"With the changes you've made in your speech and appearance," he said, "you could easily be taken for a Caucasian."

"But, I'm not a Caucasian," she responded, "and I'm not interested in starting over in another place. We discussed all of that last night and made our decision. Our future lies here." She was standing firm on the decisions of the previous night. "Where are you off to this morning?"

"I am going into town to discuss some business with Fisk," he replied.

"Should we have dinner ready for you?" she asked. "Yes, I should be back by one o'clock at the latest," he replied.

CHAPTER EIGHT

November 17, 1865 - May 17, 1866

Fisk greeted Blythington as he walked into his office. "I'm glad to see you're ready to expand again," Fisk said, "I've located a few pieces of land you can pick up at a good price."

Adam's eyes traveled around Fisk's small office. Fisk was still using the same rundown desk and broken-down chairs. A piece of oilskin was tacked over one of the windows where a pane had broken. He was sure Fisk could afford much better accommodations than his present location. He wondered why Fisk elected to remain in his dingy office.

"We can discuss the acquisitions later," he responded. "I have more pressing business to discuss first."

Fisk opened his eyes wide in surprise. What could be more urgent to Blythington than acquiring more property? "Oh?" Fisk said as he wondered what kind of pressing matter was on Blythington's mind.

"I want you to research the slave auction records," Adam said. "Mr. Lance LeBlanc purchased a slave girl named Hannah approximately nine years ago. I want to learn the identity of her previous owner."

"Why would you need to know that?" Fisk asked.

"I prefer not to disclose my reasons presently," he replied. "I may tell you later."

"You could save yourself some money and look through the records yourself," Fisk said.

"I do not want anyone to know I am interested in those records," Adam responded. "I prefer we remain the only two who know about the record search."

"You know I'll charge you a fee," Fisk said.

"I know," Adam responded. "What is your fee for this service?"

"It'll only take me an hour or so." Fisk replied. "I guess twenty-five dollars should cover it. When do you need the information."

"Today," Adam replied. "I will wait here for your return."

As he awaited Fisk's return, he read from the pocket-sized book of poetry he had thought to bring with him. He did not especially care for poetry, but it would occupy his mind. He had instructed Fisk to lock the door until his return. He did not want to be seen in Fisk's office.

Slightly over an hour later, Fisk unlocked the door. "I have your information," Fisk said. "Will you tell me now why you wanted the information?"

"I want to know what you have learned," Adam replied.

"The Negro girl, Hannah, was sold by Albert Bennett," Fisk replied. "He's the owner of Lance des Chenes. It's about twelve miles from your place."

Adam thought about the information Fisk had given to him. "How large a plantation is this Lance des Chenes?" he asked.

"It's about the size of your holdings," Fisk answered. "Mr. Bennett was accused of working for the union during the war. He probably would've been hung if Louisiana had held on a little longer. He's not hurting for money."

"His taxes are current, then?" Adam asked.

"I should say so," replied Fisk. "He's bought some more land since the war ended."

Adam took in the information. He was trying to formulate a plan. It would be difficult to purchase Bennett's plantation.

"Would you tell me what you have on your mind?" Fisk asked.

"I want you to do whatever you have to do to get that plantation in my possession," Adam replied bitterly. "I have one stipulation, though."

Fisk nodded his head and waited for Blythington to continue.

"I do not want Bennett to be killed," Adam continued. "I want Bennett to know I own Lance des Chenes. I want Bennett ruined."

"That won't be so easy," Fisk responded. "Bennett is a rich and powerful man and he's ruthless."

"Are you telling me this is more than you can handle?" Adam asked scathingly.

"I can pull it off," Fisk replied defensively, "but it's dangerous. This isn't like going after some washed up men like LeBlanc and Breaux. You'd have to sell everything you have to come up with the money to buy Lance des Chenes, and that's if Bennett would be willing to sell."

"I do not intend to part with one arpent of Southern Kingdom," Adam said adamantly. "His willingness to sell is irrelevant. I said I want the man ruined. I asked you if you are up to this. Perhaps you are not." There was sarcasm in his voice.

"There's no need to attack me," Fisk responded contritely. "I told you I can handle this." Fisk wanted to redeem his pride. "The question is, can you afford my fee?"

Adam sensed that he had pushed Fisk too far. He wanted him as an ally, not an enemy. This was not a matter of winning or losing a debate with Fisk. There was money left from the sale of the timber rights and a substantial amount from the harvest. "It depends on the amount of your fee." he answered.

Fisk smiled. He perceived that Blythington had waved a peace flag. He and Blythington would remain associates. He would be taking a risk to get Lance des Chenes for him. He wondered what Bennett had done to cause Blythington to go after him this way. It didn't matter that much to him. He stood to make money on the deal. "My fee is fifteen hundred dollars," he answered. Although Blythington had waved the peace flag, he wanted him to know better than to cross the line again.

Adam's eyes opened wide. He could afford to pay Fisk's fee, but that was a large sum of money. He regretted venting his spleen on Fisk. There would be the purchase price of the plantation in addition to the fee. He wondered for a moment if exacting vengeance on Bennett was worth the price. He recalled the pain in Hannah's eyes. Bennett would pay for what he had done to her. "I agree," he responded. "You get one-fourth today and the remainder when the land is mine."

"I'll need more than a fourth to meet my expenses," Fisk said. "I want half now and half when the deal is done."

"All right," Adam agreed. "The funds will be in your possession before noon."

"Do you want to discuss the pieces of land I was talking about earlier?" asked Fisk.

"How much land are you speaking of?" Adam asked.

"Comes to roughly seven hundred and twenty arpents," Fisk replied. "Two farms that border your property. The owners lost them for unpaid taxes. More woodland than farmland."

"Before I decide, I want to know how much your fee will be," Adam said.

"I'll include this transaction and the records search at the courthouse with my fee for the Bennett property," Fisk responded. This was his flag of truce. Fisk had made large sums of money doing business with Blythington. It wouldn't do to push him too hard. "We'll call this my Christmas gift to you."

Adam agreed to the purchase price. Fisk would take care of the details. Adam would come in the Monday of the following week to sign the papers. He wondered why Fisk was being so magnanimous.

*****

Fisk sat in his office wondering what Blythington had against Bennett. He shook his head. Blythington had certainly changed. When he had first come to Louisiana, he only wanted an impressive plantation. Now, he wanted power. Blythington had blanched at the use of coercion to purchase Seven Oaks and now he wanted to ruin a powerful man. At the rate Blythington was going, he might end up owning half of the parish. "I hitched myself to a winner when I found that man," Fisk thought to himself.

He hadn't liked the way Blythington had spoken to him.

If Blythington was to be stopped, it had to be now. In a time when railroad tycoons were earning around ten thousand dollars a year, Fisk stood to make that and more through a protracted association with Blythington. He would have to be careful to stay on his good side. Fisk scratched his head. It wasn't going to be easy carrying out the acquisition of Lance des Chenes and the ruin of Albert Bennett.

*****

"Merry Christmas," Hannah said as she cuddled up against Adam. She'd been waiting for him to awaken.

"Merry Christmas, Hannah," he responded as he placed his arms around her and kissed her. "What time is it?" he asked.

"It's about seven o'clock," she answered. "Everyone's sleeping late today."

Adam yawned. "I have to get up and get ready," he said. "I have to take Jacques and Annabelle to nine o'clock services. I hope Placide is not with them. I can tell he does not like me."

"He's probably just jealous," she said. "He wishes he could be rich and handsome like you."

"I feel uncomfortable around him," he continued.

"You've been seeing Annabelle about six months now," she said, "when do you plan on asking her to marry you?"

"Couples are supposed to court for at least a year before they can marry," he responded. "I have to wait until June to propose."

"Can't you propose now and get married in June?" she asked.

"Why are you in such a hurry for me to get married?" he asked.

"I'm not in a hurry for you to get married," she replied. "I'm in a hurry to see you accepted in local society. You're still an outsider. Marriage to Annabelle will open doors for you."

"We are doing well without acceptance in their society," he said. "Perhaps we should leave things as they are."

"We've already discussed this," she said. "Don't you want power and prestige?"

"I know what I want," he replied as he kissed her neck. "I hope you want the same thing."

Hannah gave herself to Adam. She wanted to make love to him as often as she could before her pregnancy forced them to take a hiatus from lovemaking.

"I wish I could stay with you in this warm bed," he said as they rested after their lovemaking. "We could give each other Christmas gifts all day long."

"I'm glad you feel that way," she responded, "but you'd better hurry. You're the one who insists on punctuality."

*****

Placide and Giselle were waiting with Jacques and Annabelle. "Isn't it fortunate that Placide and Giselle can be with us today?" Jacques asked. "We'll have a wonderful day."

"I hope you like what Margaret prepares for us," Adam said. "She said it will be a special surprise." Adam resented the arrogance he saw on Placide's face. Placide seemed to always study him.

"I can't wait to see what you've done with Seven Oaks, oh, pardon me, Southern Kingdom," Giselle said. "I hear it's splendid."

"I am happy to share my home with you," Adam responded. He did not take offense with her because of her mistake. "She is her usual pretty and empty-headed self," he said to himself.

"I understand you were able to purchase Paul Breaux's farm," Placide commented wryly. "That farm had been in the Breaux family for generations. Who would've suspected that Paul would sell? His accident was most unfortunate. Poor Bernadette with those six children to raise." He shook his head as he stared coldly into Adam's eyes.

Adam felt as though Placide were intimating that he was culpable in Breaux's misfortunes. The more time he spent around Placide, the more he did not like the man.

"That's unfortunate," Jacques agreed. "Poor Paul, I told him more than once strong drink would get the better of him."

"Why do we speak of sad things?" Giselle asked. "It's Christmas. A time of joy."

"It's a time to give thanks to Mary for all of the things we have," Annabelle said. "She gave us her Son."

The talk centered on happier subjects as the group made their way to church. The heated bricks did little to dissipate the cold. Adam was happy he had kept his heavy wool overcoat.

"Wasn't it an uplifting sermon Reverend Boudreaux gave?" Giselle asked later as they were walking out of the church. "I could see the angels and the baby Jesus as He lay in the manger."

"I wish Mamma could be here today," Annabelle said. "This is our second Christmas without her."

"My poor Adelaide," Jacques said, "I know she's smiling down on us today. How she would have loved Reverend Boudreaux's sermon."

Adam endured the talk about a savior. His mind and his ambition were his savior. Had it not been for his decision to come to the American south, he would be celebrating Christmas with his brothers. How they had loved to look down on him. Once again, he wished they could see him in his current circumstances.

"I'm sorry, we're ignoring you, Adam," Annabelle said as she took his hand. "I could tell you found the sermon very moving. I noticed when a tear trickled down your face."

Adam had fought very hard to remain awake during the sermon. His eyes had watered as he stifled a yawn. "It was very moving," he said. "We must be grateful for all He has done."

Annabelle squeezed his hand. "He's such a sensitive man," she thought to herself. "In time everyone will see him as I do."

*****

Hannah greeted the guests as they walked into Adam's home. She took their coats, gloves and scarves and put them away. "I hope you like what our Margaret has prepared for you," she said.

"Oh, how nice," Giselle responded happily. She looked at Hannah appraisingly. She wondered where Adam had found his lovely housekeeper. "Are you from around here?" she finally asked.

Hannah had considered reverting to the broken English she'd spoken before her lessons with Professor Pennington for the benefit of Adam's guests, but she decided against doing so. She was a free woman of color. She would not act stupid for the white folks. Giselle's question caught her by surprise. It was clear to her that Giselle had taken her for a white woman. "No, I'm not from around here," she replied. She hadn't lied. She had come to the plantation at the age of thirteen.

Placide moved nearer to Hannah and studied her. Her face looked vaguely familiar. "Weren't you here when LeBlanc owned this plantation?" he asked.

Hannah felt uneasy under Placide's scrutiny. She recalled having seen him several of the times that he had visited Mr. LeBlanc. She knew that LeBlanc had bragged to Placide about his mistress. "I was a slave on this plantation when Mr. LeBlanc was the master," she replied as she returned Placide's gaze. She was determined she would not to be cowed by the man.

"I never forget a face," Placide said triumphantly. "I knew you were LeBlanc's slave."

"How delightful to hear a Negro woman who can speak English correctly," Giselle commented airily. "It's refreshing to meet a Negro person with intelligence."

Hannah was angered by Giselle's comment but fought not to let it show. "Intelligence is so rare in us darkies," Hannah said, "It's fortunate you lived long enough to witness the anomaly."

Giselle smiled at Hannah. She was not altogether certain that Hannah hadn't insulted her. Hannah continued to smile benignly at Giselle. Giselle decided that Hannah hadn't meant her remarks to be insulting. "Although she speaks well," Giselle thought to herself," she doesn't possess the intelligence to express herself correctly. The poor wretch."

Placide stared coldly at Hannah. He seemed about to

make an angry retort.

"Everything looks so lovely," Annabelle said quickly in an attempt to ease the tension. "I love the way the red and the green look together."

"Your home looks as it did when I was a boy," Jacques said. "You've done an excellent job with the restoration."

Adam was angry with Placide for treating Hannah cruelly, but he knew Placide would call him out in an affair of honor and kill him if he took up for her. His heart went out to her. He struggled to regain his composure. "Thank you, Monsieur Dupre'," he said. "The carpenters deserve the credit. I am fortunate to have three excellent carpenters on this plantation."

"I envy you," Jacques said. "I have only old Isaiah. He does excellent work but he's grown old and slow."

"You must have come to Louisiana with your pockets filled with money," Placide commented with a wry look on his face. "Unfortunately, many of our people have been made penniless by our new government."

Adam wanted to lambaste Placide, but he held his tongue in check. "It is only an act of fate that allows me to do all of this," Adam responded. "My father left me sufficient funds to live comfortably. I am only responsible for the decision to leave England and come here."

"Good fortune seems to follow you," Placide continued. "Fate has allowed you to continue to add to your holdings."

Adam did all he could to stifle the anger he felt rising inside. "I am thankful to God for my good fortune," he responded. "It is only through His intercession that I continue to profit."

"You're a good business man, yet you credit God with your success," Jacques said. "That's an excellent quality in a young man."

"Enough about land and business," Annabelle said. "We're here to enjoy ourselves."

Mary seated the guests as Hannah had prearranged. Adam occupied the chair at the head of the table. Jacques and Annabelle sat on either side of him. Placide sat beside his father

and Giselle next to Annabelle. Hannah intended for Jacques
to act as a buffer between Adam and Placide. She hoped both
Placide and Giselle would choke on their food.

Margaret had cooked enough to feed a small army. The
seafood gumbo was delicious. She followed that up with smoked
ham, rice dressing, potato salad and candied yams. When
everyone had eaten, Ruth brought out pecan pie that she served
with coffee.

Adam sat proudly as one after another commented
on the delicious food. Hannah brought Margaret out and
introduced her as the Southern Kingdom cook. The Dupre's gave
Margaret a round of applause.

Adam invited the men to the parlor for cigars and
brandy. Hannah led Annabelle and Giselle to the library.
Annabelle had expressed an interest in looking through some of
the volumes. Ruth and Mary began to clear the table.

Placide had gotten Adam boxes of Cuban cigars duty
free as he had promised. Adam brought out a box of cigars for
his guests. Fred served brandy to the men. Placide seemed to
have lost some of his antipathy toward Adam. The day was
going better now. About an hour later, Annabelle and Giselle
joined the men.

"Adam, you have such a marvelous collection of books,"
Annabelle said. "I'd love to spend days in your library with
those lovely volumes."

"Perhaps a time will come when you will be able to read
them at you leisure," Adam said as he smiled at Annabelle.

Annabelle dropped her eyes for a moment and
then looked up at Adam. "I look forward to that time," she
responded.

"Perhaps I will finally have grandchildren," Jacques
said. "My son is taking his time about carrying on the family
name."

"Why should we hurry?" Giselle asked. "I'm in no hurry
to become fat and ugly."

"You could never be fat and ugly," Jacques said. "Just
think how delightful it would be to hold your own child in your
arms."

"We have all the time in the world," Placide interjected. "We're both young. This is a time for adventure. Children will come later."

"Just as I suspected," Jacques complained. "They rob me of my grandchildren. You wait until after my death to give me grandchildren."

"Pappa," Placide said, "you have many years yet to live. There'll be a time when you'll be surrounded by little ones."

Adam thought about what Hannah had said that morning. He could ask Annabelle to marry him now. The wedding could be held in June. The year would have passed by then. He sought a way to isolate himself with Annabelle, but nothing presented itself.

"Adam, do you own a piano?" Annabelle asked.

"Yes, it is in the ballroom," he replied. "Do you play?"

"Yes," she replied. "Please take me to see the piano."

"Would you please excuse us?" Adam said as he ushered Annabelle out of the parlor.

"It's so cold in here," she said when they reached the ballroom. "I was hoping I could play and we could sing Christmas carols."

"I can have the servants move the piano to the parlor," Adam said. "It would take too long to heat this room."

"That would be perfect," Annabelle responded with delight. "Would you do that?"

"Of course," Adam replied. "It will take only a short while."

The ballroom was cold, but Adam felt this might be the only time he would have alone with Annabelle. He took her right hand in his right hand. "I have grown to love you," he said solemnly. "I have been so lonesome here in America. The time I spend with you is the only time I feel that my life has real meaning. I hope you do not think I am impertinent, but I want you to always be in my life. Annabelle, will you marry me?"

"Oh, Adam," Annabelle responded. "I hoped that you would love me too, but we can't be married until we've known each other at least a year."

"I know I must wait," Adam said. "We can be married in

late June or early July."

"My answer to you would be yes," Annabelle responded, "but I can't give you my answer until you've asked Pappa for permission."

"I understand," he said. "May I ask his permission today?"

She smiled and embraced him. "Of course, you may," she replied.

Adam and Annabelle held hands as they made their way back to the parlor.

Hannah's heart skipped a beat when she saw them together. She quickly regained her composure and smiled as Adam walked up to her. "Is everything all right?" she asked.

"Everything is fine," he replied. "Would you please have the servants move the piano into the parlor?"

Although she had encouraged Adam to propose to Annabelle and had extolled the benefits of such a marriage, her heart ached as she watched her lover with the woman he would someday marry. "I'll have them do that right away," she replied.

"Ah, you've returned, "Jacques said with a smile when Adam and Annabelle entered the parlor. "Did you find the piano to your liking?"

"Yes, Pappa," Annabelle replied. "The servants are moving the piano into the parlor. We'll be able to sing Christmas carols."

"Magnifique," Jacques exclaimed. "It's a pity we don't have Adelaide's sweet voice." A sad look crossed his face.

"Monsieur Dupre'," Adam asked, "could I have a word with you in the library?"

"But, of course," Jacques replied.

Adam and Jacques walked over to the library. He offered Jacques a chair. He remained standing. He longed to hold Hannah in his arms as he chose the words he would use to ask Annabelle's father for her hand in marriage. "I know it may seem soon to most people," Adam began, "but I have fallen in love with Annabelle. I think she also loves me." Adam tried his best to wear an expression of love for Annabelle on his face. "Monsieur Dupre', may I please have your permission to marry your daughter?"

Jacques remained silent for several moments. Adam was beginning to worry that his request would end in a refusal.

"Annabelle is my prize," Jacques responded solemnly. "I want her to be with a man who will appreciate her and cherish her. She's a delicate flower. She'll blossom in the right hands or she'll wither and die in the wrong hands. If you're prepared to promise me you'll love her more than your own life and cherish her forever, I will give you my permission to marry her, but the wedding cannot take place until you've known one another for at least one year. If you can't love her in that manner, please bid her adieu now and walk away."

"I give you my solemn promise," Adam responded as he met Jacques' eyes.

"I know you and Annabelle will be happy together," Jacques said with a sigh. "Perhaps I will now have my grandchildren."

Adam and Jacques returned to the parlor. For the sake of privacy, Adam asked Annabelle to accompany him to the library. This thing would be difficult enough without having the entire Dupre' family looking on.

He looked at Annabelle as one who is appraising an item before its purchase. The tops of her rich young breasts barely showed, but the promise of a lovely body was clear to him. Her skin was as smooth as ivory. She was a beautiful woman; the kind of woman who would make him the envy of other men. Her sweet voice and French accent were a delight to his ears. Children produced by the marriage would be striking in appearance and extemely intelligent. She would give him his heir. She definitely would be an asset to Southern Kingdom.

He got down on one knee and took her hand as he looked up into her eyes. "Will you free my heart from a life of emptiness and consent to be my wife?" he asked.

She admired his gallantry. Ever since she was a small child, she had tried to picture her beau asking for her hand in marriage. She wasn't disappointed in Adam's proposal. He was handsome and vulnerable beneath his protective exterior and always a gentleman. Their marriage would bring out the

Adam that had been locked up for so long. "I will, Adam," she answered. "I will love you as you love me all the days of my life."

Adam stood and kissed fiancée.

"We'll be so happy together," she said.

Jacques Dupre' was beside himself with happiness when Annabelle told him she had accepted Adam's proposal. He hugged his daughter and embraced his future son-in-law.

Giselle kissed Annabelle and then she kissed Adam. "Welcome to our family, Monsieur Adam," she said.

Placide coldly shook Adam's hand. "I'll be watching," he said in a quiet voice no one else could hear. "Make sure my sister is happy, monsieur. If I find you've mistreated her in any way, I will demand satisfaction on a field of honor."

Chills ran up and down Adam's spine. Placide had declared himself. He looked at his future brother-in-law. A threat from him could not be taken lightly, and Placide had definitely made a threat.

"Monsieur Dupre'," Adam said, "I wish to set the date for the wedding."

"What day would that be, my son?" Dupre' asked.

"Please come with me to my office where I have a calendar," Adam requested.

Jacques followed Adam to his office. Adam pulled out the calendar from a desk drawer and searched for a date. "Would Saturday, June twentieth, be appropriate?" he asked.

Jacques studied the calendar and made some calculations in his mind. "That's a good day," he replied. "The gardens at Belle Bois will be spectacular at that time of the year. My staff will begin making preparations."

When they were again in the parlor, Jacques called his daughter to him. "Adam has suggested June twentieth as the wedding date," he said. "Are you in agreement?"

"Oh yes, Pappa," she said. "It'll be such a happy day."

*****

Annabelle lay awake that night thinking of how sweet

Adam had looked when he proposed to her. He had been so sincere and romantic. The proposal was even more romantic than she had dreamed it would be.

She tried to imagine how it would be when she surrendered to Adam on their wedding night. She felt that he would be gentle and would cherish all that she offered to him. She could look forward to giving herself to Adam because he would treat her tenderly.

She smiled as she thought of how they'd grow even more closely together as the years passed. She pictured Adam at her bedside holding their child for the first time. He would look down on her with tears in his eyes as he held their baby. He would do all that he could to be the warm loving father that he had missed as he was growing up.

There would be so much happiness in their future. Tears came to her eyes as she remembered her mother. "Oh, Mamma," she cried out. "You'd love Adam just as I do if you could know him." She got up from her bed, walked to a window and looked up to the heavens. "I know you approve of him, Mamma," she said "He's such a kind and gentle person. I know you'll be looking down as we recite our vows and you'll be happy for me." She could feel her mother's presence as she returned to her bed.

As she pulled the covers about her, she thought to herself, "The day would have been perfect had it not been for Placide's cold hearted treatment of Adam's housekeeper." She was still upset with Placide for humiliating Hannah. After all, the woman hadn't tried to pass herself off as white. Giselle had made a silly mistake and Hannah hadn't wanted to embarrass her. "Why did Placide feel that he had to abase the woman that way?" She had tried to speak to him but he had been short with her.

She pushed Placide from her mind. "Pappa is so happy now that he'll have his grandchildren," she thought to herself. She pictured her silver haired father with a broad smile as he bounced his grandchild upon his knee. She smiled as she contemplated all of the wonderful things that would come her way. She was still smiling as she surrendered to sleep.

113

*****

Around the same time that Annabelle was thinking dreamily of her future with Adam, he held Hannah in his arms as she wept sorrowfully.

"I am so sorry that Placide humiliated you that way," he said. "I wanted to kill him."

"You would've been foolish to try," she said between sobs. "He would've killed you. He used to entertain Lance LeBlanc with stories of his victorious duels. He has killed many men. I'm glad you didn't call him out."

"But I should have," Adam insisted. "Look how he has upset you."

"I'm not crying about Placide," Hannah responded between tears. "I know I encouraged you to marry Annabelle, but it hurt me to see you walking hand-in-hand with her. I still think it's the only way, but my heart's broken."

"I will always love only you," Adam said as he held her to himself. "No other woman will ever have my heart. I can call the wedding off if that would make you happy."

"No, Adam, you can't," she cried out. "Something like that would ruin you. If only we'd met in a different world or a different time. I could've been your wife instead of your mistress."

"Remember, you are my wife," he insisted. "You carry my child and you carry my love. We can move away and start over again. You saw how Giselle took you for a white woman."

"No, Adam," she responded emphatically. "We'd never have what we can have here. Just allow me to grieve for what we'll never have. Hold me and tell me how much I mean to you."

"Hannah, Mr. Dupre asked me to promise I would love Annabelle as I love my own life and cherish her forever," he said. " I could not make that promise in my heart. There is only one woman who will ever mean that much to me. Hannah, I love you more than I love my own life. I will cherish you forever. When I make the wedding vows to her, I will be saying them to you in my heart. How can I get you to understand that your love makes me alive? If I lose your love, I will shrivel up and die."

She buried her head on Adam's shoulder and gave in to the grief. She hated Annabelle and at the same time, she pitied her. Annabelle would be Adam's wife in name, but she would never be in his heart.

She cried long into the night. When her tears finally subsided, she asked Adam to make love to her. He was tender and gentle as he gave himself to her. She fell asleep later and dreamed of walking down the aisle with him. She was wearing a white gown. Her mother wept tears of joy as she watched her daughter wed the man she loved. Her three brothers wished her well as they welcomed the man she loved into their family.

Adam awoke early the next morning and tried not to awaken Hannah. He looked at her as he dressed. His lovely goddess lay asleep on his bed. She appeared to be smiling as she slept. He hoped she was having sweet dreams. His heart ached for her. He wished for another world and another time.

*****

"I know you came to me back in the middle of November," Fisk said as he faced an impatient Adam Blythington, "but this is taking some time. A man like Albert Bennett can't be brought down in one stroke."

"No, but I had assumed progress would have been made by now," Adam said impatiently. "It is already February and I have heard nothing."

"Things have happened," Fisk responded, "His cattle and horses have been disappearing."

"He must be aware that these things are happening," Adam said.

"He is," Fisk responded. "He just doesn't know who's taking them and where they're going. I can sell you some cattle and horses cheap, if you're interested."

"I will need them when I take over Lance des Chenes," Adam said. "I might as well purchase them from you." It was almost a certainty now that Lance des Chenes would be his.

"What else do you have planned for Mr. Bennett?"

"This one'll take some planning," replied Fisk. "It would be easier to kill him outright, but you said he has to be left alive. Bennett's gonna have an accident that'll leave him paralyzed. We have something planned."

"Make sure he isn't killed," Adam insisted. "I want him to pay for what he has done."

"What exactly has he done?" Fisk asked. "You said you might tell me later."

Adam stared coldly at Fisk. "I said I may tell you someday," he replied. "That day has not come."

Fisk admired and feared the young man in his office. This man would someday be very powerful. No one would stand in his way. "That's fine with me," Fisk said. "I was just curious."

Adam relaxed. "When is Bennett going to have this accident?" he asked.

"The next time he leaves his plantation alone," Fisk replied. "We've been watching for our chance."

"Excellent," Adam said. "I look forward to your report." He peered at Fisk. He looked more like a laborer. His looks were deceiving, though. Fisk was a dangerous man, a man one did not want as an enemy. He could tell that Fisk was intimidated. He did not want to push Fisk too far.

*****

"I know you cannot recall your date of birth," Adam said to Hannah, "but you remembered that you were born in March. I think March fifteenth would be an appropriate day to celebrate your twenty-first birthday." He pulled a small box out of his pocket and handed it to Hannah.

She was deeply moved as she accepted the small box from Adam. She opened it and looked inside. "Oh, how beautiful," she cried out. She took the ring from the box and slipped it on her finger. "It fits perfectly." She held the gold ring up for Adam to examine. The marquis cut ruby sparkled as the stone caught the light. She threw her arms around Adam's neck and kissed him with all the passion she could muster.

Hannah was in her sixth month of pregnancy. She was settled in the cottage Adam's carpenters had built for her in a remote area on the property. She had been in the cottage for two months. Adam visited her at least once a day.

"I hoped you would like it," he said. "I wanted this to be a special day for you. I wish you a happy twenty-first birthday."

"It is a special day," she responded joyously. "How did you know I was born in March?"

"You told me shortly after I came here," he replied. "How could I forget something that important?"

Her eyes grew moist. "You're so thoughtful," she said. "I don't even remember telling you I was born in March. I'm so fortunate to have your love."

"How is our baby doing?" he asked as he patted her stomach. "In a bit over three months we will be parents."

"Are you excited?" she asked.

"Yes, I am," he replied. "I only wish everyone could know of our child. I hate keeping this a secret."

"It's the only way," she said. "The law in the south doesn't permit us to marry. If you acknowledge our child publicly, you'll be run out of the area. My life would be in jeopardy and probably the baby's, too."

"You have no idea how strange all of this is to me," he said.

"You mean laws forbidding us to marry and having to keep our child a secret?" she asked.

"No, I mean loving you the way I do," he replied with feeling. "I had really never loved anyone before I fell in love with you." He took her in his arms. "I am astonished by the depth of my love for you."

"I loved my mother," she said. "It broke my heart when I was taken away from her. I never knew my brothers well; I had only seen them at a distance. They lived in the slave cabins and I lived with momma in the big house. Aside from my mother, I had never loved anyone. I certainly didn't love my mother in the same way I love you." She held him as closely as her protruding stomach allowed.

"I have to be honest with you, Adam," she said. "When I first met you, I thought you were just one more white man I'd have to serve. I tried to study you to learn your weaknesses so I could defend myself against you. I was surprised to find myself caring for you. You didn't use me like Lance LeBlanc did. You always gave back to me when I gave to you. I began to learn who you really are and I couldn't help myself. I fell madly in love with you."

"I hope to have another gift for you soon," he said.

"What's the occasion?" she asked.

"We can call it a wedding gift," he replied.

"You're marrying Annabelle," she said. "I do hope you remember her birthday next year."

Adam had run to town almost at the last minute to get a birthday gift for Annabelle. Her nineteenth birthday had completely slipped his mind. Luckily, he had told Hannah several weeks before her birthday. When Hannah asked him what he had gotten for Annabelle, he had no idea what she was talking about. Thankfully, Hannah had remembered. Forgetting his fiancée's birthday was something that would not be quickly forgiven.

"She will be my wife in name only," he said once more. "You will always be my true love. Marriage to Annabelle is only for the sake of convenience."

"Will you give me a hint about the present?" she asked.

"Not even a hint, my love," he replied. "I hope it is something that will warm your heart."

*****

Three weeks after the celebration of Hannah's birthday, Adam walked into Fisk's office. "I received your message," he said as he entered the office. "I hope you have good news for me."

"I do have some good news," Fisk said as he pointed to one of the chairs. "Have a seat and I'll tell you all about it. It's taken some time, but things are beginning to work out for us. Do you remember me telling you Bennett couldn't plant the seed he'd kept from last year because it was ruined?"

"Yes, I remember that you said something about his seed." Adam replied. He looked skeptically at one of Fisk's rickety chairs and then sat down.

"Well, he ended up having to plant that seed because he didn't have the money to buy more seed and his credit was no good at the feed and seed store," Fisk continued.

"Why would he not have credit at the store?" Adam asked. "With as much land as he owns, he should have excellent credit."

"You didn't ask the obvious question," Fisk said smugly. "Why would he have to ask for credit?"

"Yes, that is odd, "Adam reflected. "He should have substantial savings at the bank."

"Mr. Bennett doesn't trust the bank," Fisk responded. In his excitement he rose from behind his desk and started pacing. "He kept all of his money in a safe in his home. He should have trusted the bank."

"How do you know all of this?" Adam asked as he watched Fisk pace back and forth excitedly.

"Because I have all of his money," Fisk replied with a grin. "I am now independently wealthy. I really don't have to work another day in my life."

"How much money was in his safe?" Adam asked. It seemed strange to him that Fisk still occupied his rundown office if he had thousands of dollars.

"I won't say," Fisk replied, "but it's more money than I thought I'd ever see in a lifetime." Fisk saw Blythington looking around his office. "You're probably wondering if it's true that I have that much money because I still have this office." He waved his hand to indicate the shabby office. "I mustered out of the army as a corporal. If I suddenly moved to a fancy office and bought one of those fancy mansions, don't you think people would be suspicious?"

"I had not thought of that," Adam replied. He appreciated his partner's cunning.

"People aren't suspicious of you because they don't know how much money you had with you when you got to town." Fisk pointed out. "Several people know I had only a month's pay when I mustered out. I plan to work here a few more years and then return to Pittsburgh and live the good life. I might even take one of those little high yellows with me." Fisk smiled as he thought of the life he would have when he returned to Pittsburgh.

"Bennett must have reported the theft to the sheriff," Adam said. "Are you not concerned about the trail leading to you?"

"The sheriff has too many secrets of his own to come sniffing after me," Fisk replied with a laugh.

It occurred to Adam that most of the money in Bennett's safe was more than likely confederate money, which was worthless. "How much of the money was confederate money?" he asked.

"None," Fisk replied. "Bennett's a sly man. I told you before; if Louisiana had held out a little longer, he'd have been hung."

"You did tell me that," Adam said. "What did he do?"

"I really don't know," Fisk replied, "but he's been working for the union ever since Lee started losing. The union let his cotton get through the blockade. He was paid federal dollars for his cotton. He had the money to pay his taxes and even buy more land. I've known that since before the war even ended. We couldn't fire in the direction of his plantation. I don't think he ever traded the federal money he had before the war for confederate money."

Adam was in awe of Fisk. If it was true that Fisk had stolen as much money as he had implied, he was now one of the richer men in town. "I want to return to my original question," he said. "Why is it that Bennett could not get credit at the feed and seed store?"

"Because I used some of his money to persuade Gus Doucet not to give him credit," Fisk replied.

"Surely he could get a loan from one of his friends," Adam responded.

"He did," Fisk replied. "I loaned him some money." He laughed. "Would you believe the silly fool borrowed his own

money? Not directly from me, but through one of my proteges."
He smiled once more. He liked the sound of the word. "I wish
I'd been there when he borrowed the money. I was told he had
his hat in hand when he borrowed his own money." He threw
his head back and laughed mirthfully.

"Please give me the whole story?" Adam asked
impatiently. "Waiting for you to give it to me one small piece at a
time will take all day."

"Aw, you're ruining all the fun," Fisk responded.
"Okay." He took a deep breath and launched into the remainder
of his story. "Bennett borrowed money from my protege. He
bought some cotton seed, but I made sure it was doctored before
it got to him."

"How was it doctored?" Adam asked.

"How would I know?" Fisk replied flippantly. "One of
my men took care of that. Where was I?" He scratched his head.
"Yeh, I remember now. Only a few cotton plants came up. Same
with his corn. He wants more money for more seed. He'll get the
money, but that seed won't come up either."

"He can sell off some of his land to buy more seed,"
Adam said. "Why would he borrow money?"

"That's where it really gets good," Fisk replied with a
smile. "When Bennett borrowed the money, he used Lance des
Chenes as collateral. He said it would be for only a few months
or so. What makes it even better for me, Bennett has had a
gambling problem for years. He could always cover his losses
from the money he had stashed away." Fisk shook his head.
"The poor man's still losing, but he can't cover his gambling
losses anymore. I bought up all of his chits." He laughed again.
"The man's money problems keep getting worse. My men
persuaded his darkies to leave him for a while. He needs money
to hire more people so he can get his seed planted. Pitiful fool
has a hard time getting around now that he can't use his legs."
He shook his head. "That man does have his problems."

"How much longer do you think it will be before he has
to sell Lance des Chenes?" Adam asked.

"It's not a matter of him selling," Fisk replied. "I'll take
the land when he can't pay his debts. I figure another four,

maybe five weeks at the most."

*****

    In the middle of May, Adam was again in Fisk's office. Fisk was beside himself with excitement. "I foreclosed on Bennett," he said proudly.

    "You mean you now own Lance des Chenes?" Adam asked with an incredulous look on his face. "You pulled it off."

    "I told you it would take time, but I could do it," Fisk replied triumphantly. "Sixty-two hundred arpents of prime land with a mansion and barns and equipment. You can buy everything from me if you'd like."

    "What is your price for the property?" Adam asked.

    "Guess I could keep it now that I have it," Fisk replied slyly. He looked askant at Blythington and noted his discomfort. "But heck, I don't know anything about running a plantation," Fisk saw the relief on Blythington's face. "I'd run it in the ground if I kept it. That wasn't our deal anyway." He looked craftily at Blythington. "I figure five thousand dollars and half the profits from the crops this year and next year should take care of the price."

    Adam thought about Fisk's offer. For the mansion, barns, land and equipment, the purchase price was more than reasonable. "You said you might go down on the fee," he said, "How much would you charge as your fee?"

    "If you'll agree to my price," Fisk replied, "we'll call it even with what you already paid. I got more than enough from Bennett's safe to cover the rest of the fee. That man should've trusted the bank."

    "I agree to your terms," Adam responded quickly. "When do I take possession of Lance des Chenes?"

    "The papers are ready for you to sign," Fisk replied. He was beginning to wonder if he should have settled so hastily. He thought of raising his price, but thought better. Blythington could be a powerful ally or a formidable enemy. "I figured you'd agree to my terms. If you give me the five thousand, the property's yours today."

Adam made his way to the bank and withdrew five thousand dollars. He went from there to Alex Cortez's office and signed the papers. He wondered how Hannah would accept the news.

*****

"Do your remember me talking to you about a wedding present?" Adam asked as he sat in Hannah's cottage later that day. He watched Hannah as she folded clothes.

"I remember something about that," she responded.

"I closed the deal today," he said.

"What deal?" she asked.

"I purchased Lance des Chenes today," he responded. "Albert Bennett had a streak of bad luck and had to sell out."

"You did what?" she exclaimed.

"I bought Lance des Chenes," he answered.

Hannah looked as though she were about to fall. Adam ran to her and took her in his arms. "Are you all right?" he asked.

"Did you know I was born there?" she asked.

"Yes, I did," he replied. "I know Albert Bennett is your father. He will never do that to anyone again."

She began to cry. "I thought this would make you happy," he said.

"I am happy," she cried.

"I know I cannot put the property in your name," he said, "but the property is yours to do with as you please. I have to make sure the fields are profitable for the next two years. I have to give Fisk half of the profits."

She was silent for a few moments. "Is my mother still alive?" she asked.

"I have not been to the property," he replied. "I want to hitch the buggy up and take you there tomorrow."

"I wish we could go today," she said. "I know it's too far to go there and get back today."

"We will go first thing tomorrow morning," he promised.

*****

Hannah was dressed and waiting when Adam pulled up beside the cottage in the buggy early the next morning. The May day was cool and pleasant. Adam helped Hannah into the buggy and set out for Lance des Chenes.

"There it is," she said as she pointed toward a large mansion after they had traveled almost two hours. "It's been about ten years, but I remember it like it was yesterday." Tears began to stream down her cheeks as she continued to gaze at the mansion.

Adam looked at the impressive antebellum home. It was larger than the Southern Kingdom mansion. He looked for signs of activity, but saw none. "I wonder if anyone is here," he said. "It looks deserted."

"Where are the people?" she asked wistfully.

Adam drove the buggy up to the mansion and stopped. He could hear the birds chirping their songs, the insects making their noises and the cattle lowing in the background, but not a person was in sight. "Hello," he cried out.

A tall light skinned Negro man walked out from the barn. "Who you is?" the man asked.

Adam recalled his welcome at Southern Kingdom. "I'm the new owner," he replied. "Are you alone?"

"No suh," the man answered. "Evybody hiden in da bone. We dawn know whut to expeck."

"Are you Martha Bennett's son?" Hannah asked. She fought to keep her voice under control.

The man studied Hannah. "Yessum, ah is," he replied. "You knowed my momma?"

"Is she here?" Hannah asked.

"No, Mam," the man answered. "She took sick an died wintah fo last."

Hannah clutched at Adam's arm. She had always hoped to see her mother again. The news that her mother was dead struck her deeply. She fought for self-control. "What is your name?" she asked.

"Ahz Benjmin Bennett," he replied.

"Are Laban and Micah here?" she asked.

"Yessum, dey in da bone," he replied.

"Would you please tell everyone to come out," she said. "Tell them no harm will come to them."

Benjamin returned to the barn. "Da boss man's wife say fo all ya'll to come out heah," he said. "She say evyting okay."

The Negro people began to file out of the barn. Hannah recognized some of the people from her childhood. "Who's in charge of the house servants?" she asked. A middle-aged Negro woman stepped forward. "What's your name?" Hannah asked.

"Ah be Joanna," the woman answered.

"Joanna," Hannah said, "please take your staff and return to the house. Mr. Blythington and I will require refreshments shortly."

Joanna signaled her staff to follow her as she walked toward the house. Three women and a young man followed behind her.

"Who's in charge of the field hands?" Hannah asked.

"Ah is," Benjamin said. "I bin da feel han boss for tree summers."

"Mr. Blythington needs to speak with you and your two brothers," Hannah said. "Would you please show us to the plantation office?"

Benjamin, Laban and Micah walked toward the mansion. They went in through a side door. Hannah and Adam walked in behind them. "I think you'd better take over," she whispered to Adam. "For the time being, I don't want my brothers to know my identity."

Adam walked into the office and stood behind the desk. He motioned for the brothers to be seated. Hannah placed a chair beside him and sat. Adam sat down in his chair. "Mrs. Blythington and I are interested in making a profit from this plantation," he said to the men. Hannah turned to him and smiled. "Benjamin, you are the overseer. Please give me your thoughts on how we can turn a profit this year."

"Well, Mr. Biten," Benjamin began, "we ain't got nutten planted in da feels. It gone be hawd to make da profit wit out da crop."

"You may call me Mr. Adam," he said. "I know there have been problems. How quickly can we get seed in the ground?"

"It ain't plantin da seed dats da problim," Benjamin replied. "Tree times we done plant da seed and tree times da seed ain't come up. I figger if nuttin go wrong agin, in bout two weeks we kin git evyting planted."

"Then, we must get started," Adam said. "What do you need?"

"All we needs da seed," Benjamin replied. "Soons we git dat, soons we git stawted."

"You will have the seed tomorrow morning," Adam said. "Benjamin, I want you to be in charge of this plantation until I can hire a manager."

"Mr. Adam, you mean I be in charge a da whole ting?" Benjamin asked.

"For now, you are in charge," Adam replied. "When I return, I expect to see everyone working and everything running smoothly."

"Yessuh," Benjamin said.

"Is there anything else you require?" Adam asked.

"No suh, ah tink dat it," Benjamin replied.

"If anything further is required," Adam said, "send a man to Southern Kingdom. You may know the place as Seven Oaks."

"Yassuh, Mr. Adam," Benjamin answered.

After Adam dismissed Hannah's brothers, he and Hannah walked out on the large verandah in the back of the mansion. Hannah gazed at the places where she had played as a child. She recalled the voice of her mother as she trailed behind her. She saw the face of her father as he ran his hands over her body and then lay on top of her. She fought for control over her emotions. She wanted to be in the privacy of her cottage before she allowed her grief to spill out. The years of her youth spent at Lance des Chenes seemed a lifetime ago. Everything looked familiar, yet everything had changed.

"Are you all right?" Adam asked as he placed his hand

over hers. "I imagine this is all hard on you."

"Yes, it is," she replied. Adam had organized the plantation workmen so easily and so quickly. Leading was second nature to him. She had struggled to keep her composure as she spoke to her brothers and former friends. She was relieved that no one had recognized her. She had no desire to return to her former life.

She thought about her brothers. She had come close to asking Adam to make them the permanent managers and allow them to live in the mansion. That would have been a mistake. The southerners would turn against Adam if he made a former slave the manager of a plantation and moved him into the mansion.

She had not revealed her identity to her brothers. She was glad that she had held back on telling them who she was. That lifetime was over. She was pleased that her brothers would have a better life under Adam, but she had no desire to pick up where she'd left off at Lance des Chenes. It would have been different, had her mother been alive.

Adam stood by Hannah's side as she took in the place where she had lived the first thirteen years of her life. He marveled at her composure as she dealt with the news of her mother's death. He was surprised that Hannah had not revealed herself to her brothers. Had she requested, he would have made the older brother the permanent manager and allowed all three brothers to live in the mansion.

"Dere y'all is," Joanna said as she walked out the door and onto the back porch. Heah's some lemnade and cookies ah made fo y'all."

Hannah looked into Joanna's eyes. She didn't recognize the little girl who had begged cookies from her. "Don't you recognize me?" Hannah asked under her breath. She was both pleased and disappointed that Joanna hadn't recognized her. "It's true," she said to herself, "Hannah LeBlanc is no more."

"These are delicious," Adam said.

"They certainly are," Hannah added. "Thank you, Joanna."

*****

Hannah said nothing on the buggy ride back to her cottage. Adam did nothing to provoke her into a conversation. She had absorbed a lot in a short period of time and needed time to sort things out.

Adam helped Hannah down from the carriage and walked to the door with her. "Would you rather be alone?" he asked as she opened her door.

"No, Adam," she replied softly. "I need you to be with me."

Hannah walked to her bedroom. Adam followed her. She lay on the bed without undressing or removing the bedspread. He lay beside her. She moved closer to Adam and laid her head on his chest. "I thought I'd see my momma again some day," she said. "I hardly slept last night because I was thinking about our reunion." She started to say more but her body began to shake from the tears she wept as her grief poured out. "Hold me," she said as she clung to Adam. "Hold me until the pain goes away." It was nighttime before her tears subsided. "Why is there so much pain in this world?" she asked.

He had no answer for her. "I really do not know," he replied. "I wish I could make all of your pain go away and protect you from ever being hurt again."

"You're so good to me," she said as she cuddled against him. "I feel safe when I'm with you."

"May I ask you something?" he asked.

"Yes, you may," she answered in a quiet voice. "I hope I can answer your question."

"Why did you not let your brothers and the other people at Lance des Chenes know who you are?" he asked.

"It's complicated," she responded. "I wanted to throw myself into Benjamin's arms when I first saw him. He looks different, a little older, but I recognized him. The two younger boys haven't changed that much. I thought they'd see something in me and know who I was. They had no idea I was their sister.

"I used to beg Joanna for cookies. She gave me cookies today and recognized nothing about me. I looked directly into her eyes hoping there would be a spark of recognition. There was nothing. By the time we left, I was glad I hadn't told them who I am. Hannah LeBlanc is no more. I'm Hannah Blythington. I have another life and I don't want to return to the life I left behind."

"I think I understand," he said as he kissed her forehead. "I have another question."

She turned her head and smiled at him. "How many questions do you have?" she asked.

"I think this is the last," he replied. "I was prepared to make your oldest brother the permanent manager if you had asked. I would have allowed all three of your brothers to live in the mansion. I was surprised you did not ask me."

"I thought of asking that of you," she responded. "That would've been a tragic mistake. Southerners aren't ready for former slaves to run plantations and live in the plantation mansions. My brothers would've been hanged and you'd have been run out of the south.

"The time may come when that sort of thing will be accepted, but the time isn't now." She pulled herself closer to him and kissed him. "You've done so much for me and given me so much. I appreciate the gift of Lance des Chenes, but I think it would be better for you to keep the plantation."

Adam opened his mouth to protest.

"Please hear me out," she said. "Knowing that you love me enough to do that for me is a wonderful gift. I don't know the first thing about running a large place like that. You have leadership skills. I saw the way you quickly got things organized. I hope you'll teach me how to lead, but I lack those skills now."

"You lead the servants of Southern Kingdom," Adam protested.

"There's a world of difference between what I do with the servants and having the responsibility for an entire plantation. You lead, I'll be happy to follow."

Adam hugged her tightly. "My dear sweet little darling," he said. "One more question; will you ever let your brothers know who you are?"

"I knew you weren't out of questions," she said as she laughed. "No, I'll never let them know who I am. I think it's better for them and for me if we leave things as they are."

CHAPTER NINE

June 19, 1866 - (early hours) June 21, 1866

"I'm so glad that you came," Annabelle said as she greeted Robert Joubert and his fiancée, Angelina Granger, in the Belle Bois parlor.

Robert gave Annabelle a brief hug and a kiss on her cheek. Angelina embraced her old friend.

"It's so good to see you again," Angelina said as she drew her head back to look at Annabelle. "You look positively radiant. Adam must be quite a man."

"He's a wonderful person," Annabelle responded. "He's sweet and kind and considerate."

Robert cleared his throat. "I'm still here, you know," he said.

"Oh, Robert," Annabelle exclaimed. "I'm so happy that you're here. I hoped that you would come."

"I wouldn't have missed your wedding for the world," Robert said. "After all, I want to see who you rejected me for."

Annabelle's face clouded. "Why do you say I rejected you?" she asked. "I thought we'd both decided we had become dear friends and nothing else."

Robert threw his head back and laughed. "I was only teasing," he said. "I thought you'd know that. Anyway, I've found my true love." He turned to Angelina and reached for her hand.

"I'm sorry," Annabelle said as she smiled at Robert and Angelina. "I'm not thinking clearly with all the excitement about the wedding. I find my mind is in a whirl."

"I hope that Angelina is as happy as you are the day

before our wedding," Robert said. "Annabelle, you are radiant. He must be the man you've been hoping would come into your life."

"He is," Annabelle responded happily. "I was drawn more to him by his kind heart than his good looks."

"How good looking is he?" Angelina asked with a dreamy smile on her face. "He seems to have swept you off your feet."

"You read too many novels," Robert said. "The next thing I know you'll be wondering if I'm enough of a prince charming for you."

"You are my prince charming," Angelina said as she smiled sweetly at her beau. "There could be no one more handsome than you." Her expression changed. "Now, go and speak to Monsieur Dupre' and Placide. Annabelle and I want to talk girl talk."

"Girl talk, humph, "Robert said. "You two want to gossip."

"Men gossip more than women," Angelina retorted. "Now go and give us some time alone together."

Robert reluctantly left the room.

"Tell me all about your prince charming," Angelina entreated. "I want to know everything."

Annabelle filled Angelina in on how she'd felt about Adam when they met and the transition that had taken place when she got to know the man who was hidden beneath the surface. "I know he'll bloom after we're married," she said after she had told Angelina everything she knew about Adam. "He was hurt deeply as a child."

Angelina hoped her friend wasn't fooling herself about the man who was supposedly beneath the surface. From what Annabelle had told her about Adam, she wondered if Annabelle was looking at him through rosecolored glasses.

"You haven't described him to me," she said. "What does he look like?"

"He's very handsome," Annabelle answered. "He's almost as tall as Placide. He has dark hair and blue eyes. I can't wait to see them sparkle after he really trusts me."

Angelina worried about her friend. In all the time Annabelle and Adam had known each other, she had never seen his eyes light up? Robert's eyes sparkled every time he looked at her. It was easy to see the love he held for her. "I once saw him dreamy-eyed," Annabelle continued. "I asked him what he was thinking and he told me that he was thinking about me holding our child. I could see the love in his eyes that he'll have for our children. He'll be a wonderful husband and a wonderful father."

Angelina hoped for her friend's sake she was reading the signs wrong. Although she was skeptical, she was determined to give Adam the benefit of the doubt. After all, she had never even met him. Still, Annabelle was too soft-hearted when it came to the downtrodden. Any sob story would sway her heart.

Both women were startled by a knock on the door. Annabelle opened the door to find that Robert had returned.

"Monsieur Dupre' said Marie is ready to serve dinner," Robert stated.

"Is it that time already?" Annabelle asked nervously. "There's still so much to be done."

"I'll stay and help," Angelina offered. "It'll be a good experience for next month."

"It's so nice of you to offer," Annabelle responded, "but I can't take advantage of your friendship."

"Nonsense," Angelina countered. "It'll be a pleasure and I need the experience."

"I thought we were going out for a buggy ride," Robert whined.

"We have plenty of time for that later," Angelina responded. "Can't you see Annabelle needs me?"

"I give up," Robert said with a smile. "Stay and help Annabelle. I think I'll ride out to Seven Oaks and meet the groom."

"Adam renamed the plantation Southern Kingdom," Annabelle said nervously. "You'll have time to meet Adam tomorrow. He may not be in the mood for company today."

"That's odd," Robert thought to himself. "It's strange that she's worried that he won't be in the mood to meet her friends. What kind of man is she marrying? Southern Kingdom? What a strange name for a plantation." He looked at Annabelle then moved his eyes to Angelina's face. Angelina met his gaze and slowly shook her head back and forth. He could see she was also worried about Annabelle.

He looked again at Annabelle. "You're right," he said. "I'll meet him tomorrow."

*****

June 20, 1866, turned out to be a gorgeous spring day. The summer heat had not yet set in. Adam arrived at St. Landry Church well before one o'clock, which was the scheduled time for the wedding ceremony to begin. He paced up and down in the vestry of the church. Reverend Boudreaux was resplendent in his vestments. Annabelle would soon be walking down the aisle with Jacques. She would meet Adam in front of the altar. Adam pulled out his pocket watch. Five minutes remained before the ceremony would begin. He wished the time would pass more quickly. He continued with his pacing.

A few minutes later, the organ began to play. Adam turned his head and gazed toward the doors in the front of the church. Annabelle and her father would soon walk through those doors as they entered the church.

He caught his first glimpse of his bride in her wedding dress. She was wearing a white wedding gown with a veil covering her face. He still wondered why Annabelle had been so fussy about choosing her wedding gown. When all was said and done, a white gown was only a white gown.

Jacques looked like he was struggling to hold back his tears. Once they neared the altar, Jacques lifted the veil and kissed Annabelle. He wiped tears from his eyes and gazed at his daughter. When Annabelle drew nearer, Adam turned and faced her.

Adam wondered what Hannah was doing. She was staying in her cottage until after the baby was born. He had asked her to spend a few nights with him in the mansion, but she had refused him. She said she would not return until after the wet nurse was in the cottage.

He thought of the baby he and Hannah would have. He hoped Hannah would change her mind and allow the baby to stay on in the plantation house. He turned his attention to the parson. Reverend Boudreaux was speaking in Latin as he conducted the service. Adam would have preferred a simple ceremony. Marriage by a judge or justice of the peace would have been fine with him.

Reverend Boudreaux walked up to where Adam and Annabelle were kneeling and motioned for them to stand. They stood and faced the parson. Boudreaux spoke of the sanctity of marriage and all the things that marriage is supposed to entail.

Adam wondered when the parson would finally ask them to say their vows and end the dull ceremony. After an interminable length of time, it seemed to Adam, the parson finally came around to the vows.

Adam tried to look solemn as he promised to be a good and faithful husband. He wished it were Hannah standing beside him where Annabelle stood. Annabelle promised to love, honor and obey. She looked directly into Adam's eyes as she promised her eternal love.

When Reverend Boudreaux told Adam he may kiss his bride, he drew Annabelle in his arms and kissed her. Annabelle's kiss was all right but it lacked Hannah's passion. "As beautiful as she is," he thought to himself, "you would think she would have more fire."

Annabelle drew herself close to Adam and whispered, "I love you," in his ear. Her eyes glowed as she looked at her new husband.

Adam tried not to avert his eyes as he told her he loved her. He thought of the night that was to come. At least there would be some compensation for going through all of this. He looked forward to seeing his new wife's body. Many times he had tried to envision how she would look without her clothes. He would know after this night.

Several people came up to congratulate him and shake his hand. Most of the people in the church were strangers to him.

Jacques walked up to his new son-in-law and embraced

him. "You are now my son," he said. "I welcome you to my family as my very own."

Adam thanked Jacques. Before he could say anything more, Placide walked up to him. "I want to welcome you officially into our family," Placide said as he embraced Adam. As he drew Adam closer, he spoke into his ear, "If you cause my sister any distress, I will kill you, Monsieur." He stepped back and smiled at Adam.

Adam felt cold shivers run up and down his spine. Placide had warned him once before. He would have called Placide out in a duel, had he not been certain that Placide would kill him.

Giselle came up to Adam and embraced him. "Annabelle is so fortunate to have captured the heart of a handsome young gentleman such as you," she said. "Had she not caught you, I may have been tempted to visit you when Placide was on one of his adventures."

Adam quickly looked around to make sure no one had overheard. Placide was too quick to avenge his honor for Adam to welcome overtures from Giselle.

After everyone had kissed the bride and had shaken the groom's hand, the wedding party climbed into the Dupre' carriage.

Annabelle nestled against her new husband. "Wasn't the ceremony spectacular?" she asked. "Reverend Boudreaux was so touching and solemn as he read our vows. Our marriage will last forever now that Reverend Boudreaux has given us his blessings."

Adam kept his opinion of the ceremony to himself; it was long and boring. "You are right, my love," he said. "We will love each other throughout eternity."

"Oh, Adam," Annabelle said as she kissed his cheek, "you're so sweet. I could tell you were paying close attention to Reverend Boudreaux. I'm so happy you took our ceremony so seriously." She kissed him again.

Adam tried to reflect happiness to his new wife. He was hoping the time would pass quickly. There was worse to come. He had to spend a month away from home on his honeymoon.

The gardens of Belles Bois looked spectacular. Alex had worked his magic on the grounds of the plantation. All of the servants present were dressed in Dupre' livery. Adam made a mental note to make sure all his servants had livery for the next formal occasion at Southern Kingdom.

Jacques had hired an orchestra for the occasion. The bride and groom were to dance the first dance. Adam had been given formal dancing lessons while attending Eaton, but he did not feel comfortable on the dance floor. Although he knew the steps, he danced stiffly.

"Relax, my love," Annabelle said in his ear. "Allow yourself to be carried by the music."

Adam had never enjoyed dancing. As far as he was concerned, it was a complete waste of time. He smiled at Annabelle and tried to relax.

"That's better," Annabelle said. "I love to be in your strong arms."

He smiled at her again. He hoped she would like being in his arms later that night. "It has been a long time since I danced," he said. "I seem to be quite rusty."

"You'll get used to dancing, my love," she said. "We'll attend all of the dances during the social season. It'll be wonderful to show you off to all of my friends. You'll be the most handsome escort."

This was not welcome news to Adam's ears. He supposed he would have to attend the dances in order to be accepted in society. He wondered how Hannah would feel in his arms as they danced. "She has a natural grace," he thought to himself. "In no time she would know all of the dance steps."

The music stopped and Adam walked with Annabelle to a refreshment table. He was not one given to strong drink, but he wanted one now. Hannah had warned him to have very little alcohol. He was being judged by everyone in attendance. He passed up the whiskey and accepted a glass of lemonade.

"I'm so pleased you are not a drunkard," Annabelle said. "I respect a man who has self-control."

Adam agreed with her in his mind. It was taking all of his self-control to get through the wedding and the reception.

"I hope you respect everything about me," he said. "Your love means everything to me."

"I love you, Adam," Annabelle said as she pulled herself against him. "I can't believe I didn't like you the day I met you. I was wrong to feel that way about you."

"I am happy that you gave me a second chance," he responded. "Life would be very lonely without you."

"When we were walking at Southern Kingdom," she said, "I was introduced to the real Adam Blythington. You were so different. I thank God that He brought us together."

Jacques stood up and offered a toast. "Mes Amis," he said, "I wish to toast my new son." He waved his hand toward Adam. "I haven't lost a daughter; I've gained a son. May the years bring them happiness and prosperity. May there always be love in the Blythington home. May they bring me many grandchildren."

Everyone cheered. Adam bowed and Annabelle curtsied.

Placide offered a toast. "I would like to toast my beautiful sister and her new husband," he said. "May truth and love live in the Blythington home. I want to assure my precious Annabelle that her husband will live a long life, so long as he remains true and faithful to her."

After a moment's hesitation, cheers broke out once again. "You're such a tease," Annabelle scolded her brother. "Adam will be a good and faithful husband. Why must you say such things?"

Placide smiled at his sister and new brother-in-law. "May good fortune always be with you, Monsieur," he said as he raised his glass.

Adam raised his glass. Each man took a sip of his drink.

Adam looked into Placide's dark eyes. In his eyes lay death for any man who would dare to displease him. This was the third time Placide had threatened him. If this continued, Placide would meet his doom in some isolated place. He was sure Fisk could make the arrangements.

The reception ended finally and Adam and Annabelle entered the Southern Kingdom carriage. Jeremiah slapped the reins on the horses' backs and the carriage set out for home. Annabelle once again nestled against her new husband. She was tipsy from the wine she had consumed. A few more toasts would have carried her over the edge.

*****

Robert helped Angelina into his buggy. He could tell she was very upset. He too was in a quandary wondering how Annabelle had allowed herself to be deluded by Adam.

"How did she choose such a man?" Angelina asked in an exasperated tone. "She's so beautiful and so sweet. She could have done much better."

"He doesn't appear to be a friendly person," Robert agreed. "Annabelle is usually a much better judge of character." His heart went out to Annabelle. If the truth were known, he had realized Annabelle would never love him the way he loved her. He had agreed with her that they were only very good friends when he realized it was pointless to continue to try to win her love.

"She's so gullible when it comes to sob stories," Angelina cried out. "She thinks there's a kind and sensitive man below Adam's surface. He's the most egotistical, self-centered, cold-hearted man I've ever met. She's such a fool to have fallen for him."

Robert hurt deeply for Annabelle. His feelings for Annabelle had quieted and he now loved Angelina. Angelina was a sweet and loving person. Her beauty equaled Annabelle's, but still, she wasn't Annabelle. He had vowed that he would never let Angelina know his love for Annabelle had continued to simmer. "There's nothing that can be done now," he said resignedly. "All we can do is pray for her and hope for the best."

"I'll be watching," Angelina said vehemently. "I'll tell Placide if I ever suspect that Adam has been abusive."

"From the look in Placide's eyes," Robert added, "I think he'll be watching, too. It's obvious that Adam fears Placide. Adam will have to be very careful not to provoke Placide. Perhaps it'll all turn out well after all."

Angelina moved over against Robert. "I'm glad you're nothing like Adam," she said. "I can tell by the sparkle in your eyes that you do love me. We'll be very happy together."

"I do love you," Robert said as he put his arm around her. "In just another month I'll be able to express all of my love for you."

Angelina smiled up at him. "I love you, Doctor Joubert," she said.

"I love you, too," Robert responded, "but it'll be two weeks before I graduate and go into practice with Father."

"Why quibble?" Angelina laughed. "We'll be so happy together."

"Yes, we will, "Robert agreed. "Yes, we will," he said to himself. "You'll never know that you were my second choice."

*****

Annabelle grew nervous as they neared the plantation house. "I hope you're not disappointed in me," she said as she trembled against him

"How could I possibly be disappointed," he responded. "I will be gentle. This is also my first time. Please be patient with me."

"It's better than I hoped when I dreamed of marriage," she said. "We'll have our first time together. God is good to us."

Adam walked with Annabelle to his room.

"I have to prepare for the night," she said. "I need to use your bathing room."

Adam showed her the bathing room. It seemed forever to him before she came out. She was still wearing all of her clothes.

"Would you please blow out all of the lamps," she requested.

He had waited for months to see her body, and now she was asking that there be no light. He struggled to keep his patience. "I will leave only one of the lamps lit," he said. "We may need to get up during the night and the room is unfamiliar to you."

"Adam," she said, "I feel so self-conscious. What if you're not pleased with me?"

"I have the same worry," he responded.

"How could that be?" she asked. "You're so handsome."

"You are so beautiful," Adam said. "Why do you worry about me not being pleased with you?"

Annabelle slowly lay on the bed. She pulled up the bedclothes and began to disrobe beneath them. Adam stripped off his clothes and joined her. She gasped as their bodies touched. He put his arms around her and gently drew her to himself.

"I trust you," she said. She returned his kisses. When he touched her breast, she drew in a deep breath. "I'm sorry. I know I need to submit to you."

"I do not want you to submit to me," he said. "We are to become one." He had never slept with a virgin before. Hannah had instructed him to be gentle and solicitous of Annabelle's feelings.

Annabelle allowed him to touch her body. She watched him as he touched her. "Do I bring you pleasure?" she asked.

"Very much," he replied. "You are so beautiful."

She moved closer to him and began to touch his body. She was hesitant with each movement of her hands. "Do you truly love me, Adam?" she asked.

"With all my heart," he replied. "We are now man and wife."

She welcomed him as he continued to caress her body. She cried out when he entered her and held herself close to him.

Adam's mind registered the difference between Annabelle and Hannah as he made love to Annabelle.

After they had coupled, Annabelle lay close to Adam. "Did I please you?" she asked.

"In every way," he replied. "Did I please you?"

She was quiet for a few moments. "There was some pain, but Giselle told me there would be pain," she replied. "You did bring me pleasure. Giselle said it would be better once there is no more pain. You were so gentle. I do love you, Adam."

"I love you too," he responded.

She fell asleep in his arms. He wanted to go to Hannah to extinguish the fires that still burned after he had made love to Annabelle, but Hannah was in her cottage. The baby was due at any time and she would not return to the mansion for several weeks. He would be leaving for New Orleans on his honeymoon in the morning. He longed to see Hannah before he left. It would be over two months before he could hope to see her again.

It was not until early morning that he realized he had not seen Annabelle's body. She lay asleep beside him. He pulled the bedclothes back and looked at her. She did have a beautiful body, but it could not compare with the way Hannah's body looked before she became pregnant. He gently replaced the bedclothes and lay back down.

CHAPTER TEN

June 21, 1866 - July 23, 1866

While Adam's carriage made its way to the Atchafalaya River where he and Annabelle would board the paddle wheeler that would take them to the Mississippi River and on down to New Orleans, Hannah's labor pains began.

Adam had insisted Cleopatra, the plantation midwife, live with Hannah during her last month of pregnancy. This was necessary because Hannah would have no way to send for her when she went into labor.

"I knows jus whut ta do," Cleopatra said as she attempted to calm Hannah. "Dawn you worry none."

Hannah wasn't worried about the delivery of her baby. Her thoughts were on Adam. "Why couldn't he be here while his child is being brought into the world?" she asked herself bitterly. She knew the answer, but that didn't help to take away the ache in her heart. While she was bringing their baby into the world, he was leaving with his wife on their honeymoon. Although she had insisted that Adam marry Annabelle, she couldn't push away the resentment she now felt. "He should be here," she said out loud.

"Whut's dat?" Cleopatra asked.

"Nothing," Hannah replied. "I'm only rambling."

"Dat happins when da chile is commin," the midwife said. "It gonna git more worser."

"Adam!" Hannah cried out as the next labor pain took over her body, "why aren't you here with me?"

"Shugah, Mr. Adam lef fo his hunnymoon," Cleopatra said. "He ain't gone be heah. We all know he de daddy uh yo baby."

Hannah realized she had spoken out loud. She fought to remain silent. She didn't want to share their relationship with the midwife. Another labor pain racked her body. She bit her lip to keep from screaming out his name.

After the pain subsided, she thought of Adam. Maybe she should have accepted his offer to move to another place where they could live as man and wife and raise their child together. It would never be the same as their lives at Southern Kingdom, but they would have each other. She was glad he had asked her to marry him.

"You is made fo havin babies," the midwife said comfortingly. "Dis gone be more easy fo you den fo mossa da new mommas. Dat baby wantun to come out."

Hannah's body was once again gripped by terrible pain. She struggled to remain silent as the pain forced its way through her body. She lost track of time as the waves of pain swept over her. The shadows were growing longer as the pain subsided momentarily and allowed her to think once again.

"I love you so much, Adam," she said under her breath. "I wish you could be with me now. Please be thinking about me." She clenched her fists as another pain seared through her body.

"Heah he comes," Cleopatra said. "Da baby's haid done come out. Push one mo time hunny. You bout dare now."

Hannah pushed with all of her might.

"It's a lil gal," Cleopatra said a few minutes later. "You got yoseff a lil gal."

Hannah heard her daughter crying. Cleopatra cleaned off the child after she had severed the umbilical cord and handed her to Hannah.

"She gone be hongry," Cleopatra said. "It ain't gone be long befo she be wantin yo moik."

Hannah thought about the arrangement she had made for the child. Hannah's mother had told her that she always used a wet nurse because allowing a child to suckle changed the shape of the breast. "Da tit dawn look yong no mo if you lets da chile feed like dat," her mother had said. "Bes you git da wet nurse quick lack."

Hannah held her daughter closely and studied her face.

She found that the baby looked like Adam. Cleopatra took the baby from her, wrapped her in a blanket and placed her in the bassinet.

"Cleopatra," Hannah said, "please hitch the buggy and fetch Rebecca. Bring her here as quickly as possible."

Cleopatra knew Rebecca would serve as the baby's wet nurse, but she had assumed Hannah would suckle the baby for the first week or so. Rebecca had enough milk for her child and Hannah's child, but a mother always took the first week or so to bond with her baby. "Miss Hannah, dawn you wanna feed da chile fo a while yosef?" Cleopatra asked.

"No," Hannah replied. "Rebecca will feed her."

Cleopatra shook her head. "Whut kinna momma dawn wanna feed her own chile?" she asked herself. "Dat dawn be natchul."

Hannah looked at her daughter as she slept. Her hair was dark like Adam's and soft as silk. The baby would have good hair. She wondered if the baby would remain light complected. It was too early to tell. The baby's eyes were blue. She hoped the baby's eyes would retain their blue color. "You have a great future ahead of you," Hannah said to her daughter. "When you grow up, no one will ever know you're not a Caucasian. The world is yours, my darling." Hannah wanted to name her daughter Martha after her mother, but decided to wait for Adam's return before naming her. Hannah wondered what Adam would think of their child.

*****

Adam gazed at his home as the carriage drew near enough for him to see the mansion. He had endured a month away from his beloved home and his beloved Hannah. It had been a struggle, but he had acted out the part of the loving husband with Annabelle.

She chattered on about such nonsensical things. It mattered not the least to him whether a dress was made of cotton or of silk or which shoes were in fashion. She had tried on countless hats. They all looked silly to him. He wished she could have gone out alone to purchase the things she wanted. "Why does she have to drag me along?" he had asked himself on numerous occasions.

New Orleans was too crowded and there was an unpleasant odor in many of the areas. Swatting at mosquitoes seemed to be the pastime for most of the people of the city. The hotel accommodations could not compare with his mansion. The balls and galas he was forced to attend went on forever. "Boring people must be drawn to these things," he had speculated to himself.

Lovemaking no longer pained Annabelle, but she had grown no more passionate or spontaneous. She was responsive to his needs but in a very prim and proper manner. There had been no wild abandoned lovemaking.

Hannah was on his mind most of the time he was away. Their child must be born by now. If Hannah had not returned to the mansion, he would go to see her as soon as possible. He wondered if he had a son or a daughter and whom the child would resemble. He could not wait to see his child.

Making love with Annabelle had only increased his desire for Hannah. There were fires burning inside of him that only she could quench. She said her body would return to its previous beauty, but he had reservations. He would never let her know she had lost some of her beauty. Although he longed for the beautiful body that had caused him to burn with desire, his love for Hannah was not solely physical.

Hannah was standing inside the door as Adam walked into the mansion. She looked as she had before her pregnancy. It was all he could do to keep himself from taking her in his arms. "How are you, Mr. Adam and Miss Annabelle?" Hannah asked as they entered. "We've missed both of you."

"Thank you, Hannah," Annabelle responded. "Would you have someone take our baggage and packages in?"

"Yes mam," Hannah replied with a smile. She walked away to get Fred.

"Oh Adam," Annabelle exclaimed excitedly as she gazed around the room, "I have so many plans for redecorating our home. It'll be fantastic."

He looked around. In his opinion, it was already fantastic. "We can take our time doing that," he said. "We need to use our funds to expand Southern Kingdom."

"I know you have plans for Southern Kingdom," she responded, "but we need to turn our home into a showplace. People will travel from far and near when we entertain. Don't you want them to be impressed with Southern Kingdom?"

"Surely Adam will allow me to use part of my dowry to redecorate our home," she thought to herself.

He came close to telling her everything would remain just as it was, but he recalled Placide's warning. "I suppose so," he responded. "It is difficult for me to change things in my home. This is my fortress where I shield myself from the world."

"I'm sorry, darling," she said. "I'm being insensitive. I want you to always be comfortable in our home. We can make the changes slowly."

"No," he said. "I was being foolish. Please do whatever you feel you must do to convert our home into the showplace you envision."

"Are you sure?" she asked. "I don't want to upset you, my love." She raised up on her tiptoes and kissed his cheek. "You're always so kind to me."

Adam was anxious to spend time with Hannah and to see his child. "If you do not mind," he said, "I think I will go out and look over the fields. I want to make sure the crops are being tended as they should."

"Don't you want to rest after our journey?" Annabelle asked.

"Being with you has kept me refreshed," he replied. "If we are going to make changes in our home, I must make sure we have sufficient funds." He kissed Annabelle and started to turn away.

"Adam," Annabelle said, "If you have no objections, I'd like to visit Pappa while you're looking over the plantation. Please ask Jeremiah to leave the horses hitched to the carriage."

"Things are working out well," he thought to himself. "I will have time to do what I want while she is with her father."

"I will make sure he has the carriage ready for you," he

responded.

Adam walked to the carriage house and spoke to Jeremiah. Jeremiah assured him the carriage would be ready for Miss Annabelle.

He had Fred saddle his horse and rode out a short distance to inspect the cotton plants. He was sure there would be a good harvest. The cotton plants were numerous and appeared to be healthy.

When he saw Annabelle enter the carriage, he began to slowly make his way to the house. He watched as the carriage became smaller and smaller until it eventually disappeared before he spurred his horse to a gallop. As soon as he reached the house, he leaped off of his horse and tied the animal to the hitching rail.

He struggled to keep his pace to a walk. He wanted to run into Hannah's arms. She was waiting for him when he walked through the door. He took her hand and headed toward his bedroom.

"No," she said. "We'll go to my bedroom. We have to keep our love a secret from Annabelle."

She led him to a large bedroom on the second floor on the opposite end of the mansion from his room. "I thought we'd need a place where we could be alone," she said. "How do you like my new bedroom?"

"I am more interested in looking at you," he responded. "I missed you so much. I thought of you all the while I was away." He looked at her trim figure. "Are we parents?"

"We have a beautiful baby girl," she replied. "I think she looks more like you than like me."

Adam beamed. "A girl," he said. "I had assumed we would have a boy."

"Are you disappointed?" she asked.

"Not at all," he responded. "We have a daughter." There was a look of astonishment on his face. "You look so beautiful, little mother."

"Thank you," she responded. "You look so handsome. I missed you so much. I wanted you to be with me during the birth of our child. I was very upset with you for a while."

"I wish I could have been there," he said. "I know I was thinking of you at the time because I thought of you all the while I was away. When can I see our daughter?"

"I want you to see her," Hannah responded, "but I have something more urgent on my mind at this moment." She began to disrobe. Adam marveled at her body as she shed her clothes. His beautiful goddess had returned. There were no signs she had ever been pregnant.

"I see it, but it is difficult to believe," he said with awe in his voice. "You are as beautiful as you were before you were pregnant."

"I told you my momma shared her secrets with me," Hannah replied with a smile on her face. She was pleased he had noticed. It had taken a great effort to restore her body to its previous condition. He was staring just as he had before she became pregnant. "I'm glad you like my body, but I want you to do more than just look."

He undressed quickly and then caught her up in his arms and laid her on the bed. "How I missed this," he said as he felt her body against his.

She kissed him and touched him in the special way that only she could. He felt the fires of passion growing into an inferno. They were locked in their love. The fires that were ignited on his honeymoon were only ashes when at last he was quenched.

Some time later, Hannah lay beside him running her fingers up and down his chest. "While you were gone, I wondered what she was doing with the fires that burned inside of you," she said. "I wondered if you'd still want me when you returned."

"She came no where near satisfying my desire," he responded. "She could only light fires that she had no hope of extinguishing. I love you, Hannah."

"I love you, Adam," she responded. "I think I would've died had you told me you no longer wanted me."

"That will never be," he said. "I think my heart would shrivel and die without you."

They lay in one another's arms enjoying the afterglow of

their love. When they made love again, there was less urgency, but the passion was still there. Hannah held nothing back as she used the wiles her mother had taught her.

After they had rested a while, Adam asked, "What is our daughter's name?"

"I want to name her Martha," she replied. "That was my mother's name. I wanted to ask you before naming her."

"Martha," he said. "That is a beautiful name. You could have named her while I was away."

"She's our child," Hannah responded. "I wanted both of us to name her. I'm glad you want to give her my mother's name."

"When can I see her?" Adam asked.

"We can dress and go to her right now," she said. "Rebecca is with her."

*****

"She is so beautiful," Adam said tenderly as he held his daughter in his arms, "and so tiny. My little Martha. Life will be wonderful for you."

"I don't want her to ever know she's of mixed blood," Hannah said. "I want her to grow up as a Caucasian. She'll have so many things I could never have."

"We can still sell everything and move away," he said. "We can raise her together. No one will ever know you are not a Caucasian."

"You have no idea how tempted I am to take you up on your offer," she responded. "In time you'd grow to resent me for robbing you of your dream. I won't let that happen."

"I could never resent you," he said with deep conviction. "We would have land and money. We could live as well anywhere as we can here."

"You wouldn't have the power you can have here," Hannah responded sadly. "You'd miss that. You're destined for great things, Adam. I'll never stand in your way. I want for our daughter what we can't have. When she falls in love, she'll be able to live out her dreams."

He nodded his head. He knew he would never be able to change her mind. "Promise me I will always have your heart," he said. "If you will not be my wife in name, promise me you will always be my wife in your heart."

Tears filled Hannah's eyes. She looked at the man she loved as he held their child. Nothing could keep her from loving him. "I promise," she responded. "I promise I'll always love you and I'll always be yours. In a way you gave me life just as you gave life to our child. Without you, I'd still be an ignorant Negro woman with no hope. With you, I have love and I have hope. Our daughter will never be the kept mistress of a plantation owner. Our daughter will be loved and cherished by her father. She'll never know the horror of being raped by her own father."

He could only imagine the suffering she had endured. Her lot had been to be used by men who would use her but never love her. Her dread was to pass her legacy on to children of her own. "I promise Martha will never know her mother is not a white woman," he said. "I promise she will go to the best schools and she will never have to use her body in order to survive. I will always give her love and protection."

She began to weep. He held her and his child as she cried. After a while, she looked up at him.

"You have no idea what those promises mean to me," she said. "The way I was raised taught me I'd never have hope and I'd always be a slave. We rejoiced when the Emancipation Proclamation was signed, but it didn't really set me free. My mind was caught up in a pattern that was hundreds of years old. I was still wearing my chains when you got here. You freed me from the slavery that had trapped my mind. You set my mind free. It means more to me than you can ever know that our daughter is free from the time of her birth."

She took Martha from his arms and laid her in her bed. "I want you to hold me," she said. "You're so dear and so precious to me, Adam Blythington."

Adam held Hannah in his arms. She leaned against him and cried quietly. The tears she shed were of happiness for herself and her daughter.

CHAPTER ELEVEN

August 24, 1866 – September 18, 1866

Adam returned to the plantation manor after having spent most of his day monitoring the progress of the cotton harvest. The late August day had been hot and humid. Even though it was after six o'clock in the evening, the day remained extremely hot and uncomfortable. His skin felt sticky and grimy. He wanted to soak in a bathtub filled with cool water.

Annabelle greeted him as he walked into the house. "I have some exciting news," she said as she smiled up at him. "We're going to have a baby."

Adam was startled. He had found time in his day, as he did most days, to visit with Martha. In his estimation, she was the most beautiful child in the world. Her hair was a soft dark brown. She was light-complected with green eyes. Anyone who was unaware of her bloodline would not suspect she was not a pure Caucasian. Annabelle's news was welcome but unsettling. "Are you sure?" he asked.

She was mystified by his reaction. She'd thought he'd be jubilant when he learned he was going to be a father. "I'm sure," she replied. "Are you upset about becoming a father?"

He wanted to tell her he had been a father for over two months. He held his tongue. "Of course not," he replied. "I was surprised. This is great news. When is our baby due?"

Dr. Joubert said the baby will be born in late March or early April," Annabelle replied. "We have about seven months before our child will be born."

"We need to prepare the nursery," he said as he attempted to sound excited.

"We have time," she responded laughingly.

"Seven months," he countered. "I can't wait to ride the fields with my son."

"We may have a daughter," she said. "At any rate, it'll be years before our child can ride with you."

He did not want to argue with her, but if they had a son, he would make sure the child would be under his influence. He was not going to have a momma's boy for a son. "I think we will have a son," he said. "He will be the heir to Southern Kingdom."

"Will you be disappointed if we have a girl?" she asked.

He would be very disappointed if the child was not a boy. "No," he lied. "A daughter would be fine. I hear it told that daughters love their fathers deeply. It would be an adjustment for me. You are the only woman with whom I am able to let down my guard."

She was pleased with his answer. "I'm sure our daughter would cherish you just as I do," she said. "Perhaps a daughter would help you to be more open with women."

"Perhaps," he responded. He did not want to entertain the possibility that the child would be a girl.

With the birth of his heir, he would suggest to Annabelle that she move to her own bedroom under the pretext plantation business often demanded his attention during the nighttime hours. She was a very light sleeper. Sharing a bedroom with her made it difficult for him to spend time with Hannah during the night.

"Knowing you're happy with the news relieves me," she said. "I was concerned that you might not want a child."

"Why would I not want a child?" he asked. "This is great news."

"You're so kind," Annabelle said. "Our child will have a wonderful father."

*****

Annabelle lay in bed waiting for Adam to join her. It was taking longer than she had thought for him to open up to her. She remained convinced her love would heal the old wounds and allow the real Adam to surface.

She was disappointed with Adam's initial response to the news about her pregnancy. He quickly recovered but he didn't seem excited about her news. "Maybe it was only that the news surprised him and caused him to withdraw temporarily," she said to herself. "He did seem very happy once the news sunk in. That must be it."

"With all of the disappointments that have come his way, he's become defensive and vulnerable. Having a child is a huge responsibility and Adam is a very responsible man. He wants to make sure his child has the best of everything. Learning of the pregnancy caused him to wonder if he is capable of meeting the responsibility. How sweet of him. He always puts the welfare of others before his own."

She watched as Adam walked out of the bathing room and into the bedroom. He was still so young to have achieved so much. She would have to remember his possessions still didn't give him the confidence he'd lacked as a child.

Adam got into the bed and lay beside her. She hoped that he would take her in his arms. After waiting several minutes, she moved over to him. "I love you, Adam," she said as she cuddled up against him.

"I love you, too," he responded. After another few moments, he drew her to him.

Annabelle excitedly anticipated the feelings that would stir as Adam touched her body. She put one arm around his neck, kissed his lips and felt passion begin to stir.

"It has been a long day," he said. "I am sure you are exhausted, being pregnant and all."

"I feel fine," she said. "I'm only in the early stages."

"You must have your rest," Adam said as he rose from the bed and blew out the lamp.

Annabelle listened to Adam's breathing for a while. It seemed only moments had gone by when he fell into a deep sleep.

"How selfish of me," she thought to herself. "He's been working all day. I have to be careful not to be too demanding and push him away." She rolled over and within a few minutes was fast asleep.

*****

Adam was careful not to awaken Annabelle as he slipped out of bed that night. She stirred but remained asleep. He had to share his news with Hannah. He stepped carefully as he walked out of the room. Some of the floorboards squeaked as he walked toward the door. He was thankful Hannah had ordered Fred to oil the hinges. The door opened and closed without a sound. He exhaled a deep breath when he reached the hallway. He climbed up the stairs and walked as silently as possible to Hannah's room.

He knocked softly on Hannah's door. She kept her door locked because she didn't want the servants to wonder why it was locked at times and unlocked at other times. After a few moments, she opened the door.

She closed and locked the door as soon as he entered and embraced him. "I was afraid you weren't coming," she said as she held herself close to him. "I was so lonesome for you." She led him to her bed and began to disrobe.

Adam felt that his news could wait. He watched her with admiration as she removed her garments. She was even more beautiful than when he had first taken her. He was sure this was a scene that would never tire him.

When she had removed her clothing, she walked up to him and began removing his clothing. She kissed his body as she removed each article of clothing. His body was on fire by the time they lay on the bed. She continued to kiss him, driving him higher until he could wait no longer. She looked upon his face as he lost himself in her.

Sometime later, he was awakened by her soft kisses. "I am sorry I fell asleep," he said.

"Don't be," she responded. "I fell asleep, too. Making love with you grows better each time."

"It surely does," he agreed. "You feel so wonderful in my arms." He drew her closer to himself. They lay together for a while without speaking.

After several minutes, Hannah kissed his cheek. "I love you, Adam," she said. "I've never loved any other man. I really don't think I could love anyone but you." She was content lying next to her lover, but she sensed that he was holding something back. "What's bothering you?"

"You know me too well," he responded. "How do you know when something is on my mind?"

"You share everything with me," she replied. "I can tell when something has upset you and you're keeping it to yourself."

"Annabelle is pregnant," he said. "The baby is due in late March or early April."

She felt cold inside. Annabelle would have Adam's child. A part of Adam was pairing with Annabelle. She feared that the legitimate child would take Martha's place in his heart. "You may have your heir sooner than you thought," she said.

"I thought the news would make me happy," he said laconically. "It is almost as though I resent Annabelle for carrying my child. Does that make sense to you?"

"Yes, it does," she replied. "She doesn't have your love, yet she's carrying your child, your heir. I think it comes from how we feel about one another. She has the place in your life you wanted for me."

"Yes," he said. "That is how I feel. I resent her because she is not you. You should have agreed to move away with me so we could have been man and wife? You remember how Giselle thought you were a Caucasian?"

"Yes, I do remember," she replied. "I also remember how quickly Placide pointed out that I was a former slave. If we do try to live somewhere else as man and wife, someone could always come along and expose me.

"It's as I've said before, you have two mistresses, me and Southern Kingdom. You only think you could give up the one and love only the other. You'd end up resenting the one who caused you to give up the other. This way, you can have both of us. You have every part of me without giving up your other mistress."

"I do not have you the way I truly want to have you," he said. "I want you to have the place Annabelle has."

"I don't want that place," Hannah responded. "What

does she have of you? She has your name. I also have your name. I'm Hannah Blythington. She's having your child. We already have a child. The only thing I can't do for you that she can, is give you a legitimate heir."

"You could have had we moved to another state," he persisted. "We could have had our southern kingdom in Georgia, Alabama, Mississippi or any number of other states. What are the chances that someone would expose you? No one would suspect that you are not a Caucasian. You still could choose to be my wife."

"Adam, you're upset," she responded. "I have more of you than Annabelle will ever have. I've given you more of myself than Annabelle is capable of giving. What is it that you lack?"

"I have to sneak up here to spend time with you," he replied. "I want to go to sleep with you in my arms and awaken with you in my arms."

Tears began to fall from Hannah's eyes. "Adam," she cried out. "Don't you see I want that too. You've killed men to protect Southern Kingdom. Don't you realize you'll resent anyone who's responsible for you giving up Southern Kingdom? Please believe this is the only way."

"You know I respect your opinions," he responded reluctantly. "I love you, Hannah Blythington. I will always love you and I will always love our child."

Hannah clung to Adam. Tears streamed down her face. "Your love means so much to me," she said. "I hope you never turn your back on Martha."

"How could I reject Martha?" Adam asked. "She is a part of you and a part of me. I could no more reject her than I could reject myself."

He remembered something he wanted to speak to Hannah about. "I went to see Martha today," he said.

"How is she?" Hannah asked.

"She is doing fine," he replied. "I love her beautiful green eyes. She got that from you. She is so pretty."

"I saw her yesterday," Hannah said. "She's beginning to look more like you."

"Do you think so?" he asked with a smile. "She is a darling child, but I want to talk to you about Rebecca."

"Is anything wrong?" she asked with concern in her voice.

"Not really," he replied. "Rebecca is great with Martha. That is part of the problem. Martha is with Rebecca more than anyone else. I do not want her to pick up Rebecca's speech patterns. I think we should hire a white woman as a governess for Martha."

"I hadn't thought of that," she said. She had been concerned that Martha would pattern her speech after Rebecca, but she'd been reluctant to broach the subject with Adam. She didn't want Martha to have to struggle as she'd had to in order to learn to speak properly. She thought it would be better to let Adam think he'd been the one to recognize the problem. "Do you have anyone in mind?"

Adam was pleased that he had mentioned his concerns to Hannah. He was reassuring her that he had their child's best interests in mind. "I want to speak to Professor Pennington," he replied. "He may know someone we could hire."

*****

It was beginning to grow dark outdoors as Annabelle sat waiting for Adam to come home. She was certain he would be enthusiastic about her plan. The dowry her father had set for her was more than generous. As a matter of fact, it was more money than most people saw in a lifetime. Her plan was to use half of the dowry to help feed, clothe and shelter people who'd lost their homes and families as a result of the war.

The idea had come to her as she was reading an article written by Frank Klienpeter in the *St. Landry Clarion*. Mr. Klienpeter's article spoke of people, both Negro and white, who were begging on the streets. The article pointed out that many of the Negro people were without jobs and had little hope due to their lack of training and education. He urged the citizens of St. Landry Parish to become involved in helping the needy.

She would ask Adam to build a warehouse so donations

from those who were more fortunate could be stored. Those in need could then go to the warehouse and pick up food and clothing. The warehouse would be built large enough to include temporary shelter for people who had no place to live.

She heard footsteps on the porch. The door opened and Adam walked in. "How was your day?" she asked.

He grew wary. It was not Annabelle's habit to greet him at the door. "It was hot," he replied. "I guess that is not unusual for this time of the year."

She could no longer contain her excitement. "Adam, I was reading an article in the *Clarion*," she began, "and a wonderful solution occurred to me."

"Solution?" he asked, "Solution to what?"

"I'm sorry," she replied. "I should have told you more about the article. Mr. Klienpeter wrote about the people of our parish who are in such dire need. He urged those of us who are able to do all we can to alleviate their suffering."

"Who is this Klienpeter?" he asked.

"The newspaper reporter," she replied. "He wants those who can, to take part in helping the poor." This wasn't going as she had anticipated.

"Is it not written that God will help those who help themselves?" Adam asked dryly. "Those people need to find work and help themselves."

"Mr. Klienpeter says that most of them are unable to find work," she countered. "They lack the education and training."

"It does not take a great deal of education or training to work in the fields," he said acerbically. "Have you considered that most of them are too lazy to work and expect other people to take care of them?"

"There may be some who are like that," she agreed, "but most of them would work if they had the opportunity." She was becoming upset with Adam's attitude. "Doesn't your heart go out to those who are suffering?"

"Look around you," he said sharply. "Did anyone give any of this to me? Do I not go out into the fields every day and work to ensure this plantation will continue to make a profit? Giving things to people is never the solution. People do not value what is given to them. Let them earn their way."

Tears began to fall from her eyes. "There are children who are starving," she cried out. "What about them?"

"Tell them to go to Mr. Klienpeter," he replied harshly. "Since he has such a generous heart, he can feed them."

"It will cost you nothing," Annabelle said as she wept. "I intend to use part of my dowry to help those poor people."

"Not one penny of the dowry will be spent on people who are too lazy to work," he shouted angrily. "That dowry is now under my control. It will be spent as I determine."

Annabelle ran to her room, slammed the door and threw herself on the bed. Tears streamed out as she buried her head in the pillow. "How can he be so cold hearted?" she asked herself.

She searched for some reason that could explain his behavior. After some time she came up with a ray of hope. "From his point of view, he's been one of those in dire need," she thought to herself. "He was forced to work hard and take risks to get where he is now. He doesn't see that some are unable to fend for themselves. I'll help him to see there are those who can't help themselves."

*****

As was the case in 1865, the harvest of 1866 drew record prices. The mills in the northern states and England were continuing to beg for cotton. The 1866 harvest surpassed the harvest of the previous year. The cotton seeds were planted early enough at Lance des Chenes to give the plants ample time to come up and mature. James Fisk was exceedingly pleased with his share of the profits. Even after sharing the profits with Fisk, the earnings from Lance des Chenes and Southern Kingdom swelled Adam's bank account appreciably.

Eighteen sixty-seven would see the birth of his child Annabelle was carrying and further expansion of Southern Kingdom. Adam had insisted that Fisk speed up the purchase of property that lay between the two plantations. He hoped to eventually link the two plantations. The largest of the landholders between Southern Kingdom and Lance des Chenes was his father-in-law. Belle Bois took up roughly one fourth of the arpents between the two plantations.

Adam wanted to purchase Belle Bois, but he was certain Jacques Dupre' would never willingly sell his plantation. Staging an accident for Dupre' would work against Adam. Placide would inherit the plantation from his father. Even if Placide were removed, people would view Adam with suspicion. If Placide were out of the picture, and Dupre' died of natural causes, Annabelle would inherit the plantation. As Annabelle's husband, the plantation would be his. Unfortunately, Dupre' was in good health. It could be years before the property would change hands, which exasperated Adam.

The carpetbagger government had passed new laws raising the taxes the occupied states were forced to pay. Landowners who had barely managed to hold on to their land the previous year were now losing the battle. Although Adam wished to concentrate on property between the two plantations, he did pick up an additional twelve hundred and seventy arpents of land that did not meet that criteria. Even though the land he purchased was not between the plantations, all of the land adjoined one or the other of the properties. As of September 12, 1866, Blythington owned 14,560 arpents of land. He decided to invite his brothers to visit Southern Kingdom for Christmas of 1866.

*****

Adam worked in his office as he awaited Annabelle's return from a shopping trip. She was purchasing drapes for all of the windows. Her foolishness was going to cost him a small fortune, even though the money she spent was far less than her dowry. That was money he could have used for other things. He turned his attention to the drapes in his office. There was nothing wrong with them. "Why would anyone replace perfectly serviceable draperies?" he asked himself.

Annabelle had suggested doing away with the present furniture and purchasing more modern furniture. She argued that the new furniture would make the rooms seem brighter.

Thus far, he had resisted her. He admired the furniture that had come with the plantation. To him the furniture was substantial and rich looking. None of it would break easily. Adam had no idea why she wanted to replace perfectly good furniture.

When he heard the sounds of horses' hooves approaching, he rose from his desk and walked to the door to meet Annabelle She greeted him with a kiss on his cheek.

"I could only find a few things I like," she said. Fred and Jeremiah followed her into the house with their arms filled with packages.

He had no idea what could be in the packages. After almost four months of marriage, she continued to buy items for a home that to him was complete before her arrival. He wanted to curtail her spending, but he also wanted to ensure she remained content, at least until after she had produced an heir for Southern Kingdom.

"Should you be exerting yourself in your condition?" he asked. She was entering her fourth month of pregnancy.

"It's so sweet of you to worry, but I'm fine," she replied. "Dr. Joubert says I'm perfectly healthy. It'll be months before I have to take to bed."

"All the same," he said, "you should not overly exert yourself."

"My dear Adam," she said as she patted his cheek. "I'm all right. I do appreciate your concern though." She watched to make sure no harm came to any of her packages. She directed Fred and Jeremiah to take the packages into the parlor.

"I have been thinking about inviting my brothers to spend the Christmas season with us," he said. "What do you think of the idea?"

"I think inviting your brothers to visit us is an excellent idea," she responded. "I think it would be very good for them to see how successful their younger brother has become." She took his hand in hers. "I know how much it means to you to win their approval."

He thought about what she had said. Was he trying to seek the approval of his brothers? Why should their opinion of him continue to matter? She was right. He wanted to see the look of envy in their eyes when they took in Southern Kingdom. He was certain that when he had left England, his brothers were sure he was going to fail. They were only too happy to be rid of him. Had he failed while living in England, it would have reflected poorly on them. Failure in America, where none of their peers would know, meant nothing to them. He wanted to show them his empire. He wondered why it sounded so trite when Annabelle said he was seeking their favor. Wanting to gloat in his success before his brothers, who had little regard for him, was perfectly normal.

"We must post a letter to them today," Annabelle said. "There's so little time for them to make arrangements." She looked around. "There's so much to be done before their arrival."

Adam followed her gaze. Everything looked perfect to him.

He called Jeremiah into his office after he had composed a letter inviting his brothers and their families to come to Southern Kingdom. In his letter he told them he was having his bank deposit the necessary funds into their bank to cover their travel expenses. He wished he could see the looks on his brothers' faces when they received his letter. He handed the letter to Jeremiah telling him to take it to the post office at once. He also gave Jeremiah a note with instructions to his bank for the transfer of funds to cover the travel expenses. His brothers might be offended because he was paying their travel expenses but their love of money would overcome any offense and peak their interest.

*****

Annabelle picked up a piece of heavy cloth and walked to a window in Adam's office. She held the cloth next to the wall so she could see how well the cloth would match the wallpaper she had insisted on for the office. The fabric didn't match as well as she had thought while at the general store.

She set the cloth aside and considered how it would be to have Adam's brothers and their families in her home. She was prepared to dislike the brothers because of their treatment of Adam as a youngster, but, for his sake, she'd have to set her animosity aside. In order to make the proper impression on his brothers, she would have to be the perfect hostess.

Her heart went out once again to Adam. How would he be affected by having his brothers in their home? He was only now beginning to make progress and was only beginning to come out of his shell. She hoped the visit would not cause him to retreat more deeply.

Nothing on her part would get in the way of Adam and his brothers having the perfect visit. All of the guest rooms would be aired out, the bedclothes would be washed, and the rooms would have a proper cleaning.

Although Margaret was a great cook, she would ask Marie for some ideas for special dishes to prepare. The brothers and their families would be at the plantation for several weeks. Each dish had to be a delicacy. Everything had to be perfect.

Maybe, once Adam was satisfied he had the respect and admiration of his brothers the healing would begin. She hummed to herself as she set out to find Hannah.

CHAPTER TWELVE

October 10, 1866 - October 12, 1866

"How's the little mother?" Jacques asked as Annabelle and Adam entered his parlor. Jacques' left leg was propped up on a footstool.

"I'm doing fine," Annabelle replied. "If everything goes as Dr. Joubert says, you'll be a grandfather in a little over five months."

"I hope you haven't placed your faith in old Dr. Joubert," Jacques grumbled as he gazed at his left leg. 'Stay off of your leg,' he says. I missed services this morning because of that old charlatan."

"I know you don't like the inactivity, Pappa," she said, "but it is best to follow his orders. When did he say you'll be up and about again?" She hadn't responded to her father's question. She had chosen old Dr. Joubert because she couldn't bring herself to ask her old beau, although he was now a close friend, to be her doctor.

"If it was only the inactivity," Jacques moaned. "He wants me to change my diet. It would be better to die than miss Marie's delicious cooking. I'm too young to be plagued by gout. I told him it's only bruised muscles."

"Why do you see him if you refuse to follow his advice?" Annabelle asked. "Would you prefer to remain in pain?"

"You wouldn't understand," Jacques said irritably. "I had hoped he could help me."

Annabelle gave up and changed the subject. "Adam's brothers and their families are coming for Christmas," she said. "It should be a very happy occasion. We'd like you to join us."

"Forgive me, Adam," Jacques said gravely, "I don't hold

a great deal of fondness for the English. I made an exception for you because you wanted to be one of us. It would be difficult for me to enjoy the company of your family."

"Pappa," Annabelle said. "You're being unkind to Adam."

"Non, mas cheiri," Jacques responded. "Our ancestors suffered grievously under the English."

"Surely you do not mean the colonial war of rebellion?" Adam asked. "Louisiana was not one of the colonies at that time."

"I don't mean the American Revolution or the War of 1812," Jacques responded resolutely. "The English stole our property in Acadie when we wouldn't swear allegiance to the English king. We were forced to board ships to be exiled from our homes. Many of our people perished. The suffering of our people was terrible."

"I know nothing of exiles from Acadie," Adam responded.

"The English renamed our land Nova Scotia," Jacques continued. "In 1755 we were forced from our beloved land. Perhaps you've read Longfellow's poem, *Evangeline*? Longfellow knew little about us but captured some of our suffering when he wrote of two lovers who were separated by the exile. Evangeline died while waiting for her Gabriel to come to her. Many mammas and pappas never saw there little ones again. Many husbands and wives never again saw their loved ones. We were forced off of the ships in the most inhospitable places. What the English did to my people was cruel and unforgivable."

"Pappa, that was more than a hundred years ago," Annabelle said in a conciliatory tone. "Surely you can put that behind you long enough to visit with your son-in-law's family."

"Ah, the young," Jacques said while shaking his head. "It's easy for you to say, 'put this behind you.' Members of your own family perished, yet you speak of reconciliation. Adam, I think it best that I stay away from your home during your family's visit."

"Pappa, do you forget that our child will have the blood of the English in his body?" she asked. "You would turn against your own grandchild?"

"I have accepted Adam and I accept his child," Jacques replied.

"Pappa, don't force me to choose between you and my husband," Annabelle cried out. "I will never speak to you again if you do this to Adam."

Jacques glared at his daughter with bitter anger in his eyes.

Tears began to fall from Annabelle's eyes. "Come, Adam," she said. "We are no longer welcome in this home."

As she turned to leave, Jacques cried out, "Wait, mas cheiri, I can't bear to lose you." His voice faltered and his shoulders sagged. He closed his eyes and his head drooped.

Annabelle turned and faced her father. She waited patiently as he fought to control himself.

"Would you rob me of my dignity?" he asked in a voice filled with pain. "What I have said about the cruelty of the English is true. It would be even more cruel to lose my grandchild before I even set my eyes upon him. If it's your wish, I'll swallow my pride and spend Christmas in your home."

Annabelle ran to her father and threw her arms around him. "Oh my cher Pappa, I don't want you to surrender your dignity," she said while weeping. "I only ask that you accept one English family; the family of your grandchild."

*****

Annabelle wept as she and Adam made their way home in the carriage. She was torn between the love she had for her father and her love for her husband. Pappa was so dear to her. Her heart had broken when she'd seen the pain and anguish on his face that resulted when she forced him to choose his love for her over his loyalty to the Acadians. Adam would never understand the depth of Pappa's pain.

Pappa had been good to her and had loved her deeply all of her life. Her love for Adam was too new to supplant the love she felt for her father, but convention demanded her loyalty to her husband. She was now one with Adam as she had been taught.

"I really do not understand why your father carried on so about something that happened over a hundred years ago," Adam said absently.

She tried to ignore his comment as she wept. She was angry with Adam because of his insensitivity. "Would he understand if she tried to explain Pappa's feelings to him?" she thought to herself. She decided that he probably wouldn't understand.

"It really would not have mattered that much, had he decided not to visit," Adam continued.

It was all Annabelle could do to remain silent. She fought to suppress the thoughts that were coming into her mind. "Adam, I really do hate you," she thought to herself. She was immediately assailed by feelings of guilt. "I must be terrible for feeling that way about my own husband." she said to herself. "He's the father of my child."

"We come from two very different cultures," she said to herself. "There's no way Adam can understand how difficult this is for Pappa. This wasn't something Pappa had personally endured. The pain Adam suffered resulted from abusive treatment at the hands of his own family. I have to try harder to understand him."

*****

The following Wednesday, Placide tied his horse to the hitching rail beside his sister's home. He had only just learned that Annabelle had forced his father to take a conciliatory position toward the English. Placide hated the English even more than did his father. He found them arrogant and selfish. It had been difficult to work with them during the war, but the needs of his beloved south forced him to bury his hatred momentarily. He no longer needed the goodwill of the English. There were no longer blockades standing in the way of cotton shipments.

Placide rapped hard on the cypress door. Mary opened the door and invited him in.

"Is the madam in?" Placide asked in a surly voice.

"Yes sir," Mary replied, "she here." Mary was attending Professor Pennington's school, but continued to have problems with her diction.

She found Miss Annabelle in the ballroom. "Mr. Placide come to see you," she said. "He to the side door."

"Thank you, Mary," Annabelle said. "Please show him to the study. Tell him I'll be there in a moment." Annabelle supposed that Placide had spoken to their father. She'd give him a few minutes to cool down before going to see him.

Several minutes later she entered the study.

Placide looked at her coldly as she entered. "Ah, my dear sister," he said. "So soon you have forgotten the love of a father and surrendered to the English."

She had no intention of allowing Placide to intimidate her. "You speak foolishness," she responded. "I have neither forgotten the love of my father, nor have I surrendered to the English. I'm married to a man who was raised in England but is now a southerner. Although I'll always love my father, my loyalty now must be to my husband and the child I carry."

"You've caused great pain to my father," Placide said angrily. "Were you a man, I would demand satisfaction."

"Please don't think that I'll back down from you," she responded coldly. "You may demand satisfaction if you'd like. I'm not afraid to meet you on the field of honor."

He looked down at his pregnant sister. He felt that he no longer knew her. Gone was the loving younger sister he had cherished. This vixen standing before him only resembled his sister. "I want you to apologize to my father," he said. "We won't be in your home while the English are here."

"Your father?" she scoffed. "He's our father. He's able to speak for himself. I won't apologize to anyone who insults my husband."

"I had hoped you'd be sensible," he said. "I can see that you've allowed that rogue you married to turn your head."

"Leave my home at once!" Annabelle cried out. "It is you who should apologize. Don't return to this home until you're ready to make amends for your scurrilous remarks against my husband."

Placide glared at Annabelle. He thought of striking her but held himself back. A gentleman never strikes a lady. He would find a time to call Adam out on the field of honor. He had allowed him to live too long.

*****

"Adam," Annabelle cried out when Adam returned from the fields. "Please stay away from Placide."

"Why should I avoid Placide?" he asked. He attempted to sound normal as the hand of fear wrenched his bowels.

"He came here today," Annabelle responded. "He's angry because I told Pappa I wouldn't speak to him again unless he agreed to accept your family. He said he would have called me out had I been a man. Please don't go around him until he has time to cool his hot temper. I fear he'll call you out."

Adam was almost paralyzed by fear. He had heard of the duels Placide had fought. He was indomitable in a contest of weapons or fisticuffs. Although it was late afternoon, he had to go into town and speak to Fisk immediately.

"He will calm down in time. Please do not worry." Adam forced himself to say. He did not want his wife to know he was terrified. He had much more reason to fear Placide than did she.

He walked into the house to wash off some of the dust. Hannah confronted him in the hallway. "Adam," she said in a hushed and frightened voice. "I heard Placide speaking with Annabelle. He intends to kill you."

"I am going into town to speak with Fisk," he said. "Monsieur Placide has gone too far."

"Please be careful," she said fearfully. "He won't waste much time before he calls you out."

"I will," he replied. "Please tell Fred to saddle my horse. Tell Annabelle I had to go into town."

*****

"He's a dangerous man," Fisk said an hour later as he buttoned his shirt. He had opened the door of his home after hearing Blythington's loud knocks. He wanted to get rid of Blythington as quickly as possible so he could return to unfinished business with his mistress.

"If he were not dangerous," Adam said anxiously, "I would have taken care of this myself." He was doing his best to hide his fear.

"We'll take care of him tomorrow," Fisk said calmly. "After tomorrow morning, all of your problems will be gone. It's best you make yourself scarce until then." He was enjoying Blythington's discomfiture. He no longer seemed so sure of himself.

"Are you sure?" Adam asked. "I have no chance of taking him in a duel."

"No, you don't," Fisk agreed with a chuckle. "You'd be dead by the end of the day if you tried to face him. You'd better not be available for him to call you out until we take care of the problem."

*****

It was late when Adam returned to his home. He mulled over his problem as he prepared himself for bed. He wanted to spend the night with Hannah, but thought it best to sleep with Annabelle. He wanted her to believe he had no part in her brother's death. He spent most of the night awake thinking of the danger Placide posed to him. He was relieved when dawn finally arrived. If he could make it through the morning, he could live a long life.

Annabelle awakened and found her husband lying next to her. "You came home late," she said. "Is everything all right?"

"I had hoped to leave earlier yesterday afternoon," he replied, "but problems on the plantation prevented my doing so. I had to see my land manager about acquiring more land. I interrupted the poor man's supper."

"I was worried," she said.

"Please do not worry," he responded. He peered toward the window. "It looks as though it will be a pretty day. I regret that my work keeps us apart much of the time. I have nothing pressing this morning. Would you like to go for a buggy ride?" In truth, he wanted to be where Placide could not find him.

Annabelle was pleased that Adam wanted to spend time with her. He was always so busy managing the two plantations. In fact, he was often called away during the night on plantation business. He looked so tired and worried. She was concerned for him. "I'd love to go out riding with you," she said. "We can pack a picnic lunch. I hope it isn't too cold."

"I would love to spend the entire day with you," he said, "but there is pressing business I must tend to this afternoon."

"You work too hard, Adam," she responded. "You need to relax. You'll make yourself sick."

"I have a family to care for," he said. "If the plantation is not successful, what will our child inherit?"

"I still say you work too hard," she persisted. "If you don't mind, while you're taking care of your business, I'll go visit Pappa. He's been suffering with his gout."

Adam had no objections to his wife visiting her father. Placide would certainly not be there to provoke her.

"I hope he is doing better," he responded.

He hated to waste daylight hours riding in the buggy with his wife while there was work to be done, but his life would have been in jeopardy had he remained where Placide could find him.

She felt that great strides had been made. It was as rare as hen's teeth for Adam to take time out of his day to do anything that did not benefit Southern Kingdom. He had deliberately taken time out of his day so they could be together.

"Look how pretty," she said as she pointed out red leaves on a gum tree. "Fall is usually a sad time of the year for me, but when I'm with you, it doesn't seem so sad." She squeezed his arm and rested her head on his shoulder.

He wasn't the least interested in looking at leaves. He wished she would sit quietly until enough time had passed and they could return to their home.

"I hope we can do this more often," she said. "Maybe we could have a picnic next time."

"Hmm," he mumbled. He did not want to commit himself to a picnic. If he had his way, this would be the first and only time they would go out on a buggy ride.

"I wish we could have skies that color during the summer," she said. "Wouldn't you love to see blue skies like that all year round?"

He looked up at the sky. It did not seem extraordinary to him. It was only a blue sky. He pulled his pocket watch out once more. It was finally eleven thirty. If he turned the buggy around now, they would be home around twelve fifteen. Placide should be dead by now. He pulled on the reins and headed back home.

"I hope you enjoyed your time as much as I did," she said.

He nodded as he slapped the reins on the horse's back.

Adam and Annabelle returned to their home shortly after noon. They feasted on Margaret's dinner of fried chicken and dirty rice. There were homemade pear preserves to go with Margaret's fresh baked bread.

He was beginning to relax. He glanced at the grandfather clock near the doorway. "By now Placide must have met his end," he thought to himself.

"I need to be going," Annabelle said as she kissed Adam's cheek. "I want to be back home before dark."

"I will have Jeremiah prepare the carriage," he said as he stepped away from the table. "I will tell him to be extra careful with his valuable cargo."

Annabelle smiled up at him. "You're always so kind and thoughtful," she said. "I'm so happy to have such a wonderful husband."

*****

Adam watched as the carriage pulled out of sight. He pulled out his pocket watch. It was two o'clock. He was jubilant. Placide would never threaten him again. He debated whether to ride out to the fields or do paperwork in his office. A cold front had come in shortly after he and Annabelle had returned from their buggy ride. He decided to clear some of the paperwork on his desk and then devote the remainder of the afternoon to Hannah. It was a time to celebrate.

He had just stepped into his office when there was a loud knock on the door. Ruth went to open the door. Placide forced his way through the partially open door.

"Where is he?" Placide shouted. He stepped menacingly toward Ruth.

"He in da office," Ruth blurted out in fear.

Adam heard Placide's voice. He was shocked to find that Placide was still alive. He instinctively reached for his desk drawer. He stopped when he remembered he had moved the handgun to his bedroom. He rose from his desk and hurried to the office door. If he could get to the gun before Placide could get to him, he might have a chance.

Placide had spent many hours with Lance LeBlanc in the plantation office. He ran to the office and kicked it open. The door barely missed Adam as it swung around.

"You thought I'd be dead by now," Placide said as he pulled a handgun from inside his coat. He smiled menacingly. "Your henchmen failed. I killed both of them. One fell wounded, but before I killed him, he confessed that your Monsieur Fisk had hired him to kill me. I learned more about your connection with Fisk."

Glancing furtively from the corners of his eyes toward one then the other of the windows of his office, Adam silently cursed the cold front. Both of the windows were closed and locked. Placide stood between him and the only door to the office. He considered jumping through one of the closed windows but he knew his chances of escape were almost nil. He tried to steel himself for the inevitable outcome.

Adam saw cold hatred in Placide's eyes. He lowered his eyes and stared into the barrel of the gun Placide held in his hand. He fought to keep his bowels under control as his legs shook. He wanted to die with some dignity. He knew it was useless to deny his affiliation with Fisk. His voice faltered as he tried to speak. He gathered himself together and said, "Too long

I allowed you to intimidate me. Do what you must, but I shall not grovel." He heard the fear in his shaky voice.

"Oh, but you will, Monsieur," Placide retorted icily. A crooked smile crossed his lips. He enjoyed the fear he saw in Adam's eyes as he futilely searched for a means of escape. In a moment, the man's bowels would void.

"I'll kill you slowly," he said. "You'll suffer for all the harm you've done. There have been too many accidents that couldn't be explained. You're a liar and a thief, Monsieur. You're a murderer. There will be joy in heaven today and a new face in hell."

Adam looked around for a weapon. There was nothing that he could get his hands on before Placide could pull the trigger. His hope was that he would not break and beg for his life before Placide killed him. He waited for the first bullet to rip through his body.

"Lance was a good friend of mine," Placide said. "He told me he was getting the money together to save Seven Oaks. I never believed he had fallen from a horse. I knew Paul Breaux and his family. He would never willingly give up his land. That land had been in his family for generations. You had already stolen Seven Oaks but you weren't satisfied. You had to steal Lance des Chenes from Albert Bennett. Where was it going to end? Did you plan to kill my father and steal his land?"

Adam trembled with fear as he listened to his brother-in-law. "I would never harm your father," he choked out.

"You won't have the chance," Placide said. "If you weren't a coward, I would call you out on a field of honor. You are a dishonorable man. You'll die like a cur dog. That's the death you deserve."

Adam opened his mouth to speak, but no words came out.

"Not so brave now, Monsieur?" Placide asked. He knew it would be only a moment or so before Adam begged for his life. He wanted to enjoy Adam's agony before he killed him. "It's different when you're the victim, isn't it? You'll suffer as you made others suffer. When I'm finished with you, I'll find your Monsieur Fisk. He'll suffer the same fate as you." Placide smiled as he leveled his handgun.

Adam closed his eyes and made an effort to prepare himself for the bullet that was soon to smash into his body. Just as he opened his mouth to plead for his life, a shot rang out. He was baffled because he felt no pain from the bullet. He opened his eyes and watched in amazement as Placide fell to the floor.

Hannah was standing only a few feet behind the place where Placide had stood only moments before. She held a smoking handgun in her hand.

"I heard when he came in," she said in a trembling voice. "I thought I would never find your gun. I've never used a gun before. I wasn't sure I'd be able to stop him."

He was stunned. Moments before, he had been in fear of losing his life and now his adversary lay dead at his feet. Hannah had saved his life. He felt relief flowing through his body. He was amazed that he was still alive and unharmed. "I do not know what to say," he said weakly. "He was going to kill me, but you saved my life."

The relief of seeing Adam unhurt and the realization that she had killed a man overcame Hannah. She began to weep. "I couldn't let him kill you," she said as she gasped for breath. "I couldn't have lived without you. I'm sorry, Adam."

"Why are you sorry?" he asked. "You did the only thing you could do. If you had not shot him, I would be dead by now."

"I don't know why I'm sorry," she replied between sobs. "I killed a man. I've never killed anyone before." She continued to weep.

He held her until the weeping ceased. His mind was beginning to once again function properly. "We had better get this cleaned up," he said as he gazed at the pool of blood that had spread from Placide's body.

She looked at the blood on the floor in amazement. When Adam had shot Alfred Clark between the eyes, there had been very little blood. She immediately went into action. She got some rags and a bucket of water and wiped the blood off of the hardwood floor while Adam sent Fred to fetch Henry. She soon had all of the blood wiped up. She then scrubbed the floor with soapy water, rinsed it and wiped it with dry cloths.

"Yessuh, Mr. Adam," Henry said when he arrived.

Adam stepped aside and let him see the prostrate body of Placide Dupre'. "I want you to hitch one of the wagons," he said sternly. "When you have done that, take him to the graveyard and bury him. There is to be no marker on his grave. You are not to tell anyone what happened."

"Nosuh," Henry responded. "I ain't gonna tell nobody."

"Take his horse to the barn," Adam continued. "Leave him there until after dark. After it turns dark, lead his horse to Bushnell's plantation. Set him free and return to your home."

"Yessuh, Mr. Adam," Henry said.

Hannah walked in with several burlap sacks. She cut the sacks and wrapped them around Placide's body. When Henry returned, he hefted the body over his shoulder and carried it out to the wagon.

CHAPTER THIRTEEN

October 13, 1866 - October 14, 1866

Around seven o'clock the following morning, as Adam and Annabelle were finishing their breakfast, there was a loud knock on the door. Mary answered the door.

A Negro man entered. "I got to see Miss Annabelle," he said excitedly. Mary led him to the dining room.

When Annabelle saw the man, she stood up and turned to him. "What is it, Benjamin?" she asked in a voice of concern. She hoped her father's condition had not worsened.

"Miss Annabelle," Benjamin sputtered, "Mr. Placide's horse came back to Belle Bois without him."

"Slow down please, Benjamin," Annabelle said. "Is Mr. Placide all right?"

"I don't know," he answered wagging his head. "Just the horse came back."

Adam rushed to his wife's side. "Benjamin?" he asked. "Are you saying Mr. Placide's horse returned to the plantation but Mr. Placide failed to return?"

"Yes, Mr. Adam," Benjamin replied. "Just the horse came back."

Adam helped Annabelle to a chair. "This is terrible," he said. "We will organize a search party at once."

"Ruth," Adam called out. "Have Jeremiah come to me immediately."

Ruth hurried outside and found Jeremiah. Within minutes Jeremiah stood before his employer.

"Jeremiah," Adam said. "I want you to pick twenty men from among the field hands to form a search party. Saddle up horses for all of us so we may scour the countryside. I will personally lead the search party." Jeremiah left to select the men and saddle the horses.

Adam turned his attention to Benjamin. "Do you have any idea what direction the horse came from?" he asked. "Were their any signs of foul play?"

"The horse was in the barn this morning," Benjamin replied. "Nobody knows where the horse came from. I don't know nothing about no foul play."

"Was there blood on the saddle?" Adam asked. "Was the horse injured? Were there any signs Mr. Placide had been injured?"

"No, sir," Benjamin replied. "There's nothing on the saddle. The horse was just standing there."

"Placide may have only fallen from his horse," Adam said to Annabelle. "I am sure we will find him. We will search in all four directions."

"He's an excellent horseman," Annabelle responded with tears rolling down her face. "I don't think he would have fallen."

"Something may have scared the horse," Adam said comfortingly. "We want to get to Placide as quickly as possible. He may be injured."

Annabelle looked at her husband in wonder. Only two days before Placide had threatened to kill him, and today he was leading a party to search for him. "You're an exceptional man," Annabelle said as she leaned her head on his chest. "Placide wanted to harm you, yet you're concerned for his well-being."

Adam was pleased that his ruse was going so well. Annabelle was convinced of his concern for her brother. "This is not a time for holding grudges," he said. "We need to find your brother and make sure he has proper care."

Jeremiah returned to the room. "Da hosses is ready," he said.

"I hope we find Placide soon," Adam said to Annabelle. "We will search until we find him or until we lose the light. I am sure we will find him before noon."

Annabelle rose and placed her arms around her husband. "Please don't be careless," she said. "I wouldn't want you to be injured while searching for Placide."

"I will be careful," he responded. "We must be off. If Placide is injured, we must see to him as quickly as possible."

"Please have one of the servants hitch the buggy?" Annabelle asked. "I have to go to Pappa."

"I do not want you alone on the roads," he responded. "There may be dangerous people abroad. I will make sure you have use of the carriage."

Adam had Jeremiah get a field hand who was familiar with driving teams to hitch the carriage and make it available to take Annabelle to Belle Bois.

Annabelle watched from a front window as Adam and his search party took off at a gallop. Although she was worried about her brother, her heart swelled with love for her husband. She was convinced that Placide was going to call Adam out to fight him in a duel, yet Adam wasted no time going to the aid of his brother-in-law. She was married to an exceptional man.

*****

"Oh, you poor dear," Angelina said as she embraced Annabelle. "I would've been here sooner, but we only just learned Placide is missing."

Annabelle felt that it was considerate of Angelina to drive all the way out to Belle Bois, but she really wasn't up to entertaining visitors. "Thank you for coming," she responded. "You must be thirsty after that buggy ride over here. Marie has a fresh pitcher of lemonade. I can have her pour a glass for you."

"Don't worry about me," Angelina responded. "I wanted to see if there's anything we can do to help you and your family."

"That's so sweet of you," Annabelle said as she led Angelina into the parlor. "I can't think of anything. Adam is leading a search party in hope of finding Placide. He left with his men as soon as we found out Placide was missing. I pray that Adam has already found him." Tears began to trickle down her cheeks.

"I know this has to be hard on you," Angelina said as

she took Annabelle's hand in her own. "Robert would like to help search, but he won't be able to get away from the office until late this afternoon."

"I thought I heard voices," Jacques said as he entered the parlor. "I hoped it was someone with news of Placide."

"It's only me," Angelina responded. "I'm sorry it wasn't someone with good news about Placide."

"Where are my manners?" Jacques said as he walked up to Angelina. "It's so good to see you, Angelina." He put an arm around her and kissed her cheek. "You must be dying of thirst after that drive over here." He looked around. "Young Doctor Joubert let you come all this way alone?"

"I was telling Annabelle he had to stay at the office," she answered. "He's taken on most of the responsibility for the practice."

"Marie," Jacques called out, "Please have someone bring a tray of glasses with the lemonade you just made."

"Pappa," Annabelle scolded softly, "You'll awaken Giselle."

"I forgot she was asleep," Jacques responded sheepishly. "She's so heartbroken. I hope I haven't awakened her."

Delilah entered the parlor carrying a tray holding four glasses and a pitcher of fresh squeezed lemonade. Marie followed behind her.

"You didn't have to go through all that trouble," Angelina protested. "I was hoping I wouldn't get in the way."

"Nonsense," Jacques retorted, "we're pleased you came out to see us. A visit from you will help us to keep our minds occupied. The situation is distressing enough without our imaginations running away with us."

"Thank you, Monsieur Dupre'," Angelina said. "You are ever the gentleman. I hope you'll tell me if I'm in the way."

"You could never be in the way," he replied. "We appreciate your concern for our family."

As she sipped lemonade and listened to Annabelle describe how distraught Adam had been when he learned that his brother-in-law was missing, Angelina thought how odd it was that Adam had gone out to search for Placide. She recalled that there didn't seem to be any love lost between the two men.

Maybe she had judged Adam too quickly and too severely. Annabelle said he was a kind and thoughtful man once you got to know the real Adam. Obviously she and Robert hadn't met the "real" Adam.

*****

Adam divided the search party into four groups. Everyone would search until all light was gone and then meet at Belle Bois. He led his five men east in the direction of Harold Bushnell's small plantation. He wanted to make sure there would be no signs remaining of Placide's horse's hoof prints. He found a place that seemed to be the spot where Henry had released Placide's horse. He rode his horse back and forth over the hoof prints while he pretended to look for signs that Placide had passed that way on foot. After he was satisfied his horse's hoof prints had obliterated the other hoof prints, he led his men westward.

He and his men found the bodies of two men lying beside the road about fifteen feet apart. Adam dismounted and ordered his men to ride back and forth looking to see if there were any other bodies in the weeds beside the road. He was certain there were no other bodies, but the hooves of the horses would cover up any evidence that Placide had been there.

He looked around to see if there was any evidence implicating him and Fisk. Having found none, he searched through the men's pockets. In one of the pockets he found a piece of paper on which Placide's name and address were written and about one hundred dollars in currency. Adam crumpled the note and stuffed it and the money into his own pocket. He was thankful his team had come across the bodies.

The men returned after several minutes reporting they had seen no other bodies. Adam was examining the body of one of the men when they returned.

"They were both shot," he said.

The men dismounted and looked at the bodies. "I tink dis one wuz shot up close," Matthew said. "He gots da powdah burn on his face."

Adam walked up to where Matthew was standing. He looked more closely at the gunshot wound. "This must be the one who told Placide about us," he thought to himself. "Placide did us a favor when he killed him. Now, the man cannot tell anyone what happened."

"We need to get these bodies to the sheriff," he said. He had the men tie the bodies behind the saddles of two of the horses. The two men who had been riding the horses started out for town with their human cargo.

"We must continue to search for Mr. Placide," he said to the three men who remained with him. "Be careful. Whoever killed these two men may still be lurking out here."

Adam and his men searched until all the light was gone. He had insisted that they sweep far and wide. The members of his party were hopeful that one of the other teams had found Mr. Placide.

*****

Jeremiah was waiting with the other search parties when Adam arrived at Belle Bois. "We din fine nuttin, Mr. Adam," Jeremiah said. "We rode evywhere."

"We found two white mens dat been shot," Benjamin said. "I be fraid who done dat, done ketched Mr. Placide."

"You men go home and get a good night's sleep," Adam said. "Tomorrow morning at daybreak we will begin our search once again. Make sure you start where you left off today."

The men weren't hopeful that Mr. Placide would be found. They had covered more area on horseback than a man on foot could possibly have covered.

"Mr. Adam," Jeremiah said in a conciliatory voice. "I don't wanna say we ain't gonna find Mr. Placide, but we done gone more furderer din a man coulda goed on foot."

"He has to be somewhere," Adam responded sharply. "I want twenty additional men searching tomorrow. We will not stop until he is found."

Jacques Dupre' listened as his son-in-law spoke to his

men. He regretted having suspected Adam's involvement upon learning of his son's disappearance. Adam was doing all he could to find Placide. The man looked weary as he dismissed his men. Jacques was thankful Annabelle had married such a good man.

As the sounds of horses' hooves melted into the distance, Adam set out for the plantation house.

"Adam," Jacques called out.

Adam turned toward the sound of Jacques' voice. "What are you doing out here?" he asked. "This night air is not good for your condition."

"My son is missing," Jacques replied. "I had to know if there was any encouraging news."

"I wish I could give you some good news," Adam said. "We discovered the bodies of two men. Both had been shot. Their deaths may have no connection with Placide's disappearance, but we need to make sure. My men took the bodies to the sheriff. I hope he sends men out to join the search for Placide."

Jacques was even more convinced now that Adam had nothing to do with Placide's disappearance. Adam welcomed the intervention of the sheriff. "You must be exhausted, my son," he said. "Come in and have a hot meal. When did you last eat?"

"I had breakfast," Adam answered. "I did not think of food until you said something. I am famished."

Adam and Jacques entered the Dupre' home. Jacques gave instructions to Marie to have a plate of food brought out for Adam.

Adam and Jacques entered the parlor where Annabelle and Giselle were waiting. "Is there any news?" Giselle asked. Her eyes were red and swollen from crying all day.

"Nothing good," Jacques said. "Adam's party found the bodies of two men. They'd been shot."

"Oh, no," Annabelle cried out. "Placide may be dead."

"We are not giving up," Adam said. "We searched for other bodies but found none."

"Poor Adam and his men are going out again at daybreak," Jacques said. "I wish I were in the condition to go out with them."

"Don't even think of going out," Annabelle said firmly. She gazed at her husband. "Please sit, Adam. You look so tired. Are you sure you should go back out in the morning?"

"I will be all right after I eat and rest," he responded. "We cannot abandon Placide. He may be lying hurt somewhere. I am so sorry we did not find him today."

"Adam, please don't berate yourself," Giselle said. "You're doing all you can." She began to weep once more.

"I feel so inadequate," Adam said. "I am about to have a hot meal while Placide is out there somewhere. If only we had found him today."

Delilah placed a heaping plate of food before Adam. Although he felt as though he were starving, he did not allow himself to turn to the food at once.

"Please eat your food," Annabelle coaxed. "You haven't eaten since breakfast. You have to keep up your strength."

Adam allowed himself to be persuaded to eat. He quickly finished the plate of food. He was tired, but he was exhilarated. No one suspected him of involvement in Placide's disappearance. Had he waited at home while his men searched for Placide, he may have been suspected. His direct involvement, even to the point of exhaustion, ensured the good will of the Dupre' family. People were so easily fooled.

"It may be wise for you to sleep here tonight," Jacques said. "You wouldn't have to make the ride to your home."

"Unfortunately, I did not think of that earlier," Adam responded. "My men will be waiting for me at Southern Kingdom in the morning." He had no intention of spending another night without Hannah.

"If you don't mind, Adam" Annabelle said. "I'll stay here with Pappa tonight."

That would work out perfectly. "I understand you wanting to be with your father," Adam responded. "I will be getting up very early, anyway. Please be sure you get an adequate amount of rest."

"You worry too much," she responded. "I hope you can sleep. Please try to get some rest."

185

"I will try," he replied. "Our bed seems so empty without you." He hoped he had not gone too far.

Annabelle kissed him as he prepared to leave. She held herself closely to him. "Everything will be better tomorrow," she said encouragingly. "You'll see."

*****

"Are you hungry?" Hannah asked as Adam walked through the door.

"I ate at the Dupre's," he replied. He took Hannah in his arms and kissed her.

Hannah was alarmed. "Is Annabelle with you?" she asked quietly.

"She remained at Belle Bois," he replied. "We have the night to ourselves."

"I'm sure you're exhausted," she said.

"I do not think I will ever be too exhausted for you," he responded as he led her toward the stairs. "I wanted to come to you last night."

"I missed you," she said as she followed. "Does anyone suspect you had anything to do with Placide's disappearance?"

"No one suspects," he replied. "Everyone sees me as a hero who is valiantly searching for his wife's brother."

"Please be careful," Hannah said as she unlocked the door to her room. "Don't play the part too well."

Adam cleaned the road dust off of his body in Hannah's bathing room and then returned to her boudoir. His muscles ached and he felt weary, but the sight of Hannah's nude body gave him new energy. He removed his clothes and slipped into bed beside her. Her warm body sent heat waves coursing throughout his body. He held her closely and savored the way her body felt next to his.

Hannah sensed that Adam wanted to enjoy their closeness. She held herself against him and softly kissed him. Her need for him was growing but she allowed Adam to move slowly. She responded to him as he explored her body.

Adam caressed and touched Hannah as she gave herself

to him. He could see desire building in her body, but he took his time. He wanted to celebrate life with her. His opponent, who had come very close to killing him, lay dead in an unmarked grave in the plantation cemetery. Hannah had saved his life. He wanted to thank her in a special way for her bravery. He kissed and caressed as Hannah kissed him. When he was sure she could wait no longer, he gave himself to her.

Later, Adam and Hannah lay in one another's arms. They felt an extra special bond between themselves. Neither felt the need to speak. He held her closely as he felt himself drifting to sleep. As sleep was taking him, he remembered her pledge to always love him. He felt profound satisfaction as he slipped into a deep slumber.

*****

The sheriff's posse joined in the search the following day. With over fifty men searching, a large area was covered, but there was still no sign of Placide. "I don't think we're gonna find him," Sheriff Badeaux said to the men gathered that night at Belle Bois. "We've covered almost every inch of this parish."

"Perhaps we should ask the sheriffs of the surrounding parishes to join the search for him," Adam suggested. "Placide did not disappear. He has to be somewhere."

"I can ask the other sheriffs," Badeaux responded. "I don't think that's gonna do any good."

"Why do you think that?" Adam asked.

"Well," Badeaux said as he removed his hat and wiped his forehead with a red handkerchief, "I don't think Placide is anywhere near here. The kinda business he's involved in," Badeaux placed his hat back on his head and shrugged his shoulders, "well, a man makes some enemies."

"What are you implying?" Jacques Dupre' asked in an angry voice.

Badeaux had not seen Jacques standing with the men. He was beginning to feel that he was walking on quicksand. Dupre' was a powerful man in the parish. "Well, I mean in his business, a man makes some enemies," he replied. "Just seems to me that

one of his enemies has taken him. You might get a ransom note."
He shook his head and reluctantly continued. "Then again, we
might never hear anything from Placide again."

Jacques had to admit to himself that his son had made
powerful enemies over the years. He was very good at his
business. Other men resented him. There had been attempts on
his life previously. "I'm not prepared to stop looking for my
son," he said.

Adam wanted no more days of looking for Placide, but
he had to continue to play the game to keep suspicion away from
him. "I am not ready to abandon the search for Placide," he said
agreeing with his father-in-law. "We may find him tomorrow."

The field hands groaned. They'd had two days of sunup
to sunset riding. They wanted no more.

"I'd keep on searching if it would do any good,"
Badeaux said. "I think we're only wasting our time. I won't be
back out tomorrow."

Jacques appreciated the willingness of his son-in-law,
but saw how exhausted the man looked. If he didn't put an
end to the search, Adam would push himself until he ruined
his health. He heard the groans of Adam's men when he had
insisted on going on another day. "Adam," he said, "you and
your men have done enough. You have to stop and rest."

"How can I rest while Placide is missing?" Adam asked.

"You've got to stop," Jacques said softly as he placed a
hand on Adam's arm. "I don't want to lose both of my sons."

Adam forced back the smile that wanted to appear on
his face. He had triumphed. He could stop looking for Placide.
He had persevered. Jacques worried about him as he would a
son. "How can you ask me to stop?" he demanded.

"Because to continue to search will prove futile," Jacques
replied. "It pains me to agree with Sheriff Badeaux. Placide did
have some powerful enemies."

Adam dropped his head and feigned deep sorrow. "If
you feel it will do no good," he said, "we will stop the search."

He allowed the fatigue from two days of riding and a
night of passionate lovemaking to register on his face. "Men,"
he said. "Go to your homes. You can sleep until ten o'clock

tomorrow morning. Thank you for your help."

The men of Southern Kingdom rode off on their horses.

"Come on in and have something to eat," Jacques said to Adam. "You need to eat and refresh yourself. Perhaps you should stay here tonight and sleep in tomorrow."

Adam had no excuse to leave as he had the previous night. "I appreciate your hospitality," he said. "I know Annabelle will appreciate the comfort of her father and her sister-in-law."

Giselle and Annabelle looked up expectantly when the men walked into the parlor. Jacques lowered his head. He gazed at the two young women. "The news isn't good," he said. "We're calling off the search for Placide."

Giselle began to weep.

"We've searched only two days," Annabelle said. "Perhaps he will be found in another day."

"The men have covered all of the area," Jacques said. "Everyone is tired beyond endurance. The men need to rest."

"Do you think Placide is dead?" Giselle asked. "He may be injured and unable to make his way home. Please don't stop until you find him."

Jacques' shoulders sagged. He looked years older than his forty-six years. "I wish I knew the answer to that question," he replied. "I have no way of knowing." He couldn't continue.

"Our hope is that he is still alive," Adam stated. "The sheriff said we might get a ransom note. All we can do is pray and wait."

Giselle looked into Adam's tired eyes. He seemed to be physically and mentally exhausted. She was satisfied he'd done all he could to find her husband. "Please rest, Adam," she said softly. "You're so tired. I'm sorry I suggested pushing you further."

"I would not mind going out once more or many more times to find Placide," he responded. "I am tired, but Placide's safety is paramount in my mind. If going out one more day meant we would find him, I would gladly search for another day."

"I know, Adam," she said. "You've been very kind. We all appreciate what you've tried to do for us."

"I did not do it only for you," Adam said. "He is my brother-in-law. I had hoped finding him would bring peace to our family."

"We will have peace," Jacques said. "We'll welcome the family of a selfless man such as you have proven to be. We hope your family will appreciate you as we do."

Annabelle walked up to Adam and hugged him. "Don't torment yourself," she said. "It isn't your fault he can't be found. We'll pray he returns to us." Adam allowed himself to be held.

"I think we can all use some food and a good night's rest," Jacques said. "I'll tell Marie to have the food served."

The family ate in silence. Jacques, Annabelle and Giselle worried about their lost loved one. Adam was relieved because he would no longer have to search for the dead man. It was time to get back to expanding Southern Kingdom. He was pleased by the certainty that Belle Bois would one day be his.

CHAPTER FOURTEEN

November 4, 1866

"It sure is cold for a November day," Robert said as he helped Angelina down from the buggy. "We may have an early winter this year."

The temperature had dropped into the upper twenties and it was misting. Freezing temperatures during daylight hours generally didn't arrive in Louisiana until close to the end of December. Robert had reason to worry about the weather. He would be responding to the night calls for his father's medical practice.

"I saw smoke rising from the chimney as we made our way here," Angelina said. "I'll bet there's a warm fire burning inside."

Robert lifted the heavy knocker on Southern Kingdom's front door and let it drop. He waited a few moments and was about to lift the knocker again when Fred opened the door.

"Mizz Annabelle's expecking you," he said with a smile. He was fond of the Jouberts. "She settin in da parlor."

Robert and Angelina followed Fred into the parlor. Annabelle rose to greet them. "I knew the two of you would be cold," she said as she hugged Angelina and then Robert. "I had Fred put more logs on the fire. I suspected the cold front had caught you by surprise."

"It was pleasant when we left home," Angelina said with a shiver. "We didn't expect that it would grow this cold."

"Fred," Annabelle said, "Would you please ask Margaret to make a fresh pot of coffee." She turned to the Jouberts, "A hot cup of coffee should help to warm you up."

"That would be great," Robert said. The almanac said

nothing about freezing weather today.

Robert was enjoying the warmth of the fire and his second cup of coffee. Annabelle and Angelina were talking about the latest in women's fashions. His eyelids were getting heavy and he felt himself beginning to doze off. He shook his head to drive away the drowsiness. "I thought Adam would be here," he said when there was a lull in the conversation. The Jouberts' visit to Southern Kingdom had been planned a week in advance.

Annabelle's face turned crimson. "He said he had to go into town to see about some urgent business," she replied.

Robert could see she was distressed so he didn't pursue the matter further; however, he thought it was odd that Adam would have business in town on a Sunday afternoon. The silence grew heavy. "Have you heard anything more about Placide?" he asked. He regretted his question the moment it came out.

Tears sprang from Annabelle's eyes. "We haven't heard a thing," she answered in a small voice. "I hoped we would've received a ransom note by now."

Angelina saw her husband was troubled that his question had upset Annabelle. "There's still time," she said. "No news is good news."

"I suppose so," Annabelle responded. She pulled a handkerchief from her sleeve and wiped her eyes. After another long silence she continued, "Let's speak of more pleasant things. Adam's brothers will be visiting for Christmas."

"They're coming all the way from London?" Angelina asked in voice of astonishment. "I thought you'd told us Adam wasn't close to his brothers."

"Adam wants to heal the rift in his family," Annabelle responded with more enthusiasm. "He invited his brothers and their families to spend Christmas with us."

"That should be interesting," Robert said drily. He wondered if the brothers were as arrogant and cold as Adam.

"I want to show Southern Kingdom at its best," Annabelle said brightly as she warmed to her subject. "It's important to Adam that he make a favorable impression on his brothers. He was treated horribly by them as a child. He wants to show them his life turned out well."

"He wants to show off for them," Robert thought to himself. "He wants to rub his success in their faces. I wonder why Annabelle is so blind to Adam's true nature."

"What changes are you planning?" Angelina asked in an attempt to keep Annabelle's mind off of her brother. "This place is already so beautiful."

Annabelle began to share her plans with Angelina. It wasn't long before they were so absorbed they no longer noticed Robert was in the room.

Robert made his way to the library and found a book that interested him. He returned to the parlor, pulled his chair closer to the fireplace and began to read. He could hear the steady hum of the women's voices in the background. After a few pages, the warmth of the fire and the comfortable chair lulled him to sleep.

"Wake up. It's almost nighttime," Angelina said as she shook her husband. "The trip back will be even colder in the dark."

Robert opened his eyes. He wondered how long he'd been asleep. Angelina was right; the drive home would be freezing cold.

"Let me get you some quilts to bundle up in," Annabelle said. She got up and walked out of the room. She tried to locate Hannah, but she couldn't find her. She located Mary and asked her to get quilts for her friends.

"Mary's getting some heavy quilts for you," she said when she returned to the parlor. "You'd freeze to death without them in this cold weather."

"We do appreciate the quilts," Angelina said. "I'll bring them back to you soon."

"There's no hurry," Annabelle responded. "Fortunately for us we have many quilts."

The Jouberts got into their buggy and tucked the quilts about them. They were grateful for their friend's kindness. They sat as closely to one another as they could on their way home to take advantage of their body warmth and because they loved one another dearly.

*****

Another couple sat close to one another under heavy quilts as their buggy made its way home. In the moonlight, Adam could see smoke rising from the chimney of Southern Kingdom. He turned to Hannah. "Martha is amazing," he said. "She is learning so quickly."

Hannah felt safe and secure sitting next to Adam. They had spent the afternoon with Martha in the cottage. She recalled Adam's look of wonder as he played with Martha. "Did you notice her soft brown hair and milky white complexion?" she asked. "No one will ever know her mother was once a slave."

Adam was pleased that he had asked Pennington to secure a white governess for Martha. Her speech patterns would not give her heritage away. No one who did not know Martha's background would ever suspect her mother had been a slave. "Our little girl will grow up to be a fine lady," he said.

*****

Annabelle was sitting in the parlor when Hannah walked into the room. Annabelle picked up her head when she sensed that someone had entered the room.

"Hannah, I looked for you earlier," Annabelle said.

"I had to go to town," Hannah lied. "My sister was expecting a baby. I telegraphed her to see if she's all right."

"How is she?" Annabelle asked.

"She's doing fine," Hannah replied. "I was worried because she'd been sick."

"Did she have the baby?" Annabelle asked.

"Yes, she had a girl," Hannah lied again. "They're both doing very well."

"I'm glad," Annabelle said. "Have you seen Mr. Adam?"

"No, I haven't seen him since early this morning," Hannah lied once more.

"I suppose he's out in the fields," Annabelle said. "I wish he'd stay indoors on a cold day like today."

About five minutes after Hannah left the room, Adam

walked in. "It is very cold outdoors," he said.

"Did you forget the Jouberts were coming today?" Annabelle asked. "Robert had to sit and listen to us. I'm sure he wasn't thrilled to hear our chatter."

"Why did you invite them?" he asked icily. "You know I do not like them."

"No, I didn't know that you don't like them," she replied. "They've always been nice to you. What could you possibly have against them?"

"She is such a busybody and he does not know how to control his wife," he responded. "He thinks all men should be controlled by their wives. I would not be surprised to learn that he has advised you to rebel against me."

"I admit Angelina is a bit of a free spirit," she said, "but I don't think that means she walks over Robert. They love one another very much." She looked at him stonily. "Why do you think Robert would advise me to rebel against you?"

"I see the way they look at me," he replied. "They have never liked me. I do not think they agree with your choice for a husband."

"That's all in your mind," she said. "They have never said anything unkind about you. Robert was disappointed that you weren't here and, frankly, so was I. That was very rude of you."

"I cannot take time away from my work to listen to nonsense," he responded coldly. "This is a working plantation. It would be best that you visit them in their home in the future. I have no desire to become Joubert's friend."

"Adam, I want my friends to feel welcome in our home," she said. "It wouldn't take you much effort to be kind to them, and, anyway, you need to make friends. A good friend would help you to draw out of your shell."

"I am fine just as I am," he responded. "I have you and my work. I need nothing more."

Annabelle was angry and disappointed. Adam would never heal from his childhood wounds and draw out of his shell if he continued to shun people who wanted to become friends. He wasn't even trying to be nice to her friends. This was her home, too. He would have to at least make an effort to accommodate her guests. She prayed that in time her love and understanding would help him to be more trusting.

CHAPTER FIFTEEN

December 15, 1866 - December 20, 1866

Despite Adam's protests, Annabelle bought new furniture for the formal dining room and the parlor. Although the new dining room table seated more guests, Adam missed the heavy mahogany table that was in the room when he arrived. To him, the new furniture lacked the grandeur of the original furniture.

Edward, Timothy, and their families were scheduled to arrive on December twentieth, which was only five days away. Annabelle had pushed the servants to the point of exhaustion. The crystal and silver were sparkling. All of the china had been removed from the cupboards and given a thorough washing. The floors were cleaned and polished. Annabelle had checked the linen, replacing all the worn items. The bedrooms had new bedclothes. New towels were in the washstands in the bathing rooms. New draperies were hanging in the rooms downstairs and in the guest bedrooms. The mansion was ready, both inside and out.

Adam found things to do that kept him away from the mansion during the daytime. He was aware that Hannah was not pleased with Annabelle. She complained to him at night that Annabelle was trying to re-create Southern Kingdom in the image of Belle Bois. He tried his best to keep the peace. He found keeping his distance during the hours Annabelle spent working with the servants to be the best solution.

Adam and Annabelle were having a simple supper of cornbread and milk that night. "Adam, don't you love the way our home is beginning to look?" she asked.

Much to his chagrin, Adam was finding that the changes

she had made improved the overall look of his home. "I think you have done splendidly," he replied.

Annabelle glowed. She was aware that her husband had resisted the changes she was making, but had hoped he would come to appreciate the new look she was giving the mansion. "I'm happy you're pleased," she said. "I want your brothers to be enchanted by our home."

"I think they will be more enchanted by you than by our home," he said. "Edward's and Timothy's wives pale in comparison to you."

Annabelle looked closely at her husband. She wanted to make certain his words weren't empty flattery. She'd put on some weight during her pregnancy. The baby was due in slightly over three months. Adam smiled back at her. "Thank you, Adam," she responded. "It pleases me to know you still find me attractive even though I'm getting fat."

"You are beautiful," Adam protested. "I do not think you should worry about being fat. You are only showing that you are with child."

Adam's words made her feel better. "I feel as though I'm gross," she said. "I'll work at losing the extra weight as soon as our child is born."

Adam wondered if she would be able to regain her figure as Hannah had done after their child was born. He doubted she would ever be the beauty she had been before the pregnancy. Aside from representing Southern Kingdom as his wife, he did not really care what she looked like as long as she continued to be an asset. "You will always be beautiful," he said. "I am married to the prettiest woman in the entire state."

"You are so considerate," she said as she squeezed his hand.

A bright smile appeared on Adam's face.

"Why are you smiling?" she asked.

"I was imagining the look on my brothers' faces when they received my letter," he replied. "I told you their curiosity and greed would overcome any ire they might feel because of my audacity."

Annabelle wondered about the relationship between

Adam and his brothers. It wasn't love for his brothers that had prompted Adam to invite them for the Christmas season. He wanted to awe them with his possessions and his status in life. Her heart went out to her husband. She thought of the humiliation he must have endured at the hands of his brothers to drive him to feel this way. "It's my wish the three of you will have a stronger bond among you after this visit," she said. "I intend to do everything in my power to foster good will between our family and theirs."

"You may be wasting your time trying to foster good will," he responded. "Those two have looked down their noses at me for years. I want to see their faces when they realize I am doing better than both of them combined."

"Adam, this shouldn't be a contest," she said. "I'm so sorry for you. This shouldn't be a competition between you and your brothers. You are family." Tears began to roll down her face. "I wish Placide could be here to meet your brothers."

"I hope he's rotting in hell," Adam thought to himself.

"I, too, wish he could be here," he said. "I had hoped we would have some news by now."

"Pappa has all but given up," she said. "He had hoped Placide and Giselle would have a son to carry on the family name. I regret he has no other sons."

Adam had no regrets that Jacques Dupre' had no remaining sons or that Placide Dupre' had not left an heir. Annabelle was Jacques' only heir. Belle Bois would go to her at Dupre's death. "It is regretful," he said. "I have been meaning to speak to you about an idea that occurred to me." He hesitated a moment for effect. "I was wondering if you think it will be all right to give our child the middle name of Dupre' if we should have a son."

"That would be wonderful," she responded, "but his first name would have to be a saint's name. Pappa will be so pleased." She rose from her chair, walked behind Adam's chair and hugged his neck. "You're so thoughtful. Pappa says the grief would be unbearable were it not for his remaining son."

"That is so kind of him," Adam said. "He has been more of a father to me than my own father." He had no intention of giving his heir a saint's name. He would agree for now, but his son would be named after his only childhood friend, Charles Warrens.

After supper, Annabelle worked until late in the evening. She was tired from her day of activity with the servants, although she was satisfied much had been accomplished.

When Adam lay beside her that night, she told him she had a splitting headache. Adam did not mind. He had no intention of making love to her. He was thankful that with all the activity, she was sleeping more soundly than usual. He waited until her breathing indicated she had fallen asleep. Trying to be as quiet as possible, he slipped out of the bed and out of the room.

*****

Hannah took more time than usual to respond to Adam's knock on the door. "I'm sorry I took so long," she said. "I'm so tired from following the orders of 'Her Highness.'"

"She should be about finished," he responded. "I told you that you could have gone to your cottage while all of this was going on."

"I wouldn't leave the mansion to Annabelle and the servants," she said. "Thank goodness I was able to resist some of her ideas. I liked our home the way it was before she made all of the changes."

Adam had heard her arguments before. He was looking forward to the end of Annabelle's shenanigans. He especially disliked the toll this was taking on his love life. "It will soon be over," he said. "I will be happy when things get back to normal."

Hannah put her arms around Adam and held herself close to him. "I'm sorry," she said. "I know it's been rough on you, too. I haven't meant to make you suffer." She kissed him and rubbed his back. Although she was very tired, she realized he needed her. She released him, walked up to the bed and began to disrobe.

He felt desire begin to stir in his body. This was the first time in a while that she had disrobed before getting into bed. He watched as she removed her nightgown. Her body had lost none of its firmness. He was fascinated by the way her body looked in the light of the single lamp that lit the room. He began to walk toward her. She signaled him to remain where he was standing. She walked up to him and began to unbutton his shirt, kissing his chest as she unfastened each button.

By the time he stood naked before her, he felt that fire had replaced the blood in his body. He picked her up and gently placed her on the bed. He was determined to make fire course through her body, too. As he kissed her body, she began to moan and beg him to complete her. He worked his way back up to her neck and kissed her below her right ear and at the base of her neck. She turned her head to him and kissed his lips. "Now, Adam," she whispered urgently. He continued to kiss her. She pulled herself closer to him. "Please, Adam," she gasped. He made her wait no longer.

It was after midnight when he awakened. She was asleep against him. He tried to get out of the bed without disturbing her.

"What time is it?" she asked.

"It is dark outside," he replied. "It must be around midnight."

"You were so good tonight," she said. "You were driving me mad."

"I was only returning the favor," he responded. "You had me on fire before we got into the bed."

"Adam," she said emotionally, "I love you. You never leave me feeling cheated. I never dreamed making love could be this good."

"I certainly never feel cheated," Adam responded as he gently stroked her right breast. "No other woman can make me feel the way you do."

"I hope it stays that way," she said with a tightness in her throat. "I want to be the only woman who satisfies you."

"There is no other woman who can make love the way you do," he said huskily. "I think of you during my waking hours and long for you every night."

Adam got dressed and then kissed Hannah one last time

before making his way to his bedroom.
Annabelle was still asleep when he returned to the room. He crawled into the bed and lay beside her. He wished once again that Hannah were the one who was sharing his bed.

CHAPTER SIXTEEN

December 20, 1866 - January 3, 1867

Adam and Annabelle waited at the mansion for Jeremiah to return with the carriage. Adam had sent a wagon along with the carriage to carry the guests' luggage. Even though he had long anticipated the moment his brothers would set eyes on his mansion, he continued to have doubts that they would be sufficiently impressed. Annabelle sat calmly reading as he paced up and down the floor of the parlor.

"They's comin," Fred said as he rushed into the parlor. Fred was dressed in the livery of Southern Kingdom, as were all the other servants with the exception of Hannah.

Annabelle assured Adam that his brothers would be impressed. He sat beside her on the settee and picked up the book he had attempted to read earlier. He willed himself to sit there until his brothers were ushered into the room by Hannah.

He gazed around the parlor. Everything certainly looked splendid. The furnishings in Edward's home could not compare with Southern Kingdom. He composed himself and waited for the moment he would again set eyes on the two men who had mistreated him as far back as he could remember and had continued to do so until he had immigrated to America.

Hannah walked into the room leading Edward, Timothy, their wives and their children. Annabelle rose and walked over to greet the guests. Adam followed her.

"Welcome to our home," she said with a warm smile on her face. Adam loved the way she spoke as she greeted his brothers. She sounded to him like French aristocracy.

"Yes, welcome to our home," he added as he shook hands with his brothers and drew hugs from his sisters-in-law.

"We hope you enjoy your stay."

Edward had put on weight and his hair was thinner. Timothy looked about the same as he had roughly two years before.

"It is splendid to see where our cotton comes from," Timothy said. "We heard of these cotton plantations."

"Your plantation does look impressive," Edward said. "You must have over one thousand acres."

"I own fourteen thousand, five hundred and sixty arpents of land to be exact," Adam responded.

Edward's jaw dropped. "How did you acquire so much in such a short while?" he asked.

"I invested my money in land," Adam replied. "The timber on the land is worth a fortune. With the price of cotton as it is, the harvests have brought in more than most men can accumulate in a lifetime." He failed to mention the incredible sum he had received from Jacques Dupre' as Annabelle's dowry.

"Perhaps we should have sold the business and invested in the American south," Timothy said as he studied his younger brother. "It seems that you have grown quite rich."

"When we find time, I would like to take you to Lance des Chenes, another plantation we own," Adam said proudly. "I had to hire a manager to run that plantation. We stay very busy."

"Another plantation?" Edward asked. "Extraordinary." He gazed around at the interior of the mansion. The interior was as impressive as the exterior. He wondered how his younger brother could have managed so well. He and Timothy had expected Adam to fail abysmally.

"It seems we underestimated your talents," Timothy said. "Had you remained with the firm, you might have used your skills to multiply our fortunes in England." He marveled at the success of his younger brother.

He and Edward had speculated that Adam had used the last of his money to lure them to America in hopes that they would accept him once again into the firm. They had misjudged their younger brother. The servants were dressed in matching livery. He could only guess at the cost of the furnishings in this one room.

Adam had become rich beyond any expectations. Annabelle was wearing the latest French fashions. Adam was dressed in an expensively tailored English suit. Timothy felt that his business suit did not compare well to the suit worn by his younger brother.

"Leaving England was the best decision of my life," Adam said. "I hope the firm is continuing to do well."

"Very well," Edward responded. "We are doing better than when Father ran the firm."

Adam smiled. He enjoyed the discomfort of his brothers. He could tell they were envious. "I am very pleased to learn you are doing well," he said. "I often wondered if you were purchasing some of Southern Kingdom's cotton."

"It is possible," Timothy said. "We have bought a great deal of cotton from the American south." From what he had seen and heard, Adam did indeed control a kingdom.

"Where are my manners?" Adam asked. "Hannah, would you please have the servants show our guests to their rooms."

"Please let us know if you need anything," Annabelle said. "We'll eat supper at six o'clock. I hope you'll like the okra gumbo. It's the perfect meal for a cold day such as this."

*****

Ruth and Fred showed the Blythingtons to their rooms. Edward and Timothy were green with envy. The bedrooms they were assigned in the mansion were more impressive than anything they had in their own homes. Both of their homes could fit into the mansion with plenty of room to spare.

Edward's wife, Hilda, gazed in wonder at the rich draperies, rugs, and other things in their bedroom. Their two boys were given a bedroom next to theirs and the three girls a room across the hallway.

Mary told Hilda that the oldest daughter, Alice, could have her own bedroom should they think that necessary. Hilda was awed by the splendor of her surroundings. She asked Mary to let Alice have her own room.

Timothy and his wife, Bernice, were given a bedroom beside Edward, on the opposite side from Edward's sons. Their two sons were given a bedroom across the hallway from their bedroom.

Edward and Timothy were amazed. Although they and their children occupied six of the upstairs bedrooms, there were still several more unoccupied rooms. The mansion was larger than many hotels.

Ruth and Fred showed the Blythingtons the private bathing facilities. Servants began filling the copper bathing tubs with water. The Blythingtons bathed and dressed for the evening.

Edward, Timothy, Hilda and Bernice met in Edward's room. "I have nothing to wear that can compare with what Adam's wife was wearing," Hilda said as she regarded the clothes she was wearing. "We must go into the city and purchase new dresses."

"We cannot afford to buy new wardrobes," Edward responded with exasperation in his voice.

"I certainly will not stay here and wear the rags I brought," Bernice said. "Timothy, you must take me into town to purchase new clothes."

"The clothes you brought are new," Timothy responded. "Adam is a rich man. You cannot expect us to compete with him."

"Did you not say on our trip to America that you supposed he was a failure?" Hilda reminded Edward. "If you would have used him in the firm as you should have, with his business sense, we would all be rich now."

"We were mistaken about him," Timothy responded. "If we would have only known."

"You should have known," Hilda continued. "The two of you were so sure of yourselves."

"All of that cannot be helped now," Edward responded. "We do not have the money to buy new clothes for everyone. The clothes you have were perfectly acceptable around our English friends." Before his trip to America, he thought of himself as wealthy.

"Our poor English friends," Bernice interjected. "I shall be embarrassed to join Adam and his wife for supper wearing rags."

"Rags," Edward said angrily. "We brought trunks filled with appropriate clothing. Surely you can pick something suitable to wear for supper."

*****

Hilda and Bernice were dressed in the best of what they had brought with them. They were both surly as they started for the dining room.

Annabelle had changed into an emerald green evening gown. Adam was wearing another finely tailored English suit with a vest that matched Annabelle's gown. Annabelle's jewelry glittered in the candlelight. Edward and Timothy realized they would not have peace for some time to come.

"Please make yourselves at home," Annabelle said.

Hannah seated the visiting Blythingtons. Hilda and Bernice checked Hannah out as they sat. They felt the dress she was wearing was better than what they had brought from England. They could not even compete with the servants. Edward and Timothy would pay for their humiliation.

"I hope you enjoy the okra gumbo," Annabelle said. "It's a mixture of Creole and Cajun cuisine."

"Delicious," Edward said as he took a spoonful. "I do not think I have ever tasted anything this good."

"I am pleased that you like the gumbo," Adam said. "We have pecan pie for dessert. Please leave some room for the pie. Our Margaret is an excellent cook."

"Your gown is beautiful," Hilda said to Annabelle with obvious envy in her voice. "Is it a Paris original?"

"We're fortunate to have excellent boutiques in our city," Annabelle responded. "If you would like, we can go shopping tomorrow."

Edward and Timothy blanched. Adam noticed their discomfort. "I am sure you ladies brought sufficient clothing," he said, "but I would be delighted if you would accompany

Annabelle on a shopping excursion. Since you will be doing me a favor, please charge everything to my account."

Hilda and Bernice smiled. "How kind of you," Bernice said. "We could not possibly impose on your hospitality."

"No imposition," Adam responded. "As you can see, Annabelle is in the family way. I would be comforted to know she is with two ladies who will see that no ill befalls her."

"There is no need for you to incur that expense," Edward said. "Our wives brought trunks of clothing with them."

"What woman would pass up the opportunity to have new dresses?" Annabelle asked with a smile. "Please say you'll come with me."

"What shall we do with the children while you go shopping?" Edward asked.

"Surely you and Timothy can see to the children for a short while," Hilda replied acrimoniously.

"I have the perfect solution," Adam interjected. "The children are old enough to benefit from formal tutoring. They can attend classes with our Professor Pennington while you are away."

"Professor Pennington?" Timothy asked. "Who is he?"

"Adam engaged a professor to teach English lessons to our employees," Annabelle replied. "He'll tutor our children when they reach the proper age."

"It is settled then," Adam said before his brothers could protest further. "Annabelle will enjoy the company."

Edward and Timothy thought it would be in their best interest to allow their wives to accompany Annabelle.

*****

Squeals of delight rang out when Annabelle and her group returned from Opelousas with the carriage filled with packages. Hilda and Bernice were enthralled with Annabelle. Annabelle had used her influence to press the hard worked seamstresses at Madame Comeau's to complete a gown for each of her sisters-in-law and several more were on order. Hilda and Bernice could barely wait to show their new gowns, hats and shoes to their husbands. Fred and Jeremiah carried the packages to their bedrooms.

"Isn't this exquisite," Hilda bubbled as she held her new gown up for Edward to examine. "We spent a king's ransom today and Annabelle did not even blink an eye."

Edward had assumed that Annabelle would allow his wife to purchase one dress and perhaps a new hat. He was amazed by the packages of clothing strewn on his bed. "There must be at least six new hats as well as pairs of shoes, corsets, stays and undergarments," he said to himself. "Adam is even wealthier than Timothy and I had presumed." He no longer felt as though he were a wealthy merchant. He felt he was now the poor relative accepting charity from his rich younger brother.

His eyes were drawn back to the bed where Hilda was excitedly opening her packages. "You will be fit to have audience with the king wearing that gown," Edward said with awe in his voice.

Bernice burst into the bedroom without knocking. She was wearing her new gown. "I feel immensely rich," she said as she turned to show Hilda her gown. "I have never worn anything so magnificent. What do you think of this one for the Christmas Ball?"

Hilda took in Bernice's appearance. "You look so beautiful," she exclaimed. "I must change into my new gown." She ordered Edward out of the room so she could change her clothes.

Edward walked to Timothy's bedroom. Timothy opened the door in response to his knock. "Do you feel as frayed as I do?" Timothy asked his older brother as he walked into the room. "Bernice was speaking of a Christmas Ball and galas we are to attend."

Edward shook his head. "I brought nothing that I can wear to a formal event," he said. "Perhaps we should suggest to Adam that he take us on a shopping trip." He snickered at his attempt at humor. "Hilda will expect me to dress in proper attire. We came prepared to meet a pauper and now we must dress for the king." He laughed outright this time.

"The transformation in Adam is greater than anyone

would believe," Timothy said. "It will be a relief to get back to London where we have the respect of our peers."

"I would suggest we leave earlier than planned," Edward said, "but Hilda and Bernice would likely object. We are scheduled to be here until two days after the new year to suffer through this indignity."

*****

Bernice and Hilda preened like peacocks as they entered the dining room. "You look lovely," Annabelle said as she walked up to meet them. "Those gowns look fabulous on you."

"Thank you," Hilda responded as she grinned from ear to ear.

"Silly fop," Edward said to himself. "Going on so about a gown. One would think she has never worn fine clothing." He shook his head as he watched his wife.

Bernice blushed under Annabelle's praises. "It is embarrassing to watch my own wife go on so," Timothy thought to himself.

"Please be seated," Adam said. "I thought it would be a splendid idea to retire to the ballroom after we have eaten. Annabelle can play the piano as we lend our voices to Christmas carols."

"It will be such fun," Bernice exclaimed. "Timothy and I used to sing Christmas carols with our neighbors each Christmas. I do miss it so."

"Miss it so," Timothy said indignantly. "You were the one who insisted that we discontinue the practice."

Bernice favored her husband with a dark look. Timothy looked away and returned his attention to his meal.

Edward and Timothy picked at the meal of chicken fricassee', potato salad, homemade bread and fig preserves. Hilda and Bernice hurried through their food. They wanted to see the grand ballroom Annabelle had spoken of earlier.

As they entered the ballroom, Timothy turned to Edward and whispered in his ear. "You could fit your entire house into this room," he said.

Edward was not pleased that Timothy had not mentioned his own home in comparison to the ballroom. "It is perhaps three times the size of your house," he whispered sharply to Timothy.

Adam heard his brothers as they whispered to one another. He was pleased that his success was having an adverse effect on them. "Please excuse the appearance of the ballroom," he said contritely. "Annabelle has not had the opportunity to purchase new furniture for this room."

The visiting Blythingtons surveyed the fabulous room. It compared favorably to the richest ballrooms in England, yet it was unsatisfactory for Adam and Annabelle.

Annabelle began to run her fingers over the piano keys. She commenced playing a Christmas carol and Hilda and Bernice began to sing. Adam joined in with his rich baritone and his brothers followed. After several songs, Ruth brought in mugs of hot chocolate for the group.

"Everything is going so well," Annabelle said to Adam that night in the privacy of their room. "Hilda and Bernice seem to be having a wonderful time. Did your brothers enjoy their day?"

"You have been magnificent, my love," Adam said. "You are an asset to Southern Kingdom."

"Asset?" Annabelle thought to herself. "I hope I'm more than only an asset," she said petulantly. "The cattle and horses are assets."

"I only meant you have comported yourself so well," Adam responded. "You are my beloved wife."

Annabelle smiled. She regretted having been cross with Adam. "I'm pleased that you consider me to be an asset," she responded. "I'm sorry I was cross with you. You haven't answered my question. Are your brothers enjoying themselves?"

"We spent much of the day riding over Southern Kingdom," he replied. "This plantation is much larger than most of the estates in England. We are riding over to Lance des Chenes tomorrow."

"Did they enjoy the ride?" Annabelle persisted.

"They were green with envy," he replied. "They were

so sure of themselves in England. They treated me shamefully. I enjoyed seeing the looks on their faces as we toured the plantation."

"Do you want to gain their friendship or get even with them?" she asked. "It would be pleasant to visit them in England some day."

"I will never return to England," he stated flatly. "My home is here. I only wanted them to know how successful I have become."

"I thought this visit would be a wonderful time for you and your brothers to get to know one another better," she responded. "They are your family."

"I have no intention of ever seeing them again after this visit," he said. "You and the children we will have are my only family." He wanted to add Hannah and Martha to the list but thought better.

"Edward and Timothy may have recognized their mistake," she said. "They may want to make amends."

"Those two cold fish," he laughed. "Their thoughts of me are purely financial. They have no more love for me than I have for them."

"I was under the impression this visit would reunite your family," she responded. Tears trickled down her cheeks. "I miss Placide terribly. How can you not want to reconcile with your brothers?"

"How can there be a reconciliation?" he asked. "We were never close. Edward and Timothy would turn against one another if it were financially expedient. My only purpose for this visit was to impress upon them that the brother they branded as a failure is much richer than they can ever hope to be."

*****

"How far is Lance des Chenes from here?" Edward asked.

"It is only twelve miles away," Adam responded. "We can cover that distance in a little over an hour at a canter."

Edward and Timothy were already sore from riding

over Southern Kingdom. Neither had ridden in years. They were not looking forward to a twelve-mile horseback ride.

"Would it be possible to use the carriage?" Timothy asked. "I am rather sore from yesterday."

Adam laughed. "I had not stopped to think that you two are unused to riding," he said. The carriage would be too comfortable for his purposes. He told Jeremiah to hitch the horses to the buckboard. There would be room on the seat for all three of them. Although there were saddles at Lance des Chenes, he wanted to use his handtooled saddle, which could ride in the back of the buckboard.

Adam enjoyed watching the irritation of his brothers as they bumped along in the buckboard. They were probably wishing they were on horseback.

"I say," began Timothy, "the young woman who directs your household servants is striking. I think I would be tempted if such a beautiful woman lived in my home."

"She is spectacular," Edward agreed. "I would give one hundred pounds to spend a night with her."

"I, too," ventured Timothy. "Adam, where did you find such a splendid creature?"

"The story is too long and boring," Adam replied. "I am fortunate to have her at Southern Kingdom." He was seething inside at the thought of either of his brothers touching Hannah.

"I am amazed that your wife allows such a beautiful creature to live in your home," Edward said. "Are you not tempted, old boy?"

"I am a happily married man," Adam replied. "Hannah is very competent in the performance of her duties."

"Is she married?" Edward inquired.

"She is not married," Adam replied. Although he was pleased that his brothers found Hannah attractive, he was not happy with the direction the conversation was taking.

"Would you mind if I asked her to allow me to spend some time with her?" Edward asked. "It is not often one finds such a striking woman."

"Hannah would be offended if she knew we were having this conversation," Adam replied irritably as he contemplated spilling Edward out of the buckboard. "She is not that kind of woman. She comes from a Christian home."

"Dash it all," Timothy said. "It would be my luck she would be inaccessible."

Adam thought of Hannah as the buckboard rolled along. "She is a striking creature," he said to himself. He would never let either of his brothers touch her. He was tempted to tell them he made love to her almost every night just to see the look on their faces. That should make them even more envious, but he was unwilling to entrust his brothers with his secret.

"Is that Lance des Chenes?" Timothy asked as the large mansion came into view.

"Yes, it is," Adam replied.

"You own two mansions?" Edward asked with awe in his voice.

"Yes, I do," Adam replied calmly. "My plan is to acquire all of the land between the two plantations."

"You already own two plantations," Timothy said with awe in his voice. "Why would you want to acquire more land?"

"Power, prestige and money," Adam responded. "Why do you strive to do more business than the other export and import firms?"

"In order to have a better standard of living," Edward replied.

"You live better than most of the people in England already," Adam pointed out.

"I see what you mean," Edward responded, "but I would be content with what you now own."

"Perhaps," Adam said. "I am not content. I will be the largest landowner in the parish. I will be the most powerful man in the parish, perhaps the entire state."

Edward and Timothy gazed at their younger brother as he told them what he intended to accomplish. He did not look at all like the groveling man who had asked them to buy out his share of the mercantile firm. The man who shared the buckboard with them was a powerful and determined version of that man. Neither knew why, but a cold shiver ran up and down their spines.

Roger Manual, the man Adam had hired to manage Lance des Chenes, stepped out from the barn as they approached. "Mr. Blythington," he said. "It's a pleasure to see you."

Manual was efficient in managing the plantation, but there was something about the man that bothered Adam. He could not put his finger on just what it was that bothered him.

Edward, Timothy, this is Roger Manual," Adam said. "He is the manager of Lance des Chenes. Mr. Manual, these are my brothers."

Edward and Timothy shook hands with Manual. "This is a rather large operation," Timothy said. "It must keep you rather busy."

"Six thousand, two hundred arpents," Manual answered with pride in his voice. "Some of the richest soil in the entire parish."

"Would you please have someone remove the tack from the buckboard and saddle horses for the three of us?" Adam asked. "We want to look over Lance des Chenes."

"Of course, Mr. Blythington," Manual responded. "Do you want Joanna to get the cook to fix a meal for you before you ride out?"

Adam looked at his two brothers. They seemed more than willing to eat before riding over Lance des Chenes. He pulled out his pocket watch. It was only nine o'clock. "Ask Joanna to make a pot of fresh coffee," he replied. "We will return around one o'clock for dinner."

Edward and Timothy groaned inwardly. Although the temperature of the December day was only in the forties, the humidity and lack of sunshine made it seem much colder. It would have been nice to sit in a warm house and eat a hearty meal. They had already seen more of Lance des Chenes than they wanted. The thought of riding horses over harvested fields on a cold day did not give them great pleasure.

Edward and Timothy looked around as they sat in the dining room sipping their coffee. The antebellum mansion at Lance des Chenes was even more impressive than that of Southern Kingdom. They wondered why Adam had not made this his home.

"I purchased Southern Kingdom a year before I acquired Lance des Chenes," Adam said after watching his brothers as they appraised the mansion. "My heir will reside in this mansion when he comes of age. He will manage this plantation to gain experience. When I die, he will inherit all that I own."

"You may have more than one child," Edward said.

"My property will not be divided," Adam said firmly. "My firstborn son will own all of my property."

"You resented being the younger brother," Timothy interjected, "yet you would make arrangements for only one child to inherit from you. I find that somewhat at odds."

"My other children will each inherit a substantial sum of money," Adam responded coldly. "I will not have my land divided."

"Would it not be better to wait for a warmer day to survey this property?" Edward asked as he looked at the horse he was expected to ride.

"We do not know that we will have a warmer day before you leave," Adam replied.

Edward and Timothy followed their younger brother reluctantly as he led them away from the protection of the barn.

The wind began to blow from the east and the temperature continued to drop as the Blythington brothers rode over the property that comprised Lance des Chenes. Edward wanted to see no more of the fields and woodland. In his opinion, Adam owned as much property as the wealthiest of the landowners in England. As the temperature dropped, he became more sullen. It infuriated him to know the brother he thought so little of possessed so much wealth. "Adam, are you not cold?" he asked.

Adam felt the cold east wind, but the unhappiness of his brothers warmed his heart. "There is a bit of a chill in the air," he agreed. He pulled his pocket watch out. It was only eleven thirty. "We have not seen even a fourth of the property."

About an hour later, Adam led his brothers back to the main house. "We can have dinner and then take the buckboard back home," he said.

"I can no longer feel my ears," Timothy said acrimoniously. "The cold is as damp here as it is in England."

"I hope you do not intend for us to leave this house until we are sufficiently warmed," Edward said. "My feet and hands are frozen. That wind cut right through my clothes."

"I thought you two were enjoying yourselves," Adam responded. "What do you think of Lance des Chenes?"

"It is unfortunate that we did not get to see the cotton growing in the fields," Timothy replied. "I would have liked to see the cotton on the plants."

Edward was too cold to wish for anything other than a hot fire. "I will tell you what I think after I have warmed sufficiently," he replied. "It is too cold to stand out here and chat."

Edward and Timothy devoured the hot vegetable soup the cook had prepared. Adam watched as his brothers ate their meal. They no longer intimidated him. They were suited for the work in their firm and nothing else. His wealth was now much greater than theirs. He came close to feeling pity for them, but remembered how contemptuous of him they had been before he left the firm. They deserved to be humiliated.

After eating, Edward pulled a chair in front of the fireplace and sat. Timothy pulled up another chair and sat beside him.

"We had better be getting back," Adam said about half an hour later. "It will only grow colder if we wait. I do not think you want to be on the road in an open buckboard after dark."

"Surely we can wait a bit longer," Edward said peevishly. "My feet have not sufficiently warmed."

"If we do not leave now," Adam warned, "We will face a very cold ride home."

Edward and Timothy pulled themselves away from the fireplace and walked outside with Adam. The buckboard was hitched and waiting for them. The temperature had continued to drop.

"It is bloody freezing out here," Timothy whined. "Could you not send someone for the carriage?"

"We do not want to be out after dark," Adam reminded

them. "In just over an hour you will be able to warm yourselves at Southern Kingdom."

Edward and Timothy pulled their coat collars up. Adam was pleased that he was wearing the wool longjohns Hannah had advised him to wear. He was warmer than his brothers. He smiled as he slapped the reins on the horses' backs. The buckboard lurched and then set off toward home. Adam felt like closing his coat collar, but he did not want his brothers to know he felt the cold.

"What a pleasant day for riding this has been," Adam said. "The cold weather keeps the mosquitoes away."

"I would prefer to swat at mosquitoes than freeze my arse off," Timothy said as his teeth chattered. "I find it difficult to believe you enjoyed riding in this weather."

"We had a beautiful blue sky and brilliant sunshine part of the day," Adam commented cheerfully.

"We had a bloody cold wind," Edward said irascibly. "Most of the day was cloudy. Did you do this to punish us for the way we treated you in England?"

"Not at all," Adam replied warmly. "I thought you would like to see the fields where your cotton grows. I wanted to show you the wide open spaces of America."

"I have seen all of the wide open spaces I am going to see," Timothy said grumpily. "When we get to the plantation, I will not move from the fire until I am thoroughly thawed. I have never been so cold in my entire life."

"England has colder weather than Louisiana," Adam responded.

"I did not ride all day in the cold in England," Edward said bitterly. "I am only exposed during the brief trip to my office and then home again."

"I do apologize," Adam said lightly. "I had not stopped to think I am more used to our weather and being outdoors than you are. I will soon have you before a roaring fire."

*****

"I say, this fire feels wonderful," Edward said as he

stretched his hands out toward the roaring fire in the fireplace of the Southern Kingdom mansion. "It was frightfully cold on our way back here. Timothy and I were certain we would freeze before our journey ended."

"Why do you go on so?" Hilda asked in exasperation. "We were exposed to the weather as we walked from the boutique to the theater. It was not that cold."

"You did not remain outdoors all day," Edward said irritably. "You were out in the cold for only a short while."

"It was very cold," Timothy added testily. "The wind easily blew through our coats."

"You are not being nice to your host," Bernice said unequivocally. "You should be thankful Adam wanted to show you this wonderful plantation."

"I must come to my brothers' defense," Adam said. "They are not used to being out in the weather. I should have taken them in the carriage."

"But that would have meant we would have been out in the cold," Hilda said testily. "It would have been reprehensible for the men to use the closed carriage while we were exposed to the elements. I know you would not want a woman in Annabelle's condition exposed to inclement weather."

"You could have remained here while we used the carriage," Edward said angrily. "Is it necessary that you continue to shop every day?"

"What a horrid thing to say," Hilda responded furiously. "Annabelle took us to pick up a few things and attend a matinee. You would prefer that we sit here all day and wait for you?"

"I think we'll all feel better after we eat some of Margaret's delicious seafood gumbo," Annabelle said consolingly. "It's the perfect meal for this kind of weather."

"Annabelle is right," Adam said. "The gumbo will help to warm you. Margaret makes a delicious seafood gumbo."

Adam smiled as he witnessed the discomfort of his brothers. They were arguing with their wives and between themselves. The two men he had reckoned to be invincible were only paper tigers.

Adam led the way to the dining room. After everyone

was seated, Mary and Fred began to serve the food.

"I cannot wait until tomorrow night," Bernice said. She looked like a child anticipating a gift.

"What is so special about tomorrow night?" Timothy asked warily.

"Annabelle and Adam are having the annual Southern Kingdom Christmas Ball tomorrow night," Bernice replied. She looked as though she were about to get up from her chair and dance a jig. "We told you about the ball night before last."

"I remember now," Timothy responded abjectly. "Adam, do you think it would be possible for Edward and I to go into town tomorrow and purchase formal attire?"

"It will be difficult to acquire formal wear at this late hour," Adam replied. He stroked his chin as though deep in thought. "Perhaps something can be done, though. I will take you to my tailor tomorrow morning. If we get there early enough, he and his staff may be able to complete a suit of clothes for each of you as a favor to me."

"How early," Edward asked.

"We would have to be there by seven o'clock," Adam replied. "He would have to begin immediately with measurements."

"Would we have to travel in that cold buckboard?" Edward asked fractiously.

"Since we do not have to take saddles with us," Adam replied, "we can use one of the buggies. We will be much more comfortable."

Edward began to calculate the amount he would have to pay a tailor to come up with formal attire at the last minute. He was upset with Adam for not using a buggy for their trip to Lance des Chenes. "Why did he insist on taking saddles along when there were many saddles available at Lance des Chenes?" he asked himself.

"To show my contrition for the discomfort you suffered today," Adam said, "I will cover the expense of the new attire."

"That will not be necessary," Edward protested. "Timothy and I have sufficient funds to cover the expense."

"I insist," Adam continued. "You are my guests. I want

to prove to you that I am truly sorry for your discomfort. Paying the tailor is the least I could do."

*****

The tailor had not been pleased when asked to make two suits with accessories in one day. Adam had to pay more than three times the normal price. Edward and Timothy spent the morning at the tailor's shop trying the suits on as the tailor's assistants worked on them.

Adam, Edward and Timothy joined their wives for dinner at the Hotel Bienvenu dining room and then took in an afternoon performance of The Merchant of Venice. The English visitors were astonished that a troop of actors they had seen perform in England were performing in Opelousas, Louisiana.

"Well done," Edward said to Adam as he applauded. "This is getting to be a small world. We saw that troop perform King Lear in London."

"We get many superb actors out here," Annabelle said. "Steam ships and locomotives have made the world much smaller."

"Oh Annabelle," Bernice said as she smiled broadly, "they were even better here than when we saw them in England. I wish Timothy would sell his share of the business to Edward and move out here."

Timothy overheard Bernice. He chose not to respond and make a scene. He made a mental note to erase the notion from her mind as soon as he could speak to her privately. He would insist on returning to civilized London.

"I could help you to acquire some land, Timothy, if you choose to remain in Louisiana," Adam offered.

"Would that not be wonderful?" Bernice responded. "We could be rich like Adam."

"Are you really planning to remain here?" Edward asked Timothy after only hearing part of the conversation. "What about the Import and Export business?"

"If you ask me," Hilda joined in, "you should remain here with Adam and Timothy. It should not be difficult to dispose of a successful mercantile business."

"That would be wonderful," Annabelle interjected. "With my poor brother's wife grieving, I have no one with whom to share my time. We could be together almost every day."

"There is enough land available for both of you," Adam said, knowing his brothers had no intention of remaining in America. "We could get to know each other better. Your children would be welcome to attend classes with Professor Pennington."

"It will be so good to get away from the fog and factory smoke of England," Hilda said. "Edward, why would you not send a cable today?"

"We will discuss this later," Edward responded frigidly. "We were not intending to make Louisiana our home." Edward was embarrassed. People were beginning to stare in their direction. He had no intention of remaining in Louisiana. He had been counting the days and looking forward to returning to his gentlemen's clubs where he was looked up to and respected. He had no desire to walk in his youngest brother's shadow.

Adam helped Annabelle up the steps of the carriage. He was enjoying himself thoroughly. He turned to the side and studied his brothers as they sat facing their wives. It was clear they were not enjoying themselves.

Bernice and Hilda continued to discuss the prospect of remaining in Opelousas as the carriage took the party to the tailor shop. In their minds' eyes they saw themselves in the near future as being rich and pampered with dozens of servants. They would go shopping almost daily with Annabelle. Their husbands would soon be as rich as Adam.

"We have had nothing but problems ever since we arrived here," Edward whispered to Timothy. "Now, we must disabuse our wives of the notion of remaining in this country. We have never said we do not wish to return to England."

Timothy was thinking of what Adam had achieved in such a short period of time. If he and Edward worked together, they should be able to acquire a fortune.

"Timothy, did you hear me?" Edward hissed.

"Oh, sorry," Timothy replied. "I was deep in thought."

"I hope you were not thinking of remaining here," Edward whispered angrily. "We have a successful business in England that awaits our return."

Timothy turned red. He had been thinking of remaining in the south. "Would it be such a bad idea to remain here?" he asked. "The two of us together should be able to do much better than our younger brother."

"No!" Edward replied much louder than he had intended. He gazed around to find the other people in the carriage staring at him. "Why did I ever agree to come out here?" he asked himself. "If the others have their way, I will never return to my home. Even Timothy has abandoned me."

Adam was pleased as he listened to the exchange between his brothers and with the conversation between Annabelle and his sisters-in-law. It was going to be a wonderful evening.

*****

"You two look so handsome," Annabelle said as Edward and Timothy walked into the parlor. "I'm sure all the ladies will ask you to write your names on their dance cards."

"They had better not wander too far," Hilda commented as she gazed upon her husband in his formal coat and tie. "Edward had better restrict his name to my dance card."

"There may not be room for his name on your dance card," Adam said. "You and Bernice look lovely tonight."

Hilda and Bernice smiled brightly. "I am sure the men will not bother to notice us with your lovely wife in the room," Bernice responded. "She will be the most beautiful woman there."

"That's not true," Annabelle said. "I'm fat and pregnant. Hilda and Bernice, you do look lovely. I'm sure Adam's English family will turn many heads. Adam hadn't told me how handsome his brothers are and how beautiful the two of you are. It will be like having royalty in our home."

Bernice and Hilda were flattered. Edward and Timothy smiled warmly at their sister-in-law.

"You are not fat," Hilda responded. "Your condition gives you a certain glow."

"You're very kind," Annabelle said.

"It is you who are kind," Timothy added. "We would have come to America sooner had we known Adam had married such a beautiful and gracious woman."

Bernice shot a pair of daggers at her husband. He had not told her she was beautiful, yet he was fawning over Annabelle. She gazed at Annabelle. She saw no guile in the way she was conducting herself. She would speak to Timothy later about proper conduct.

"Thank you," Annabelle said, "I take that as a compliment from a man who has the good sense to have selected such a lovely woman as his wife."

Bernice smiled. Annabelle had accepted the compliment graciously and had put Timothy in his place.

"Our guests will soon arrive," Annabelle said. "Perhaps we should make our way to the ballroom. We would like for all of you to stand with us in the receiving line."

The six people made their way to the ballroom. The couples paired up and stood in line to receive the guests. As the guests arrived, they were led to the receiving line by Fred and Hannah. Adam introduced his guests to his brothers and their wives.

Several ornate chandeliers brightly illuminated the interior of the ballroom. Timothy gazed up at the dozens of candles that glowed around the room. He had never seen so many candles in his entire lifetime.

The orchestra was set up on a raised platform on the north side of the ballroom. Tables covered with serving dishes of fried shrimp, oysters, catfish, chicken and many other regional delicacies were set up along the west wall of the ballroom. Several of the field hands were called upon to man the food tables and serve the drinks and canapés. All of the servants, with the exception of Hannah, were dressed in Southern Kingdom livery.

"Everything looks so lovely," Giselle said as she arrived on the arm of her father-in-law. "Adam, you look so handsome." She let go of Jacques' arm and walked up to Adam. She embraced him and kissed his cheek. "We must get together sometime," she whispered in his ear.

Adam was caught off guard. He had flirted innocently with Giselle when he had first met the Dupre's, but he had been more careful once he found out Placide was an excellent duelist. The words Giselle had spoken sounded very much like a proposition to him. Although he considered her a scatterbrain, she was a beautiful and tempting woman. With Placide out of the way, he might consider spending some time with her.

Hannah caught his eye as he was thinking of Giselle. It seemed to him that she was reading his thoughts. He was unwilling to trade Hannah for Giselle. He smiled at Hannah and she turned her attention back to the guests.

"It's good to celebrate Christmas again," Jacques said as he shook Adam's hand. "This is our first Christmas ball since Adelaide passed away. We must leave the dead in God's hands and pay attention to the living."

"I am happy you chose to come," Adam said. "It will be all the more festive with you here."

Jacques smiled as he gazed upon his tall son-in-law. "He's such a good husband for Annabelle," he said to himself. "He's such a good man. "

"We will have joy tonight," he said to Adam.

"I would like for you to meet my brothers and their wives," Adam said. He took Jacques to where Edward, Timothy and their wives were receiving guests. "Monsieur Dupre', these are my brothers Edward and Timothy." Jacques shook hands with the two brothers. "This is Edward's lovely wife, Hilda, and Timothy's lovely wife, Bernice. I would like you to meet my father-in-law, Monsieur Jacques Dupre'."

Jacques kissed the hands of each of the Blythington ladies as he bowed before them. He shook Edward's, and then Timothy's, hand. "I'm so pleased to meet Adam's family," he said. "He has become a son to me."

Hilda and Bernice were captivated when they met Jacques.

"Now we know where Annabelle gets her good looks,"

Hilda said. "Your wife must have to watch you closely to keep the other ladies from stealing you away."

Jacques was sad for a moment and then brightened up. "My Adelaide went to meet the Lord two years ago," he said. "It was she who gave Annabelle her beauty."

"I am so sorry," Hilda said contritely. "Please forgive me."

"You meant no harm," Jacques responded kindly. "There's no need for you to apologize. Perhaps, with your husband's permission, you would consent to dance with me later."

Hilda smiled brightly. "Edward had better not object," she said to herself. "I am sure Edward has no objections," she said as she glared at her husband. "I will be honored to dance with you."

Bernice was feeling left out. "I am so sorry about the passing of your wife," she said.

"Thank you for your sympathy," Jacques responded. "Perhaps you would also honor me with a dance if your husband doesn't object."

Bernice looked coldly at Timothy. "I have no objections," Timothy responded hastily.

"Then it is settled," Jacques said. "I will have two lovely dance partners."

Hilda resented Bernice for barging in. It was obvious to her that Jacques had intentionally left her out. Why did she have to work upon the man's sympathy so he would consent to dance with her?

Adam was pleased with the way the evening was turning out. Members of the classes haute of St. Landry Parish society as well as several state and local dignitaries, were in attendance. Hannah was proven correct in her assessment of his marriage to Annabelle. Influential people, who would have shunned the ball had he not been married to her, traveled several miles to be in attendance.

Adam glanced toward his brothers. They stood apart from one another near the food tables. As far as he could tell, they had not spoken to one another since the beginning of the ball. He noticed they each held a glass of champagne. There would be some severe headaches in the morning.

Jacques was dancing with Bernice at the moment. Hilda glared at her from the edge of the dance floor. It appeared that both women were intrigued by the silver-haired Frenchman. Jacques smiled as he whirled Bernice around on the dance floor. He was oblivious of the friction between the former close friends.

"What do you think of the party?" Annabelle asked as she walked up to Hilda's side. "I'm so happy you and Bernice could be here."

"It is a wonderful party," Hilda responded as she kept an eye on the dance floor. "I wish Bernice were not making such a fool of herself over your father."

Annabelle glanced in the direction of Bernice and Jacques. There was nothing out of the ordinary as far as she could tell. "What has she done?" she asked.

"She as well as forced herself upon the man," Hilda replied. "Jacques is only dancing with her out of sympathy."

"How do you know this?" Annabelle asked.

"When he arrived here, he asked me to dance with him," Hilda answered irritably. "Bernice whined to him because he had taken no interest in her. Because he is a gentleman, he could not say no to her. She is so pathetic."

Annabelle found it odd to hear the note of jealousy in Hilda's voice. She glanced again at her father. He seemed to be enjoying himself immensely. There was no evidence that he had sympathy for Bernice. She searched for something innocuous that she could say. "It's wonderful to see Pappa enjoying himself," she said hoping to defuse the argument between the English ladies. "He's been so sad since Mamma's death."

"He would enjoy himself much more if that silly woman would leave him alone," Hilda said angrily. "Perhaps you could tell her he prefers to dance with me."

Annabelle found herself in an untenable position. She had nothing to gain by taking up for either of the women and much to lose. "Pappa is a very capable man," she said. "I'm sure he knows what he's doing."

"You have not seen the way he looks when he takes

Bernice's hand and leads her out to the dance floor," Hilda went on. "One can easily see it pains him to divide his time between the two of us."

"This is such a lovely party," Sophia Landry said as she took Annabelle's arm. She turned toward Hilda. "Would you please excuse us? Senator Barnes' wife wants to speak to Annabelle."

"Hilda," Annabelle said, "Would you please excuse me. I'm afraid my duties as hostess must separate us for a moment." She fled before Hilda could say anything further. She was happy her old friend had pulled her away from Hilda's quarrel.

Adam overheard the exchange between Annabelle and Hilda. Things were going better than he had expected. His brothers and their wives were all quarreling.

Around three o'clock in the morning, those guests who were not staying at the mansion overnight began to leave. Those who had come from far away, or who were in no condition to travel, were making their way to the guest bedrooms. Annabelle begged her father to remain in one of the guest rooms but he insisted on returning to his home. He bowed to Bernice and Hilda as he prepared to walk through the door. "I have had a lovely time," he said. "It's been some time since I've had so much joy. Thank you very much for entertaining an old man."

Both women smiled broadly as Jacques told them good night.

When the door closed behind Jacques, Hilda turned to Bernice. "I do not see why you humiliated yourself by insisting that he dance with you," she said angrily. "Was it not clear to you that he extended the invitation only to me?"

"You are the one who made a fool of herself," Bernice replied. "He told me I felt so light in his arms. It was plain to see he only felt pity for you."

Edward and Timothy rushed to their wives. "This is not the way ladies should conduct themselves in public," Edward said. "Bernice, apologize to Hilda for the cruel things you said to her."

"It is Hilda who should apologize for the things she said to Bernice," Timothy stated angrily.

"What is wrong with you, Timothy?" Edward asked.
"Do you not want harmony between our families?"
        "Not at the expense of my wife's feelings," Timothy
replied. "Those things Hilda said to Bernice were cruel. She
should apologize."
        The few guests who remained stopped to watch the
argument between Adam's brothers. Edward became aware that
people were staring. "We will continue this discussion in our
chambers," he declared as he stalked off.
        "You see what you have done," Hilda said to Bernice.
"You have upset Edward."
        "I do not care whether or not he is upset," Bernice
responded. "My husband agrees with me that your behavior was
atrocious."
        Hilda glared at Bernice. It seemed to Timothy that Hilda
was on the verge of attacking his wife physically. He stood
between the two women. "I think it best we all retire to our
chambers," he said. "Bernice and I will be going to our room.
Unless you apologize, I do not think there is any need for us to
discuss this further."
        Timothy took Bernice's hand and started for his
bedroom. Hilda made a move to follow and then decided to
remain and speak to Annabelle.
        "I am sorry for the uncivilized behavior of my brother-
in-law and his stupid wife," Hilda said to Annabelle. "She is
acting most uncivilized."
        Annabelle didn't know what to say. She was amazed at
the behavior of Adam's English family. "Maybe she's just tired,"
Annabelle responded. "We'll all feel better in the morning."
        "Edward will chastise Timothy for his behavior," Hilda
said. "This sort of thing would never have happened in England.
Bernice must be affected by the American independent nature. I
must speak to Edward." She turned on her heel and walked off
toward her bedroom.
        "It was a lovely evening," Adam said as he stood by his
wife's side.
        "I don't know what got into Bernice and Hilda,"
Annabelle said. "They're both married women. Why would they

argue over who Pappa preferred as a dancing partner? I don't think it made any difference to him which of the two was on the dance floor with him."

"Your father is a handsome man," Adam said. "Perhaps the two women were infatuated with him."

"Don't be ridiculous, Adam," Annabelle responded. "They've been married many years and have children."

"Perhaps our American independence has affected them," Adam said with a grin. "Edward and Timothy were also quarreling tonight."

"That's not at all what I wanted," Annabelle said sorrowfully. "I hope a good night's rest clears their heads."

*****

Elsewhere in the mansion, Hilda was haranguing Edward about the events that had transpired during the course of the evening. "Edward, you cannot allow Timothy and Bernice to talk to me that way," she said after telling him her version of what had taken place after he left the ballroom. "I am the wife of the senior partner. Are you going to allow them to treat me disrespectfully?"

"I had hoped Timothy would come to our room so we could clear the air," Edward responded. "I will speak with him in the morning."

"I will not be able to sleep until you have put them in their proper place," Hilda insisted. "You must get Timothy in here at once."

Edward was tired and had a severe headache. He regretted that the champagne had flowed so freely. He would have preferred to wait until morning to speak to his brother. He realized Hilda would not allow him to sleep or even rest until he spoke to Timothy. Resignedly, he walked to Timothy's room and knocked on the door.

Timothy opened the door and looked coldly at his brother. "What do you want?" he asked angrily.

"I would like you to come to my chambers so we may speak about the events that occurred this evening," Edward replied in a tired voice.

"Edward, if you want to speak of the events of this evening, you may come into my bedroom and discuss the things you have on your mind with Bernice and me," Timothy responded bluntly. "I shall not leave this room."

"I am the senior partner," Edward rejoined arrogantly. It was inconceivable that his younger brother would speak to him this way. "We will discuss this in my chambers."

"We are not at the office," Timothy responded flatly. "We are equals in this home."

"We will never be equals," Edward spat out. "Your very existence depends on my magnanimity."

"Your magnanimity?" Timothy shot back. "I work for every farthing I receive. Do not forget I am a partner in the firm."

"A junior partner," Edward said as his anger continued to grow. "I do not need you. I can hire a lackey to do your work."

"You may have to hire a lackey," Timothy retorted as he glared at his older brother. "Bernice and I have discussed the possibility of remaining here. With my share of the business, I should be able to acquire a substantial amount of property."

Edward regretted the angry words he had spoken. Timothy could not be easily replaced. It would be difficult to come up with the money to buy Timothy's share of the business, which might mean someone outside of the family could buy his share and enter the firm. That would be terrible. Edward hated Hilda for forcing him to deal with the situation now instead of waiting until the morning as he had originally proposed.

"I think we should all get a good night's rest and discuss this in the morning," Edward said. "We do not want to act in haste." He walked away and returned to his room.

"Did they apologize?" Hilda asked.

"I will not discuss this further," Edward said menacingly. "Your meddling may cost me a large sum of money. I cannot afford for Timothy to leave the firm."

"You can buy him out," Hilda rejoined.

"It would take a great deal of money to buy him out," Edward responded. "We might even have to go in debt."

"We can sell the firm and stay here," Hilda continued.

"Your share of the business would be enough to purchase more land than Adam owns."

"I am not staying in America," Edward responded unconditionally. He was exhausted and wanted Hilda to leave him alone. "My life is in England. Anyway, why would you want to remain here with Bernice?"

"We would own more land than Timothy," she replied. "She would have to look up to me."

"We are returning to England and that is final," Edward snapped. "I must get some rest. I must find a way to convince Timothy to remain with the firm."

"Do you mean you will not demand an apology?" Hilda asked tempestuously. "I will not be married to a man who allows people to get away with insulting his wife."

"I do not give a damn about your apology!" Edward shouted. "This stupid argument may cost me my business. Now, shut your mouth and let me sleep."

Hilda opened her mouth to protest, but stopped when she noted the anger in her husband's eyes. She would speak of this at another time when he was more receptive. He would pay dearly for the way he had spoken to her this night. She made up her mind to patch things with Bernice. Bernice would be her ally in her war with Edward.

In the meantime, Bernice was working on Timothy to convince him to remain in America. "I am not a farmer," Timothy replied in response to his wife's appeal to him to sell-out his share of the business and purchase a plantation. "I detested riding over the land with Adam. Furthermore, I do not know the first thing about growing cotton."

"What did Adam know about farming when he left England?" Bernice asked. "He has become very prosperous. The people who work for him farm the land."

The more Bernice spoke, the more Timothy became convinced he should not remain in America. The two days he had spent on horseback had taught him he did not want to spend his days on a horse's back overseeing a large estate. His position in the firm had no physical demands nor did it require much in the way of leadership skills. Why would he leave a comfortable position to live in a place where there was great risk of failure?

"I am not cut out for that sort of life," Timothy confessed. "Our lives in England are very comfortable. I am unwilling to risk losing all I have acquired."

"Only a few moments ago you told Edward we were considering remaining here and now you tell me you are afraid of failure," Bernice cried out. "Have I married a coward?" She expected Timothy to deny he was a coward and declare his willingness to begin a new life.

Timothy considered Bernice's accusation. He had never viewed himself as a coward, but he preferred to be called a coward rather than lose his comfortable lifestyle. "I do not think I am a coward," he replied. "I weighed all the possibilities and concluded I am more suited for life in a mercantile firm than life on a plantation."

"In the few moments we spoke of this matter you weighed all the possibilities?" Bernice asked incredulously. "You did not have time to weigh everything in that short while."

"I have and my mind is made up," he responded hoping his wife would accept this as the last word. "I must get some rest so I may make amends with Edward in the morning."

Bernice was furious. She was sorry she had argued with Hilda. Hilda was her one true friend. She would find a way to patch things with Hilda. Hilda would help her to get the better of Timothy.

*****

Bernice stood inside her room with the door ajar as she watched for Hilda early the next morning. She hoped Hilda would leave the room before Edward. After ten minutes of watching and waiting, Hilda stepped out of her room. Bernice walked out of her bedroom trying to make it seem only to be a coincidence the two had exited their rooms simultaneously, and began to walk toward the stairway. As she did so, she maneuvered herself beside Hilda, drew a deep breath and then plunged into her carefully rehearsed speech. "I feel badly about our argument," she began.

Hilda smiled. "Such a stupid argument," she responded. "We have been friends far too long to let something so silly drive us apart."

"Yes, we are good friends," Bernice agreed. "I would hate to continue to be at odds with you."

"You are so right," Hilda agreed.

"I am very upset with Timothy," Bernice began. "He was very rude to me last night."

"Edward was terrible," Hilda confessed. "He said some horrible things to me."

"The things we must endure," Bernice said sympathetically. "Why must men be such tyrants?"

"I need your help," Hilda said. "I want to make Edward suffer for the way he treated me."

"We will think of something," Bernice responded. "Perhaps you can help me with Timothy."

Hilda smiled as she walked down the stairs with Bernice. Things were back as they should be. Bernice was not her enemy. Bernice was her ally against her true enemy, Edward.

*****

Edward kept his eyes closed until he heard the bedroom door close. He dressed hurriedly, walked across the hall to Timothy's room, and knocked softly on his door. Timothy opened the door and the two men faced one another.

"I want to talk to you about last night," Edward said.

Timothy feared that Edward had come to tell him he was no longer wanted in the firm. "I hope we can make amends," he said.

"That is what I want," Edward agreed as he let out a sigh of relief. "We both said things we did not mean."

"Yes, we did say some foolish things," Timothy agreed. "I have no intention of remaining here in America."

"Neither have I," Edward responded. "I cannot wait to return to England. I hope Hilda gets this silly notion of remaining in America out of her mind."

"Bernice has been ranting about selling out and purchasing land in America," Timothy said. "I do not see myself as a farmer. The two days we spent on horseback with Adam were enough to convince me I do not belong here."

"I am pleased we can continue as partners," Edward said as he smiled at his younger brother. "I do not want anyone other than you as a partner in our business."

Timothy smiled back at his older brother. He no longer resented Edward for being the senior partner. It was wonderful to have someone else to accept responsibility for the difficult decisions. He looked forward to resuming his life in England. "I think I will appreciate working in our firm more than I did before we came here," he said. "I never thought I would yearn so much for a holiday to end."

"This holiday may still have financial rewards," Edward stated boldly. "I have given some thought to striking a deal with Adam to purchase all of his cotton directly from him. We could pay Adam more for his cotton and still get the cotton at a price lower than the buyer would sell to us."

"Just the kind of thinking that keeps us ahead of the other export and import businesses," Timothy responded. "You are a brilliant man, Edward."

Edward was pleased with himself and with Timothy's remarks. The partnership was again on solid footing and he had regained the respect of his younger brother. "We must speak to Adam about our proposal," he said. "He grows many bales of cotton. Think of the profits we will reap."

Timothy was thinking of the profits. Edward was once again proving himself a shrewd businessman. Blythington Import and Export had a brilliant future with Edward at the helm.

"I think we are in for some rough sailing," Edward stated. "Our wives are not happy with us. We need to meet them with a united front. It will be many weeks before we again enter a safe port." He was pleased with himself for coming up with nautical terms to describe the situation with their wives.

"I am sure you will keep the ship on course," Timothy

said with a smile. He was happy to once again be on good terms with his elder brother. He preferred facing Bernice's ire to Edward's anger.

*****

Adam smiled as his brothers and their wives entered the dining room. It was clear they were at odds with one another. Hilda and Bernice must have gotten over their argument. They were speaking conspiratorially with one another. Edward and Timothy were discussing business.

"I trust you had a good night's sleep," Adam said to the group in general. Judging by the looks of his guests, he doubted anyone had gotten much rest.

Edward gazed at his youngest brother. Adam certainly looked well rested.

"I am not used to being up that late," Timothy said.

"It may have been the champagne you drank," Bernice said as she gave her husband a harsh look.

Edward was bent on showing Hilda her anger made no difference to him. "I slept very well," he said. "It was a lovely party."

Edward's remarks irritated Hilda. "Your eyes are as red as embers," she said. "You certainly do not look well rested."

"Hilda, are you ill?" Edward asked solicitously. "You look very pale this morning. Perhaps you should return to our room after you have eaten. I would not want you overtaxing yourself."

"I am quite well," Hilda responded irritably. "Bernice and I had a wonderful time at the ball."

"I'm so happy you enjoyed yourselves," Annabelle chimed in. "I think most of our guests enjoyed themselves. You're the only ones who are up for breakfast."

"I should be sleeping in." Timothy thought to himself. "I feel horrible."

"Is it usual for guests to sleep through breakfast?" Edward asked hoping to change the subject.

"Some won't rise until late in the afternoon," Annabelle

replied. "There's no need to be up until one is thoroughly rested."

"They are wasting daylight," Edward commented. "This would not do in England."

"We are not in England," Hilda responded irritably. "There is nothing wrong with resting after a party."

Edward was miffed. Hilda was always chagrined if he remained in bed past breakfast. She was only attempting to abase him.

"I would not mind returning to my bed," Timothy commented. "I certainly could use more rest."

Edward was upset with Timothy for agreeing with Hilda. "I hope you do not take your sloth with you when we return to England," he said. "I need a partner who is able to work long hours when necessary."

Timothy noted the tone in Edward's voice. "I am willing to work whenever required," he said with a note of annoyance in his voice. When he saw the look on Edward's face, he regretted the tone he had taken. "I only meant there is nothing pressing today."

"Bad habits should never be developed," Edward lectured. "Once a habit is formed, it takes weeks and much effort to break."

"You sound like an old maid school teacher," Hilda commented. "Why must you be such a stuffed shirt?"

"I was only pointing out that bad habits are too easily acquired and difficult to break," Edward replied petulantly. "It is best to guard one's self against such habits."

"For heaven's sake," Hilda responded testily. "Why can you not be like Adam? He makes scads of money and enjoys his life. Why must you always be so sullen?"

"I am neither a stuffed shirt nor am I sullen," Edward responded. "Timothy and I built a sound business by making sure our work habits are above those of our competitors."

"You inherited the business," Hilda rejoined. "I do not think it has grown significantly since your father's passing."

Edward regretted arguing openly with his wife before

these people. It was not like him to reveal his personal life to anyone. His head was pounding and he was very tired. The visit had gone badly almost from the outset. He yearned once again for his life in England.

"I apologize to my host and hostess for our bad manners," he said. "Hilda, if you wish to continue this discussion, we may do so in the privacy of our room."

"I have nothing to hide," Hilda responded loudly. "After the way you treated me last night, I should not even speak to you."

Edward noticed that some of the other guests were beginning to walk into the dining room for a late breakfast. He sat beside Timothy and asked for a cup of black coffee. He was developing a taste for the brew.

"The morning is going terribly," Edward said quietly to Timothy. "Hilda is in a foul mood."

Timothy did not think he was faring any better with Bernice. "I only want to get home to England," he responded. "Bernice has been upset with me ever since we arrived."

"Do you get the feeling Adam is aware of our discomfort?" Edward asked.

"Now that you mention it," Timothy replied, "he not only seems to be aware, he appears to be enjoying himself thoroughly at our expense."

"Do you really think so?" Edward asked. "How could he have known our wives would be upset with us?"

"You have a point," Timothy replied. "He did nothing to provoke our wives. Perhaps we are imagining things."

"It is difficult to think clearly with all of the things Hilda has been doing," Edward said. "The sooner we get home, the sooner our lives will return to normal."

"Yes," Timothy responded as he gazed at his formerly obedient wife. "Things must return to normal."

Edward watched as Hilda and Bernice followed Annabelle to the parlor. He finished his coffee and addressed his youngest brother. "Adam," he said, "if you can spare a moment, Timothy and I would like to discuss a business proposition with you."

"I can always find time to discuss business," Adam responded. "We might be more comfortable in my office." The three men walked to his office.

"Please be seated," Adam said. "Would you care for a good cigar? I got these from a man who trades with Cuba."

"Those are very expensive in England," Edward replied. "I would like to try one."

Adam handed a cigar to each of his brothers. After the cigars were lit and the room began to fill with smoke, he stated, "Edward, you spoke of a business proposition."

Edward leaned forward in his chair. "As you know, we import cotton," Edward began. "We get our cotton from someone who purchases cotton here and then sells the cotton to us. We were thinking we could purchase the cotton directly from you and eliminate the middle man."

"I can see that you could purchase the cotton more cheaply that way," Adam agreed. "You would increase your profits." He intertwined his fingers and surveyed his brothers. He waited for them to spell out the terms of their proposal.

"You would also increase your profits," Edward continued. "We would pay you more for your cotton than the buyer. That way it's beneficial for everyone."

"That may be beneficial," Adam agreed. "How would you calculate the price you would pay me for my cotton?"

"I am sure we could come up with something that would be satisfactory for everyone," Edward replied. "We can work on the details later."

"There will not be a later," Adam said calmly. "I have been pleased with the prices offered by my buyer. I will not sever my ties with him unless your offer makes it worth my while. We will work out an agreement now or there will be no agreement."

Edward turned to Timothy. He was becoming annoyed. "Have you given thought as to how to successfully negotiate this arrangement?" he asked in hopes that Timothy might have an answer. He was finding that Adam was a shrewd businessman.

Timothy desperately searched for an answer. "I thought

perhaps a penny per pound above what the buyer would pay you, Adam," he replied. He was pleased with himself for coming up with what he thought was a satisfactory solution.

"That would not make it worth severing my ties with my buyer," Adam responded. "My buyer gives me top prices."

"Do you have something in mind?" Edward asked. "I am sure we can reach an agreement." He did not feel as confident as he had upon entering Adam's office.

"Yes, I do," Adam replied. "We will share the profit made by eliminating the middle man."

"I was thinking of an arrangement that would be more profitable for the firm," Edward responded. "After all, we take a risk that the prices will drop before we dispose of the cotton."

"We all know the textile mills are clamoring for all the cotton they can get," Adam countered. "We can do business if you are willing to agree to my terms."

Things had not gone as Edward had planned. He felt belittled by his youngest brother. "Timothy and I will need time to discuss your offer," he said.

"That is no problem," Adam said. He looked at the clock on a shelf in his office. "It is now twelve minutes past nine. We will meet again in one hour. If you agree to my terms, I will sell all of my cotton directly to you. If not, I will continue to do business with my buyer."

It angered Edward that Adam seemed so sure of himself. This was not the same man who had stood in his office timidly negotiating the sale of his share of the business. He felt he was being diminished in Timothy's eyes. "Come, Timothy," he said as he rose from his chair.

Timothy rose and obediently followed his older brother out of the room.

Once they were safely in Timothy's room, Edward began to vent his spleen. "Did you ever encounter such arrogance?" he asked. "He would have made a great deal of money at one cent a pound."

"Are we going to reject his offer?" Timothy asked.

Edward was tempted to reject the offer on principle. Where did Adam get off treating him disrespectfully? Still, even halving the middleman's cost would assure Blythington Import and Export a substantial profit. "No," he replied. "We will accept his offer." A thought entered his mind. "Perhaps we can negotiate with Mr. Dupre' to allow us to purchase cotton directly from him. He may not demand as much of the middleman's fee."

"Excellent," Timothy responded. "We could grow rich."

At ten o'clock Edward knocked on the door of Adam's office. Adam opened the door and motioned for his brothers to be seated.

"We will agree to your terms," Edward said. "We do have a condition."

"What is your condition?" Adam asked. He wondered what trivial condition Edward was adding in an attempt to save face.

"You must sign a contract agreeing to sell all of your cotton to Blythington Import and Export for the next five years."

Adam smiled as he gazed on his brothers. He already intended to sell all of his cotton to his brothers if they met his price. He would be a fool to sell any portion of his harvest for less. "You do drive a hard bargain," he responded. "I agree."

Timothy was aware Edward's condition meant nothing and was only an attempt to save face. He felt sorry for Edward. He had never before seen his older brother beaten so handily.

"I am pleased that you added that condition," Timothy said to his older brother after they had left Adam's office. "You showed him you are a shrewd businessman."

Edward studied his brother's face to determine if he was being patronized. Timothy seemed to be sincere. "It was best to lock him into the agreement for a specified amount of time," he said, "and we have to be sure he does not sell part of his harvest to another firm."

*****

The Blythingtons gathered in the parlor Christmas morning. There were gifts for all of the adults and for the children. The children squealed with delight as they opened their presents. Adam gazed upon the tall Christmas tree standing in the corner of the parlor. The strings of popcorn and red bows adorning the tree made a pleasant sight. Only nine days remained before his brothers and their families would return to England. He smiled as he reflected on the quarrels he had been privileged to witness. His brothers would have problems with their wives for months to come.

Edward sipped eggnog spiked with rum as he gazed at the Christmas tree. The days were passing by much too slowly. His head still ached from the Christmas Eve festivities at Belle Bois. Champagne had flowed much too freely. Hilda and Bernice danced again with Jacques but managed not to quarrel. He wondered if it was possible to book earlier passage back to England. "It is no use to even attempt to do so," he said to himself. "Hilda would never agree."

Timothy sat beside Edward as he gazed at the Christmas tree. The sounds of the children's laughter as they opened their presents caused his head to ache more severely. It would be many hours before he could lay his aching head upon his pillow. Bernice was only a few feet away physically, but miles away emotionally. He wanted to dance with her at the Christmas Eve ball, but she only had eyes for Jacques. He missed the comfort of his wife's arms.

Timothy decided to look for a time when he could be alone with Edward. He would beg his brother to seek an earlier return to England. The visit to America had gone on much too long.

The children were munching on bonbons Fred and Mary had brought into the room. "Please don't eat too much, children," Annabelle begged. "Margaret is preparing a delectable Christmas dinner."

Timothy's stomach lurched at the mention of food. The champagne he drank at the Christmas Eve ball had left his stomach in turmoil. The thought of sitting at a table piled with food was revolting.

Hannah walked into the room followed by Jacques and Giselle. Two Belle Bois servants trailed with arms filled with gifts. "Je vous souhait joyeaux de Noel," he said. "Merry Christmas."

Annabelle rushed to her father and wrapped her arms around him. "Merry Christmas, Pappa," she said. "I'm so happy you came." She turned and hugged her sister-in-law. "Merry Christmas."

When Annabelle released her, Giselle walked up to Adam and embraced him. "I'm angry with you," she whispered. "You still choose to ignore me."

Adam did not know how to respond. He was relieved to find that Hannah had left the room. Visiting Giselle at her house would be unwise and meeting with her at Belle Bois would be foolhardy.

Hilda and Bernice brightened when they saw Jacques. Bernice's face looked radiant as she gazed at Jacques. Timothy groaned.

Edward stood and shook hands with the older man. "Merry Christmas," he said. He quickly returned to his eggnog. His goal was to dull his senses as much as possible for the remainder of the day and possibly the remainder of the visit to America.

"Merry Christmas," Adam said. "Welcome to our home. Would you like some eggnog?"

"Do you have something stronger?" Jacques asked. "I need something to ease my aching head. I had forgotten I am no longer a young man."

"You may find the eggnog has just the right ingredient," Adam responded.

Fred poured a glass of eggnog and handed it to Jacques. Jacques took a sip. "Indeed," he remarked, "the perfect ingredient." He took another sip and smiled. "I'm beginning to feel better already."

He turned to the servants who still held the gifts. "Place them beneath the tree," he instructed. He turned back to the London Blythingtons. "Would you be so kind as to open your gifts?"

Bernice and Hilda were the first to open their gifts. Jacques, heeding Annabelle's advise, had gotten identical ivory brooches for each of the ladies. She had advised him this way neither of the ladies would feel slighted. He hadn't understood why one or the other would feel that way, but he followed his daughter's advice nevertheless.

"Oh, how beautiful," Hilda exclaimed. She noticed the one Bernice held in her hand was indistinguishable from the one she held in her own hand. "I guess he was afraid to hurt her feelings," she said to herself. She was unwilling to reopen the wounds resulting from their arguments earlier in the week.

Bernice looked at Hilda as she pinned the brooch to her dress. She felt sorry for Jacques. The poor man was forced to purchase a brooch for Hilda identical to hers to keep her from whining. "It is lovely," she said sincerely to Jacques. She wished she could convey to him her sympathy for Hilda's behavior. Perhaps she would find time later in the day.

Timothy watched as his wife pinned the brooch to her dress. Bernice had not shown very much excitement for the present he had given her. "What is it that causes her to make a fool of herself over this old Frenchman?" he asked himself.

Hannah walked into the room. "Dinner is served," she said. The guests began making their way to the dining room. Timothy walked next to Edward. "I do not think I will be able to eat a thing," he said. "The champagne from last night has my stomach upset."

Edward was sure he felt about the same as Timothy, but was annoyed by Timothy's confession. "Perhaps you should have had less to drink," he said remonstrantly. "A gentleman knows his limitations."

Timothy thought of pointing out his brother's hypocrisy, but stopped himself. He had no desire to revisit the controversy that had followed the Southern Kingdom ball.

*****

"Do you think it would be possible to book earlier passage back to England?" Timothy asked his older brother that afternoon.

"I think it is impossible," Edward replied. "Even if we could, do you think Hilda and Bernice would agree?"

Timothy groaned. "I find it difficult to believe Bernice is the same woman who arrived with me," he said as he shook his head. "She no longer shows affection for me."

Edward grimaced. "Not only Bernice," he said. "Hilda has been cold to me since our argument following Annabelle's ball. I have never known her to remain angry for this long."

"Could we try to get earlier passage?" Timothy asked mournfully.

"These things are booked weeks, if not months, in advance," Edward replied. "There is no chance of leaving earlier." He shook his head. "I am beginning to wonder if Hilda will accompany me on my return to England."

"Why did we ever agree to come here?" Timothy asked. "We were doing very well in England. I fear Bernice will never be the same."

"If this continues after we are home," Edward commented, "I will seek a mistress. A man needs certain things."

Timothy was aghast. He had never heard his brother speak this way. He thought about what Edward said about a mistress. Having a mistress was better than waiting for a coldhearted woman to show affection. "Perhaps I will seek a mistress also," he said.

Timothy remembered Edward's proposal to speak to Jacques Dupre' about eliminating the middleman and selling directly to Blythington Import and Export. "Have you spoken to Mr. Dupre' about selling directly to us?" he asked.

Edward was upset with himself. He had completely forgotten. The spiked eggnog and the whiskeys he drank after dinner had made him slightly tipsy. Even so, he was alert and his words were not slurred during his conversation with Timothy. He should have no problem speaking with Dupre'.

Jacques was sitting across the room conversing quietly with Annabelle. Edward stood and made his way across the room to Dupre' and his daughter.

"Pardon me, Monsieur Dupre'," he said. "May Timothy

and I have a few moments of your time?"

"Of course you may," Jacques said as he rose. "Would you please join us?"

"We would like to have a private discussion with you if you do not mind," Edward responded.

Jacques frowned. He couldn't imagine why Edward and Timothy would need a private meeting with him on Christmas day. "Please excuse me," he said to Annabelle. He turned to Edward. "Perhaps our hostess wouldn't mind if we meet in the library."

Annabelle nodded her approval.

Jacques walked to the library followed by the two brothers. He opened the door of the library and allowed the two men to enter before him. He closed the door and sat in a stuffed chair. "I am at your service," he said.

Edward was going to stand but decided it was safer to sit. His legs were wobbly. "We have a business proposition for you," he began.

"Couldn't this have waited for another day?" Jacques asked. "It's Christmas day."

"Perhaps," Edward replied. "Since you are already here, we thought it would be acceptable."

The expression on Jacques' face clearly indicated his distaste for conducting business on Christmas day. "What do you have in mind?" he asked as he reminded himself these men were family.

"We would like for you to sign a contract agreeing to sell all of your cotton directly to Blythington Import and Export," Edward replied. His tongue felt thick in his mouth. He wished he had waited for another day to approach Dupre'. Why had Timothy insisted it had to be today? Timothy was acting like Hilda, forcing him to do things when the time was not appropriate.

"Why would I do that?" Jacques asked.

"We would give you a penny a pound more for your cotton than if you went through a middle man," Edward replied. "With all of the cotton you sell, that would represent a great sum of money."

"My buyer is a family friend," Jacques responded. "He has handled my business satisfactorily for years. Our families have known one another for generations. I make a satisfactory profit and his business sustains his family. I find no need to alter my agreement."

"Do you not see you will get more money for your cotton?" Edward said irritably. "Do you not understand you can make more money if you sell directly to us?"

"As I have said," Dupre' continued, "I'm satisfied with the arrangement I have with my buyer."

Edward realized he had allowed the alcohol to affect his behavior. He wanted to excuse himself and ask for a meeting later in the week. He doubted Dupre' would agree to another meeting. He could see Timothy's look of dismay out of the corner of his eye. He was irritated with himself and with Dupre' for turning him down. He fought to regain control.

"Perhaps you failed to understand my proposition," Edward said. "Would you be more interested if I told you we can halve the cost of the middle man?"

"I have made my position clear," Jacques responded coldly. "I will continue to do business with my buyer." He rose from his chair. "I think it's best we return to the others."

Edward watched as Dupre' walked out of the room. Timothy closed the door behind Dupre'.

"That did not go well," Edward said.

"No, it did not, "Timothy agreed.

Edward felt anger rising once again. He would not have spoken to Dupre' if Timothy had not insisted. "I did not think it would be a good idea to speak with Dupre' today," he said. "I wish you had not insisted that we speak to him today."

Timothy's head dropped. He had insisted on nothing. Responding to his brother's accusation would solve nothing, though. Edward was not being himself. He wondered how many glasses of eggnog and whiskey his brother had consumed. He wanted to put the entire American episode in the past.

"I apologize, Edward," he said soothingly. "I should have known better."

Edward was deeply shamed. Timothy had done nothing

wrong, yet he had apologized. He vowed to drink no more, at least until after he returned to England. He needed all of his faculties about him to make it through the remainder of his sojourn in America.

"It would be best if we both forget about this," Edward said. "It is always difficult for an Englishman to deal with a Frenchman."

"Quite right," Timothy agreed. "I should have considered that."

When they returned to the parlor, Dupre' was speaking with his daughter. "There you are," Annabelle said smiling.

"I was telling Annabelle of your most generous offer," Jacques said with a broad smile on his face. "She insists I'm too set in my ways. It could be so. Although I'm not in a position to accept, I do appreciate your offer."

Edward examined the smile on the Frenchman's face. There was no duplicity in his expression. Dupre' was treating the matter as though it had never happened. He sighed with relief. "Monsieur Dupre', I appreciate you taking the time to hear us out," he responded. "Perhaps you would reconsider our offer at a later date."

"I'll keep your offer in mind," Jacques said. "It's my desire that there be harmony between our families."

Edward and Timothy understood what Dupre' meant. For the sake of Adam and Annabelle, he was willing to forgive and forget. There would be no reconsideration.

*****

Adam observed Giselle as she walked out of the door that led to the verandah. He waited several minutes before following after her. He found her on the verandah sitting in the wooden swing. "I see you also needed fresh air," he said as he walked toward her.

"The day is so pleasant," she responded gaily. "I couldn't resist the urge to sit in your swing and enjoy the beautiful sunshine."

Adam sat beside her on the swing. They remained silent

for several moments.

"Don't you find me desirable?" she asked as she turned and looked into his eyes. "Twice I've asked you to meet with me. You've made no response."

Adam was no longer having sexual relations with Annabelle because of her condition, but that posed no problem since Hannah was satisfying his desires. There was no reason to complicate his life by having an affair with Giselle; nevertheless, he felt an overpowering desire to make love to the woman who had shared Placide's bed. "What a way of putting him in his place," he thought to himself.

"It is impossible to meet with you at Belle Bois," he replied, "and it would bring suspicion if I were to visit you at your home. Besides, I have no idea when you are at your home."

"There are other places," she responded as she looked at him coyly. "A man with your resources should have no problem coming up with a solution."

A warning bell went off in his mind as he considered her challenge. He had no real need for her, and the man he wished to cuckold was dead. Why would he feel a need to injure Placide further? As a moth drawn to a flame, he felt himself drawn to the widow of the man who had cowed him. Knowing Placide lay dead in the plantation graveyard was not enough. He wanted to demean Placide further by planting his seed in the woman who had been his wife.

He thought of renting a room in one of Opelousas' hotels, but rejected the idea. People would see them together at the hotel. It would be only a matter of time before news of their liaison reached the ears of Annabelle and Jacques or, far worse, Hannah.

He thought of the cottage where Martha lived with Rebecca and her governess. The solution was to build a cottage where he could meet with Giselle. It would have to be a sufficient distance from the main house so as to remain undetected by Hannah, yet it would have to be close to the road so as to be accessible by buggy for Giselle. He would select the site and set Daniel and his crew to building the cottage immediately.

Giselle studied Adam as he sat quietly beside her. She was beginning to think he had little interest in pursuing her.

"It will take a few weeks," he finally said, "but I have found a solution. How do I get word to you when the time is right?"

She smiled brightly. She had been intrigued with Adam since she'd first met him. She'd been very careful not to arouse Placide's jealousy. Now that Placide was dead, too much time had elapsed to have any hope he remained alive, she could unleash her desire for Adam. She felt no loyalty to Annabelle. If Annabelle were taking proper care of her husband, no woman could steal his affection from her.

"I've been many weeks without a man," Giselle pushed on. "I have no wish to wait any longer. There has to be a way to meet sooner."

"It would be too dangerous," Adam said. "Your reputation is at risk." Adam did not care in the least about her reputation. He did not want to risk his relationship with Hannah.

"Doesn't the danger add to the desire?" Giselle asked. "I can't wait any longer."

"Please believe me when I tell you I want to be with you," Adam responded, "but as a gentleman, I cannot expose you to the risk. We must wait."

Giselle pouted as she sat beside him. She would have to resign herself to waiting the few weeks. She decided to try one more gambit before giving in. "Perhaps one of your brothers would find me attractive," she said. "The younger one is very handsome."

"You would not think of giving yourself to Timothy?" he asked incredulously.

"I want a man who isn't afraid of wanting me," she replied heatedly. "I have already waited weeks. Why must I wait any longer?"

"This is getting out of hand," he thought to himself. "I will get a room in one of the hotels," he said. "How do I get word to you?"

"You won't have to get word to me," she replied. "I'll

engage a room at the Blanchard Hotel in Eunice tomorrow." She thought for a moment. " It'll be registered under Mr. and Mrs. Byron Olivier. I'll tell the clerk my husband has been delayed. If you want me, meet me there at one o'clock."

Adam did not like having Giselle dictate terms to him. He had no intention of letting any woman control him, yet her threat of giving herself to Timothy caused him to throw caution to the wind. "We will meet this one time at a hotel," he said firmly.

"Perhaps there'll be no desire to meet again after this first time," she said challengingly.

Adam smiled. He would give her more pleasure than she had ever found in Placide's arms. Hannah had taught him how to please a woman. She would desire to meet with him again. He would put Placide out of her mind once and for all.

*****

"Is something bothering you?" Hannah asked as she lay in Adam's arms that night.

"No," he replied. "Why do you ask?"

"You seem distant," she replied. "It's as though your mind is some other place."

Adam became uneasy. He had tried to meet all of her needs as they made love, although he had wondered how Giselle would compare to Hannah. He had the uncanny feeling she could read his mind.

"I have a lot on my mind," he responded. "With the attention I must give my brothers, I have been neglecting plantation business."

"Are you sure that's all that's going on?" she asked. "You seemed distracted when we made love."

He pulled her body closer to his own. "I am sorry," he said. "I did not mean to cause you any concern. Everything will return to normal once my brothers and their families have returned to their own homes. This visit is wearing me thin."

Hannah recalled how he had given himself to her with wild abandon even though he was exhausted from pretending to search for Placide. As tired as he was, he had given her his full attention. Her instincts told her another woman was involved.

She had watched as Adam slipped out to speak with Giselle and she had looked out of the window to see them sitting together on the verandah swing. She suspected Giselle was trying to entice Adam into having an affair with her. Making love to the wife of the man who had tormented him would be very tempting to Adam.

She hoped the affair would be short-lived. She couldn't bear to have Adam abandon their child. Her first impulse was to draw away from him. As she lay in his arms, she evaluated their relationship. No other woman could satisfy him as she did. Their relationship was more than just sex. He relied upon her for advice. He shared his dreams with her. He would always come back to her. She drew closer to him and kissed him passionately.

"What was that about?" he asked.

"It's about how much I love you," she replied. "You're the only man for me."

Adam was filled with an acute feeling of guilt. How could he cheat on her after all she had done for him? He truly loved her. His relationship with Giselle was only out of spite for Placide.

"I love you, Hannah," he said. He tried to drive Giselle from his mind as he made love to Hannah once more.

*****

"There is some plantation business I must see to," Adam said to Edward and Timothy the following morning. "You are welcome to ride with me if you wish."

Both men groaned. "Would you mind terribly if we stayed in?" Edward asked. "Timothy and I have business to discuss."

Adam doubted Edward and Timothy had much in the

way of business to discuss, but he was relieved to get rid of the two for the day.

As he walked out to the barn, he tried to decide whether to take a buggy or ride his horse. He figured the hotel would more readily accept the story of Giselle being his wife if he arrived in a buggy carrying luggage, but it would be difficult to convince the people of the plantation he was riding over the fields should he take the buggy. He gave orders to Fred to saddle his black stallion, Diablo.

The stallion settled into a comfortable lope as he rode toward Eunice. He had allowed about half an hour leeway in case problems arose. He could easily kill half and hour in town before going to the hotel. The day was sunny and cool; a perfect day for an outing. He hoped he would not encounter anyone he knew, but he had a story prepared. He would tell anyone he met he was looking at a bull he was thinking of purchasing.

As he neared the town, he slowed the stallion to a walk. He would arrive at the hotel around one o'clock if he took his time. He preferred to ride slowly instead of risking being seen in town.

Once he was in town, he rode to the livery stable and told the attendant he would return in a few hours. He did not want to leave Diablo tied in front of the hotel for fear someone would recognize the horse.

At five minutes to one, Adam walked into the hotel and stepped up to the desk. "I am Byron Olivier," he said. "I believe my wife is waiting for me."

The desk clerk gave Adam a long look. "She's in room two oh six," he said. "I'll send the boy outside for your luggage."

"I was detained in Sunset," Adam said. "My wife came ahead with all of our luggage."

"So she did," the clerk said. "She told me you were detained. I hope it wasn't too great an inconvenience."

"Only business," Adam replied. He wanted the clerk to stop asking questions. He hoped Giselle had thought to bring luggage with her.

Adam tried to keep himself calm as he walked up the stairs. Giselle was a beautiful woman, but was this affair worth the risk he was taking? He recollected the times Placide had intimidated and belittled him. He hoped Placide could look down from heaven or up from hell and see her lying naked in his arms. Who had won in the end? He would thrust the dagger through Placide's heart by having sex with his wife.

Giselle responded instantly to his knock on the door. She was wearing only a red robe. "Were you seen by anyone we know?" she asked with concern in her voice. Despite the fact it had been her idea to use the hotel room, she was questioning the wisdom of meeting this way. There was too much risk of being seen.

"I saw no one I know," he replied.

She was relieved. If they could return to their homes without being seen, the meeting would be worth the risk she'd taken. She walked up to Adam and wrapped her arms around him.

"I often wondered how it would be in your arms," she said, "even while Placide was still alive."

"I thought the two of you had a perfect marriage," he responded.

"He was away too often," she said. "There were fires he didn't put out." She stood on her tiptoes and brushed her lips against his.

He felt desire growing in his loins. He drew her closer and kissed her passionately. He could feel her body responding through the thin garment she wore. She began to breathe more rapidly as she responded to his fervor.

"We'll be more comfortable on the bed," she said breathlessly as she pulled herself away.

Adam watched as she moved her shoulders and allowed the robe to slip to the floor. Her body resembled Hannah's with the exception of her creamy white skin. He recalled her reluctance to bear a child because it would disfigure her body. He agreed her body was well worth preserving.

Giselle kept her eyes on Adam as he studied her body. She could tell he was pleased by what he was seeing.

"Take off your clothes and come to me," she said huskily.

Adam began to disrobe. His fingers fumbled at the buttons on his trousers.

"Come here and let me help," she said as her eyes gleamed.

He walked to the edge of the bed where she sat. She unbuttoned each of the buttons, touching him as she did so.

He fought to control himself. He wanted to make sure he brought her pleasure before releasing himself.

When his clothes lay on the floor beside the bed, she lay on the bed and made room for him. He felt the fire in her body as she pressed against him. Her body was soft and yielding yet firm and strong. He resisted the temptation to enter her. He explored her womanhood and was quickened by her response to his touch. He felt his own desire grow as she gave back to him.

"That was fantastic," she said some time later as she lay next to him. "There are no fires left burning. I think I've met the lover of my dreams."

Adam compared the experience with Giselle to making love with Hannah. Giselle had satisfied him completely, as had Hannah. He had never dreamed Giselle could make love with such reckless abandon. Although he could never share his life with her as he had with Hannah, he did not want this to be the last time he would make love to her.

"I was surprised by the depth of your passion," he said. "I had no idea how amorous you could become."

"You haven't disappointed me, Adam," she said. "Do you remember I questioned whether or not I'd want to meet with you again?"

"Yes, I do remember something about that," he replied.

"You've passed the test," she said with a smile on her face. "I've never been so satisfied before in my life. For all Placide's swagger, he mostly saw to satisfying himself."

Adam was affronted by her comment about passing the test, but he was lifted by her comment about giving her more satisfaction than Placide.

"I wondered if making love to you would be worth the risk I was taking," he stated bluntly.

"Is it?" she asked. She was no longer smiling.

He allowed a few moments of silence before he answered. "You are an excellent lover," he responded.

"You haven't answered my question," she persisted.

"It was worth the risk," he said. He felt desire for her beginning to grow again. Pulling her gently to him, he explored her body once more.

Giselle smiled at him. "I can't believe you're not worn out from our lovemaking," she said as she responded to his touch.

Adam took his time making love to her the second time. He did not allow himself to be released until he was sure she was sated.

"If only I had met you before I married Placide," she said. "It would've been perfect." She was quiet for a moment and then asked, "You haven't mentioned Annabelle; does it bother you that I'm her sister-in-law?"

"No," Adam replied bluntly, "Does it bother you?"

"It should, I guess," she responded, "but it doesn't. Is she a good lover?"

Adam thought for a while. "I prefer not to discuss Annabelle," he said.

"I told you that you are a better lover than Placide," she said. "Why won't you answer my question?"

"It would hurt Annabelle if she knew about us," Adam replied. "She does her best."

Giselle read her answer in his response. Annabelle couldn't satisfy a man like Adam. There would be many more occasions in the future for lovemaking with him.

"What do you think Placide would say if he knew we have made love?" Adam asked.

"He wouldn't say a thing," she replied soberly. "He'd kill both of us."

"You must be of the opinion he will not be returning," Adam said. "Otherwise you would not take this risk."

"He hasn't been seen in almost three months," she responded. "He won't be coming back."

Adam repressed a smile. He was confident Placide

would never return.

*****

Adam followed Giselle's buggy at a distance until she returned to her home. It was not safe for a woman to be out alone after dark. It was already dark when he turned toward Southern Kingdom.

As he rode to his home, he thought of the time he had spent with Giselle. While it was true that they were excellent together in bed, there was nothing more to their relationship. They had not spoken to one another as two people in love. They had discussed their desire for one another as dispassionately as though they were speaking of the weather. Yet, as he thought of her seductive body, he could feel the heat rise in his loins. He only had to think of how her naked body felt as they made love to become aroused.

He decided he would speak to his carpenter before turning in for the night. Daniel, the head plantation carpenter, responded to Adam's knock on his door. "Yessuh, Mr. Adam," Daniel said when he recognized the man at his door.

"I have a job for you and your crew," Adam said. "I want you to build a hunting cabin in the woods on the northeast side of the property. We will choose the location tomorrow. I want a cabin that will be warm in the winter and cool in the summer."

Daniel had not known Mr. Adam to be a hunter but had no reason to question his orders. "We kin bill it fo you, Mr. Adam," he responded. "We got to finish up on da lil bone fuss."

"I want you to drop everything and get this done," Adam ordered. "This will be your top priority."

"Yassuh, Mr. Adam," Daniel responded. "Whutever you lack."

*****

The night was turning cold as Adam entered his home.

Annabelle smiled as he walked in. "I was beginning to worry," she said. "I hope you don't have to go out again tomorrow. You must be very tired."

Adam could not tell his wife he was indeed very tired but refreshed. Making love with the wife of his nemesis was very invigorating.

"I am tired," he responded. "The cattle appear to be doing very well. It will soon be time to begin preparations for spring planting."

"Pappa says you're one of the better planters in the parish," Annabelle stated. "He said you're doing remarkably well for a man who knew nothing of farming before he arrived here."

"You know I value your father's opinion," he responded. "That means a great deal to me."

Annabelle walked up to Adam and kissed his cheek. "You must be famished," she said. "Margaret has supper ready. I told her to prepare her delicious vegetable soup. It'll help to warm you up."

Adam and Annabelle walked to the dining room arm in arm. The London Blythingtons joined them shortly after they entered.

"Everything smells so good," Edward said as he walked into the room. He turned toward Adam. "I hope you had a very profitable day."

"It was a good day," Adam responded. "How was your day?"

"Timothy and I were able to go over our strategy for the new year," Edward replied. "Bythington Import and Export will be even more successful next year." He noted the look of disapproval on Hilda's face. "I cannot wait to leave here," he said to himself as he turned his head away from Hilda. "Things will return to normal once we are back home."

*****

Later that night, Hannah lay on her bed thinking about Adam. She had little doubt he had met Giselle somewhere and they'd had a tryst. Adam avoided her and wouldn't look her in the eye. She doubted he would be coming to her room that night.

The thought of Adam with Annabelle in his arms was difficult to endure. The thought of him with Giselle in his arms brought sharp pain. She tried to rationalize his interest in Giselle. Placide had come very near killing him. Even though Placide was dead, because of all he had done to Adam before his death, cuckolding him would be hard to resist.

She recalled how Adam stood trembling with his eyes closed as he waited for Placide's bullets to strike him. "What a blow that must have been to his pride and his manhood," she said to herself. "Having a love affair with Giselle would do much to assuage his pride."

Even though she was able to excuse Adam's behavior, it still hurt her to think he needed another woman after all she'd given to him. She kept her body looking fit and always strove to respond to his every need. She continually sought to find ways to arouse his desire for her.

As she lay in the dark, she listened for his footsteps. She dozed off after several hours. Adam still hadn't come to her.

Morning came at last. She took particular care in getting herself ready for the day. She wanted to look her best for Adam.

She went to the kitchen to make sure Margaret had a good breakfast prepared for Adam. Mary was buttering biscuits and Ruth was helping Margaret remove a cornbread from the oven. "Did Mr. Adam ask for cornbread?" Hannah asked.

"Mr. Adam, he done et sum biskits and fig perserves and took off," Margaret replied. "He say he got to git tings going early tadey."

Hannah's heart dropped. It wasn't like Adam to leave without telling her goodbye. She tried her best not to let her disappointment show.

Day after day passed without a word from Adam. On the sixth day she heard a soft knock on her door. She rushed to the door hoping it was him. Her heart leaped when she saw him standing in the dark hallway.

"May I come in?" he asked sheepishly.

"Of course you may," she replied. "This is your home."

Adam entered the room and closed the door behind him. He stood awkwardly for a few moments. "I guess you want to know why I have not come sooner," he said with his eyes downcast.

"I already know why you haven't been with me," she responded.

He lifted his head and looked into her eyes. "How could you?" he asked. "Did someone tell you something about me?"

"No one had to tell me a thing," she replied. "I read the signs."

"What signs?" he asked. "Am I that transparent?"

"Not to most people," she replied. "Sometimes I can read your thoughts."

He walked to the bed and sat down. "I guess you hate me now," he said. "I cannot blame you."

"Hate you? No, I don't hate you," she responded levelly. "I love you. You already know nothing can stop me from loving you."

He leaned against the headboard and closed his eyes. He opened his mouth to say something but changed his mind and remained silent.

"Why did you stay away from me?" she asked. "Why didn't you come to me? I've missed you so much."

"You said you know what I did," he replied. "You cannot know and ask me why I did not come to you."

"I know you're having an affair with Giselle," she said softly. "I know you're probably going to keep on seeing her."

His jaw dropped. "You do know," he said with a look of incredulity on his face. "Someone must have seen us."

"As far as I know, no one else even suspects," she responded. "I hope no one else finds out about the two of you."

He let that soak in. He lifted his head again and looked into her eyes. "Are you going to ask me how I could have done this to you?"

"I don't have to ask," she replied. "I already know why you went to her."

Adam was amazed. At that moment, he would have

believed in the power of crystal balls. He was speechless.

"I saw when she flirted with you at the ball," Hannah continued. "When she came here Christmas day, she got you to sit with her in the swing. I could tell from the way she was acting, she was spinning her web. That wasn't when I first discovered she wanted you in her bed. The way she looked at you, even when Placide was around, spelled that out clearly. Some of the bad feelings Placide had for you were caused by his jealousy. He knew Giselle wanted you. He wanted you dead long before he walked in here that day to kill you."

Adam felt small. Hannah loved him deeply and he had cheated on her. He had no right to her love. He rose from the bed. "I am sorry I hurt you," he said. "I have no right to expect forgiveness."

"Are you leaving?" she asked in a pained voice as he took a step toward the door.

"Do you want me to stay?" he asked shamefacedly.

"Yes Adam, I want you to stay," she replied. "I want you to stay with me forever. I know I can't have that. I'll settle for you spending the night with me."

"How can you still want me to be with you?" he asked. He was unable to look into her eyes.

"Because I know who you are and I love you," she replied. "I told you I know why you went to her."

"Why do you think I went to her?" he asked.

"Because of the way Placide shamed you," she replied. "I saw you before I pulled the trigger and killed him. You think you were robbed of your pride and your manhood."

"You knew how scared I was that day?" he asked shamefully.

"Who wouldn't have been scared?" she responded. "You had no way of escaping. He was going to kill you. The danger was real. A lesser man would have begged for his life."

"I came close to begging for my life," he admitted. "I may have had you not shot him."

"You wouldn't have begged," she said positively. "You're not a coward."

Adam mulled over what she had said. Perhaps he was not a coward, but he had cheated on Hannah. "None of that excuses what I have done to you," he said. "Are you not hurt by what I have done?"

"I was dying inside until you came to me," she replied. "I can't deny that you hurt me deeply. What hurts even more is I know you aren't finished with her."

"I will tell her I will see her no more," he said. "I have not been with her since that first time."

"Do you love me, Adam?" she asked. "Do you really love me?"

"More than my own life," he replied. Tears trickled down his cheeks. "I know you must not believe me after what I have done."

She searched his eyes as she weighed his response. "I believe you," she said. "You aren't like most men, Adam. There's something inside of you that keeps on pushing." She hesitated. "I can't ask you to stop seeing her until whatever it is inside of you that pulled you to her burns out."

"I will tell her it is over," he insisted. "I was wrong to go to her."

"It'll pass," she said. "If you stop before it passes, she'll still have power over you. I know you'll never love her."

"You tell me it hurts you, yet you tell me to continue," he responded. He was baffled.

"I'm the only woman you'll ever love," she said emphatically. "I have to share your body with other women, but I'll never share your heart. Your heart belongs to me. I have to accept you as you are or reject you out of hand. I love you too much to reject you."

"I do not deserve you," he responded gently. He was awed by the faithfulness of the woman standing before him. "How can you still love me?"

"Because you were made for me and I was made for you," she replied. "It's that simple."

Adam put his arms around Hannah. "I do love you," he whispered in her ear. "I love only you. I will always love only you."

"I need you, Adam," she said. "Please make love to me."
He was amazed that she still wanted him that way,
knowing he had been with Giselle. He caught her up in his arms
and carried her to the bed. After they made love, he lay awake
thinking of the things she had said. He marveled at the woman
who lay in his arms.

*****

The January day was cold and overcast when the
London Blythingtons boarded the paddle wheeler that would
take them to Baton Rouge. There, they would board the
seagoing vessel that would return them to England. Edward
had supervised the loading of the luggage to make sure no
last minute hang-up would keep them from leaving on time.
"You must come again," Adam said as he shook
Edward's hand. "Perhaps your next visit could be in the
springtime when everything is growing."
Edward found the thought of returning to his
brother's home repulsive. "I have enough problems from this
trip to last for some time to come," he thought to himself.
"It will be some time before Timothy and I can find time for
another holiday," he said. "I am sure you recall how things
quickly pile up."
"Perhaps Hilda and Bernice could take a holiday without
you and Timothy," Adam suggested. "I am sure Annabelle
would love to have them spend more time with her."
Edward blanched. The last thing he wanted was
Hilda spending more time with Adam and Annabelle. He
turned to gauge Timothy's reaction. It was clear Timothy was
in agreement. He returned his attention to Adam. "I am sure
Timothy would agree with me," he said. "Hilda and Bernice
have many commitments in London. It would be impossible for
them to find the time."
"Not that we do not appreciate your offer," Timothy
added as Adam shook his hand. He hoped Bernice and Hilda
had not overheard Adam's offer.
Adam had no intention of inviting Hilda and Bernice to

return without their husbands. He was as tired of the London Bythingtons as Edward and Timothy were of him. Even though he enjoyed seeing the discomfort of his brothers, it was not to the point that he wanted to endure another visit.

"I wish Edward had decided to stay," Hilda said bitterly as she bid Annabelle good-bye.

"We'll miss you," Annabelle responded. "I'm so pleased to have met your family. I hope you'll come again."

Edward heard the exchange between his wife and Annabelle. "There is no way I would stay and it will be a cold day in hell when I come back here," he said under his breath. He wished Hilda would stop talking and let Adam and Annabelle disembark.

"I wish your father had been here to see us off," Bernice said. "He is such a gallant man."

"He had business to attend," Annabelle responded. "I'm sure he would've loved to be here."

"He would surely have been here," Hilda thought to herself, "if Bernice would not have made such a fool of herself over him. I am sure he wanted to see me off."

"I will miss you," Bernice said as she hugged Annabelle. "The time passed too quickly."

"Not quickly enough," Timothy thought to himself. "Say your good-byes, woman, so we can leave this place."

"I'll miss you," Annabelle responded. "I regret there's so much distance between our families. I hope you'll return soon."

"It is difficult to get Timothy and Edward to leave the firm even for a short while," Bernice replied sadly. "I fear it will be a long time before we return." She stopped and thought for a moment. "I have an excellent idea, Hilda and I could return without them." Her face lit up at the thought of visiting the American Blythingtons without the encumbrance of husbands.

Edward and Timothy groaned inwardly. "I will make sure Hilda never again steps foot in America," Edward whispered to Timothy.

"I agree," Timothy whispered to Edward. "I have gotten

more problems than I need from this trip."

Adam and Annabelle waved as the paddle wheeler churned away from the dock and made its way downstream.

"I hope this visit helps to heal the rift in Adam's family," Annabelle thought to herself.

"Edward and Timothy will catch hell from their wives for a long time," Adam thought gleefully. "I hope Edward and Timothy think about how rich I am every day for the rest of their lives. I hope those two toads feel small in their little offices."

CHAPTER SEVENTEEN

March 14, 1867 - March 18, 1867

    "Miss Hannah," Henry said excitedly, "Dares a Negro man been axin questins ta da feel hans bout Alfred Clark. He say he investigatin Mr. Clark's disperance."

    "What do you know about him?" Hannah asked.

    "He say he fum da Linken Freedim Ciety," Henry replied. "Da hans say he wans ta talk ta me. I come to see you when I heahed bout him."

    "Relax, Henry," Hannah said soothingly. "I'll tell you exactly what to say to him. When he questions you about Clark's whereabouts, tell him Mr. Clark spoke with Mr. Adam and Mr. Adam offered him two thousand dollars to leave Southern Kingdom and never return. Tell him Mr. Clark said he would leave and never come back if Mr. Adam would give him five thousand dollars. Tell him Mr. Adam gave Mr. Clark the five thousand dollars and he left as he said he would.

    "Let him know you and I were both in Mr. Adam's office when Mr. Clark accepted the money. If he asks you where Mr. Clark went, tell him when you last saw him, he was heading for the road."

    Henry nodded his head. He had listened very carefully to her instructions. "I sho does preciate you, Miss Hannah," Henry responded. "I dawn want Mr. Adam ta git mad at me."

    "Everything will be all right," Hannah said. "I'll speak with Mr. Adam."

    "Tank you Miss Hannah," Henry responded with relief in his voice.

    After Henry left, Hannah wondered at her meeting with

Henry. He had come to her with the problem of the investigator. When LeBlanc had been the plantation owner, she and Henry had been equals. He managed the field hands while she managed the house staff. Henry would have no more thought of calling her Miss Hannah as calling Jeremiah "mister." Her relationship with Adam and her education under Professor Pennington had given her distinction in the minds of the Negro people of the plantation. They looked to her now as the true wife of their master.

*****

"I expected someone to come here asking about him eventually," Adam responded when Hannah told him about her conversation with Henry. "I thought someone would have been here much sooner. As long as Henry stays with the story you gave him, everything will be all right. That was clever thinking on your part."

"I hope Henry doesn't get nervous and say more than I told him to say," she stated. "When he came to me, he looked like he'd seen a ghost."

"I am sure Henry's fear of me is greater than his fear of the investigator," he responded. "I think he will stay with the story you gave him."

"We may have to get rid of this one, too," she said. "He'll be dangerous if he learns too much."

"We will do what we have to do," he responded gravely. "It would be best to avoid complicating the situation by having yet another come to investigate this man's disappearance."

"Why don't you send word out to the man to come and meet with you?" she asked. "The sooner he leaves, the better."

"I do not want him to get suspicious," he replied. "I want him to get the story from the field hands before I speak with him. I will only confirm what he has already learned through his investigation."

*****

"I've been wanting to talk to you," the investigator said

to Henry. "My name is Caesius Brooks. I represent the Lincoln Freedom Society. One of our men hasn't been heard from in over a year. You may remember him; his name is Alfred Clark. I tracked him to this plantation. I understand he spent some time talking to the people on this plantation about organizing a labor movement."

Brooks stopped talking and waited for Henry to respond. Since he'd been asked no specific question, Henry remained silent.

"Are you afraid to talk to me?" Brooks asked.

"I ain't feared uh nobody," Henry answered belligerently. "You din ax no questin."

"Did you speak to Mr. Clark?" Brooks asked.

"I sho did," Henry replied and once again became silent.

"What did you think of Mr. Clark's effort to organize the workers?" Brooks asked.

"Da tings he sayed sounded good," Henry replied, "but he lit out ah heah real fass lak."

"Do you mean he left in a hurry?" Brooks asked. "Why did he leave?"

"Mr. Adam say he give him two tousan dollahs to leave," Henry replied. "Mr. Clark say he go and dawn come back ifin Mr. Adam give him five tousan dollahs. Mr. Adam gived him da money and he lit out ah heah. I tink Mr. Clark, he dawn care bout nuttin but hisself."

"Are you saying Mr. Clark accepted a bribe from Mr. Blythington?" Brooks asked incredulously.

"Dats zackly what I's sayin," replied Henry. "He kounit git outtah heah fass nuff."

"Did Mr. Blythington tell you this?" asked Brooks.

"I wuz dere," Henry replied as he recalled his disappointment when Clark agreed to abandon the field hands for five thousand dollars. "I kounit bliebe my ears when Clark tole Mr. Adam fo five tousan dollahs he gone light out and nevah come back."

"All of this seems very strange," Brooks said. "I would never have believed Mr. Clark could walk out on his commitment to our society. Are you sure he took the money and left promising never to return?"

"I done tolt you whut happint," Henry replied in an irritated voice. "Evahting happint jus lack I sayed."

"Do you mind if I continue to look around?" Brooks asked. "He may have left something behind that would give me some idea as to what took place."

"Dis place blongs ta Mr. Adam," Henry replied. "Befoe you goes pokin roun, you bettah ax Mr. Adam."

"Where can I find him?" Brooks asked.

"You kin go to da house and ax Miss Hannah," Henry replied.

Henry was relieved when Brooks left him and headed for the big house. He'd stuck to the things Hannah had told him to say. When the workers had asked earlier about what had happened to Clark, he had told them Clark had left after accepting a bribe from Mr. Adam. Some of the field hands might suspect there was foul play in the disappearance of Mr. Clark, but no one would voice their suspicions. Brooks was getting no more out of the field hands than he'd gotten from Henry.

*****

Hannah opened the door in response to Brooks' knock. "May I help you?" she asked.

"I hope so," Brooks replied. "I'm Caesius Brooks. I'm with the Lincoln Freedom Society. I'm looking for Mr. Blythington. Henry told me I might find him here."

"Mr. Blythington isn't in at the moment," Hannah responded. "He should be returning shortly."

"Do you mind if I wait?" Brooks asked.

"Not at all," Hannah replied. "I'll show you to his office."

Brooks had hoped to be left alone in Blythington's office so he could rummage around for anything that looked suspicious. Hannah offered him a chair and then sat and waited with him.

"Are you familiar with Mr. Alfred Clark?" Brooks asked.

"I met him the day he left here," Hannah replied.

"Do you know anything about his disappearance?" Brooks asked.

"What do you mean by his disappearance?" Hannah asked. "He left here on his own accord that evening and never returned."

"We haven't heard from him in over a year," Brooks responded. "I'm investigating his disappearance."

"As I said previously," Hannah continued. "I wasn't aware Mr. Clark had disappeared."

"Do you know what happened to him?" Brooks asked.

"I only know he accepted five thousand dollars from Mr. Blythington and then left promising never to return to this plantation."

"Mr. Blythington offered Mr. Clark five thousand dollars to leave this plantation?" Brooks asked.

"Mr. Blythington offered Mr. Clark two thousand dollars to leave and never return," Hannah replied. "Mr. Clark told Mr. Blythington if he raised the amount to five thousand dollars, he would leave and never return."

"Did Mr. Blythington tell you that story after Mr. Clark disappeared?" Brooks asked.

"Henry and I were in this room when Mr. Blythington spoke with Mr. Clark," Hannah replied patiently. "He left after Mr. Blythington gave him the money. We haven't seen him since that time."

"Are you sure that's what happened?" Brooks asked. "Mr. Clark was dedicated to our cause."

"Are you implying that I'm a liar?" Hannah asked challengingly. "Henry and I were here during the meeting between Mr. Clark and Mr. Blythington."

"Why did Mr. Blythington want you and Henry to be present during the meeting?" Brooks asked.

"Mr. Blythington would be the one to speak to about his reasons for Henry and I being in attendance," Hannah replied.

"Did he give you a reason?" Brooks asked.

"He said he wanted to show Henry that Mr. Clark wasn't as dedicated to his cause as he pretended to be," Hannah replied. "He said he wanted me as a witness in case anyone came here inquiring about Mr. Clark."

"How could he be certain Mr. Clark would accept the money?" Brooks asked.

"Again," Hannah replied, "that's a question you'll have to ask Mr. Blythington."

"Mr. Clark came here to show former slaves how to truly be free," Brooks said. "As a white woman, you couldn't understand what it was like to be enslaved. I find it difficult to believe the son of a runaway slave would betray his people. Mr. Clark was a personal friend of mine. I don't think he accepted a bribe. I think you're hiding something. I intend to find out what really happened."

Hannah was pleased that Brooks took her to be a white woman. This was evidence to her of the changes that had taken place in her life since meeting Adam. She was upset that he continued to question her veracity. "I'm only an employee of this plantation," she responded. "Mr. Clark speaking to the other employees about organizing meant nothing to me. If you choose to waste your time searching for something that doesn't exist, suit yourself. I did notice you used the past tense when you spoke of your friend. Did you mean you and Mr. Clark are no longer friends?"

"No, I don't mean that," Brooks replied sharply. "I don't think there was a bribe. I think someone would have to kill Mr. Clark to make him give up our cause."

Hannah laughed. "I don't mean to make light of you or your Mr. Clark," she said. "You hold him in such high regard. Have you ever considered what you'd do if someone offered you a fortune to turn your back on your cause?"

"I would never betray the cause," Brooks replied defensively. "It's so easy for you white folks to say something such as that. You have no idea what it's like to be a slave."

"Have you ever been a slave, Mr. Brooks?" Hannah asked. "Have you worked from sunup to sundown toiling in the fields?"

"My father ran away from a plantation in Georgia," Brooks replied defensively. "He told me and my brothers and sisters the horrors of slavery. I want to make sure my people are truly set free."

Hannah thought of her years in slavery. She hated the institution that had caused so much suffering for so many people. The young man standing before her was filled with ideals and secondhand knowledge about slavery. He wanted the slaves to rebel against their former masters and ask for higher wages and better conditions, but he had nothing better to offer the people if the landowners refused to implement changes or if they decided to run the former slaves off and hire immigrants to work the land. Education was the only thing that was going to truly set her people free. Ignorant people, whether Negro or white, would always remain at the bottom.

"I don't want to belittle your cause," Hannah said. "I think you're well meaning, but I really don't think you know the first thing about how to lift your people out of their quagmire. If the people don't work, they can't eat. The people know nothing about business or commerce. Even if they were able to take over the plantation, they would have no idea how to operate the business side of the plantation."

"We could teach them how to do that," Brooks said defiantly.

Hannah laughed once more. "How can you teach them what you don't know?" she asked. "Your cause is doomed to failure unless you can come up with real solutions to the problems of the Negro people."

"We do have real solutions," Brooks responded angrily. "You white people are all alike. All you do is put us down."

"I'm not putting you down," Hannah responded. "You have good intentions, but that's all you have. Recruit people to your cause who can teach the Negro people arithmetic, reading, writing and how to operate businesses. Those are the things that will set your people free."

*****

Adam walked through the door and found Hannah speaking with a Negro man. "Is there a problem?" he asked.

"No, Mr. Blythington," Hannah replied. "Mr. Brooks is

asking questions about Mr. Clark."

"Mr. Clark?" Adam asked with a bemused look on his face.

"The young man who was here talking about organizing the field hands," Hannah responded.

"Oh, now I remember," he said. "Is he not the fellow who accepted the money to vacate his cause?"

"Mr. Blythington, I'd like to ask you some questions if you don't mind," Brooks said. He took an instant dislike to Blythington.

"Certainly," Adam responded. He sat behind his desk and made himself comfortable.

Brooks cleared his throat. "My name is Caesius Brooks," the man began. "I represent the Lincoln Freedom Society." He gazed at Blythington to assess his reaction.

"Please go on," Adam said as he nodded

"Mr. Clark was a member of our organization," Brooks continued. "We've had no contact with him in over a year. He was last seen at your plantation."

"You speak of Mr. Clark in the past tense," Adam observed. "Has something happened to him?"

"That's what I'm here to find out," Brooks replied. "No one has seen him or heard from him in over a year. We find that very strange."

"What does that have to do with me?" Adam asked.

"Mr. Clark was a very dedicated man," Brooks replied. "Frankly, I don't believe he would've abandoned our cause voluntarily. I'm here to learn what happened to him while he was on your plantation."

"I can only tell you what Henry, my field hand supervisor, told me about him and the brief conversation we had in this office," Adam responded. "Aside from that, I know nothing about Mr. Clark."

"What did Henry tell you about Mr. Clark?" Brooks asked.

"Henry told me that Mr. Clark was attempting to organize the field hands," Adam replied. "I asked Henry to arrange to have Mr. Clark meet with me in this office. I asked

Hannah and Henry to remain in this office as witnesses to what would transpire in our meeting."

"Why would you feel that witnesses were necessary?" Brooks asked.

"I was convinced Mr. Clark had a price," Adam replied with a smile. "It was a simple matter of learning what amount would cause him to abandon his principles. I wanted Henry here to witness Clark accept money to desert his cause. I wanted Hannah present as a witness in case someone, such as yourself, came around later asking questions."

"It's difficult for me to believe that Mr. Clark would accept money to abandon our cause," Brooks said skeptically. He was beginning to wonder if Blythington had really found Clark's Achilles heel. "That goes against everything he stood for. Please tell me about your meeting with Mr. Clark?"

"Mr. Clark sat where you are now sitting," Adam began. "Henry sat in that chair." He pointed to a chair across the room and to his left. He moved his arm and pointed to the opposite side of the office. "Hannah sat in that chair where she is now sitting. Mr. Clark explained his cause to me. I listened to him for about half an hour and then offered him five hundred dollars to leave and never return. We went back and forth about the amount of money until I offered him two thousand dollars. At that point, he told me for five thousand dollars he would leave and never return."

Brooks groaned inwardly as he listened to Blythington's story. Could it be possible that his good friend had accepted money from this man? "What was Henry's reaction?" he asked.

"Henry was devastated," Adam replied, again smiling. "I think he believed Clark was here to show the Negro people a better way of life."

Blythington's story was coinciding with the accounts of Henry and Hannah. They had either rehearsed their stories very well or they were telling the truth. He recalled Henry's anger when he related his disappointment in Clark. "What was Hannah's reaction?" he asked.

"You may ask her that question," Adam replied. "I do not think it surprised her that Clark's fidelity could be purchased."

"Do you think everyone has a price?" Brooks asked.

"I would like to be able to speak to you about the purity of mankind," Adam replied. "Unfortunately, it has been my experience that everyone does have a price. One only has to discover the price of a person's integrity."

Brooks shook his head. He hoped Blythington was wrong with his assumption. He wondered if there was a price for his own integrity. "That's a jaded way to look at life, isn't it?" he asked. "Don't you believe there are truly good and honest people in this world?"

"There were four people in this office when Mr. Clark sold his integrity for five thousand dollars," Adam replied. "You have spoken to two of us. Feel free to question Henry about our meeting. I do wish Mr. Clark would contact you so you might ask him that question."

"I do too," Brooks said as he thought about his friend. "I'd like nothing more." He sighed and then brought his thoughts back to the meeting. "I already spoke to Henry. Do you mind if I look around?"

"I have nothing to hide," Adam replied, "but I do not want anyone searching through my property and I do not want anyone stirring up my employees."

"I had not thought to ask Henry how Clark arrived here," he thought to himself. "I must speak to him as soon as possible."

"Your employees are free to listen to me if they choose," Brooks responded. "We are a free people."

"You are correct," Adam agreed. "If the employees want to meet you somewhere away from my property and on their own time, they may. I will not have you speaking to them on my property nor during their work hours." He stood to indicate the meeting was at an end.

"Thank you for your time, Mr. Blythington," Brooks said after he rose from his chair. "This isn't finished."

Adam watched as Brooks walked out of the office. He sat at his desk for a few minutes before addressing Hannah. "Please make sure Brooks is out of the house," he said. "I want to make sure he does not overhear us."

She rose from her chair and left the office. "He got on his horse and rode toward the road," she said when she returned. "You can speak freely."

"I never thought to ask Henry by what mode of transportation Clark arrived on this plantation," he said. "We need to make sure there is nothing on this place that connects us with Clark. I have a feeling Brooks is going to come back and snoop around."

"I'll send Fred to find Henry," she responded. "We can meet when he gets here."

"Thank you, Hannah," he responded. "Please let me know as soon as he arrives."

As he waited, he tried to concentrate on the paperwork that lay on his desk. He looked up when Hannah walked in with Henry. "Please sit down," he said.

Hannah and Henry sat. "Henry, how did your meeting with Mr. Brooks turn out?" he asked.

"I tink it wuz good, Mr. Adam," Henry replied. "He sho do ax a lotta questins."

"What did you say to him?" Adam asked.

"I tolt him dat Mr. Clark done took da five tousan dollahs an lit out," Henry replied. "He axed me ifin I wuz sho."

"Good," Blythington said. "We need to make sure our stories match."

"Yassuh," Henry responded.

"Henry, do you remember how Clark arrived on this plantation?" Adam asked.

"He come on a hoss," Henry replied.

"Do you mean to tell me we have his tack in our barn?" Adam asked.

"Yassuh," Henry replied. "We been usin da hoss and da saddle."

Adam struggled to control himself. He was upset with himself for overlooking something as important as this. "I want to see the horse and the saddle immediately," he said.

"Da saddle in da bone," Henry responded. "I kin ketch da hoss and bring it in da bone."

"Do so right now," Adam said. "I will meet you in the barn."

Henry left to carry out his employer's orders."

"Do you think Brooks can identify Clark's horse and saddle?" Hannah asked.

"I have no idea," Adam replied. "I do not want to take that chance. I cannot believe I overlooked something that simple. Killing Brooks will only complicate things. We need to get rid of that horse and saddle."

"Brooks is smart," she said. "He may be watching the plantation."

"We will have to wait until after dark before we can do anything," he responded.

Adam walked to the barn and met with Henry. He inspected the horse and saddle. The saddle resembled many of the other saddles in the barn. At first glance, there did not seem to be anything extraordinary about the horse or the saddle. Henry lifted the left stirrup. Adam noted the initials "LFS" stamped into the leather. He examined the horse more closely. There was a small brand on the left rump of the horse showing the same initials. Once again, he chastised himself for his lapse. Evidence that Clark had not left of his own free will was clearly waiting to be uncovered by the investigator.

"Henry," Adam ordered, "I want this horse and saddle locked in a stall until nightfall. Brooks is not to be allowed on this land until we have destroyed the evidence."

Henry sensed that Mr. Adam was very upset. He didn't understand what could've upset him. To him, Clark's horse and saddle were indistinguishable from the other horses and saddles on the plantation, but he knew better than to question Mr. Adam's reasoning.

"Yassuh, Mr. Adam," Henry responded.

"After it is dark," Adam continued, "I want you to take the horse and saddle out to the most remote corner of this property. You are to shoot the horse and then bury both the horse and the saddle. Be sure you are not followed."

The order startled Henry. "Mr. Adam?" he asked, "is you show you wants ta do dat?"

Adam was displeased with Henry for questioning his order. His first impulse was to lash out at the Negro man. He decided instead to explain the necessity of carrying out the order. "Henry," he began, "it is very important that we get rid of the horse and saddle. They both carry the markings of the society Brooks represents. At a glance, Brooks will know this was Clark's property."

Henry had seen some scratches on the saddle leather, but they'd made no sense to him. He wished he'd paid more attention in Professor Pennington's classes, but it was all he could do to stay awake as the professor went on. He didn't understand how such insignificant markings could identify the horse and saddle, but he understood the sense of urgency in his employer's voice. "I's gone make show dey ain't gone be foun," he said. "You kin blieve dat, Mr. Adam."

"Be sure that no one follows you," Adam added. "Brooks may be watching us now."

"Yassuh, Mr. Adam," Henry responded.

*****

Brooks was watching through his spyglass as Henry led the brown horse into the barn. He thought little of the incident until he saw Blythington walk to the barn shortly after. He wondered if the horse could have been the one issued by the society to Alfred Clark. He decided to wait until after dark and then make his way to the barn to examine the horse.

Brooks waited until well after dark before climbing down from the tree from which he had been watching the plantation buildings. The darkness of the night and his unfamiliarity with the terrain caused him to stumble several times.

As he approached the vicinity of the barn, he saw the silhouette of a man on horseback leading another horse. He tried to get close enough to identify the man. He ran in a crouched position in the direction of the silhouette. In his haste, he tripped over the roots of an oak tree and banged his head against a large exposed root.

When he regained consciousness, he had no idea how long he had been lying beneath the tree. He lifted his head and tried to stand, but the world began to spin. He lay for a while longer and then once again attempted to rise. The world was no longer spinning, but he had difficulty getting his bearings. He discovered that his legs were still too weak to support him and dropped down to his knees. As he knelt rubbing the knot on his forehead, he looked toward the barn. The man and the horses were no longer there.

After kneeling for several minutes, he stood and made his way into the barn. Horses occupied several of the stalls. In the darkness he couldn't distinguish the colors of the horses, let alone examine them for familiar markings. He would have to devise a plan that would allow him to go into the barn during daylight hours. He decided to return in the morning and speak with Henry.

Brooks cautiously retraced his footsteps. He found his horse in the thicket where he had left it tied. As he rode, each step his horse took caused his head to pound. He was hungry and weary. He hoped the people at the house where he was staying would have food waiting for him.

*****

Henry felt an aching deep in his bones as he unsaddled his horse. In only a couple of hours it would be time to begin the day. He wanted to get as much sleep as possible before the start of the new day.

It had taken him most of the night to dig a hole large enough to bury the horse. He felt badly about shooting a perfectly good horse. The horse and saddle were now buried in a remote place on the plantation away from Brooks' prying eyes.

The bed felt good as he lowered his body onto the corn shuck mattress. His wife stirred but didn't awaken. He listened to Ellen as she slept. He was glad he didn't have to lose sleep while she asked a bunch of questions. In a short while he drifted off to sleep.

It seemed his head had barely touched the pillow when

he felt Ellen shaking him.

"Is you gonna stay in da bed all da day?" she asked as she shook her husband. "Whut kinna feel boss you is stayin in da bed lack dat?"

Henry's body ached as he lifted himself from the bed. It was going to be a long day. "Jus fix sumptin ta eat," Henry said. "I gotsta git stawted."

Ellen quickly fixed breakfast for her family. They needed to eat well to have energy to chop the cotton all day long in the late spring heat. She gazed at her husband as she stood before her wood stove. His eyes were red and he was moving slowly.

"Is you sick?" she asked. "You show dawn look good. Whut time it wuz you got back heah?"

"I dawn got no pockit watch," Henry replied crossly. "Soons I could I wuz in da bed."

"You sho duz look a sight," Ellen observed. "You sho you din git you some likker?"

"Jus fix da food, Woman," Henry responded. "I got no time fo nunnah yo lip."

Ellen put her head down and concentrated on her cooking. Henry was in no mood to discuss his business.

Henry ate his breakfast in silence and then walked out to the barn.

"I been looking for you, "Fred said as he came up to Henry in the barn. "Mr. Adam say he want to talk to you. You best come quick."

Henry groaned as he started for the big house. He hoped he had no other important things to handle for Mr. Adam. He had decided he'd set the field hands to working and then find a tree to nap under.

Hannah opened the door and let Henry into the house. "He's in his office," she said. "He's been waiting for you."

"Whut duz dese people tink I is?" Henry asked himself. "Dey sends me off ta berry a good hoss in da middle eh da night and dey specks me up bright an early."

"Were you able to complete your task?" Adam asked as Henry walked into his office.

"Yassuh, Mr. Adam," Henry replied. "I done jus whut

you tolt me."

"Good," Adam responded. "I know you must be tired. You may tell Matthew to supervise the field hands while you get some rest."

Henry smiled brightly. "I show duz tank you, Mr. Adam," he said. "I kin hawdly keep mah eyes opent."

As Henry was making his way to his cottage, he was enjoying his good fortune until he spied Brooks coming up the drive. He groaned inwardly as Brooks dismounted and headed his way.

"Mr. Blythington said he has nothing to hide," Brooks said. "I want to take a look in the barn."

Henry doubted that Mr. Adam had given Brooks permission to search the barn. "You best ax Mr. Adam fore you goes in da bone," he responded.

Brooks saw Blythington as he walked out on the side porch.

At the same time, Adam saw Brooks and began walking toward him. "I hoped you had completed your investigation," he commented.

"I'd like to take a look in the barn and perhaps look at some of your horses," Brooks responded. "I don't remember what you answered when I asked you how Mr. Clark left this place."

"You did not ask that question of me," Adam responded.

"How did Mr. Clark leave?" Brooks asked.

"Perhaps Henry would know that answer," Adam replied. "I did not follow him outside."

"Henry?" Brooks asked, "can you tell me what sort of transportation Mr. Clark was using when he left here?"

"He wuz ridin on a brown hoss," Henry replied.

"Was the horse pulling a buggy?" Brooks asked.

"I done sayed he wuz ridin on da hoss," Henry replied irritably. "Wunnit no buggy."

"Are you sure you saw him ride away?" Brooks asked.

Henry was tired and frustrated. He'd lost almost an entire night's sleep because of Brooks' prying and now Brooks was keeping him away from his bed. He'd had enough of

Brooks.

"I is sho," Henry replied tersely. "I done seed Clark ax fo da money to light outta heah. Mr. Adam say you kin look in da bone, I shows you da bone. I ain't ansing nunnah yo questins no mo."

"Mr. Brooks," Adam said, "you may look in the barn. You may look at the horses. I have no idea what you expect to find. I agree with Henry; your questions have become tiring."

Henry followed Brooks as he headed for the barn. Brooks went from stall to stall. He stopped when he came upon a brown horse in one of the rear stalls. "I want to look closely at this one," he said. He examined the horse thoroughly and then frowned.

"Sumptin wrong wit da hoss?" Henry asked.

"No, not really," Brooks replied. "This horse looks a great deal like the one Mr. Clark was riding."

"Dats Mr. Adam's hoss," Henry responded emphatically. "Clark ain't nevah done rode on dat hoss."

"I know it isn't Mr. Clark's horse," Brooks said defensively. "I only said it looks like his horse."

"Well, it ain't, "Henry said triumphantly. He was beginning to enjoy Brooks' discomfort.

Brooks cast an angry look at Henry and began to look at the saddles. After examining them closely, he stood and faced Henry. "Do you have any other saddles?" he asked.

"Dems all da saddles we's got," Henry replied.

"Where are the other horses?" Brooks asked.

"Deys in da hoss pasta," Henry replied.

"Would you take me out to the horse pasture?" Brooks asked.

"Dats da one rat nex ta da bone," Henry replied. "When you walks outta da bone rat dere, you be in da pasta."

Henry watched as Brooks rode his horse from one group of horses to another. After looking over the horses, Brooks rode slowly back to the barn. He dismounted and walked up to Henry.

"Are you sure those are all the horses?" Brooks asked wearily.

Henry stepped closer to Brooks. "I gone break yo bones iffin you ax me one mo questin," Henry said as he towered over Brooks. "You done seed all da hosses. I done tolt you all da tings I knows. You kin git outta heah and go look fo yo frin. You ain't gone fine him heah."

Brooks took a couple of steps back. He could see that Henry was angry and exasperated with him. "Where could he have gone?" he asked fearfully.

"I specks you needs to go lookin fo him," Henry replied. "He ain't heah, dats fo sho."

Brooks shook his head slowly. If Clark had indeed accepted the bribe and left the plantation, he had no idea where to start looking for him. He hated to acknowledge that his friend had accepted the five thousand dollars to betray the cause. Everything he could think to do that would gain knowledge of Clark's whereabouts had been done. He had come to a dead-end. He thought of the words he had chosen. He hoped his friend hadn't ended up dead. "It is possible he took the money and started a new life." Clark's family would be devastated when they heard the news.

CHAPTER EIGHTEEN

March 20, 1867 - March 27, 1867

"Adam!" Annabelle cried out. "Our baby's coming."

Adam stirred from a sound sleep. He had only been in their bed about an hour. He was weary from the hours he had spent in Hannah's bedroom. "Are you sure?" he asked.

"Of course I'm sure," she replied.

"I will send someone for Dr. Joubert," he said as he slipped into his clothes. He left the bedroom, ran down the hallway where the house servants were quartered and pounded on Fred's door.

"Yessuh," Fred said as he gazed at Adam through bleary eyes.

"Go into town and get Dr. Joubert," Adam said. "Tell him it is time."

Fred hurriedly dressed and then ran out of the house to saddle a horse. In a matter of moments, he was galloping off to town.

Adam ran into Hannah as he was hastening back to his room. "Perhaps we should get Cleopatra in case Dr. Joubert can't be located," she said. "She'd know what to do until he gets here."

"That may be best," he agreed. "Please send someone for her."

Hannah went to Mary's room and roused her from her bed. "I need you to go and fetch Cleopatra," she said. "Miss Annabelle is having her baby."

Mary dressed without delay, ran to Cleopatra's small house on Shady Lane and awakened her. "Miss Hannah say it's time," she cried out. "She say you gots to hurry."

Mary waited as Cleopatra dressed behind the blanket that was strung out to divide the room. After a few moments, she walked out from behind the blanket and picked up her satchel of "birthing" tools.

Mary returned to the plantation house with Cleopatra at her heels. Cleopatra rushed into the master bedroom. "I gone take care of you, Miss Annabelle," she said. "Dawn you worry bout nuttin."

Adam paced back and forth as he waited for the arrival of his first legitimate child. He looked at his watch. Annabelle had been in labor over three hours. Once again, he wished for a boy. He would have his heir. He wondered why it was taking so long. He considered going into the bedroom but decided against it. Hannah would soon come out and tell him how the birth was advancing.

Several minutes later, Hannah walked out into the hall where Adam was pacing. "She's doing fine," she stated. "Cleopatra told me Annabelle is a woman who's built for having babies."

"How long before the baby will be born?" he asked.

"It's difficult to tell," she replied. "I was in labor with Martha for a little over eleven hours."

"I had not realized it had taken that long," he responded. "I regret I was not there with you."

"I do too," she said. "How I wished you had been there with me."

Hannah turned and walked back into Annabelle's bedroom. Adam began pacing up and down the hall once more. His thoughts were centered on the child Annabelle was bringing into the world. He wanted a healthy and intelligent son. He would make it clear to Annabelle the shaping of the boy's life would be left entirely to him. He envisioned his son riding over the fields of Southern Kingdom with him. He would raise the boy to be strong and self-reliant. He would be a worthy heir to Southern Kingdom.

Annabelle cried out as another contraction tortured her body. "It gone be soon, Missy," Cleopatra exhorted. "You bout dere."

Annabelle gazed around the room after the pain subsided. "Where's Dr. Joubert?" she asked once again. "He should be here by now."

"Don't you remember, Fred returned without him?" Hannah replied. "He said Dr. Joubert was called out to deliver another baby."

"I remember now," Annabelle exclaimed. "Did he speak to young Dr. Joubert?"

"I don't think he thought to go and see him," Hannah replied. "He spoke to Dr. Joubert's wife. Maybe she'll ask young Dr. Joubert to come."

"I hope so," she said weakly. "Where's Adam?"

"He's out in the hallway," Hannah replied. "He's waiting just outside the door."

"He wants a son," Annabelle said faintly. "I hope we have a boy." Before she could say anything further, another contraction battered her body. She cried out once more from the pain.

"He comin now," Cleopatra said excitedly. "It gone be ovah soon."

Annabelle pushed and the baby's head appeared. She cried out in pain as her baby made his way into the world.

"Jus a lil more," Cleopatra urged. "You bout done."

Annabelle felt excruciating pain as Charles Dupre' Blythington passed from her body and cried out to all the world he had been born.

"It's a boy," Hannah said as she looked upon the naked infant. "You have a son."

Hannah opened the door and walked out into the hallway. "Your wish came true," she said to Adam. "You now have your heir."

Adam wrapped his arms around Hannah and kissed her lips. "This is what we wanted," he said.

Hannah returned his kiss then quickly pulled herself away from him before any of the servants appeared. She was happy for Adam, but saddened because she hadn't brought forth his heir. "Yes, it's exactly what we wanted," she responded.

"Where is Fred?" Adam asked. "Please send him to Belle

Bois to tell the good news to Jacques Dupre'. He now has the grandson he has been hoping for."

"I'll find Fred," Hannah said as she turned from Adam. She was filled with trepidation as she thought of Adam's heir. She prayed the birth of his son wouldn't take his love away from Martha.

"Mr. Adam, you kin come in now," Cleopatra said. "Yo boy wiff Miz Annabelle."

Adam walked into his bedroom and saw his son lying in Annabelle's arms. It was difficult to determine who the boy favored. The child had dark hair but he and Annabelle were both dark-haired. His face was red and his eyes were closed. It was too early to ascertain.

"How do you like your son?" Annabelle asked as she smiled weakly.

"He is wonderful," Adam replied.

"Would you like to hold him?" Annabelle asked.

"I think I should wait until he is older," Adam replied. "I do not want to hurt him."

"You won't hurt him," she responded. "You only need to make sure you support his head. His neck won't be strong enough for the first few months."

He lifted his son and held him against his shoulder. "He is so small," he remarked. "It will be some time before he is able to ride with me."

"He'll be able to ride with you soon enough," she responded. "You can teach him to ride in the barnyard. I want him to stay with me until he's older."

"He will begin his lessons with Professor Pennington when he is four years of age," he said emphatically. "When he is five, he will accompany me during the mornings and have his lessons during the afternoons."

"Adam," Annabelle implored, "please allow him time to be a child."

"This child is my heir," he responded in a firm voice. "He will be taught the skills he needs to take over after I am gone. I want him to manage Lance des Chenes when he reaches the age of eighteen. He must grow up to be a leader. A woman cannot teach him to be a man."

"Don't you want our son to have a soft heart?" she asked
as tears began to roll down her cheeks. "He has to learn how to
be a friend and how to love."

"I will teach him those things," he replied coldly.

Annabelle came near to telling Adam he couldn't teach
their son things he didn't know. She held her tongue. "Hopefully
he'll change his mind after he spends more time with our son,"
she thought to herself.

He took her silence for acquiescence. He was pleased to
have settled the matter once and for all.

"This son will be raised by his father," he said to himself.
"Any other children who are born of the marriage may be raised
solely by Annabelle. That really does not concern me. Only
this son will be the heir to Southern Kingdom. Charles Dupre'
Blythington, all of this will be yours some day."

"I still think he should have a saint's name," she said.
"Remember, you had to agree to abide by the rules of the church
before we could be married."

"His name is Charles," Adam responded forcefully. "I
will not give in to the silliness of the church."

He had insisted on naming his son Charles, but
she'd hoped he would give in when he held the child in his
arms. "Charles is such a formal name for a petite baby," she
commented. "Perhaps we should call him Charley."

He shook his head. "He must be worthy of his position
in life," he responded. "We shall call him Charles."

Her heart was saddened. Adam was determined to raise
Charles in his image. She wanted to demand that Adam recant
his decisions, but felt too tired to argue. She would work in
subtle ways to make sure Charles would be softhearted.

Adam handed Charles back to Annabelle and sat in a
chair. He watched as his wife held his newborn son. "You have
so much to learn," Adam said to himself while he watched
Charles as he lay sleeping at his mother's side. "You will learn
how to run our kingdom." He recalled Alfred Clark's visit
to Southern Kingdom. "You will learn how to defend our
kingdom."

"Let me see him," Jacques said as he entered the bedroom followed by Giselle. "I want to hold my grandson." He walked to the edge of the bed and looked down on his daughter and his little grandson. "Mon petite enfant. I'm your grandfather."

Annabelle had fallen asleep. She awakened when she heard the sound of her father's voice. "Isn't he wonderful?" she asked.

"Mangifique," Jacques replied. "He's magnificent. I have a grandchild. I can now die happy." Jacques lifted Charles from beside his mother and sat in a rocking chair with him. "How long I have yearned to rock my own grandchild. If only Placide were here to see him." Tears began to roll down his face. "I fear that we'll never again see Placide."

"Oh, Pappa," Annabelle said. "Do we have to be sad at a time like this?"

"You're right, mas Cheiri," he replied as his countenance brightened. "It's a time for joy."

"I want to hold him, too," Giselle said as she took the infant from Jacques' arms. "He looks so much like our Placide." She met Adam's eyes and gave him a wicked look.

Adam was not pleased with Giselle's comparison of Charles to Placide. "I find he favors Annabelle," he said.

"What have you named him?" Jacques asked.

"Charles Dupre' Blythington," Annabelle replied. "Adam thought you'd want a Dupre' to follow after you."

Jacques smiled as tears flowed from his eyes. "Adam, you're so kind," he said. He couldn't continue.

"The Dupre' line will go on forever," Adam responded. "It is the least I could do to show my recognition of all you mean to us."

Tears trickled down Jacques' face. After several minutes, he regained his composure. "It's wonderful that Annabelle married such a kind man," he said. "I lost one son, but I thank God He has given me another. The two of you have given me a grandson. My heart overflows with joy."

After hearing her father express the joy of having Adam as a son, Annabelle lamented the cross words she'd had with Adam. "He's not trying to keep Charles away from me," she thought to herself. "He wants to make sure Charles has the proper training to succeed him as the owner of Southern Kingdom. The poor man had all of this responsibility thrust upon him with very little preparation. He only wants to make sure Charles is prepared when the time comes for him to manage all of his father's property."

*****

"I came as quickly as I could," Dr. Robert Joubert said as Hannah led him into the master bedroom. Angelina walked in with him. "It seems God chose last night to increase the population of St. Landry Parish. Father hasn't returned home yet. Mother told Angelina you had sent for him."

"Cleopatra was very capable," Adam said coldly. There was something about this young doctor that really set him off.

"I'm sure she is," Robert responded. "Still, I would've preferred if a competent physician had been here."

"There was no need," Adam stated frostily. "Cleopatra has delivered the children of our plantation for years."

Robert chose to let the matter drop. "How are you feeling?" he asked Annabelle.

"I feel fine," she replied. She was once again upset with Adam. "Why did he have to be so insulting to Robert?" she wondered angrily.

"May I hold him?" Angelina asked. Charles was feeding happily at his mother's breast.

"As soon as he's filled his stomach," Annabelle answered with a smile. "He seems never to have enough."

Robert moved closer to Annabelle's side. He felt her forehead and then held her wrist. "There's no fever and your heartbeat is strong," he commented. "You don't seem much the worse for the ordeal you've been through."

"Cleopatra said I'm made for having babies," Annabelle responded. "I would've made a good brood mare."

"I hope I have an easy time when my turn comes," Angelina said with a happy smile.

Annabelle looked at her friend closely. "Are you going to have a baby?" she asked.

"Yes, I am," Angelina answered, "but I'm not pregnant yet. The good doctor here agrees that we can have several children."

"How many children do you want?" Annabelle asked.

"Maybe a dozen," Angelina replied. "Wouldn't it be great to have a house full of children?"

"Adam, isn't that wonderful?" Annabelle asked. "A house filled with children's laughter."

Adam did not want to be dragged into their conversation. "Wonderful," he stated absently.

Charles pulled his head away momentarily from his mother's breast. Angelina reached down and took him into her arms. "He's so sweet," she cooed. "I can't wait to hold my own baby."

*****

"How do you feel about fathering your heir?" Hannah asked as she lay in Adam's arms that night.

"Strangely, I feel no different," he replied. "I guess it will take some time to adjust."

"I guess it's different with men," she said. "My adjustment to motherhood was immediate."

He remained silent for a short while. "How do you feel now that Annabelle's child is born?" he asked apprehensively.

It was her turn to be silent. She turned so she could see into his eyes. "Does it make you feel any differently about Martha?" she asked nervously.

"Somehow, I knew that was what you were wondering," he replied. "No one can ever take her place. She is my first child. I wanted to acknowledge her as my child to the world. You are the one who insisted her birth be kept secret."

"Do you really mean that?" she asked. This was what she had hoped for but had doubted would happen. She feared now that Adam had his legitimate heir, Martha wouldn't mean as much to him.

"What kind of man do you think I am," he asked in a hurt voice, "if you could think I would stop loving Martha with all of my heart?"

"A lot has changed," she said.

"Nothing has changed between us," he cried out. "I love you and I love Martha."

She held her tongue. He was still having an affair with Giselle. That was a change that had taken place since Martha's birth. Giselle had some strange hold on him. He had never again spoken of her, but she noticed at times he made love with less fervor. His heir coming into the world was a great change.

"No, nothing has changed," she agreed weakly. "It would break my heart if you were to reject Martha."

"That will never happen," he said firmly. "No one can take your place and no one can take her place."

Hannah wished she felt sure of herself. She still hoped Adam's fixation with Giselle would burn itself out. The birth of the son who'd be the heir to Southern Kingdom had caused her to feel insecure about her place with Adam.

"What are you thinking?" he asked. He turned her face toward his so he could look into her eyes. He discovered she was crying. He gathered her closer to himself. "What are you thinking?" he asked softly.

"Things I don't want to think," she answered. "I'm wondering if you still love me."

"Of course, I love you," he replied as he kissed her tears away. "I could never love any other woman. Why would you wonder if I love you?"

"Why indeed?" she thought. "Another woman and a child for his wife shouldn't cause me to wonder? Is he that obtuse?"

She felt his manhood stiffen as he lay next to her. Part of her wanted him to move away from her and part of her wanted to make love with him. He made no move to take her. The next step would be up to her.

The love she felt for Adam welled up inside of her. She ran her fingers lightly against his chest. Her breathing grew deeper as he began to caress and kiss her body.

"I love you," he said hoarsely. "I use that word with no woman but you."

Her heart was gladdened. She believed he was being truthful. She surrendered herself completely to the man she loved.

*****

Adam waited until he could hear Annabelle breathing deeply. When he was satisfied that she was fast asleep, he rose from the bed and put his robe on. Annabelle sat up in bed with a jolt and looked around. She felt the empty space where shortly before he had been lying. "Where are you Adam?" she called out loudly.

"I am here," he answered. "I was thirsty. Would you like something to drink?"

"No, thank you," she replied fretfully, "I was having a bad dream."

He returned to the bed and sat down. He wanted her to go back to sleep so he could meet with Hannah, but he felt he had to say something. "Tell me about your dream," he said.

"It was awful," she sobbed. "Placide had returned." She hesitated a moment.

"How could a dream about Placide returning be bad?" he asked. His stomach was beginning to churn. Had she dreamed about Placide finding him with Giselle?

"I know it sounds strange," she continued. "Placide was very angry at you and wanted to kill you. I was begging him not to shoot you." She stopped and searched his face in the weak light. "He was telling me why he wanted to kill you when I awoke."

"What reason did he give?" he asked tensely.

"Oh, Adam," she cried out. "It was terrible. He said you were a scoundrel. He said you turned Giselle against him."

"Why would you dream such a thing?" he asked. He fought to make his voice sound normal.

She tried to look into his eyes in the dim light. "The dream seemed so real and disturbing," she said. "Please hold me."

He lay beside his wife and held her. He was soaked in his own perspiration. He was thankful she could not see him in the darkness.

"I know you didn't turn Giselle against him," she wept. "I'm so sorry that kind of thing could have even entered my mind."

"You cannot control your dreams," he said consolingly. "Your dream may have been caused by something you ate."

"Yes," she agreed hopefully. "It had to be something I ate."

He lay in his bed holding Annabelle until she again drifted off to sleep. He thought of making another attempt to go up to Hannah but decided it was best to remain with his wife. She would be very disturbed if she awakened again and found him gone.

CHAPTER NINETEEN

April 4, 1867 - June 21, 1867

"All I am to you is a cheap whore you make love to in a shack!" Giselle shouted.

Adam was caught by surprise. She had met him at the door when he arrived. She had almost torn his clothes off in her haste to make love. She had held nothing back as they made love, but now, she was shouting at him angrily.

He looked around the room. While this was not the finest of houses, it certainly was not a shack. "What do you want?" he asked in exasperation. "I am married to your sister-in-law. I cannot take you out dining or to the theater."

"You could bring gifts," she replied angrily.

"You accuse me of treating you like a whore," he exclaimed, "yet you ask for gifts. Is that not hypocritical?"

"Not to pay for the sex, you ass!" she shouted once more. "To show your affection. You never even tell me you love me."

"You have never told me you love me," he responded.

"Perhaps I would if you said it first," she responded petulantly.

"Do you love me?" he asked.

"Why do you choose to change the subject?" she asked acrimoniously.

"Why are you angry and what do you want of me?" he asked. "I have no idea why you turn from lover to shrew so quickly."

"Shrew!" she shouted. "How dare you. I've had all I can take of you, Mr. Adam Blythington." She rose from the bed and began to dress.

Adam rolled off of the bed and slipped into his drawers. Whatever was eating away at her was beyond his comprehension. Maybe it was time to terminate the relationship.

"You won't beg me to stay?" she asked in a playful voice. "Have I satisfied your desire already?"

He shook his head. "Who are you?" he asked. "One moment you are shouting at me and the next you are suggesting that we make love."

"Don't I excite you?" she asked teasingly as she began to disrobe. "Have you tired of me so soon?"

Adam watched as she slowly removed one article of clothing after another. Seeing her beautiful body caused his loins to stir. He felt himself once more being pulled into her web.

When Giselle was completely naked, she walked over to Adam and pulled down on his drawers. "Surely you don't plan to make love in those," she said. Her eyes teased him as she began to touch him.

He pulled her hand away and removed his underwear.

She moved her nude body against his. "Isn't this better than quarreling?" she asked.

He gathered her up in his arms and laid her on the bed. He felt fervor for her growing as she ran her hands over his body.

After they were both spent, they lay in one another's arms. She kissed his neck and blew softly in his ear. "Would you have let me leave?" she asked.

He remained silent as he went over the argument in his mind. "Would I have let her leave?" he asked himself. "Yes, I had almost wished she would walk out of my life. I lack the power to walk away from her, but I would have allowed her to leave."

"You haven't answered," she reminded him softly.

"I was so exasperated that I do not know what I would have done," he finally answered. "Why do you get so angry at me?"

She stiffened, but she caught herself before she lost her temper once more and then softened. "Perhaps it's that I want more of you than I can have," she replied. "Would you leave

Annabelle for me?"

He was flabbergasted. "You know that is not possible," he replied. "What would Jacques say to such a thing?"

"Don't you find it strange?" she asked. "Your concern is more for the reaction of your father-in-law than that of your wife."

He thought a while. "I am more concerned about his reaction because of the effect it would have on both of our lives," he finally replied. "Your reputation would be ruined. You would be an outcast."

"We could sell everything and move away," she implored. "We could go where no one would know our past."

He reflected on the irony. He had asked Hannah to move away with him to a place where no one would know their past; where they could live as man and wife. Now, Giselle was asking the same thing of him.

"What about Charles?" he asked. "I could not leave my son and Annabelle would never consent to letting me leave with him."

"There's always a price for love," she said as she ran her fingers slowly down his chest. "We could make love any time we pleased. Wouldn't you like that?"

Her magic was working again as she gently touched his flesh. He felt himself responding to her touch. Another moment and he would agree to anything. He took her hand in his. "I will not leave my son," he said forcefully. "He is of my own flesh."

"We'll take him with us when we leave," she said as though everything were settled. "Annabelle won't know until after we're gone."

Adam found himself in the horns of a dilemma. He did not want this day to be the last day he would hold Giselle in his arms and feel her flesh against his own, but he was not going to leave everything he had worked so hard to create. He was not going to leave Hannah. If the choice was between Giselle and Hannah, Hannah would win out. Hannah was his soul mate.

"I am not leaving Annabelle," he stated with finality. "I will not leave Southern Kingdom." His heart ached at the thought of never again seeing Hannah.

"Then we have nothing further to discuss," she said crossly. "You've made your decision."

Once again, she rose from the bed and dressed. Adam jumped up from the bed and dressed before she could change her mind. He was not sure he could keep his resolve if her flesh touched his own again.

Giselle walked out of the door without saying another word. Adam hurried out to the small barn behind the house and hitched her horse to her buggy.

No words were exchanged until she was seated in the buggy. "I'll be here again next Wednesday afternoon if you're interested," she said teasingly. She slapped the reins on the horse's back and rolled away.

Adam watched the buggy move down the path until it disappeared into the distance. He knew he would be returning the following Wednesday afternoon.

*****

Even with the English nanny's help, Annabelle was finding her new role as mother very demanding. Charles slept during the day and cried most of the night. She'd refused Hannah's offer of a wet nurse. She was beginning to have second thoughts about her decision.

It seemed that her head had just touched the pillow when she felt a hand on her shoulder. She opened her eyes and struggled to clear her mind.

"Charles is crying again, Mrs. Blythington, " the nanny said. "I've diapered him. I think he's hungry."

Annabelle groaned as she lifted her head from the pillow. She rose slowly from the bed. She was exhausted, and making matters worse was the nausea that plagued her the last few mornings. She wanted to be cross with the nanny but she knew Matilda was only doing her duty. "Thank you, Matilda," she responded. She wearily made her way to the nursery.

She felt her anger rising as she walked past the bedroom Adam had chosen to sleep in temporarily. He claimed it was difficult for him to concentrate on plantation business without rest. Charles was now almost three months old. Adam had moved out of her bedroom before Charles was two weeks old. He had only spent two nights in her room since that time. "How convenient for him," she thought angrily to herself. "Does he think I have no need of rest?"

She struggled to control the resentment she felt toward her husband. She'd been told that her moods affected her milk. In the short time it took her to reach the nursery, she composed herself.

"How is my boy tonight?" she asked as she lifted Charles. He stopped crying and studied his mother's face. She moved over to the nursery rocker and sat, exposing a breast for him to suckle. Her head drooped several times as Charles nursed.

"Please stay asleep for mommy," she whispered softly as Matilda took the child from her.

"I'm sorry I had to wake you, mum," Matilda whispered. "I couldn't get him to stop screaming. He does have a bit of a temper."

Annabelle patted Matilda's shoulder and then began the short walk back to her room. She didn't want to waste a moment before getting back into her bed. There was no telling when Charles would demand his next meal.

"You startled me," she said to Adam when she came across him in the hallway.

"I arose when I heard a noise," he said nervously.

"Charles was crying," she responded crossly. "I had to get up to feed him. I'm so sorry we interrupted your peaceful slumber. "

"That must have been what I heard," he said with relief in his voice. "How is he?"

"He still sleeps all day and cries most of the night," she replied grumpily. "Not that his crying would bother you."

"I am sorry he awakened you," Adam said unconvincingly. "Perhaps you should have accepted Hannah's offer of a wet nurse."

She felt resentment rising and fought to control her tongue. In her state, she'd say something she'd regret. "Good night, Adam," she responded coldly. "I, too, need rest."

Adam watched his wife as she made her way to her bedroom. "She is not getting her figure back as quickly as she thought," he said to himself. He had made love to her only twice since Charles' birth. In his mind's eye he compared Annabelle's body to Hannah's body. Hannah's body was fresh on his mind, being that Annabelle had bumped into him as he was returning from her room. Annabelle lost out in the comparison.

*****

"You look so tired," Angelina said a few days later, as she embraced her friend.

"Charles keeps me up most of the night," Annabelle responded. "I refused a wet nurse because I wanted him to bond with me. I didn't stop to think that I'd be up most of the night."

"Poor Annabelle," Angelina said sympathetically. "You'll make yourself sick. Do you think you should change your mind?"

"My hope is that he'll soon begin to stay awake during the day and sleep at night," she replied. "I want my son to know his mother."

"Are you sure you'll be all right?" Angelina asked.

"If I can get past the nausea, I think I'll be fine," Annabelle responded. "Nausea and exhaustion are difficult to endure."

"Why are you nauseated?" Angelina asked. "Nursing a child shouldn't cause nausea."

"Maybe it's something I ate," Annabelle replied. "I've been nauseated all week."

Angelina covered her mouth with her hands. "Oh no," she exclaimed. "Have you had relations with Adam since Charles' birth?"

"He came to me twice last month," Annabelle replied, "but it can't be what you're thinking. I'm still nursing Charles."

"Oh, but it can be what I'm thinking," Angelina said earnestly. "It happens rarely, but women do get pregnant while nursing."

Annabelle began to cry. "It can't be," she sobbed. "Charles is only an infant. I will never again be rested."

Angelina moved over to the sofa where Annabelle sat and put her arms around her friend. "I'm so sorry," she said. "I'll ask Robert to come and examine you."

"Please don't be offended," Annabelle said. "I'd feel more comfortable with his father. Robert was once my beau."

"He's a doctor now and a happily married man," Angelina said. "What will you do when his father retires?"

"I don't like to think of that time," Annabelle replied, "but until that time, I'll feel more comfortable with the elder Dr. Joubert."

*****

"The sow is pregnant again," Adam said contemptuously as he walked into Hannah's room. He found Annabelle repugnant with the extra weight she was carrying.

"What sow?" Hannah asked.

"Annabelle," Adam replied, " she is pregnant again."

"I know you don't love her," Hannah responded angrily, "but you owe her more respect than that. She's done nothing to you to deserve that sort of treatment."

Adam was taken aback. He had not expected Hannah to rise to Annabelle's defense. "I thought you resented her," he responded lamely.

"I don't resent her," she responded. "Why would I resent her? She's a young girl who fell in love with a man who'll never love her in return. She's the mistress of this plantation in name only. Treat her with respect. She's given you your heir and now she'll have another child for you. Do you want her to leave you and return to her father?"

He had not considered that Annabelle would even think of leaving him. Divorces were almost unheard of. If she left him and returned to her father's home, Belle Bois would never be his. "I will have to mend my ways," he said uneasily. "I had not stopped to weigh the harm I was causing to my dream of owning Belle Bois."

"Sometimes you should stop to consider the harm you're doing to other people," she thought to herself. Although she continued to love him deeply, his callousness put her off. What was to stop him from turning on her and Martha?

He saw that Hannah was deep in thought. He sensed his behavior had caused a rent in their relationship. He searched his mind for a means by which he could regain her favor. "You must think I am heartless, speaking of Annabelle in that manner," he said apologetically. "I confess what I said was deplorable. It is true that I have not treated Annabelle fairly. I shall make amends."

Hannah hoped he wouldn't make too many amends. He was spending more nights with her since he had moved out of Annabelle's bedroom. Now that she'd convinced him to be more considerate with Annabelle, she couldn't turn around and tell him to be only marginally considerate.

"Am I forgiven?" he asked contritely.

She smiled up at him. "Of course," she said. She moved to him and rested her head on his chest.

He put his arms around her, bent down, and kissed her. "Please do not turn your back on me," he said emotionally. "I know I do not deserve your love, but I cannot live without you."

"I'll always love you," she responded. "Nothing could kill my love for you." She took his hand and gently pulled him toward the bed. "Aren't you going to show me how much you love me?" she asked.

Adam smiled happily. The moment had passed. Hannah still loved him.

*****

"How could you have gotten her pregnant again so soon?" Giselle asked contemptuously. She moved away from him and pulled the sheet up to cover her nakedness. "I would keep you satisfied if you'd spend more time with me."

Adam could not tell her it was Hannah who kept him satisfied, not Annabelle. "She is my wife," he said. "She would think it strange if I did not go to her."

"I think she's asexual," she said. "It's difficult for me to picture Annabelle in an aroused state."

"Why do you speak so disparagingly of her?" Adam asked. "She is your friend."

"I only pretended to be her friend for Placide's sake," she replied. "I hate her and all of the little rich girls like her. She should have refused to have your child and kept her figure. Now that she's pregnant again, she'll always be fat."

It upset Adam to think his wife would continue to be fat. He wanted a beautiful and shapely woman to present to the world as the mistress of Southern Kingdom. For a moment he thought of divorcing Annabelle and marrying Giselle. She would make a suitable mistress. He pushed the thought from his mind. The community would ostracize him should he divorce Annabelle and, even worse than that, he would lose all hope of becoming the master of Belle Bois.

"Annabelle does you no harm," he said. "It would grieve her should she learn about our affair. She does love you."

"She knows nothing of love," Giselle huffed. "You would need no other woman if I were your wife. You only stay with her because I don't have riches to offer you."

"You have a large piece of property and a beautiful home in town," he said. "You are not poor. Why are you so bitter?"

"My father was only a poor sharecropper up in north Louisiana, Mr. Blythington," she spat out. "I don't have a plantation with which to lure you. Placide married below his station in life. I would have done well had he not gotten himself killed. Now, I have no hope of Belle Bois ever being mine."

It surprised Adam to learn that Giselle had a poor upbringing. Her mannerisms were that of the rich. "You do not act or speak as a sharecropper's daughter," he said. "I was of the impression you were the daughter of a planter."

"I studied the speech and manners of the rich since I was a child," she responded. "I was determined to free myself from my roots. I saw the desperation in my mother's eyes. I didn't want to live the life my mother had settled for."

"Annabelle never mentioned your austere background,"

Adam said.

"She knows nothing of my past," Giselle responded. "I wanted no one to know my past." She remained silent for a few moments and then continued soberly. "My father killed my mother in a jealous rage. He accused her of having an affair with the man who owned our land. That man was only one of the men my mother was bedding. They'd come around when my father was out in the fields or in town. She was ten years younger than my father. He got her pregnant when she was only fifteen. She was still a goodlooking woman when she died.

"He was already drunk when he killed her, but he sat at the kitchen table and drank the remainder of his bottle of whiskey. My mother lay dead on the floor in a pool of blood while he finished his whiskey. I wanted to run away, but he said he'd kill me too if I didn't stay and sit at the table with him. He left the house after he drank all of the whiskey. I heard as he rode away into the night. I learned the following day that he'd broken into our landlord's house. Shots were fired and my father was killed. I guess that was a fitting end for his empty life.

"My mother's death left me with a deep sense of loss, but I felt no remorse when I learned my father had been killed. He was a very mean and angry man. He'd put my mother through a living hell.

"I was only sixteen at the time. My father's fat sister wanted me to move in with her family. She only wanted a slave. She had eight children and my uncle was even more of a bully than my father. I packed the few things I had and left. I had given no thought to what I'd do for food and shelter.

"Placide met me a month later in a saloon in Alexandria. I was hired as a singer, but the owner wanted me to be nice to the customers. I knew what he meant by nice, but I refused to go to bed with any of them.

"Placide was the first man who slept with me. I was young and beautiful. He came to see me every night, but I refused to give him what he wanted. I knew I had only one chance of getting what I wanted. I told him he'd have to marry before I'd sleep with him. After a week, he asked me to marry him. He said he wanted my answer that night because he'd completed his business in Alexandria and was returning to his home.

"I didn't love him, but I loved what his money could do for me. I agreed to marry him, but with one stipulation. No one would ever know my past. I knew he was a wealthy man and I felt his family would look down on me. I would have none of that. He agreed to keep my past secret. He concocted a story about me being the orphaned daughter of a wealthy businessman. That would explain why my family would never come to visit.

"We were married two days later by a judge. He kept his word. Jacques and Annabelle have never learned of my humble beginnings."

Adam was impressed by the dispassionate recitation of her history. It was as though she were telling him about something she had read in a newspaper. He felt a kinship with her. She had freed herself from a life she had found wretched and had made something of herself. He put his arm around her and drew her closer. She did not resist.

"Must we quarrel?" she asked after a while. She nuzzled his neck and pressed her body against his.

The touch of her soft skin stirred him deeply. He felt a quickening in his loins as he allowed his hands to explore her body. No matter how angry he became with her, he could never resist her.

Some time later Adam awakened to feel Giselle's fingers lightly touching his face. She kissed him when she saw his eyes open.

"I'll miss this when my year of mourning is over," she said. "I'm convinced you'll never leave Annabelle and marry me."

"What do you mean?" he asked. "There is no reason for us to ever stop."

"Surely you don't think this is all I want," she responded. "I'm twenty-three. I'm growing no younger. I have to consider my options."

"Options?" he asked anxiously.

"I need to find a suitable husband," she answered

simply. "I intend to grow rich, and since I don't have the means to earn riches, I must marry a rich man."

Adam was stunned. He had not given much thought to their future. He assumed she would remain satisfied with their arrangement. He found the thought of never again touching her beautiful body unbearable. The thought of another man lying with her was disturbing. "It would have been better if I had never gotten involved with her," he thought to himself.

"Would it be that easy for you to discontinue our relationship and marry another man?" he asked.

"One does what's necessary," she replied. "I married Placide."

"But you loved him," Adam countered. "Could you meet someone else who you would truly love?"

"Loved Placide," she scoffed. "I told you I married him for his money. He thought only of himself. His idea of a woman was someone who he could use when he needed and then put back on a shelf. I don't need love for marriage."

"Surely you do not intend to live the rest of your life without love?" he asked.

"The closest I have ever come to loving a man is what I feel for you," she mused. "I could be content with you. You're very demanding, but you're also very giving. You don't ask more of me than I'm willing to give."

Adam considered what she had said about love. He pondered his feelings for her. He would never love her as he did Hannah, but the thought of losing her was heavy on his heart. "Would you consider continuing our relationship after you are married?" he asked hopefully.

She propped herself up on one elbow and stared into his eyes. "That would be difficult for me," she responded after a while. "I couldn't give enough of myself to my husband if I continued to see you." Tears began to run down her cheeks. "I would continue to see you if it were possible, but I wouldn't be able to stand another man's touch." She moved closer to Adam and pressed her body against him.

He felt more tenderness for her at that moment than he had at any other time during their relationship. "She is such a complex woman," he said to himself. "Will I ever know who she really is?" It occurred to him that her mourning period would end in just about five months. He held her more closely.

"We must enjoy the time we have," she said after a while. "Placide hasn't even been declared dead."

Adam's heart was gladdened. There was more time. Although he knew with certainty Placide was dead, no one else but Henry and Hannah were sure of his death. The coroner would have to make the pronouncement before Giselle could remarry. As far as the law was concerned, she was still married to Placide. He felt a deep sense of relief.

"We must," he agreed. He was determined to give Giselle all the pleasure he could bring forth in the time they had left. He caressed her gently. He felt as though he had been given a reprieve. There was still time.

CHAPTER TWENTY

July 20, 1867 - September 3, 1867

Adam rode slowly through his fields on a July day in 1867 surveying the cotton stalks showing their white fiber in the hot sun. He watched as the pickers dragged their heavy sacks down the rows plucking the fiber from the bolls. The weather had been cooperative for planting and growing. He could see healthy plants covered with white all the way to the tree line far off in the distance.

There had been no further problems since Brooks' investigation back in March. From what Henry had been able to learn, Brooks had packed up and headed back east. "I hope that is the last we hear from those people," Adam said to himself. "I will have to be more careful in the future. That could have been a costly mistake."

Giselle was growing more demanding. She was not satisfied meeting him at the cottage every week or so. He felt that meeting more often would pose a great risk for both of them. She claimed he was taking her for granted. "Why did I allow myself to get involved with her?" he asked himself. "Hannah gives me all I need." He had often thought of ending the affair, but had a sense of loss each time. Giselle's body continued to excite him.

His thoughts turned to Hannah. Since their talk about his affair with Giselle, Hannah had never again spoken of Giselle or indicated she had a problem with the affair. There were no hurt looks or accusations. He would have felt less guilt over the dalliance with Giselle if Hannah were not so accepting.

He could hear the dinner bell in the distance calling all the hands to dinner. He touched his spurs lightly to Diablo's ribs and turned the horse toward the plantation house. He had not felt hunger before he heard the bell, but now he was famished.

The field hands were spread out under shade trees eating their meals. He could see rice and gravy, sausage and beans piled high on the plates. "If I ate that much," he commented to himself, "I would have to stop to take a nap." It amazed him that the workmen could return to the hot fields in the afternoons after such a heavy meal.

Hannah smiled up at him when he pulled Diablo to a stop at the hitching rail. "Margaret just made a big pitcher of lemonade," she said. "I'm sure you could use something cool to drink after being out in that hot sun. I'll bring you a glass."

Adam sat on the swing on the verandah. Although he had been in the south for over two years, he still could not stand to eat until he had cooled off. Hannah came to him and handed him a tall glass of lemonade. "Thank you," he said. "You are always so thoughtful."

She smiled at him and then looked around to make sure there was no one close enough to overhear. "Nothing is too good for my man," she said. "I want to make sure all your needs are taken care of."

He returned her smile, but immediately felt guilty about his affair with Giselle. He looked in Hannah's eyes and saw no reproach there. He drank down some of the cool liquid while thinking of something to say in response to her comment. What could he say? How could he possibly justify his infidelity to Hannah? "The lemonade is delicious," he finally said lamely.

"I'm glad you think so," she responded. She turned her attention back to seeing to the needs of the field hands.

Adam rose from the swing and went into the house. Annabelle was sitting in one of the rockers in the parlor. She smiled when she saw her husband. "Ruth," she called to the servant standing nearby. "Please have Margaret set the table."

Adam bent over and kissed his wife's cheek. "How are you feeling?" he asked.

"I feel wonderful for an elephant," she replied. "Only seven more months to go."

"You are still beautiful," Adam said. "Once the child is born you will quickly regain your figure." He instantly realized that any reference to her figure was unwelcome. Although she was only about two months pregnant, she had not lost the weight she had gained while carrying Charles.

"I hope so," she said shaking her head. "I feel as though I'm as fat as a cow."

He tried to think of something he could say to comfort her. He regretted he was not skillful at making small talk. He could again think of nothing.

"Is you hongry Mr. Adam?" Margaret asked as the couple entered the informal dining room.

"I am hungry," Adam admitted, "but not enough for one of those field hand dinners. I will serve my own plate." Even when he asked Margaret to serve him a modest amount, she heaped the food on his plate.

"I think I'll only sit here and keep you company while you eat," Annabelle said. "I'm not very hungry."

"Miz Annabelle," Margaret scolded, "we done went ovah dat befoe. You got to eat fo da baby. I gone fix you a plate."

It was useless to protest. "Only a small helping, please," Annabelle called out as Margaret headed back to the kitchen.

Annabelle chatted as she and Adam ate their meal. She had reached the conclusion that she'd have to initiate the conversations at mealtime and could expect only a few words in return from her husband. She was disappointed that he hadn't gotten better at opening up to her. She was beginning to feel uneasy about his reticence.

"I must return to the fields," he said as he laid his fork across his plate. "There is much to be done."

"You're working too hard," she protested. "Why don't you hire an overseer as Pappa and the other planters have done? You would have more time to relax and spend time with your family."

"An overseer would not be as concerned with the plantation as I am," he replied. "Besides, I would have to pay the overseer. That money can be better applied elsewhere."

"Also," he said to himself, "it would be more difficult to find an excuse to meet with Giselle and the last thing I need is more time with you."

*****

The fields were fallow once again. The harvest had been bountiful. The cotton was loaded on ships and dispatched directly to Blythington Import and Export. Eliminating the buyer's fee had increased the year's profit.

Adam felt the wind against his face as Diablo trotted down the headland. It was warm for this late in the season. He thought of Hannah and then of Giselle. While he would never love Giselle as he did Hannah, he could not get her out of his mind.

"I need to go into town and speak with Fisk," he said to himself. "I have to keep my mind occupied. Perhaps buying more property will release my mind long enough to free myself of Giselle."

It was still morning. He headed for the house to change into something more appropriate for going into town.

He cleaned up and changed quickly and was about to step out of the door when Annabelle called out to him. He turned toward her and watched as she made her way to him. Although she was a little less than five months pregnant, it seemed to him she was even larger than when she had been pregnant for Charles. Her face was puffy and her hair was scraggily. He felt like telling her to lose weight and take better care of her appearance but decided it would be best to remain silent. Annabelle had become very disputatious lately.

"Will you be back home late?" she asked.

"Why do you ask?" he countered.

Annabelle strove for self-control. Adam had grown distant since Charles' birth. "Don't you recall Pappa and Giselle are coming for supper tonight?" she asked. "They'll be here around five o'clock. I had hoped you would be here."

He had totally forgotten Jacques and Giselle were coming for supper. Annabelle invited Jacques, but Giselle insisted on accompanying him. She said it would give her an opportunity to be with other people. It made him uncomfortable when Annabelle and Giselle were together. Giselle was aware of his discomfort and found it amusing. He was always worried Jacques or Annabelle would pick up on her double entendres.

He was tempted to tell Annabelle his business would keep him in town late, but he wanted to see Giselle, even though he would have to control himself around her.

"I will be here," he said. "I will put off my trip to town until tomorrow. I have business to attend to there." It would do him no good to ride into town in hopes of getting Giselle off of his mind since he would be dining with her tonight. He decided instead to go to his office and do some paperwork.

*****

"How was your sugarcane harvest?" Adam asked his father-in-law. He cared little about the harvest, but he was trying to keep his mind and his eyes off of Giselle. She had chosen to wear a dress with an inappropriately low cut neckline. Her lovely breasts were temptingly revealed. It was a wonder to him that Jacques had not chastened her. Jacques seemed to be unaware.

"Better than I had expected," Jacques responded. "The yield was excellent and the prices held. I had feared the market would drop."

"Will you plant more sugarcane acreage next year?" Adam followed up as he struggled to keep his eyes turned away from Giselle.

"No," Jacques said as he shook his head. "Cotton prices are higher than ever. Although I made a small profit with the cane, I can make more on cotton. I think I'll plant more cotton next year."

Giselle leaned over as though to listen more intently to what Annabelle was saying. Adam caught the movement out of the corner of his eye. He felt his heart pounding in his chest. "She knows exactly what she is doing to me," he said to himself.

He forced his attention back to Jacques and found him waiting for a response. He groped for something to say. "Our cotton yield was excellent," he said.

"That's good," Jacques said with a puzzled expression.

"I asked if you were going to plant sugarcane next year."

Adam struggled to recover. "As I was saying," he said as he attempted to keep his voice level, "our yield was excellent and the cotton prices are rising. Our profits would decrease if I planted sugarcane."

"Oh, I see, "Jacques responded. "I'm sorry I interrupted you before you finished. I apologize."

"No apology necessary," Adam said with relief in his voice, "I should have spoken more clearly." From the corner of his eye, he could see Giselle smiling. She knew she had caused him to become flustered.

After the meal, Adam and Jacques retired to the library to smoke cigars. "Are you hoping for a girl this time?" Jacques asked after they'd sat silently for some time enjoying their cigars. "Annabelle says she'd like a daughter."

"I already have a daughter," Adam thought to himself. "Now that I have an heir, I do not care what it is."

"A daughter would be fine," he said. "She would be good company for Annabelle while I am out in the fields with Charles."

"It will be some years yet before Charles accompanies you to the fields," Jacques returned.

"He will begin to go out with me in the mornings when he is five," Adam responded in a matter-of-fact manner. "He will be old enough by that time."

"Placide was eight when I began to take him with me," Jacques said. "I suppose he could have come with me earlier."

"I want my son to run Southern Kingdom when I am gone," Adam responded. "He will get his formal education from Professor Pennington and I will teach him how to run a plantation. He will be ready when it is his time."

"I suppose it's because he knew nothing about farming before he came here that he wants Charles learning so early," Jacques thought to himself. "He'll temper his opinions as time passes."

"I'm sure you'll do what's best for Charles," he said.

Adam took Jacques' words for agreement with his decision to begin Charles' education at a young age.

Giselle peeked her head into the library. "Are you two going to puff on those smelly cigars all night?" she asked. "Annabelle and I are dying for male companionship."

Adam and Jacques got up and walked with Giselle to the parlor. Giselle made sure she sat across from Adam.

"I would suggest to you that you go into the nursery and kiss Charles goodnight," Annabelle said, "but I don't want to risk awakening him. Hopefully, he'll sleep all night."

"Does he usually sleep all night?" Giselle asked.

"Almost always," Adam replied. "He is no trouble at all."

"Speak for yourself," Annabelle thought to herself acerbically. "He usually sleeps during the daytime and stays awake at night," she answered in an irritated voice. "Adam doesn't know he cries at night because he sleeps in his own room."

Annabelle had told Giselle about Charles' sleeping habits. Giselle smiled sweetly as she searched Adam's face. She could tell Annabelle had upset him.

"He's such a precious child," she said. "I'm sure he'll soon reverse his pattern and allow both of you to sleep peacefully."

Jacques pulled out his watch. "I'm enjoying the company, but it's getting late," he said. "We must be getting back to Belle Bois."

Adam and Annabelle walked to the carriage with Jacques and Giselle. Giselle accidently allowed the back of her hand to press against Adam's groin as he was helping her into the carriage.

*****

Hannah waited anxiously for Adam to come up to her room. She had helped Mary and Ruth to serve supper to the Blythingtons and their guests. It was a wonder to her how Mr. Dupre' and Annabelle failed to notice Giselle flaunting her body for Adam and flirting with him all evening. "How could they not have seen?" she asked herself. "It was as plain as their noses."

Adam was playing a dangerous game. Mr. Dupre' was no fool. If he even suspected what was going on between Giselle and Adam, there would be a confrontation. After all, Giselle was the widow of his deceased son.

She was trying to decide whether or not to speak to Adam about Giselle. He had a lot to lose if the affair were to be discovered by Mr. Dupre'. She had resolved never again to speak of Giselle with Adam, but he had to be warned. She decided to wait until after they made love to broach the subject. He was always more receptive after his desires were sated.

She heard a soft knock on her door and hurried to open it. "I'm glad you were able to come," she said as she ushered him in. "I missed you last night."

"I missed you, too," he said as he held her closely.

She couldn't help but notice he lacked his usual urgency. Was his mind still on Giselle? "You must be tired," she said. "Come and lie down."

"I am tired," he said as he sat on the edge of the bed. "It has been a trying day."

She sat beside him and waited for him to go on.

"I know it is unfair to you," he began, "but I must speak with someone about Giselle. You are the only one I can trust." His shoulders sagged and his head drooped. "I should never have started this with her." He hesitated once more. "I am making a fool of myself."

She detected the anguish in his voice. She didn't know whether she should say something or wait for him to continue. She remained silent and waited for him to proceed.

"I want to stop seeing her," he continued after some time, "but she has some sort of hold on me. I am playing a fool's game." He lay back on the bed and covered his eyes with his hands. She lay beside him and held his hand.

Afer a while, he opened his eyes and looked at her. "You should be angry with me instead of showing me understanding," he almost shouted. "I am a louse."

"Would it help if I were angry with you?" she asked. "Would you feel better if I shouted at you and called you names?"

"At least I would not feel so guilty," he muttered. "I am acting like a heel, and yet you continue to love me. Am I not causing you pain?" His voice rose as he asked the question.

"Pain? Yes, Adam, you're causing me pain," she replied. "It tears my heart out every time I think of the two of you together."

"I am sorry," he said sincerely.

"Please let me finish," she said firmly. "Even though your affair with her causes me a lot of pain, I still feel sorry for you because I know the game she's playing with you. She's the cat and you're the mouse. You're only a diversion for her. She can't even begin to look for another man until Placide's pronounced dead by the coroner and she's gone through a satisfactory period of mourning. She's bored and you're her amusement while she bides her time."

"She told me she will start looking for a husband as soon as she can," Adam admitted. "Instead of feeling used, I was euphoric because of the time I can still have with her. I know I am acting stupidly. I do not know how to walk away from her."

"Do you love her?" Hannah asked tightly.

He was silent for a while as he mulled over her question. "We have never mentioned the word 'love,'" he replied. He saw no reason to hurt Hannah by telling her the truth. "I admit there is a strong physical attraction, but it has nothing to do with love." He stopped himself and thought over his relationship with Giselle. "No, I do not love her. "

She considered his answer. "Then, what is her hold on you?" she asked.

"She drives me mad with desire," he admitted in a small voice. "I am the puppet and she pulls the strings. How did I ever allow myself to become this way?"

"Because she has no heart," Hannah replied. "She's a brilliant actress. The person you see is the persona she coldly and deliberately sets before you."

Adam recalled how easily Giselle slipped from one mood to another. There was no real connection. Giselle was loving one moment, angry the next, and then captivating moments later. "She is a brilliant actress," he admitted. He was astonished. Although Hannah had spent little time with Giselle, she knew her well. "She keeps me off balance. I find myself wishing she would walk out on me, yet hoping she will be with me forever."

"Listen to me, Adam," Hannah said gravely. "She's playing a dangerous game. I watched her tonight. She's intrigued by the game. She exposed her bosom to you and flirted with you in front of your wife and your father-in-law because the danger of being caught excites her. It's all a game to her, but a very serious game. I noticed how difficult it was for you not to stare at what she had on display. Mr. Dupre' is no fool. Although he may not have said anything tonight, he was aware of her behavior. He's a wise man, which makes him wary. A wise man always lets out enough rope for the guilty man to hang himself."

Adam considered her words. "Do you think he suspects us?" he asked worriedly.

"No, I don't think so," she replied. "He watched you closely. You reacted to her display as most normal men would have, but you were a gentleman. You didn't stare or make excuses to be alone with her. I'm almost positive he suspects that Giselle is up to something."

Adam breathed a sigh of relief. "I have got to end it with her," he said. He was convinced he would put an end to the affair now that his father-in-law was suspicious. "I will tell her tomorrow afternoon when I see her."

Hannah shook her head and stared into his eyes. "Don't be a dupe, Adam," she said. "Mr. Dupre' may have her followed. You shouldn't meet with her again."

"But what will she think?" Adam questioned. "She may be angry enough to go to Jacques."

"She'll figure out it's over," Hannah replied patiently. "You owe her no explanation. She could have cost you everything you've worked so hard to build by her behavior tonight. She likes flirting with danger, but she's not foolish enough to disclose her secret. She has too much to lose."

"She will be hurt," Adam offered lamely.

"Adam!" Hannah exclaimed. "Come to your senses. She'll be angry because the mouse escaped the trap. She doesn't like rejection and she won't take that well, but she'll keep her mouth shut. Be thankful you got out before you were found out."

Adam pulled Hannah closer. "I do not deserve you," he said tenderly. "You are my love and my treasure. I can always count on your wisdom."

She nuzzled her head against his chest. He cupped her chin in his hand and pulled her mouth up to his. He felt heat rising in his loins as she returned his kiss.

"What would I do without you?" he asked when they stopped for air.

"You'll never have to answer that question," she replied as she unbuttoned his shirt. "I'll be yours forever."

*****

"I had just about given up on you," Fisk said as Adam stepped into his office. "That new son of yours must really be keeping you busy. How long has it been?" He scratched his head and squinted as though looking inward. "Must be about a year."

"It is no business of yours if it has been a year, a month, or a day," Adam thought to himself. He glanced about Fisk's office. There were pictures on the walls and the chairs were sturdier. As his eyes continued to travel, he saw Fisk had a new desk and he no longer kept his papers in boxes. There were two wooden filing cabinets in a corner of the office.

He realized it had been a long time since he had been in Fisk's office. The visit from the brothers and their families and his preoccupation with Giselle had cost him precious time. His stomach churned when he thought of Giselle. If he hurried, there would still be time to meet with her. "No," he said to himself. "I have got to heed Hannah's advice."

"What happened to your plan to invest as little money here as possible and return to Pittsburgh as a wealthy man?" Adam asked as he swept his hand indicating the pictures on the wall and the new furniture.

"I found myself a white woman," Fisk replied while smiling broadly. "Real pretty little thing. No more high yellows.

She wants to marry me. I figure another three or four years and I can put together enough money to take her back with me and buy one of those fancy houses where the rich folks live. She says she can teach me how to be refined." He shook his head and laughed. "Never thought a woman like that would be interested in me."

"Are you not concerned your new lifestyle will draw attention to you?" Adam asked.

"Nope," Fisk asserted smugly. "I'll continue to live in the house I'm renting. Won't change the outside of the office. She says she's willing to wait a few years for the good life."

Adam regretted allowing himself to surrender to curiosity. He had no interest in the man's life aside from acquiring land for Southern Kingdom. He wondered why Fisk had not left for Pittsburgh with the money he had taken from Bennett's safe. "What do you have that would interest me?" he asked.

"I'll have to look," Fisk replied. "Couldn't count on you anymore so I started doing legitimate business. Doesn't bring as much money in as working with you, but I've been making a pretty good living."

"Has anything been made available between my two plantations?" Adam asked.

"Three parcels," Fisk replied uneasily. He avoided meeting Adam's eyes.

"Had I not told you I was interested in any property that becomes available in that vicinity?" Adam asked coldly.

"Adam, you've got to understand you haven't been around in over a year," Fisk replied nervously. "You made it pretty clear you didn't want me to go to your place."

"You could have sent a messenger," Adam responded with a hard edge to his voice. Fisk had never dared to call him by his first name before.

The two men stared at each other for several moments. Finally Fisk averted his eyes. "Too late to do anything about that now," he said defensively. He moved toward the file cabinet. "I can see if there's anything now."

"How much land did you broker in that locality?" Adam

asked frigidly. "We need to see about getting that land back."

"Get it back?" Fisk asked himself. He was taken aback. "How would it look if I sold land and then something happened to the buyers? That kind of thing wouldn't be good for my business. Can you imagine the attention that would bring my way?"

"Things have really changed," Adam thought to himself. "Fisk is now worried about his reputation." He stared coldly at Fisk as he contemplated the latest developments.

Fisk grew uneasy under Adam's scrutiny. "Think of the trouble I could be in," he said appeasingly. "I've got to get through a few more years out here." He wished he had made wiser decisions with the money he had taken from Bennett's safe.

"It appears I need to take my business elsewhere," Adam leveled. "I need a land dealer who has my best interests at heart."

Fisk understood the ramifications of Adam doing business with another land broker. Adam would search for the most ruthless man he could find. He could very well end up as a target. Adam was not the sort of man to cross. "I don't think there's a need for that," he replied apologetically. "We might be able to make a deal on some of the land." He smiled hopefully at Adam.

"All or nothing," Adam responded. "I want to buy up all the land between Southern Kingdom and Lance des Chenes."

Fisk's head drooped. He had made a grievous mistake by failing to contact Blythington when those parcels came on the market. Georgina had encouraged him to forsake his old ways and become a legitimate broker. He should have known better than taking advice from a woman.

"I'll see what I can do, Mr. Blythington" he said solemnly. "It'll take some doing. My fee may be more than you're willing to pay."

"Maybe I can discourage him by charging a high fee," he thought to himself.

Adam allowed a crafty smile to spread across his face. Fisk was back to addressing him by his surname. "Your fee will be higher than you can expect for legitimate brokering," he said definitively, "but be assured, you will not gouge me. I will not allow you to place any obstacles in my path."

All hope left Fisk. He had one of two choices. Do business with Blythington or have him killed. He considered having Blythington murdered. That would take care of him once and for all. "Much too risky," he thought to himself.

He recalled the time he sent three men to murder Placide Dupre'. The men were found dead and Dupre' vanished from the face of the earth. He suspected that Blythington had a hand in Dupre's disappearance. "If the attempt fails, or he even suspects double-dealing, he'll come after me," he said to himself. "Much safer and more profitable to do business with him. It's like doing business with the devil, though."

Fisk shuddered and then pulled one of the file cabinet drawers open.

*****

"I hadn't expected to see you today," Jacques said as Adam walked into the Southern Kingdom mansion. "Annabelle said you were in town on business."

"Where is she?" Adam asked as he glanced around the room.

"Charles once again demanded her attention," Jacques replied as he studied his son-in-law's face. "I hope things went well for you in town."

"It took less time to complete my business than I anticipated," Adam responded.

"You must have encountered Giselle on your way back from town," Jacques said as he looked into Adam's eyes for his reaction. "She's decided to spend a few days at her home."

"I did not see her," Adam responded. He sensed that his father-in-law was on a fishing expedition. "I came part of the way through the fields."

"Ah, well, I'm sure she'll be returning in a few days," Jacques said. "She seems to get bored quickly in town."

"Boredom has never been one of my problems," Adam

said. "There is always much to occupy my time."

"Oh, Adam, you're home," Annabelle said pleasantly as she walked into the room. "I thought you would be all day in town. Did everything go as you had hoped?"

"There were a few problems," Adam replied, "but nothing that could not be overcome."

"Are you hungry?" she asked. "I can ask Margaret to fix something for you."

"Thank you, but no," he replied. "I had something in town."

"I have to be getting along," Jacques said. "There's much to see to at home."

"But Pappa, you only just arrived," Annabelle protested. "Please don't leave so soon."

"I was planning to inspect the cows Henry purchased at the auction last Tuesday," Adam said before Jacques could respond. "Since it is such a mild and sunny day, perhaps you would like to ride out with me,"

"It is a beautiful day," Jacques agreed. "An outing on a day like today may be just what I need."

"It's not at all as I suspected," Dupre' thought to himself as he followed Adam out to the barn. "Giselle left only a short time before I did. There wasn't enough time for her to rendezvous with Adam." He shook his head. "Giselle will get in trouble one day with her flirting. She'll encounter a man who isn't a gentleman like Adam."

Adam was grateful fate had placed his father-in-law in his home at this time. His resolve to remain away from the cottage and Giselle had weakened. The yearning had grown so strong, had it not been for Jacques' presence, he would have found himself again in Giselle's arms.

*****

Giselle slapped the reins on the horse's back when she spotted the cottage off in the distance. "Adam will be very excited today," she laughed softly to herself as she urged the horse to hurry.

"Last night was hilarious. The way he struggled to keep his eyes off of me. It's fortunate Jacques was preoccupied and failed to notice."

Much to her dismay, Adam wasn't waiting in the small barn to unhitch the horse from the buggy. She thought he might be waiting for her in the cottage, but discounted that notion. His horse was nowhere in sight. She tied the reins to the top rail of the pen and made her way to the cottage. "He's late," she exclaimed when she entered the cottage. She stomped her foot. "Today of all days."

She pondered which would be best; undress and wait for him in the bed or curl up on the sofa to wait. "He may be only a few minutes late," she supposed. "I don't want to waste any time." She took off her garments and folded them neatly on a chair.

She got in the bed and lay back on a pillow to wait. "I'll let him see my body and burn with desire before I give in to him," she decided as payback for causing her to wait on him. "I'll make him beg."

She awoke with a start. The shadows were lengthening and Adam still hadn't arrived. She mulled over the things that might have befallen him. It had to be an accident or something pressing had come up. "He wouldn't dare insult me by deliberately allowing me to come all this way only to be stood up," she fumed. "He had better have a good reason."

She hastily dressed and went out to her buggy. She became even angrier as she convinced herself this was Adam's way of brushing her off. "He had better have a very good reason," she cried out angrily.

*****

"How is my favorite sister-in-law?" Giselle asked Annabelle the following Sunday afternoon as she removed her coat and handed it absently to Ruth. "I grew so bored in town. I couldn't stay there a moment longer."

"I'm doing very well," Annabelle replied. "Will you be spending some time with Pappa?"

"No," Giselle responded. "I was thinking I hadn't stayed overnight in your beautiful home. I thought it was time I rectified the oversight and spent a few days with you."

"You're certainly welcome in our home," Annabelle responded graciously. She was puzzled. Giselle had never before expressed a desire to pay an extended visit to Southern Kingdom. While it was true Giselle was capricious, she was also very finicky. "Why would she choose to stay in a home with a crying baby?" she asked herself.

Moses Dupre', Giselle's coachman, followed her in carrying a large trunk.

"Where do you want him to put my things?" she asked.

"I'll have Hannah get one of the upstairs bedrooms ready for you," Annabelle replied. "I don't think you'd want to be down here with Charles. He may keep you awake." She turned to Moses. "You may set the trunk down here."

"Set it there and go and get the rest of my things," Giselle dictated to Moses. "Be careful not to muss anything."

"You'd think he'd know what to do by now," she said as she turned her attention back to Annabelle. "They act like children."

Annabelle wondered how long her sister-in-law was planning to stay. She had been looking forward to a Sunday afternoon nap. Now, she'd have to entertain her brother's wife. She tried to look at the bright side. "At least I'll have another woman to talk to," she thought to herself.

Moses brought the remainder of Giselle's things into the house. As he turned to leave, she said, "You will remember to come here Friday afternoon to get me?"

"Yes Mam," he replied. "I'll be here Friday."

"Mary," Annabelle said as she turned to one of the servants, "Please find Hannah and ask her to select a room for Mrs. Giselle. Please tell her I'd like for Mrs. Giselle to have an upstairs room."

"Yesum," Mary responded. She left in search of Hannah.

"Where's Adam?" Giselle asked as she unpinned her hat.

"We have a mare in foal that's having problems,"

Annabelle replied. "Adam is with Henry and Jeremiah in the barn."

Giselle excused herself and went to the powder room to refresh herself. She wanted to look her absolute best when Adam walked in. She was disappointed to learn he was out in the barn, but this would work out even better. He would be very surprised to see her when he walked in.

Giselle returned to the parlor and made small talk with Annabelle as she waited for Adam. She had already waited over an hour, and was growing restless.

"How much longer do you think it will be?" she asked Annabelle.

Even though Annabelle was tired, she'd been doing her best to entertain her sister-in-law. She was not altogether clear what Giselle was asking. "How much longer will what be?" she asked.

"How much longer before Adam comes in?" Giselle asked irritably. "It's rude to keep company waiting."

Annabelle was perplexed. She had assumed Giselle had come to visit with her. Why would she be concerned with how much longer it would be before Adam came into the house? "Why would that concern you?" she asked.

Giselle realized she had committed a faux pas. She searched her mind for a reply that would allay Annabelle's suspicions. If Annabelle were to be watching her closely, it would ruin her plans for the week. "Please forgive me," she replied contritely. "I apologize for my bad manners. I was thinking of the poor mare. She must be in terrible pain. I hate to think of poor dumb creatures suffering so. I'm in such agony for the ordeal to be over for her."

Annabelle regretted the tone she'd taken with Giselle. If she hadn't been so fatigued, she would have realized Giselle's distress. Ladies who lived in the city were not used to the ways of nature. "I should beg your forgiveness," she responded. "This sort of thing is commonplace for me. I hadn't stopped to consider how difficult this must be for you."

*****

Hannah burned with anger as she helped Mary and Ruth make the room ready for Giselle. She had chosen the room farthest from her own for Giselle. "I should've known she wouldn't let Adam out of her trap that easily," she admonished herself. "I should've advised Adam to meet with her and tell her it was over. I've got to think of a way to thwart her."

Hannah tried to come up with a plan as she instructed the servants to dust off the furniture, air out the room and get fresh water and towels for the bathing room. She remembered Adam was in the barn with Henry and Jeremiah. "I've got to go and warn him," she said to herself.

She hurried down the back stairs and made her way to the barn. She was relieved to find that Adam was still in the barn. As she closed the door behind herself, she saw the foal attempting to stand. She watched for a moment as the foal struggled to its feet.

Adam was watching wearily as the young colt made its way unsteadily to its mother. It had been a difficult birthing, but both mare and foal were now doing well. From the corner of his eye, he spotted Hannah. "Is something wrong?" he asked tiredly.

"I have to talk to you about an urgent matter," Hannah replied.

Adam knew Hannah well enough to recognize she had something important on her mind. Henry and Jeremiah were going to stay with the mare and the foal for a while to make sure they were all right. "We can go to the office," he offered.

Hannah shook her head. "I think we should go to the corncrib."

He thought it was odd that Hannah had suggested the corncrib, but he trusted her judgment. He nodded his head almost imperceptibly and then followed her.

Hannah latched the corncrib door after they were inside and turned to Adam. "Giselle's in the house," she said. "She intends to spend a week over here."

His face turned white. He walked over to a stool that stood beside the corn sheller and sat down. "Why?" he asked. "She has never spent a night with us before."

"She's upset with you because you snubbed her," Hannah replied. "I think she wants to make you pay for ending the affair. She wants to make you crawl to her so she can reject you. She may even want to have sex with you in the home you share with your wife as a way of proving some foolish point to herself."

"Why did I ever go to her in the first place?" he asked dejectedly. "I already had all I needed." He bowed his head and sat slumped on the stool.

"We have no time for that," she responded more sharply than she had intended.

He lifted his eyes and looked at her. "Why are you angry with me?" he asked. "I did what you told me to do. Is it my fault she will not take no for an answer?"

Hannah battled to control her temper. Scolding him would only make matters worse. It peeved her that he was seeing himself as a victim. He had made some very bad decisions that had led to this dilemma. "I'm not angry," she replied appeasingly. "I only meant we need to come up with a way to solve this problem."

"What should we do?" he asked forlornly. "I will do whatever you think is best."

Hannah was exasperated with Adam. He was acting out of character. Where was the strong decisive man who had built Southern Kingdom? This man was weak and indecisive. "What's happened to you, Adam?" she cried out. "You've stood against men who would've killed you, yet you're ready to fall apart when you're challenged by a scheming woman? Have you surrendered your manhood to her?"

She could see her words stung Adam. He glared at her and fire burned in his eyes. He straightened his spine as he sat upon the stool and then rose to his feet after a moment. "If you were a man, I would kill you," he said coldly.

She stood her ground and stared back into his eyes. "I'd choose death over watching the man I love cringe in fear," she said. "I'm pleased to see the Adam I know hadn't gone far."

Adam felt the anger begin to subside. A smile touched his lips. "That did get my attention," he said. He moved toward her and took her in his arms. "I feel as though I have returned from a long journey."

She held on to her man. She was deeply relieved. "I'm glad you're back," she said. "I've missed you."

"You had better return to the house before you are missed," he said. "I will be in momentarily. Giselle will lose this battle."

Hannah held onto him a moment longer and then leaned her head on his chest. "I believe you," she said with a smile on her lips. She stood on tiptoe and kissed him passionately. Her heart was lighter than it had been in months.

*****

"There you are, Adam," Giselle said as Adam entered the room. She studied his face for the impact her surprise made on him.

"It is good to see you," Adam said lightly. "You are looking well." He turned toward Annabelle. "If you two will excuse me, I will go and clean up."

"Are they both all right?" Annabelle asked.

"There were some difficult moments," he replied, "but it ended well. We now have a healthy young filly."

"That's wonderful," Annabelle responded. "Giselle was very worried."

Adam returned his attention to Giselle. "Is that so?" he asked.

Nothing was going as she had planned. Adam was supposed to be disquieted, not she.

"The poor dear was moved by the mare's suffering," Annabelle interjected. "I'm afraid I was insensitive as I was telling her about the foaling process. This is something new to her."

"Oh, I understand, "Adam said as he gazed steadily into Giselle's eyes. "It is not as though she were some farmer's daughter. I do hope you feel better now."

Giselle lowered her eyes. "You bastard," she said to herself. "You know my father was a sharecropper."

"It's a relief to know the ordeal is over and they're doing well," she responded. She watched Adam's back as he walked away. There was something different about him. She was beginning to question the wisdom of her decision to spend a week at Southern Kingdom. Oddly though, she felt a greater attraction for Adam.

*****

"Don't you think you should've stayed in your room tonight?" Hannah asked as she closed her door behind Adam. "What if Giselle comes looking for you?"

"Why should I have remained in my room?" he inquired of her. "I want nothing further to do with her."

"I'm almost certain she'll go to your room tonight," Hannah replied. "She'll think it's strange when she finds you're not there."

"I locked my door before I left," he responded. "My room is too near Annabelle's for her to knock loudly or call out to me. There is no way she can know I am not there."

"She'll know," Hannah declared. "Somehow she'll know."

"This is confusing," Adam said. "On the one hand you tell me I should not be alone with her, and on the other you tell me I must be in my room because you think she will come to me tonight."

"You'll have to face her and tell her the affair is over," Hannah said earnestly. "This is the only way she'll agree to leave you alone."

"I will go, but first you must satisfy my desire," Adam said as he pulled her more closely. "It will be easier for me if I am satisfied when she comes."

"There's no time, and besides, she'll sense you've been with another woman," Hannah responded. "A woman can always tell."

Adam considered her words for a moment. He had gone to Hannah after spending the afternoon with Giselle. Was she telling him she knew each time he had been with another woman? Did women truly sense these things? He kissed Hannah passionately and then left her room.

As she leaned her back against her door, Hannah wondered if she'd done the right thing. She had been aware of Adam's need when he kissed her. Had she left him burning with desire for her only to have Giselle take advantage of the desire she'd kindled?

*****

Adam returned to his room, undressed and slipped under the covers. He tossed and turned restlessly as he tried to fall asleep. All evening he had looked forward to spending the night with Hannah. He felt desire for her burning in his loins.

He heard a soft tapping on his door and hoped Hannah had changed her mind and had come to ask him to return to her room. He heard another soft tap. "Come in," he called out softly. He saw the silhouette of a woman's body in the dim light as the door opened.

The woman moved quickly to his bed and slipped in beside him. "I couldn't sleep," he heard Giselle say. "I wanted you to love me." She removed her nightgown and drew her body closer to him.

He struggled to control the overpowering desire he felt thrusting through his loins. His body thrilled as he felt her flesh against his. His hands seemed to take on a life of their own. It was as though he watched as they touched her breasts and manipulated her flesh. He heard moaning coming from deep down in his throat. He pressed his mouth against hers and listened to the sound of heavy breathing coming from his lungs. His mind sought to detach itself from her while his body cried out for more. He surrendered and his last hope of resistance slipped away.

"That was wonderful," she said contentedly some time later as she lay next to him. "I missed you. We are so good together."

Adam wanted to push her away, but it felt wonderful to have her next to him once more. He felt a heavy sense of guilt for letting Hannah down.

"Adam, don't you think we're wonderful together?" she asked in a small voice. She waited for his answer. After a few more moments of silence, she felt her temper begin to flare.

Adam felt her body stiffen. He knew an outburst would follow shortly. "If you have any hope of this relationship continuing," he warned, "I would suggest you learn to control your temper. I will not be a puppet on a string for you or for anyone."

She squelched her anger. There was an edge to Adam's voice she hadn't heard before. "You could at least answer my question," she responded soothingly.

"We are wonderful together," he acknowledged, "but I am unwilling to put up with the baggage that comes with our lovemaking."

"Baggage," she blurted out. "What baggage?"

"Keep your voice down," Adam said in a hushed but firm voice. "Annabelle's room is only two doors down." He waited a few moments for Giselle to grow calm. "By baggage I mean the mood swings and the dangerous games."

"I could force him to explain," she thought to herself, "but that would only prove his point."

"I'll have to give that some thought," she said tersely. "Perhaps it would be best we put an end to our affair."

"I have given that a great deal of thought," he responded evenly, "and I have concluded, under the present circumstances, it is best that it ends."

After all the times she had made him dance to her tune, she couldn't believe what she was hearing. He was no longer under her control. If she wanted the relationship to continue, she would have to give in to his demands. Placide was a strong man, but he had always given in to her. How could Adam dare to give her an ultimatum. She began to move away from him, but she stopped herself. In her heart, she knew he would allow her to leave without a further word.

"I have a full day ahead of me," he said when she did not give him an answer. "I suggest you retire to your room so we may both get some sleep."

"Just like that?" she asked unbelievably.

"Just like that," he replied calmly. "I will not risk losing all I have and I will not be embarrassed. I am not your play toy."

"Am I to be your play toy?" she asked disconcertingly. "Are you telling me I must do your bidding if we are to continue?"

"We are to be equals in a relationship that gratifies both of us," he replied. "I expect you to give no more to me than I am willing to give to you. I will be treated with respect and I will treat you with respect. I will not risk my reputation or my property."

"Make love to me once more and I'll give you my answer," she said coyly. "You may decide you don't want to be without me."

"As I said previously," Adam stated emphatically, "tomorrow will be a full day. We must both get some sleep. I hope you can find your way back to your room."

Giselle wanted him more than she had ever in her life wanted a man. She wanted to feel his muscular body as he sought to please her. "You can be such a hard man," she said finally. "I agree."

"One more time and we must both get some rest," he said.

Giselle surrendered her body to his gentle care. She felt herself being carried on clouds of ecstasy. It no longer mattered to her that she couldn't manipulate him.

*****

Adam was surprised to see Jacques' carriage pulling up before his home when he came in from the fields for his dinner. It was highly irregular for Jacques to visit on a Monday, especially at noon. As he stood waiting for the carriage to come to a halt, he wondered what had brought his father-in-law to Southern Kingdom.

Jacques descended from the carriage and made his way

over to Adam. "I guess you're wondering what brought me this way," he said as he shook Adam's hand. "I went to town to see Giselle but her servants told me she's here."

"Yes, she is here, "Adam responded. "She arrived here yesterday afternoon. She must be in the house. Come on in. I am sure Margaret prepared a delicious meal. Please stay and have dinner with us."

Jacques followed Adam into the house. "Oh, Pappa," Annabelle said when she spied her father. "What a pleasant surprise." She walked over to him and hugged him warmly. "We were just sitting down for dinner. I'll have Hannah set another plate."

"I didn't mean to impose," Jacques said. "I brought something for Giselle."

"You know you're not imposing," Annabelle responded. "Giselle is in the dining room. I'm sure she'll be pleased to see you."

Giselle was astonished to see her father-in-law. An alarm bell went off in her mind. "There's something on his mind," she said to herself. "He doesn't trust me around Adam." She rose from her chair, went over to Jacques and kissed his cheek. "It's so nice to see you," she said.

"I was thinking about how much you've gone through in the past year," Jacques stated, "what with Placide's disappearance and all. I know the experience has been difficult for you."

Giselle heard the words he was saying, but she knew something very different was running through his mind. She waited patiently for him to get to his point.

"The waiting must be especially difficult," he continued. "I thought a tour of Europe would help to cheer you up. I took the liberty of asking my sister Elaine to go along as your traveling companion. This will be good for both of you. The poor woman has gone no where since Harold's death." He pulled a ticket from his coat pocket and handed it to her. "Your ship will be sailing Monday of next week."

"I would've jumped at the offer of an expense paid tour of Europe a week ago," she thought to herself. "I really don't want to be separated from Adam now." She wanted to tell her father-in-law she wasn't interested in a tour of Europe, but she knew the matter wasn't open for debate. She wouldn't inherit a penny from Placide's estate until after he had been pronounced dead. Although she had the free run of the estate in town, including the servants, all expenses were paid by Jacques. Without Jacques' largess, she would be forced to live as a pauper.

"He suspects there's something between Adam and me," she thought to herself. "This is his way of removing the source of the problem. He's worried that I'll embarrass him with Adam or with some other man." Although he had always been a gentleman with her, he had taken her measure. She'd been stupid to flirt with Adam around him. Nothing had gone unnoticed. She could see Adam out of the corner of her eye. The tour of Europe wasn't making him happy either.

"That's so thoughtful of you," she said. "It's such short notice, though. It may be best to postpone the trip so I may make all the preparations."

"Yes, it is short notice," Jacques agreed. "I'll take you home so you may begin the preparations today."

"You've sealed the cage," Giselle said to herself. "I won't even have one more night here to say good-bye to Adam. I underestimated you, Monsieur Dupre'."

"You're so kind," she said. She sought to keep her displeasure with him out of her voice. "At least we can have a pleasant meal before we leave." She was hoping to have a moment alone with Adam to arrange a meeting at the cottage before boarding the ship.

"There's always time for a delicious meal," Jacques said, "especially with my beloved daughter and son-in-law. He sat down beside Adam.

Giselle picked at her food as she groped for some means of having a private word with Adam. She gazed in his direction. Jacques was keeping him engaged in conversation. She was beginning to despair until an idea planted itself in her mind. Jacques wasn't keeping an eye on her. She'd leave a note in Adam's room telling him to meet with her at the cottage the following afternoon. The note would be safe from Annabelle since they no longer shared a room. Her spirits lifted.

"I need to go upstairs and pack my things," she said.

"Do you need any help?" Annabelle asked.

"No," Giselle replied, "Most of my clothes are still packed. It'll only take a moment." She hurried to her room and packed her clothes. After the clothes were packed, she wrote a note for Adam asking him to meet with her at the cottage at two o'clock the following afternoon. No one was in the hallway when she reached Adam's door. She placed the note under his pillow and slipped out of the room unseen. She was smiling when she reentered the dining room.

"Everything is packed," she said. "Annabelle, would you please have your servant take my trunk out to the carriage?"

"I will tell Fred to bring your trunk down," Adam said.

"Thank you," Giselle responded. "She turned back to Annabelle. "Thank you so much for your hospitality. You were so sweet to allow me to stay, especially since you had no notice that I was coming."

"It was our pleasure," Annabelle responded. "Please come and visit us when you return from your trip."

"I will," Giselle rejoined. She turned to Adam. "Please take good care of Annabelle and Charles. They're very special to us."

"Yes, of course," Adam said. "I hope you enjoy your stay in Europe."

"I hope to be caressed by warm sea breezes," she responded. She hoped Adam would understand she wanted him to caress her once more before she was forced to leave. "I hope I don't cry with homesickness each night when I lay my head on my pillow." "Adam, please look under your pillow," she said under her breath. "We can be together at least one more time before I leave."

*****

Hannah couldn't believe her good fortune as she stood in the hallway listening to Jacques. Giselle would be leaving soon on a tour of Europe. She'd be gone for up to a year or maybe even longer. That should give sufficient time for Adam to clear his head.

She almost felt sorry for Giselle as she watched her pick at her food. She noticed that Giselle continued to glance furtively toward Adam. "She wants a moment alone with him," Hannah thought to herself. "That's not likely to happen the way Jacques's keeping him occupied."

As she studied Giselle's face, she saw a change come over her. There was now a smile on her lips. "She's come up with a solution," Hannah thought to herself. "There's a reason for her sudden good cheer."

She followed Giselle at a distance as she made her way upstairs to pack. It occurred to her that the only recourse left to Giselle would be to leave a message for Adam. Jacques was watching Adam too closely for her to communicate openly with him.

"Where would she leave the letter to ensure it would come to Adam's attention?" Hannah asked herself. "It would have to be left where it wouldn't be seen by others."

There was only one place she could think of that fit the criteria. She made her way quickly to Adam's bedroom and hid in the bathing room. She left the door ajar so she could observe Giselle when she came in.

A few minutes later, she watched as Giselle stole quietly into the room, pulled back Adam's bedspread, lifted his pillow, and clutched it to her breast. Giselle held the pillow up to her nose as though she were inhaling Adam's scent. She then placed the pillow back on the bed and replaced the spread.

Hannah waited for Giselle to leave and then walked beside the bed where Giselle had stood only moments before. She pulled the bedspread down, slid her hand beneath the pillow and discovered the note Giselle had hidden there.

Hannah lifted the note to her eyes. She could smell the scent of Giselle's perfume. She read the message and then crumpled the note in her hand. "You'll wait in vain for him, Giselle," she said to herself. She smiled happily.

A few minutes later, she placed the paper in the grate of

the fireplace in her room, struck a sulphur match and touched it to the note. The flames quickly licked around the paper and soon all that remained was ashes. "Just like the ashes of your affair," she said to herself. She walked up to the mirror and checked her appearance. After she was assured she looked her best, she went downstairs to witness Giselle's departure.

CHAPTER TWENTY-ONE

January 7, 1868 - February 26, 1868

Winter of 1868 had set in cold and wet in south
Louisiana. Temperatures had dropped below freezing five days
in a row in mid-February. Several inches of snow had fallen
followed by sleet only a couple of days after the snow had
melted. Some of the local planters said this would mean fewer
insects during the warmer months.

Adam pulled the collar of his heavy coat more tightly
around his neck after a sudden wind gust blew through the
buggy. He was driving the buggy this morning, hoping it would
give him some protection from the cold winds. The City of
Opelousas finally appeared in the distance as the buggy topped a
slight hill. "I hope Fisk has a fire going in his office," Adam said
to himself. His feet felt like they were encased in a block of ice.

Fisk had bought two of the three parcels of land back,
but the new owners had refused to sell unless they made a profit.
He was angry with Fisk for selling the land to them in the first
place. He had argued unsuccessfully that the extra cost should
have been deducted from Fisk's fee.

The last of the three landowners, Adam thought of them
as interlopers, was refusing to sell. It was Fisk's opinion that
Adam should be satisfied he was able to buy two of the three
parcels and leave it at that.

The two Fisk had managed to purchase added up to
twenty-three hundred arpents. The remaining tract was twenty-
six hundred arpents. Adam was unwilling to accede to the loss
of the land.

Adam's cold fingers pained him when he knocked on the
door to Fisk's office. No one responded to his knock. He rapped

his cold knuckles harder on the doorframe. It was much too cold
to be standing here waiting for Fisk to open the door. Adam
wiped frost off of one of the windowpanes with his gloved hand
and looked inside. He saw no one in the office. "Where could he
be?" he asked himself. He pulled his watch out to check the time.
It was nine thirty. "Fisk should be here," he muttered.

This is not the kind of weather to expect a client to wait
outdoors," he grumbled angrily. His nerves began to fray. "I told
him I would be here."

"I'm sorry I'm late," Fisk said as he appeared beside
Adam. He rubbed his hands together. "It sure is cold."

Adam was startled. He had not seen Fisk coming up
behind him. "A good businessman must always be prompt," he
said angrily. He struggled to get his temper in check. It would be
necessary to have his wits about him for the meeting with Fisk.

"I just had to have another one of Georgina's biscuits,"
Fisk said casually. "Had another cup of coffee, too. Sure didn't
want to leave that warm kitchen to get out in this cold."

Adam waited impatiently as Fisk unlocked the door. He
followed him into the cold office. Much to his displeasure, he
discovered there was no fire in the Franklin stove. He shivered
involuntarily as he sat in one of the chairs and pulled his coat
tightly about himself. He wanted to make an angry comment
about the cold office but held his tongue. "Part of Fisk's strategy
may be to get me off balance," he said to himself.

"I talked to Bernhart again," Fisk said after he sat behind
his desk. "He still refuses to budge. Says he intends to hold on to
the land and pass it on to his sons when he's gone."

"Have you anything in mind with which to encourage
him?" Adam asked. "It was not so long ago a situation such as
this would have posed no problem for you."

"Well, times are different now," Fisk said as he leaned
back in his chair. "Now that everything's getting back to normal,
it ain't so easy to do those kinds of things." He watched to see
how that would set with Blythington.

"I suppose you have done your best," Adam conceded.
"Sometimes we have to live with our disappointments." Fisk
was lying. It was less than three years since the end of the war.

Louisiana was still under Military Governor Benjamin Flanders. Things were not even close to normal. He lifted his hat from the chair beside him and began to rise from his chair.

"He's giving up much too easy," Fisk said to himself. "I know he isn't gonna give up on that land." He searched Blythington's face for something that would give him a clue as to what he was thinking. His face was impassive.

"Now, hold on there," Fisk said fretfully. "I didn't say we couldn't get the land. I said it won't be easy."

Adam sat back down in his chair. "What do you have in mind?" he asked.

Fisk had nothing in mind. Legitimate business was bringing in plenty of money without the risks and headaches. His girth had expanded with Georgina's good cooking and he was enjoying his new lifestyle. He felt Blythington's eyes boring into his head. "I can have some of the men come up with an accident," he said speculatively. "He might decide his health is worth more to him than the land."

"Can you get that done without implicating yourself or me?" Adam asked. He knew Fisk was only hypothesizing and had not thought through any plan.

"I'll have to talk to some of the fellas and work on it," Fisk replied. "We'll have to do some careful planning." He felt himself being pulled into a place where he didn't want to go. He thought once more of having Blythington eliminated and then recalled how he had pretended to give up so easily.

"He already has someone else lined up in case I won't work with him," he thought to himself. "I wonder who that could be." Several names came to mind but he ruled them out. "It's got to be somebody from out of town."

"Springtime will be here soon," Adam said. "I want to put my men to planting that land simultaneously with my other property. I cannot make money with fallow ground."

"That's cutting it pretty close," Fisk opined. "Doesn't leave me with much time to persuade Bernhart."

"If you feel it cannot be done within that time frame, just say so," Adam responded. "I know someone who can get the job done."

"There he goes again," Fisk said to himself. "He's got somebody lined up. Probably someone who would cheat his own mother to make a dollar." He got out of his chair, walked to the potbellied stove and began to place kindling on the grate. He had to buy a little time so he could think things out. In a few minutes he had a large fire going. "That oughta make this place feel better soon," he said. "Nothing like a hot fire on a cold day."

Adam sat quietly and gazed at Fisk as he waited for him to continue. He was willing to allow the silence to go on indefinitely.

"Can you tell me who you've lined up for just in case I don't come through for you?" Fisk asked nervously. "You want to make sure it's somebody you can trust."

"Indeed, I can tell you," Adam replied evenly, "but I choose not to divulge that information; however, he did indicate to me he is eager to prove himself. I would prefer to keep our arrangement; that is, if you feel you can deliver."

Fisk walked back to his chair and sat down. "What have I done to deserve this mess?" he asked himself. "I'll do whatever it takes to get the land," he said in a hollow voice, "but you'll have to agree to pay all of the extra expenses. I'll have to hire some men to change Bernhart's mind."

"My father always said one gains more knowledge and is more likely to retain the knowledge when one pays for one's own mistakes," Blythington stated flatly. "Had you acted as we agreed, you would not be faced with this problem. I will only pay a fair fee for your involvement."

Fisk felt anger begin to boil. "Damn it!" he exclaimed, "can't you get it through your thick skull you had stopped coming around. How was I to know you were still interested? You're pushing me too far." He glared at Blythington.

Adam gazed calmly at Fisk. He waited for him to vent his anger. After a while, Fisk seemed to wither.

"If I recall correctly," Adam said, "You came to me asking me to do business with you. You made several guarantees. In return, I agreed to purchase land only through you. I kept my word and I trusted you to keep your word. Are you telling me now you no longer value my business?"

"Don't you understand, Mr. Blythington," Fisk implored, "I want your business, but you're asking me to take all of the risks and pay all of the extra costs. Do you think that's fair to me?"

"This is a matter of principle," Adam responded tranquilly. "I kept my word and now I expect you to do the same. I am unwilling to pay the price of your betrayal."

"Betrayal?" Fisk responded incredulously. "Are you calling what I did betrayal? I simply sold land that came on the market to interested buyers."

"Yes, I do call what you did betrayal," Adam replied. "You guaranteed me you would make sure I had first refusal on all parcels of land that became available between and surrounding my two plantations. Do you recall your guarantee?"

"Yes, but things changed," Fisk said weakly. "You should be able to understand that."

"Nothing changed," Adam responded sharply. "I did not tell you I was no longer interested in our business arrangement."

"Can't you at least meet me half way?" Fisk asked. "Just a little help with the extra expenses. I've done a lot for you."

"My position is clear," Adam said definitively. He placed his hat on his head and rose from his chair. "You have made money from our transactions in the past and you stand to make a great deal more money from me in the future, that is, if you intend to honor my business."

"It's not good to push someone too far," Fisk shot back like a harried beast.

"I appreciate you bringing that up," Adam said coldly. "We can have a profitable relationship for the duration of your stay in Louisiana or we can become enemies. Think carefully before you make your decision. I am a man of my word. I give you my word I shall deal forthrightly with you should you choose to continue our relationship. On the other hand, should you choose to become my enemy, I give you my word I will deal ruthlessly with you."

Fisk felt a cold hand reach into his stomach and squeeze tightly. He had never before in his life encountered eyes that held more evil. In all his years in the war he had never felt death as imminent as he did now. "I didn't mean I wanted for us to be enemies," he said placatingly. "I hope you didn't take anything I said that way. I guess I should've told you when the land came on the market like I had said I would. You're right; it was my fault. I oughta have to pay for my mistakes. I'll get the land for you and I'll keep an eye out for anything else I can do for you."

"Very well," Adam said. "I will be waiting to hear from you soon."

Fisk slumped back in his chair after the door closed behind Blythington. "I just sold my soul to the devil," he said disconsolately. He pulled a drawer of the file cabinet open and drew out a bottle of whiskey. He lifted the bottle to his lips and took a sip. The whiskey was warm going down but he still felt the iciness in the marrow of his bones. "That man would kill me without blinking an eye." He resolved to be careful not to anger Blythington in the future. "I got to make some money and hightail it back to Pittsburgh as soon as I can. Maybe there I'll be free of him." Once again he raised the bottle to his lips, but this time he drank a large swallow of the fiery liquid.

*****

Wilson Bernhart was having supper with his wife and two sons when the side door to his house was kicked open and four men wearing white sheets and brandishing handguns entered. "Get out of here!" Bernhart cried out as he rose explosively from his chair. He lunged for the rifle he kept in the corner of the kitchen.

One of the men moved quickly, took hold of him and shoved him violently toward the kitchen table where his wife and two sons sat.

"Sit down and no one'll get hurt," the man nearest him growled in a deep voice.

Bernhart remained standing and glared at the man. "You have no right to be in here," he said courageously. "I've heard about your organization. Men don't hide their faces; only cowards."

The man who'd manhandled Bernhart swiped his gun barrel across his face. Blood dripped from the tear the barrel left on his face. "The man said for you to sit down," the hooded man said threateningly.

"What do you want with us?" Bernhart asked as he seated himself. "We don't have anything worth stealing and we ain't been doing anything with Negro folks except hiring them to do work around the place." He lifted his hand and felt his face. There was a deep gash where the gun barrel had struck. There was blood on his hand when he pulled it away.

"We come to tell you to sell out and move back where you come from," the man who appeared to be the leader of the group said. "We taking our state back from you Yankees. All ya'll are doing is coming here and taking our land."

"We came here to raise our boys where there are still wide open spaces and to get away from the long winters," Bernhart shot back indignantly. "You have no right to tell me where I can live. I served as a captain with the Army of the Potomac defending this nation."

"I don't care if you crossed the Potomac with George Washington," the leader said crossly, "you don't belong here."

"You seem to have forgotten you're still under martial law," Bernhart countered. "You can't get away with this sort of thing."

"You might not live long enough to tell the law," one of the men who hadn't spoken previously said.

"If something happens to me, Mary and my boys will still have this place," Bernhart parried. "You still won't have my land."

The man who appeared to be the leader pulled a knife from a fold in his sheet and held it against the younger boy's throat. "Is your land worth your boy's life?" he asked.

The boy looked at his father with fear in his eyes. Bernhart measured the distance between himself and the man. "Hanks's throat would be cut before I could get to him," he thought to himself.

"Will!" his wife, Mary, cried out. "Nothing's worth all of

this. Please don't let them hurt Hank."

"Did Fisk order you to do this?" Bernhart asked. "He's been trying to buy our land back."

"Fisk? Order us?" the leader shouted, "You don't know nothin about nothin. We don't take orders from nobody. We oughta kill the bunch of you and be finished with you."

"Will, please do whatever they say," Mary pleaded. "We can sell out and start over somewhere else. Don't make them hurt Hank."

"If I do what you ask, will you leave us alone?" Bernhart asked. He would tell them whatever they wanted to hear and then go to the law in the morning.

The leader smiled. "I know what you're thinking," he said. "You're thinking we'll leave here tonight and then you'll go to the law in the morning. Isn't that what you're thinking, Blue Belly?"

Bernhart sat quietly and gazed at the leader.

"I asked you a question," he said loudly. "Answer me."

"I wasn't thinking anything like that," Bernhart lied. These men were smarter than he'd thought. "I was only thinking I want my family to be safe."

"That's a good answer, boy, but you're lying," the leader said gruffly. "You think you're smarter than we are. You think you can get around us." He gazed coldly into Bernhart's eyes for a few moments. "I'll tell you how this is gonna work. You have no idea who we are so you won't know whether or not we're watching you. We'll be watching, and if anything goes wrong, your boys are gonna die. Is that starting to get into your head, boy?"

"I understand," Bernhart answered evenly. Another plan was taking shape in his mind. "I'll put Mary and the boys on the first train they can catch going back home, and then I'll go to the law," he thought to himself. "They can't hurt them if they can't get to them."

"You're still thinking, huh, Blue Belly?" the leader began. "I can see it in your eyes. Ya still thinking that we're dumb. If you make one move to send these boys anywhere until after this place is sold and all your belongings are packed, get ready to bury them. That goes for your sweet little wife, too."

Bernhart slumped in his chair. He'd fought enough battles to know when he was defeated. It wouldn't be smart to take on the Klan. He looked around the room. Mary had the place looking like home. He would miss the house and his land, but losing his wife and his boys was too high a price to pay. "All right, you win," he said sadly. "We'll sell the place and move out."

"Now, you're starting to think right, boy," the leader of the men said jubilantly. "Just remember, we'll be watching. If you want those boys to grow up to be men, don't try nothin stupid."

The leader moved his knife away from Hank's throat and returned it to the fold in his sheet. "Come on, fellows," he said. "We'll leave these people to themselves. They probably need time to clear their bowels." He threw his head back and guffawed.

The men filed out of the house. When the leader reached the door, he turned back to the Bernharts. "Like I told you, Blue Belly," he said menacingly, "we have our people watching you."

Mary and the boys huddled around Bernhart as soon as the door closed behind the men. "Would those people really kill us, Pa?" Willy, the older of the boys, asked as he clung to his father.

Bernhart searched for something he could say to comfort his family. "God was protecting us," he said.

"You're going to go and speak to the land agent first thing in the morning, aren't you?" Mary asked.

He considered the possibility of getting the law to intervene. A picture of the man holding the knife against Hank's throat came into his mind. "Yes, Mary," he said abjectly, "I'll go and see him first thing in the morning."

*****

Two days later Blythington received a letter from Fisk.

He opened the envelope and removed the message. The note read:

Come to my office at 9:00 tomorrow morning.

There was no signature and there were no other markings on the paper. "Tell him I will be there," Adam said to the man who delivered the letter. The messenger walked away wordlessly, mounted his horse and headed back for town.

"I hope he has good news," Adam said to himself. He reread the note. "If it were good news, he would have written that in the message. He must want to tell me he cannot get the owner to sell." He gave more thought to the message. "He has changed his mind about our business association. How am I going to find someone to replace him?"

He slept fitfully that night. He awoke with a start around two o'clock in the morning. He had dreamed he was in a chair in Fisk's office with his wrists and ankles bound tightly. Fisk was holding a knife to his throat. Although the night was cold, his clothes were soaking wet. After he reassured himself it had only been a dream, he lay back down and tried to go back to sleep. Roughly an hour later, he awoke in terror with his hands protecting his throat. The nightmare had returned.

"It must mean he wants to kill me," he thought anxiously. "If he indicates to me he no longer wants my business, I have to do away with him before he gets someone to kill me."

Once again he was faced with the possibility of having to engage someone to replace Fisk. "I have no idea where to even begin," he thought to himself. "I do not even know with whom to speak of such a thing. I surely cannot ask Fisk." He was caught in the horns of a dilemma.

He deliberated whether to go to Hannah's room and spend the remainder of the night with her or to get a good book from the library and read until dawn. He did not want to go back to sleep because the dreams were frightening.

He was halfway to Hannah's room when he changed his mind and headed for the library. Nothing on the shelves caught his interest. He continued to search the shelves until he finally settled upon Edgar Allen Poe's short stories. He sat down to read in one of the overstuffed chairs in the library.

He had no idea how long he had been asleep when he heard a male voice say, "There he is men. Grab him and tie him up before he gets away." Adam opened his eyes and jumped from his chair. He was not going to be taken without a fight. Instead of the hooligans he expected to find, he discovered there was no one in his vicinity. He listened but he did not hear the sounds of the footfalls of fleeing men. He looked for the man whose voice he had heard, but turned up nothing.

In a quick search of the house, he found no unlocked windows or doors. There was no one downstairs and no evidence anyone had entered his home. The man he heard had apparently evaporated into thin air. "It must have been another dream," he said to himself wanly. He walked over to the grandfather clock in the parlor. It was four o'clock.

He considered going upstairs to continue his search, but felt that was unnecessary. "There has to be a reason I am having those dreams," he said to himself. "This may be some cosmic force trying to warn me."

Hannah opened her door after his second knock. "Is something wrong?" she asked sleepily when she saw him standing in the hall.

He was beginning to feel foolish. "No, not really," he replied, "but I had some very disturbing dreams." He halted for a moment and then continued shamefacedly, "it was probably something I ate."

Hannah held him tightly. "Dreams can be very real," she said. "Come to bed and lie down."

Adam felt better now that he was with Hannah. He lay back on the bed and closed his eyes. The dreams no longer seemed as menacing. "It must be something I ate," he said to himself.

She curled up beside him and cradled him in her arms.

He nestled his head against her breast and soon fell asleep. She listened to his even breathing for a while and then felt her eyelids growing heavy. A few moments later, she was fast asleep.

*****

"It's time to wake up," Hannah said as she gently shook Adam.

"Is it morning already?" he asked as he tried to rub the sleep out of his eyes.

"It was already morning when you came up here," Hannah replied lightly. "You must be exhausted."

"I feel much better," he responded. "I must have fallen asleep almost immediately."

"You were asleep in only a few moments," she said. "Were you bothered by more of those dreams?"

"You must have driven them away," he replied with a smile. He pulled her close and kissed her lips. "I should have come up here earlier."

"Why didn't you?" she asked. "You know my door is always open to you."

"It was already after two," he replied. "I did not want to disturb you."

"So, losing almost an entire night's sleep was better?" she asked.

"No," he replied. "I hoped to go back to sleep and rest peacefully, but the dream returned. I wish I had come to you earlier."

"Would you like to tell me about your dream?" she asked.

"I feel foolish now," he replied, "but it seemed so real last night."

Hannah waited. She wasn't sure he would continue.

After several moments, he continued, "I dreamed I was bound in one of the chairs in Fisk's office. He held a knife to my throat. I was sure he was going to kill me."

"That's terrible," she said. "That must have been very disturbing."

"Yes, it was," he responded. "I fell asleep once again and had the same dream. When I awakened, I was trying to protect my throat. Later, I fell asleep in a chair in the library. I awoke when I heard a man telling his men to tie me up before I could get away. There was no one near me when I opened my eyes, and I did not hear anyone running away. All of the doors and windows were locked. I saw no sign that anyone had gained entry."

"Oh, poor you," Hannah said. "No wonder you looked so frazzled." She moved closer to him and held his hand. "Do you have any idea why you're dreaming about Fisk harming you?"

"He sent a messenger here yesterday with a letter telling me to meet with him at nine o'clock this morning," Adam replied. "There was no explanation on the note for the meeting."

"Do you have any idea why he wants to meet with you?" she asked.

"I was hoping he arranged the purchase of some property we spoke of," he answered, "but there is the possibility he wants to tell me he is no longer interested in my business."

"There's more to this than Adam is telling me," she thought to herself. "Did he have an altercation with Fisk?"

"What makes you think he wouldn't be interested in your business?" she asked.

Adam wondered what she would think if he told her the whole truth. He concluded he would tell her only part of the truth. "Fisk has changed his lifestyle," he replied. "He is now married and he is satisfied handling smaller transactions. He says there is too much risk in dealing with large amounts of land."

"He's not very bright," Hannah stated. "There's more money to be made with the larger transactions. What are you going to do if he breaks off your arrangement?"

"He will be difficult to replace," Adam replied shaking his head. "I have no idea where to begin to search for a replacement. I do not travel in the same circles as those people."

"I wish I could help you," she said, "but I don't associate with those people either."

*****

The late February day turned out to be warmer than

it had been in several weeks. Adam told Fred to have Diablo saddled and ready.

"You aren't eating," Annabelle said after watching for several minutes as Adam picked at his food. "Are you feeling ill?"

"No, Annabelle, I am not ill," he replied. "I have to go into town on urgent business. I am only preoccupied."

Since Charles was now sleeping at night without waking her, and she was in her last days of pregnancy, Annabelle was much more rested, and more kindly disposed toward Adam. "I hope things go well for you," she said. "I'll say a prayer for you."

"Thank you," he said absently, "that is very kind of you." He glanced up at the clock on the mantle. "I must be off. I have to be in town for a nine o'clock appointment." He rose from his chair and kissed Annabelle lightly on her cheek. "I do not expect to be home for dinner."

"Be careful," she said as she looked up at him. "He's looking gaunt," she said to herself. She bowed her head right then and prayed for her husband's safety and for his day to go well.

*****

"I wonder what is in store for me," Adam mused as he tied Diablo to the hitching rail that stood in front of Fisk's office. He gathered himself together in preparation for the meeting with Fisk. He was determined to project boldness and confidence.

"Come on in," Fisk said from the doorway. "I brought a jug of hot coffee from home and some cups. Should warm you up after that ride."

"The ride was pleasant," Adam responded easily, "but I would welcome a hot cup of coffee." He waited as Fisk poured coffee into two mugs.

"I have cream and sugar if you want some," Fisk said.

"Black is fine," he responded. He sat on one of the chairs and calmly sipped his coffee. He was intent on Fisk being the first to bring up the issue of the meeting.

"That cold hearted bastard's not even gonna ask me why

I sent for him," Fisk said to himself. "He knows I have to dance to his tune." He appraised Blythington. "Expensive suit and boots. Damn it! I helped to make him what he is today and now I got to do what he says or else. I'd like to see him knocked off of his high horse." He finally accepted that Blythington was going to wait all day, if necessary, to be told the reason for the meeting.

"I reckon you're wondering why I asked you to come here today," Fisk stated.

"I was enjoying my coffee," Adam responded. "Did your wife make the coffee?"

"You arrogant jackass, you know damned well who made the coffee," Fisk thought to himself. "Sitting there like you don't have a worry in the world."

"Georgina made the coffee," he replied.

"Excellent coffee," Adam said. "Please give Mrs. Fisk my compliments."

"I got the land for you," Fisk blurted out in exasperation. "It wasn't easy, but Bernhart is selling out."

"When do we sign the papers?" Adam asked.

"Not so much as a thank you," Fisk thought irritably. "They're ready now," he replied. "I was able to get him to sell it for the same price he paid for it."

Adam examined Fisk's face. He saw he was hiding something. "You paid far less for that land than Bernhart did," he said to himself. He was about to press Fisk to tell him the truth when he recalled his dreams. "You did well," he said. "Are the papers at Cortez's office?"

"Yeh," Fisk replied as he struggled to hide his relief. He'd been worried that Blythington would challenge him about the price. "You can sign um any time you're ready."

"I will go there now and give him a bank draft," Adam said. "Of course, the draft will include your usual fee." He rose from his chair and started for the door.

"It's always a pleasure doing business with you, Mr. Blythington," Fisk said as he came up to Blythington and offered his hand. "I'll be keeping an eye out for more land in that area."

Adam shook Fisk's hand and then left his office.

"I got one over on you," Fisk said out loud. "You're not

as smart as you think."

Adam mounted his horse and headed toward Cortez's office. "He thinks he outsmarted me," he thought to himself. "I only set the hook a little deeper." He was elated by the way the meeting had gone. He now had the land and Fisk was happy doing business with him again. "It all worked out very well." He wished he could whistle.

CHAPTER TWENTY-TWO

February 28, 1868 - March 30, 1868

     Annabelle got over her reticence quickly when the labor pains began to torture her body. Dr. Robert Joubert listened intently to her heartbeat. "You're doing very well," he said when the pain subsided. "It'll only be a few more minutes." Robert had come in his father's stead because Dr. Allan Joubert's painful gout had rendered him unable to travel.

     The windows were opened wide to let in whatever breeze would blow in. The late February day had turned out hot and humid. Robert wiped perspiration from his brow with his handkerchief.

     "Why isn't Adam here?" Angelina asked when he walked over to the window where she stood watching storm clouds gather. She was trying to decide whether to close the windows against the impending storm or leave them open to allow air into the room. Annabelle's nightgown was soaked with her own perspiration.

     Adam had sent Fred into town to fetch Dr. Joubert. When Robert arrived, he was told that Adam was out in the fields. "He should be here," Robert replied. "No one could have kept me from your side when Alice was born."

     "I'm so mad at him," Angelina said. "I don't know why Annabelle continues to put up with him. If I were her, I'd give him a piece of my mind."

     Robert smiled. Angelina and Annabelle were nothing alike temperamentally. Angelina was not a docile creature. He had no doubt Adam would've had difficulty with her.

     "Why are you smiling?" Angelina asked.

"I was thinking about what you said," he replied. "Adam would behave very differently with you as his wife."

Angelina opened her mouth to comment but broke off when Annabelle cried out. Robert hastily returned to her and bent down to determine the degree of dilation. To his amazement, the top of the child's head was beginning to appear. The midwife had told him when Charles was born Annabelle had experienced a relatively easy delivery, especially for a first child. She would be in labor less than three hours for this child.

"The baby's coming," he said. "Try to help him along. Push as hard as you can."

The infant inched his way out. Soon the baby's entire head was out. Robert took hold of the infant's head and turned the baby until he was facing toward him. "Just a little more," he said.

Annabelle cried out as she complied with Robert's orders. "He's coming," Robert repeated. "Another minute or so and it'll all be over."

In less than a minute, Robert held the infant in his hands. He gently slapped the baby's bottom. The child gave a startled cry and then grew silent.

"You have a beautiful baby boy," Robert said as he held the child close to Annabelle so that she could see her son.

"He's beautiful," Annabelle said softly.

After Robert severed the umbilical cord, Angelina took the baby from Robert and cleaned him. A few minutes later she laid the boy next to his mother.

"Is something wrong with him?" Annabelle asked with alarm in her voice. "He's not crying."

Robert examined the infant carefully. He appeared to be perfectly normal. He was an unusually quiet child, though. "He seems fine to me," he said. "Some infants are placid. Be grateful you have a baby who'll let you sleep."

The look of concern left Annabelle's face.

"He's not at all like Charles," she said. "Charles came into the world screaming and demanding."

"Have you chosen a name for him?" Angelina asked.

"Yes," Annabelle replied. "We'll name him Adam Paul

Blythington, II. I think we'll call him Paul. A child needs to have his own name."

A loud clap of thunder resounded outside as though to announce Paul's birth. Ruth, who had been hovering nearby, rushed to a window to pull it shut as the rain began to pour down. Angelina left Annabelle's bedside and gave Ruth a hand with the windows.

"We have a choice between getting wet or smothering," Angelina said loudly so as to be heard over the sound of thunder. "Maybe we should leave a crack in the windows so some air can come in." An exceptionally loud clap of thunder made the windows rattle. As she gazed out the window, she could see the tops of the live oak trees swirling from the blowing wind. "It looks like we're in for a bad storm."

A loud cracking noise could be heard. A large branch from a pecan tree standing near the house fell to the ground. Annabelle lifted her head from the pillow and gazed outside at the raging storm. "Ruth, please get Fred, Mary and Hannah to help you close all the shutters," she said with obvious concern. "I hope Adam's not out in this weather."

"I hope he was hit by lightning," Angelina said to herself. "At the very least, I hope he's getting soaked to the bone."

Robert moved rapidly to one of the windows and began to close the shutters. Ruth hurried out of the room to find Hannah and the other servants. The house shook from the next thunderclap.

"There wasn't a cloud in the sky when we got here," Robert said. "We may be in for another cold spell. That usually happens when bad weather comes up so suddenly."

"I hope not," Annabelle moaned. "Especially after the cold of January and the earlier days of this month." She drew Paul more closely to protect him from the impending cold.

"I don't think you need to worry so soon," Angelina laughed as she watched her friend's protective instinct toward her son. "It's still hot in here."

Just as quickly as the storm had come up, it subsided. Robert opened one of the shutters and peered outside. Water was still dripping from the roof and the trees, but the sun was shining brightly. Everything looked freshly bathed. The sky was cobalt blue. He opened one of the windows to test the temperature. Cool air wafted into the room.

"I guess I was wrong," he said. "It turned out to be exactly what we needed." He opened the window wider and relished the feel of the cool air on his face.

The door opened and Adam Paul Blythington, the first, walked into the room. Water dripped from his clothes. "Mary told me you had a boy," he said in a matter-of-fact manner.

"Would you like to hold him?" Annabelle asked.

"I must change into dry clothes," he responded disdainfully. "I am needed in the fields." He turned to leave the room.

"May I have a word with you?" Robert asked politely.

"Time is money," Adam replied coldly. "There is much to be done. Perhaps some other time."

"Your wife just had a child for you," Angelina cried out furiously. "Surely you can take a little of your precious time to comfort your wife and hold your son."

"I will thank you to mind your own business," Adam said as he glared at her. "I have never interfered in your life and I will not tolerate your interference in mine."

"Adam, your attitude toward my friends is contemptible," Annabelle cried out in a hurt voice. "They were only showing concern for me and our child."

Adam turned his attention from Angelina to his wife. His face registered fury as he glared down at her. Without another word, he turned and stomped out of the room.

*****

After changing into dry clothes, Adam searched for Hannah. He found her opening the shutters in one of the upstairs bedrooms. She saw immediately that something had upset him. She continued with her work while waiting for him to tell her what was on his mind.

Adam held back until she had opened both sets of

shutters in the room before he spoke. "May I have a moment of your time?" he asked.

"Of course," she replied. "You know I always have time for you."

"I would feel more comfortable in your room," he said. "Do you mind if we go there?"

Hannah followed him to her room. Once they were in the room, she locked the door and waited for him to speak.

"When I came in from the field to change clothes," he began, "Mary told me Annabelle had delivered her baby." He felt anger again begin to boil. He composed himself before he continued. "That young Doctor Joubert and his opinionated wife were in the room with her when I went in." He balled up his fists. "I do not know why some people refuse to mind their own business." He began to pace up and down the floor.

Hannah watched him as he paced. She knew when he was agitated like this it sometimes took him a while to reach his point.

He ceased pacing and faced her. "Annabelle asked if I wanted to hold the baby," he continued. "She could see I had come in only because my clothes were wet and she knew I was busy supervising the work in my new fields. There is plenty of time to hold the child later." He shook his head as he recalled the doctor's vile wife. "I think she only did that to embarrass me. I told her I had to get out of the wet clothes and return to the fields." He began pacing once again. He moved to one of the windows and gazed outside. Several minutes passed before he turned back to Hannah. "People like her make me so angry."

"Are you talking about Annabelle or Mrs. Joubert?" she asked.

"They both made me angry," he replied, "but I was speaking of Mrs. Joubert. She raised her voice at me and accused me of not caring about my wife and my child. Does she declare herself to be a mind reader? What makes matters even worse, Annabelle agreed with that ill-mannered busybody. She did not wait until we were alone but said that in their presence. I am her husband yet she betrays me."

"I would be very upset if he had shown no interest in

my child," Hannah thought to herself. "How could he think his attitude toward the child was proper?" She listened to him as he continued to rail against Annabelle and Angelina.

"I have half a mind to go down there this moment and throw them out," he said forcefully. "What do you think?"

Hannah was preoccupied with her own thoughts. The question startled her. "Think about what?" she asked.

"Were you not listening to me?" he asked. "Should I go down and throw the Jouberts out?"

"I don't think it's a good idea to throw them out," Hannah replied, ignoring his question about whether or not she was listening. "The Jouberts are important people in St. Landry Parish society. Making enemies of them wouldn't be wise."

Adam was chagrined by the lack of compassion in her voice. "Do you not agree that they wronged me?" he asked accusingly.

Hannah considered treating him gingerly, but decided to be forthright with him. "I don't blame them for being upset with you," she said soberly. "If it had been me who had just given birth to your child, I would have been very angry with you."

"Do you not understand I was wearing wet clothes and I was busy with very important work?" he lashed out. "How could you agree with them?"

"Don't raise your voice to me, Adam," she said coldly. "You asked my opinion. I refuse to agree with you when you're wrong. You showed no more concern for what Annabelle had just gone through or for your child than you would have for a piece of furniture. What you did was very cold hearted and cruel."

Adam was taken aback by the hard tone in her voice. "Do you really think I acted cruelly?" he asked. His deportment changed from angry to shamefaced.

"Yes, I do," she replied. "What kind of man refuses to even look at his newborn son? Are you that busy?"

"It is only that I have less interest in him now that I have an heir," he said defensively. "Surely you can understand that."

"Will you lose interest in Martha now that you have an heir?" she asked. "What if I became pregnant again? Would you show no interest in our child?"

"That is not the same thing," he sputtered. "You know I would always love our children."

"How can I know that?" she asked in a hard voice. "How is this child different from Martha or any other child I might have for you?"

"Surely you know it is different," he replied defensively.

"It's not different," she said flatly. "I think you need to stop trying to justify your behavior and examine your heart. There has to be something missing in a man who shows so little interest in his newborn son."

Adam dropped his eyes and studied his feet. He had run out of arguments. If Hannah, who loved him unconditionally, felt he had acted deplorably, then it was the truth. She would have agreed with him had he been right. It was difficult to admit he was wrong.

"What should I do?" he asked earnestly.

"You should go downstairs and see your wife and hold your son," she replied in a relieved tone. She hadn't been sure Adam would admit he had erred.

He held her in his arms for a moment and then turned for the door. Before he opened the door, he turned back to her. "You love me enough to tell me when I am wrong," he said soberly. "I want you to know how much I cherish you."

"I love you very much," she said. "Now, go and make amends."

*****

Surprise registered on the faces of Annabelle and the Jouberts when Adam opened the door and stepped back into the room.

"How are you feeling, Annabelle?" he asked.

"I'm fine," she replied as she looked wonderingly at her husband.

Adam moved more closely to the bed. He bent down and gazed at his slumbering child. "He looks so peaceful," he said. "Not at all like Charles."

"No, thank heavens," Annabelle responded. "He may let me get more sleep than Charles did."

Adam reached his hand out and stroked the baby's head gently. "May I hold him?" he asked.

"Of course you may," Annabelle answered with a smile. "He's your son, too."

He lifted the child and held him against his shoulder. Hannah had taught him how to hold a baby when Martha was an infant. "He is so small," he said.

"Yes, but he'll grow to be a man like his father," Annabelle said happily. "I hope he takes his time getting there, though."

"Yes," Adam agreed. "It will be some time before he becomes a man."

He lay Paul back down beside Annabelle. "I must return to the fields," he said. "If there is an emergency, please send someone to get me. I will let Fred know where to find me."

"I'll let you know," she responded. "I think we're both doing well; wouldn't you agree, Robert?"

Robert had been mesmerized as he watched Adam with Paul and Annabelle. Adam didn't seem to be the same man who'd been in the room earlier. "Mother and child are doing very well," he managed to get out.

Adam walked out of the room and closed the door behind him.

"Who was that man?" Angelina asked. "Did he go out and send someone else in his place?"

"Adam's a very sensitive man," Annabelle said. "He probably took the time to think about his behavior and realized he had acted badly. You'd like him if you took the time to know him."

"He may have realized he had gone too far and was in jeopardy of losing his claim to Belle Bois," Angelina said to herself. "He seemed sincere but I think he's only a consummate actor."

"If you say so," she responded, "but how can we get to know him when he avoids us?"

"He's not avoiding you," Annabelle said. "He works

much too hard. I've told him to take more time to enjoy life, but he says he's determined to build a large plantation for our children."

"This is already a large plantation," Robert said. "How much more does he want?"

"He says he won't be satisfied until Southern Kingdom and Lance des Chenes are combined," she replied.

"He owns Lance des Chenes too?" Robert asked with awe in his voice. He thought for a moment. "Belle Bois is between the two plantations."

"Since Placide left no heirs, we'll inherit Belle Bois when Pappa passes away," she replied. "I hope that's a long time from now."

A shiver ran down Robert's spine. "I hope so, too," he said solemnly. "I sincerely hope so," he thought to himself.

*****

Robert stuffed all of his medical appurtenances into his black bag. "Send for me if there's even the slightest problem," he said to Annabelle. "You went through that much more easily than I had anticipated."

"Cleopatra said my body was made for having babies," she joked. "I would've made a good brood mare."

"You're no brood mare," Angelina reproved. "That's the second time you've said that. I won't have you talking that way about yourself. You're a lovely young woman with two beautiful baby boys. I wish I were built like you. It seems it took weeks for Alice to come out."

"It'll be easier the next time," Robert said.

"Spoken like a man," Angelina retorted. "You should carry the next one."

There were hugs and kisses before Robert and Angelina were allowed to leave.

"Be sure to send someone to me immediately if there are any problems," Robert told Ruth from the buggy. "I'm not expecting anything to go wrong, but anything can happen."

"Yassah, Doc Robit," Ruth responded. "Don't you worry

none."

Robert took the reins in his hands and called out, "Get up, old girl, we're going home." The buggy began to roll down the drive.

"I hope you can get a good night's sleep," Angelina said. "You must be exhausted. What time did you come in this morning?"

"It was around two o'clock," Robert replied. "It seems most people decide they need a doctor when it's nighttime."

"I told you that you could have chosen the law," she picked, "but you decided you wanted to be the great healer."

"You wouldn't have it any other way, and you know that," Robert said as he put his arm around his wife. "Maybe we can work on making the baby tonight."

"Work?" she asked. "When did that become work?"

Robert laughed heartily. "I love you," he said warmly. "Life with you only gets better."

Angelina leaned her head against his shoulder. After a while she sat up. "Adam is a strange one," she said. "That little show when he returned to the room was for our benefit. I can't believe Annabelle doesn't see through him."

"I think she sees what she wants to see," Robert said sadly. "It's hard for her to admit to herself she married a despicable character. I feel so sorry for her."

"I noticed she's given up hope that Placide's still alive," she said.

"Why do you say that?" he asked. "I must've missed something."

"Don't you remember when she said Placide didn't leave any heirs?" she asked.

Robert shook his head. "That one passed right by me," he said. "Adam would be much more careful around her if he were still here."

"Adam would be dead by now," she stated flatly. "Giselle told me he was angry with Adam and wanted to call him out. It was fortunate for Adam that he disappeared."

Robert felt another shiver run down his spine. "I wonder if he had a hand in Placide's disappearance," he pondered out loud.

"I don't think so," Angelina replied. "He and his men spent days looking for Placide. He insisted that Sheriff Badeaux join in on the search. He almost made himself sick looking for Placide."

"I remember now," he said. "Maybe things would've been better between them had Adam found him."

"Maybe," she agreed as she moved closer to him and leaned her head on his shoulder. "But I doubt it," she thought to herself.

*****

In late March, Adam watched as the horses pulled his new Cyrus McCormick plows through the fields. He had seen an advertisement in a Virginia newspaper he happened to come across and decided to purchase seven of the machines for his own fields. Four worked the Southern Kingdom fields and the other three were used at Lance des Chenes.

Many of the other planters ridiculed the machinery, but he was interested in implementing modern farming methods in his fields. The plows cut the soil preparation time by more than half. The horses were now pulling the harrows down the rows digging out the weeds within inches of the young cotton stalks. The cotton would require less hoeing by the workers.

Henry recommended the hiring of many more hands for the additional fields. With the new plows, he cut the number Henry had recommend by one fourth. "If McCormick would invent a mechanized cotton picker," he thought to himself, "I could let half of the workers go. A penny saved is a penny earned."

He could not understand why so many people resisted change. "We are living in a wonderful age," he thought to himself. "One of these days something may even be invented to replace the horse." He thought of a locomotive on iron wagon wheels. "That machine could pull dozens of plows." He embraced the wave of the future.

Henry pulled the lever to lift the harrows when he came

to the end of the row. He sawed at the reins and called out to the horses. The horses turned sharply and were soon headed in the opposite direction down another row. Adam watched as Henry bounced on the seat mounted between the wheels of the machine. Before long, Henry was headed back in his direction. It amazed Adam when he thought of the speed of the machine. The horses were pulling Henry down the rows much faster than a man could walk at full speed, maybe even faster than many men could run.

Adam made a mental note to make some inquiries. He wanted to learn more about modern machinery. Not only would he own the largest plantation in the area, he would have the most modern plantation.

Diablo responded immediately to the pressure of Adam's heels and began to canter down the headland. In a short while, the large barn came in sight. Adam wanted to eat an early dinner and then go into town to speak with Fisk.

He had not heard from Fisk since the purchase of the Bernhart property. Adam thought he might have to prod him to get him to continue his search for more land. He had been giving serious thought to finding a replacement for Fisk. The first step was the most difficult; finding someone who could point him in the right direction.

CHAPTER TWENTY-THREE

June 13,1868

Fisk was busy with a customer when Adam walked into his office. "Mr. Blythington," he said distractedly, "I'll be with you as soon as I take care of Mr. Chautin's business."

Adam sat in one of the chairs and waited for Fisk to complete his business. After half an hour, it became clear to him that Fisk was stalling. "He wants to make me wait on him," he said to himself. "He knew what time I would be here. This is all about who controls whom."

"I have some business to take care of in town," he said as he rose from his chair and set his hat on his head. "I should be back in an hour or so."

Fisk looked at him nervously. "No need to leave," he said. "We were just finishing up."

"There is someone I must see," Adam said. He looked at the pocket watch he held in his hand. "I am already late for the meeting. I will return after I conclude my business."

A stunned expression settled on Fisk's face as he watched Blythington walk out of the door. His first thought was that Blythington was only upset because he had made him wait. He had meant to make Blythington cool his heels. The man was in need of some humbling. His second thought was unsettling. Blythington may have decided to meet with the man he had spoken about earlier. "I know he's got somebody just waiting to steal my business," he said to himself. "Why did I have to play that childish game and make him wait?"

*****

Adam was not sure where he was going to go for an hour, but he was not going to be available to Fisk for that period of time. He strode briskly toward the courthouse.

A large, swarthy man was sitting in a buggy on the east side of the courthouse square. The man looked directly at Adam. Adam wondered if Fisk had people watching him. He ruled that out. Fisk had not known in advance that he would walk out of the office.

"Mr. Blythington, may I have a word with you," the man called out when Adam reached the side of the buggy. The man was already stepping down.

Adam scanned quickly to his right and then to his left. He turned his head and looked to his rear.

"I didn't mean to startle you," the large man said. "I only want to talk over a business proposition. I'm Norman Gertzer."

Adam found his voice. "Surely you do not mean to conduct business out on the street?" he said. He felt uneasy. He was not sure this was the type of man with whom he would want to conduct business.

"My office is two blocks from here," Gertzer said. "You can ride with me or follow me there. It's your choice."

Adam hesitated.

"I know what you're thinking, but I only want to talk to you," Gertzer said in a straightforward manner. "I have a proposal I hope you'll find interesting. I mean you no harm."

"It would be difficult for him to do me harm in broad daylight in the middle of the city," Adam said to himself. He crossed over to the opposite side of the buggy and climbed in.

Gertzer remained silent as they drove to his office. Adam scrutinized the man. He was even larger than he had first appeared. The man's suit was cheap but clean and neat. He was freshly shaven and his black hair was combed down neatly. He wondered what was on Gertzer's mind.

"Come on in and take a seat," Gertzer said a few minutes later as he opened the office door. "I think what I have to offer will be beneficial to both of us."

Gertzer walked to a wooden filing cabinet, pulled open a drawer, removed several folders, and then sat behind a wooden desk. He placed the folders on the desk and opened the one that lay on top.

Adam sat in one of the chairs in front of the desk.

"I'll get right to the point," Gertzer said. "No use beating around the bush. I want to be your land agent."

"What makes you think I need a land agent?" Adam asked. "James Fisk has worked as my agent for years."

"I know that, Mr. Blythington," Gertzer responded evenly, "That's why I wanted to talk to you. I did some work for Fisk a few times." He looked at Blythington and let that soak in. "I struck out on my own when Fisk decided to serve a different clientele." He met Blythington's gaze. "He came here one evening just as I was closing up. I could tell he'd been drinking. He's usually a very careful man, but that evening he let the whiskey do the talking."

Gertzer looked at Blythington to gauge his reaction.

Adam nodded his head for Gertzer to continue.

"You'd been in his office that day," Gertzer continued. "He was hopping mad. Said you were going to push him too far some day. He wanted to know if I'd be interested in a plan he had for bringing you down a peg or two. I asked him what he had in mind, but he wouldn't say. I guess he thought better of it once he sobered up. I haven't heard from him since."

"Why are you telling me all of this?" Adam asked.

"As I said," he answered, "I want to be your land agent. Fisk doesn't want to take any chances now that he's married and wanting to go legitimate. I figure you can use a man who can get you what you want at the right price."

"Fisk would be a difficult man to replace," Adam said. "He keeps abreast of what is available and he has many contacts."

"I know what's available," Gertzer responded slapping his left hand on top of the folders. "I know what you want. I've been looking for land between and around your two plantations. Now that Fisk is legitimate, I have the contacts who matter."

Adam considered Gertzer's statement. The only reservation he had was a nagging suspicion Fisk had set this up. "How do I know Fisk is not behind this?" he asked.

"I'll tell you how," he replied. "If you accept my offer, the first thing I'm gonna do is eliminate Fisk."

Adam was taken aback. "Why would you do that?" he asked.

"Cause he'd get in the way," Gertzer replied abruptly. "Even though he no longer wants to handle your business, he'd get mad if you went to another agent. He'd put out a contract on you and on me. To him it would be kill or get killed."

"Do you have other clients?" Adam asked. "I require someone who would be loyal and who would put my needs first and foremost."

"That's no problem," Mr. Blythington. "I'm making money on some small deals. I might not look like it, but I'm an ambitious man. I figure doing business with a rich man like you who wants to get even richer will get me what I want. I'd be looking out for both of us."

"My next question is, how do I know whether or not I can trust you?" he asked.

"You don't," Gertzer replied evenly. "Not anymore than I know if I can trust you. You're the only man who can get me what I want. I'm the only man who'll get you what you want. I think it would be best for both of us to trust each other. I'll live up to my part."

"I would like to give your proposal some thought," Adam said. He began to rise from his chair.

"I don't want to sound pushy, Mr. Blythington," Gertzer said, "but you don't have much choice. Fisk is already thinking of having you killed. Once an idea like that gets stuck in his head, he worries it over until it happens. You don't have much time before it'll happen."

Adam felt a cold chill. He recalled the nightmares. "He does want me dead," he said to himself. "That is why I dreamed those dreams."

"Would you mind showing me what you have in those folders?" he asked. "It may be prudent for me to entrust you with my business."

Gertzer smiled broadly. He handed the open folder to Blythington. "That's a large piece of land," he said as he extended his arm and pointed his finger. I can get that for you at a reasonable price. I have some others that'll probably interest you."

The information was impressive. Gertzer was well prepared. Adam wondered how long it would take before Gertzer eliminated Fisk. He shuddered involuntarily. He did not want to know.

*****

Several things were on Adam's mind as he made his way back to Fisk's office. He had been thinking of replacing Fisk, but Gertzer had come out of nowhere. He was not positive the man was not sent by Fisk.

He recalled the day he met Fisk at the courthouse. Fisk had come out of nowhere. Somehow, the right people came his way at the right time. He could say the same thing about the land he purchased. He just happened to be at the right place at the right time when the land became available.

He had to credit his good fortune to the cosmic force that had given him the warning dreams. "Fate is working for me," he said to himself. "It is impossible for me to fail."

Before walking into Fisk's office, he struggled to compose himself. It would not be easy to face Fisk knowing he had agreed to his murder. He did not want to do anything that would alert Fisk.

Fisk was sitting behind his desk when Adam entered the office. He pulled out his watch and checked the time. "He was gone over an hour," he said to himself. "I wonder what he did while he was gone. I'll bet anything he didn't have any business in town. He wasn't gone long enough to talk to anybody else about land."

"I am glad to see we are alone," Adam said sarcastically. "I trust Mr. Chautin is a satisfied customer."

"We were just going over some last minute details," Fisk

said. "Chautin is a worry wart. It takes half an hour with him to do what I could do in five minutes. Nothing's ever easy with him."

"I imagine you must deal with some difficult people," Adam said.

"And you're the most difficult," Fisk said to himself. "It comes with the business," he responded. "Some are easy; some not so easy."

"I have heard nothing further from you about land purchases," Adam said pointedly. "When last we spoke, you indicated you would conduct a vigilant search."

"I've been doing all I can," Fisk responded. "You've gotta understand things are more settled now. Not as many large tracts of land on the market. What little there is isn't anywhere near your land. I'm doing all I can."

Adam felt like telling Fisk it really did not matter, but he knew that would make Fisk suspicious. "I do not want excuses," he said adamantly. "I want results. What happened to the man who wanted to go home a rich man?"

"That man is making plenty enough money on legitimate business," Fisk said to himself. "That man has a wife now and wants to live a long and comfortable life. No more risks for me. I don't want to die and I don't want to spend the rest of my years in jail."

Adam shook his head and looked toward the ceiling.

"I told you, Mr. Blythington," Fisk said nervously, "I'm doing all I can do."

"That is not satisfactory," Adam said scathingly. "I will return next week. When I return, I want to hear you say you have a purchase ready for me."

"This time you've gone too far," Fisk said to himself. "I'm not taking any more of this from you. You're a dead man."

"I'll do my best," he said. "I hope I'll have something for you."

Adam felt the hairs on the back of his neck rise. He had seen a look in Fisk's eyes that frightened him. He rose from his chair and turned to walk out the door.

"Don't forget your hat," Fisk called out. "A gentleman

wants to always be at his best."

Adam picked up his hat and set it on his head. "Thank you," he said. "I look forward to hearing from you."

"In a few days, you won't hear anything ever again," Fisk said to himself. He felt better than he had in months. He looked forward to the supper Georgina would prepare for him.

Adam mounted Diablo and made for Gertzer's office.

*****

"I didn't expect you back so soon," Gertzer said as he looked up at the man who walked into his office. "Have a seat."

"I have only a moment," Adam said calmly. "I will remain standing."

"What can I do for you?" Gertzer asked.

"Fisk told me he has nothing for me," Adam replied.

"That's no problem," Gertzer responded. "I have plenty of land lined up."

"That is not why I came to see you," Adam said coldly. "Fisk made a veiled threat as I was preparing to leave his office. I sense he intends my immediate demise."

"That is a problem," Gertzer said as he stroked his chin. He was impacted by the coldness in Blythington's eyes. "Is he still at his office?"

"He was when I left," Adam replied.

"Leave all of that to me," Gertzer said. "Fisk isn't going to live long enough to set anything in motion."

"Thank you," Adam said in a tone that would suggest he had made a normal business transaction. "It seems our meeting was fortuitous."

"I'm glad to be able to help," Gertzer said with a broad smile on his face. "I told you this would be good for both of us." He had learned an important fact about Blythington's character; the murder of another human being was only business to him.

*****

James Fisk looked up from the property description

he'd been reading when he heard his office door open. Norman Gertzer was standing in the doorway.

"I haven't seen you in a while," Fisk said. "I heard you'd opened your own office. How's business?"

"I learned a lot from you," Gertzer replied with a smile as he walked in and shut the door behind him. "You were a good teacher."

"There's plenty enough business for both of us," Fisk said. He appreciated the compliment. "You might be able to help me with one of my problem clients."

"Which one is that?" Gertzer asked as he walked up to Fisk's desk.

"Adam Blythington," Fisk replied. "He's gotten too big for his britches. I think something needs to be done about him."

"Like what?" Gertzer asked. He was now within arm's reach of his prey.

"You said I taught you a lot," Fisk replied. "When a problem looks like it's getting too big, what did I teach you to do about the problem?"

"You always said the problems should be eliminated," Gertzer replied with a broad smile on his face. He reached beneath his coat and withdrew a hunting knife. "That's one of the reasons I'm here."

Fisk knew of Gertzer's reputation with knives. "Are you crazy?" Fisk asked. "Put that thing away." He started sliding his right hand along the top of his desk. He always kept a loaded handgun in the top desk drawer.

"Keep your hands out where I can see them," Gertzer ordered. "You taught me to watch the man I was gonna eliminate very closely. I know about the gun in the top drawer."

Fisk stretched his hands out to the middle of the desk. "If it's money you want," he said, "I can give you a thousand dollars right now and more later. I was gonna ask you to kill Blythington."

"I'll be doing all of his work from now on," Gertzer said. "I can make more money with him than I could with you and besides, I like that kind of work."

Fisk knew how much Gertzer liked killing. He had used

him several times to get rid of nagging problems. "You won't get away with this," he said. "I've got connections with Sheriff Badeaux. He'll hunt you down."

"No one will ever know who killed you," Gertzer said.

Fisk saw he had nothing to lose by making a move for his gun. His hand reached the drawer pull at the same time the knife's blade plunged into his neck. He fell sidewards and landed hard on the wooden floor.

Gertzer stood over Fisk, withdrew the knife from his neck and rolled him over on his back.

Fisk looked up at the knife and then stared into Gertzer's eyes. Fisk's lips moved as he attempted to form words. "Why?" he finally asked.

"You should have known you couldn't walk away from the devil," Gertzer replied. "You sold your soul a long time ago."

"Isn't that what you're doing?" Fisk whispered.

"Yeh, but I learned from you," Gertzer replied. "I know I can't turn back." He got down on one knee and slid the knife across Fisk's neck. He watched as the life bled out of his former colleague and then bent over and wiped the knife on Fisk's coat.

Gertzer returned the knife to the sheath attached to his belt in the small of his back and rose to his feet. He recalled what Fisk had said about giving him the thousand dollars now. He rifled through the desk drawers until he found the money. A broad smile spread across his face after he counted the money. It had been a profitable afternoon.

CHAPTER TWENTY-FOUR

June 14, 1868 - June 29, 1868

Adam sat back in his office chair reading the account of Fisk's death in the *St. Landry Clarion*. Gertzer had been true to his word. When Adam left Gertzer's office, Fisk had only about an hour remaining of his life. The article read:

The body of James Alexander Fisk was discovered in his office late yesterday afternoon. The deceased was twenty-seven years of age.

Mrs. Georgina Fisk, wife of the deceased, said she grew anxious when her husband failed to appear for supper. She went to his office and discovered his body lying on the floor in a pool of blood.

Mrs. Felix Brown, who lives near the office where the body was discovered, says she heard what sounded like a woman's screams. Mrs. Brown stated, "I ran in the direction I thought the screams were coming from. I saw a woman covered in blood kneeling next to a man's body. I tried to help but she kept on screaming. When I saw I couldn't do anything for her, I ran to tell the sheriff. I don't know how something like this can happen in our city."

Sheriff Glenn Badeaux and deputies, Roscoe Taylor and Alton Delafosse, were on the scene until late Tuesday night. When asked if the killer had left helpful clues, Sheriff Badeaux stated, "We're looking at everything carefully. We don't want to miss anything . Since he was murdered in the late afternoon or early evening, many people were still outdoors. Someone must have heard something or seen something. We want to talk to all of the people who saw Mr. Fisk yesterday. I'm sure that we'll find something."

When pressed for a time frame as to how long he thinks it will take to apprehend the perpetrator, Badeaux stated, "It's hard to say in something like this. I want everybody to know that we will not rest until his killer is found."

"You will be a very tired man," Adam said confidently to himself. "You will never know what happened."

He reread the newspaper account and noticed something he had overlooked on his first reading. Sheriff Badeaux wanted to speak with everyone who had been in contact with Fisk on the day of his murder. He had not stopped to think he might be questioned about his connection with Fisk. "Who would know that I saw him that day?" he thought to himself. He recalled that Chautin had seen him in Fisk's office.

He considered waiting for Badeaux to seek him out. "It is wiser that I make contact with him," he said to himself. "The last thing I want to do is cast suspicion upon myself." He pulled out his pocket watch and checked the time. It was too late to go today. He would go into town and see Badeaux first thing in the morning.

*****

Flies buzzed around on the walkway in front of the sheriff's office. Adam recalled the statements the planters had made about the freezing weather reducing the number of insects. "I wonder how many were here last year," he thought to himself. He was trying to keep his mind off the impending interview with Sheriff Badeaux.

"I must not appear to be nervous," he said to himself. "I really know nothing of Fisk's death."

He pushed the door open and stepped into the office. A thin bald man wearing a deputy sheriff's badge looked up at him. "Can I help you?" he asked.

"Yes," Adam said, "I read the account of Mr. Fisk's death in the paper. Sheriff Badeaux said he wished to speak to everyone who had contact with Mr. Fisk on the day he died."

"The sheriff should be back soon," the deputy said. "You can take a seat if you want to wait."

"Do you have any idea how long he will be?" Adam asked. He had hoped to be done quickly with the matter.

"He's talking to the mayor," the deputy replied. "Everybody's upset about the murder."

Adam sat in one of the chairs that were lined up against the front wall of the office. "I would have brought something to read, had I known I would have to wait," he said to himself. He rose from his chair and began to read the wanted posters that were tacked up on one of the walls. He was about half-way through reading the posters when the door opened.

"Sheriff," the deputy said obsequiously, "this man says he has information about the murder."

Badeaux turned and faced Adam. "You have information on Fisk's murder?" he asked.

Adam was miffed with the deputy. He had not said he had information. "I am afraid there has been a misunderstanding," he replied. "I read about the unfortunate incident in the paper. The article stated you wished to speak to all who saw Mr. Fisk on that day."

Badeaux searched Blythington's face for several moments. "Haven't we met?" he asked. "Your face is very familiar."

Adam blanched. Badeaux remembered him from Placide's disappearance. "I asked you and your deputies to help search for my brother-in-law, Placide Dupre," he replied.

"Yes, I remember now," Badeaux said. "What an unfortunate incident. We still haven't heard from him."

"It is very sad," Adam said. "We continue to hold out hope for good news."

Badeaux shook his head. "I don't want to disappoint you, son," he said, "but it's like I said when we stopped searching. He was involved with some rough people; he's never gonna be found."

"I hope Fisk's murderer is apprehended," Adam said. "By what I gleaned from the article, you feel certain his killer will be found."

Badeaux looked Blythington in the eye. "I couldn't tell the reporter we'll probably never know what happened," he said. "Whoever did this knew what he was doing."

"Do you have any suspects?" Adam asked.

"Everyone's a suspect," he said. "I've been in this business long enough to know not to trust anyone. His wife could have done it, but we didn't find a knife. She'd have to be a good actress to pull it off. That kind of thing does happen. It could even be you." He stared into Blythington's eyes.

Adam was not expecting anything like this. He did his best to meet the sheriff's gaze.

After a few moments, Badeaux chuckled. "That makes you uneasy, doesn't it?" he asked. "I went to Baton Rouge for some training. The instructor said that would make just about anyone confess."

"I guess it would work on the guilty party," Adam replied.

"Deputy Nolan says you have some information," Badeaux said changing the subject. "I sure could use some help on this thing,"

Adam wondered if repeating the question was part of Badeaux's Baton Rouge training. "As I told you previously," he said, "I came in response to your request. I was in Mr. Fisk's office on the day he was murdered."

Badeaux seemed to ponder his statement. "As a matter of fact," he said after several moments, "you were in Fisk's office twice that day."

Adam was thrown off balance. He opened his mouth to ask Badeaux how he knew he had been in Fisk's office twice that day, then recalled he had seen Chautin only a few yards from the office when he returned. "That is correct," he responded levelly.

"Did you and Fisk argue that day?" Badeaux asked bluntly.

"Could Chautin have heard us arguing?" he asked himself. He took a chance Chautin had been out of earshot by that time.

"Mr. Fisk is," Adam corrected himself, "was my land agent. I was in his office that day to ask him if he knew of any available land near my own."

"That's strange," Badeaux said as he rocked back on

his heels. "You didn't answer my question. Were you and Fisk arguing Tuesday?"

Adam met his piercing gaze. "No, Sheriff," he answered, "We did not argue."

"Why did you leave his office and then return later?" Badeaux asked.

"He was busy with a client, Mr Chautin," he replied. "I had other business in town. I told Mr. Fisk I would return later in the afternoon."

"What kind of business did you have?" Badeaux asked. "Did you speak to anyone in particular?"

"Several people may have seen me speaking to Gertzer," Adam told himself. "I may have been seen going into or coming out of his office. Best to tell the truth." "I went to see Mr. Norman Gertzer," he replied.

"So, you left the office of one land agent only to go to the office of another land agent," Badeaux said accusingly. "Isn't that odd?"

"Why would that be odd?" Adam asked. "I felt that Fisk was moving too slowly. I was considering taking my business elsewhere. Gertzer was only the first of many with whom I was intending to speak."

"Did Fisk know you were thinking of firing him?" Badeaux asked.

"I was not actually firing him," Adam replied. "He was not my employee." He looked at Badeaux squarely. "In answer to your question, I did tell Fisk I was going to replace him if he did not take more interest in my needs."

"Is that when you argued?" Badeaux asked.

"As I stated earlier," Adam replied levelly, "we did not argue. I told Fisk I would return next week. I was going to evaluate the situation at that time."

"Did you say that to Fisk?" Badeaux asked.

"Yes," Adam replied.

"Do you have any idea who wanted Fisk dead?" Badeaux asked.

"We only had a business relationship," Adam replied. "I have no idea who would have wanted him dead."

Badeaux smiled. "I already talked to Mr. Gertzer," he said. "I wanted to see if you would tell me the truth."

Adam began to relax and then became guarded once again. Badeaux was much too sharp to be unguarded around him.

"I appreciate you coming in," Badeaux said. He shook his head. "I was almost certain you weren't gonna come in on your own. I thought I had a good suspect." He shook his head once more. "It sure would make the taxpayers happy if I could solve this thing."

*****

"Freedom is precious," Adam told himself when he was out of the sheriff's office. Badeaux was a much more thorough interrogator than he had previously believed. "I wonder if he really thought I was guilty?" he asked himself.

The urge to go to Gertzer's office to ask him what he had told Badeaux was powerful. "That is just the thing Badeaux would be looking for," he told himself. "He would become even more suspicious."

He untied Diablo's reins, set his left foot in the stirrup and lifted himself upon the horse's back. He touched his heels lightly to the horse's sides. Soon, he was out of town. He slowed the horse from a canter to a walk. He needed to gather his thoughts. His mind was exhausted. It seemed to him that Badeaux had been determined to find something that would connect him to Fisk's murder. "I wonder what Gertzer told him?" he asked himself. "It must have been much the same as what I said or he would still have me in his office." He once again felt the urge to speak with Gertzer.

He nudged Diablo and was soon moving along at a canter as he headed back home. The sun was bright but the air was cool. He looked around at the young cotton stalks growing in the fields, the lush pastureland and the thick woodland as he rode along. He appreciated the countryside more than he had in some time. He had been in Badeaux's office only about half an hour but it had seemed like hours. He was beginning to feel hungry. "I hope Margaret has something good to eat," he said to himself. The farther he traveled from Badeaux's office, the better he felt. All was well with his world once again.

*****

During the first two weeks after Fisk's murder, the *St. Landry Clarion* printed several articles giving updates on the progress of the investigation. There was much speculation as to who committed the murder and why. Only one story appeared the third week. Someone said he had seen a band of Gypsies camped west of the sawmill. Another person ran with that rumor and said he had seen three men dressed as Gypsies enter Fisk's office on the evening of his death.

By the fourth week, people had become bored with the story and had moved on to other things. Samuel Hargroder, the town barber, discovered Harold Cummings, a successful young local attorney, in bed with his wife. Mr. Hargroder returned to his home in the middle of the afternoon, which was unusual for him, and found his wife and Cummings in one another's arms in his bedroom. Hargroder, who thankfully was not an accurate marksman, had taken his handgun out of a drawer and shot Cummings. The report of the shooting in the *Clarion* said Cummings' dignity suffered more than his person, being as he would recall the incident every time he sat.

Five weeks after the murder, Adam rode into town to meet with Gertzer. It was around nine o'clock when he saw the courthouse dome in the distance. He had not scheduled an appointment with Gertzer, but felt the land agent would make time for him.

He knocked on the office door and waited. After a few moments, he looked in one of the windows. Gertzer was nowhere to be seen.

"Hello there," he heard a voice calling in the distance. He turned toward the sound of the voice.

"I was looking through some records at the courthouse," Gertzer said as he drew nearer carrying several documents.

A short time later he unlocked the door and ushered

Blythington into the office. "I've found several properties that may interest you," he said. He spread the documents out on his desk. "These are two and three hundred arpent farms. One's only a hundred arpents, but they're all in the area that interests you. I think we can persuade the owners to sell at a reasonable price."

Adam pulled a chair near the desk and looked over the documents. He got up and gazed at a map on Gertzer's wall that identified all of the sections in St. Landry Parish. "I am interested in these," he said as he continued to study the map.

"I thought you would be," Gertzer said. "Two of them border Belle Bois. "You might want to start getting land out that way, being as you'll own that, too, one day."

"This man can read my mind," Adam said to himself. "The thought had crossed my mind," he said.

"I know these are only small amounts," Gertzer said, "but the way I see things, folks'll be a lot less suspicious if we keep it small. If we go up against the big landowners, that would bring a lot of attention to what we're doing. When the time comes, we'll handle them."

"I was thinking about acquiring large farms," Adam said, "but I see your reasoning. It would be best to proceed cautiously, at least until people forget about Fisk's murder."

Gertzer chuckled. "I think people have just about forgotten already," he said. "Everybody's talking about Hargroder shooting Cummings in the seat." He threw back his head and laughed deeply as though he were picturing the scene of the shooting. "I wondered when Hargroder would catch him. Most of us knew what was going on. Cummings wasn't her first."

"I hope Sheriff Badeaux has a short memory," Adam said.

"No such luck," Gertzer responded. "He'll never stop looking. That story about the Gypsies might be just the thing to put him on a false trail. I feel sorry for any Gypsies who were around here that night."

"Why do you say that?" Adam asked. "There were no Gypsies around Fisk's office."

"I know that and you know that," Gertzer said. "but if the fellow who says he saw them identifies them, Badeaux'll see to it they hang for Fisk's murder."

"Surely he would not hang innocent men," Adam said.

"How do you think Badeaux has stayed in office this long?" Gertzer asked. "Somebody gets hung every time there's a murder. St. Landry hasn't had an unsolved murder case in years."

"Do you mean he trumps up charges against innocent men to keep his job?" Adam asked. He was appalled that this sort of thing was perpetrated against innocent people. "How can he get away with that?"

Gertzer found it amusing that Blythington didn't recognize he was condemning innocent people to death to achieve his goals. "Judge Cormier works with him," he said. "Cormier's been in office about thirty years."

"Do you mean Badeaux could choose to accuse you or me of any murder in order to have a conviction?" Adam asked.

"We don't have anything to worry about," Gertzer replied. "He only picks people who are too poor to defend themselves or tramps passing through. You're too rich and powerful for him and I know too much."

Adam was relieved. Badeaux could do whatever he wanted as long as it did not affect him or his property.

CHAPTER TWENTY-FIVE

November 10, 1868 - January 5, 1869

The diet and exercise were working even better than Annabelle had hoped. She looked at her nude reflection in the full-length mirror in her bedroom. She noted that her stomach was flatter and her hips were slimmer. She turned sidewards and looked again. A few more inches and she'd return to her pre-pregnancy figure.

She prayed she wouldn't become pregnant again any time in the near future. Two babies in less than two years was hard on her body. She had worn almost nothing but maternity clothes during the past two years. It was great to be able to wear regular clothes again.

Because of the infrequency of Adam's visits to her room, there was only a slim chance she would become pregnant. He had been an ardent lover on their honeymoon and during their first year of marriage, but he showed little interest now in making love. She may have suspected there was someone else in his life, but he spent no more time away from home than he had during the first year of marriage. It could be the hard work and long hours required to run the large plantation were taking their toll on his libido.

She enjoyed the times they made love, but she didn't long for him to complete her. If the truth be told, her dread of having another child this soon after her other two took most of the pleasure away. Maybe in another two years or so she'd feel differently.

She turned away from the mirror and began to dress. She and her two boys were spending this early November

Saturday afternoon with Robert and Angelina. After she finished dressing, she walked over to the nursery.

Paul was dressed in a sailor suit. He looked up at her, smiled, then crawled toward her. She lifted him up and kissed his cheek. "How's mamma's little man?" she asked as she squeezed him tenderly.

"If I can get Charles to stay still long enough," Matilda said, "I'll have him ready." He struggled to get out of her grip. "I've never seen two full brothers who are less alike."

Charles broke away from Matilda and ran for the door. Annabelle took hold of him just before he made it through the open doorway. "Where do you think you're going, young man?" she asked as she picked him up and kissed his cheek. Charles squirmed but she held him firmly.

"Please hold him for me, Mum," Matilda requested as she shut the nursery door. "It'll make it easier for me to get these clothes on him." She held a sailor suit identical to the one worn by Paul, except for its size. Several minutes later and after much struggling, Charles was dressed.

"You'll want to wrap them warmly," Matilda suggested, "It's a mighty cold day."

"Thankfully, Jeremiah is taking us in the carriage," Annabelle said. "It'll at least keep us out of the wind."

"I told Ruth to heat up some bricks," Matilda said. "They should hold their heat in the quilts."

"You're always so thoughtful," Annabelle responded as she hugged Matilda. "Whatever would we do without you?"

Matilda beamed from the praise of her mistress. "I only want for you and the boys to be comfortable," she said. She caught a movement out of the corner of her eye and heard a loud wail.

Charles had jumped on Paul's back and was trying to ride him as though he were a horse. "Get off of him," Matilda cried out. She rushed over and lifted Charles from Paul's back.

Annabelle rushed to Paul and picked him up off of the floor. In a matter of moments, he was quiet once again.

"I want ride horsey," Charles cried out as he strained to get away from Matilda.

At that moment, Mary opened the door and stepped in. "Evatang be reddy, Miz Annabelle," she said. "Jermia out front."

"Are you sure you don't need me to come with you?" Matilda asked. "Charles can be a handful."

"We'll be just fine," Annabelle replied. "It's only for one afternoon."

*****

When she saw the carriage pull up beside her house, Angelina rushed outside to meet Annabelle. "Let me help you with them," she said as she took Paul in her arms. "We need to get these babies out of this cold weather."

Robert came up behind her and took Charles in his arms. "Nasty weather," he said. "It was such a beautiful day yesterday." He hurried back into the house with Charles.

"Get those boys near the fire," Angelina ordered as she scurried in with Paul. "We don't want any colds or, God forbid, pneumonia."

"We were wrapped up in layers of quilts," Annabelle said, "and the hot bricks gave us some warmth."

Jeremiah walked in with several bricks in his arms. "We gotta get dese bricks hot fo da ride back," he said. He squatted by the fireplace and began to place the bricks where the fire would heat them.

"You must be freezing," Angelina told him when he finished his task. "There's a fire going in the kitchen fireplace. Why don't you go warm up and I'll make some hot chocolate for you."

"Dats mighty kinda you," Jeremiah responded. "Dat hot choklit would be mighty good rat now, but I got to git dem hosses in da stable firse." He rose from the hearth and went back outside.

"Annabelle, if you'll excuse me for a few minutes," Angelina said, "I'll fix us each a cup of hot chocolate. That would be just the thing to warm you up."

"Let me help you," Annabelle offered.

"No, you stay here and get the babies warm," she

responded. "It won't take me long."

"I don't know why I bother to hire a maid and a cook," Robert said. "She does most of the work herself."

Robert heard the cooing of a child. "Alice must be awake," he said. He left the room and returned shortly with eleven month old Alice in his arms.

"She's so beautiful," Annabelle exclaimed. "May I hold her?"

Annabelle took Alice from Robert's arms and held her gently. "Those blue eyes," she said. "She'll be a heart-breaker."

Charles, who had been trying to pull books down from the bookshelves, suddenly demanded his mother's attention. He toddled over to her and took hold of her skirt. "Hold me," he cried out as he pulled on her skirt. "Hold me."

Annabelle handed Alice back to her father and scooped Charles up in her arms. As soon as he realized his mother had given him her complete attention, he said, "Down, I go down."

"He gets that from his father," Robert said to himself. "He only wanted her to stop paying attention to Alice."

Annabelle set the boy down and he hurried back to the bookcase. "I know you're not interested in reading those books," she said laughingly as she took his hand and led him away from the bookcase. "Here, play with these." She took several toys out of a bag and handed them to Charles."

Charles played with the toys a short while and then began to throw them at Paul. One of the toys struck Paul. His bottom lip began to quiver. He looked up at his mother and started crawling toward her.

Annabelle sat in one of the rockers in the room and sat Paul upon her lap. Charles hurried to her side. "Hold me," he said as he lifted his arms for her to take him. She lifted him to her lap. He began to shove Paul. "Paul down."

"Stop that," Annabelle scolded. "You'll have to learn to share."

Charles pulled his arm back and slapped his brother's face. Paul buried his head in his mother's bosom and cried softly.

"Why did you do that?" Annabelle scolded. She set Paul on the floor and then walked to one of the stuffed chairs and sat Charles down. "You will sit in that chair until you learn to behave properly." She took Paul up in her arms once again and returned to the rocker.

Charles beat his hands against the sides of the chair and shouted loudly. "Mamma mean, mamma mean," he shouted out over and over again.

Angelina walked back into the room and took in the scene. She set the tray of cups filled with hot chocolate on a small table near the bookcase and took Paul from Annabelle. "If he were mine," she said as she nodded toward Charles, "I'd slap his little bottom. He's having a temper tantrum."

Annabelle walked over to Charles, took him in her arms and returned to the rocker. "He's not a bad child," she said. "He only needs a little attention."

Angelina shook her head in disbelief. "His bottom needs attention," she said to herself.

Charles tired himself out with his screaming. The young boy was soon asleep in his mother's arms. Annabelle rocked him a while longer and then went into the nursery and lay him on the bed. "I'll probably regret this tonight when you refuse to sleep," she said to herself.

When she returned to the parlor, she took Paul from Angelina and sat with him. He sat quietly and watched the faces of the grownups as they spoke.

"A good friend of ours will be dropping by," Robert said. "He's a fascinating man. I think you'll enjoy meeting him."

"Who is this friend?" Annabelle asked.

"Frank Klienpeter," he replied. "He's a reporter for the *Clarion*."

"This will be a treat," Annabelle said. "I've read many of his news reports. He and I have much in common."

"Oh," Angelina interjected. "What do the two of you have in common?"

"He has written several articles urging people to help the destitute," she replied. "I wanted to use half of my dowry to erect a building where people could bring food, blankets and clothing for the poor. I hoped it would be large enough to have rooms where those who needed to get out of the weather could stay."

"That's an excellent idea," Angelina said. "There are empty warehouses here in town that could be used for that purpose. Maybe you could rent one of them."

Annabelle looked down at the floor. "I no longer have the funds for such an undertaking," she said sadly.

Angelina and Robert were sure her dowry had been substantial, but said nothing. They saw the sadness on her face and guessed she had approached Adam about her idea, only to be rebuffed.

"That must be him now," Robert said when he heard a knock at the door. He rose from his chair and walked to the door.

"I hope I'm not intruding," Klienpeter said when he saw Annabelle with the child on her lap.

"Not at all," Angelina said as she hugged his neck. "Annabelle is one of your admirers."

Annabelle blushed bright red. "What must he be thinking?" she asked herself. She was hoping Mr. Klienpeter wouldn't take Angelina's comment the wrong way.

"I've read many of your articles in the *Clarion*," she said. "I agree with your campaign to help the poor." She hoped that would explain to him what Angelina meant by admirer.

"Unfortunately, many tell me they agree," he responded, "but few become involved."

She blushed once more. Shamefully, she was in that number who agreed with him but did nothing.

Klienpeter sensed Annabelle's discomfort. "I'm sure in your case," he said, "you do all you can to help."

"Yes, I'm doing all I can," she agreed to herself, "but still it's nothing."

"There's more hot chocolate in the kitchen," Angelina said. "I'll get a cup for you. We all need something to warm our insides."

Annabelle studied Klienpeter out of the corner of her eye. He was tall with a muscular build. He had dark hair and a dark, neatly-trimmed beard. His eyes caught her attention. It wasn't their shape or their color that made them intriguing. She could see a deep intelligence and a curiosity in them. They seemed to miss nothing. They were penetrating, yet kind at the same time.

Klienpeter sat in a stuffed chair across from Annabelle. "I was hoping Robert would make the introductions," he said.

"Oh, I'm sorry," Robert responded quickly. "Angelina will scold me for my bad manners. Annabelle, this is my good friend, Frank Klienpeter. Fritz, this is Annabelle Blythington. She's a very dear friend."

"I'm delighted to make your acquaintance, Mr. Klienpeter," Annabelle said. She was puzzled that Robert had called him Fritz.

"Please call me Fritz," Klienpeter said. "It's always a pleasure to meet a kindred spirit."

He had seen the puzzled look on her face when Robert had called him Fritz. "I'll bet you're wondering why Robert called me Fritz," he said with a smile.

"I had wondered," she admitted.

"Robert and I were at the University of Louisiana together," he began to explain, "Three of us had parents with good taste, who named each of us Frank. Robert thought we needed new names so he'd know which of us was being referred to when someone spoke of Frank. Since I have a German surname, I became Fritz. Like the mustard plaster he uses, it stuck."

"Would you prefer that I call you Frank?" she asked.

"No," he replied after thinking for a moment. "I hope we become good friends. All my good friends call me Fritz."

She didn't know why, but she was extremely pleased he wanted to be good friends. "Then Fritz it shall be," she agreed. "Are your parents from Germany?" She was dismayed by her own question. A lady was not supposed to be so forward.

"Actually, I'm only one-sixteenth German or maybe even less," he answered with a smile. "My mother is a Boudreaux."

"That explains the dark hair and dark eyes," she thought to herself.

"Enough about your background," Robert said. "I wanted to pick your brain concerning law enforcement in this parish; especially Sheriff Badeaux and Judge Cormier."

"Why do you want my opinion?" Fritz asked cautiously.
"Have you heard something?"

"When you give me a look like that," Robert responded,
"I know you're up to something. I was only wanting your
opinion, but I can now see you're working on something. Spill it
out."

Fritz looked at Robert and then at Annabelle.

"You can trust her," Robert said. "She'll keep what you
say in confidence."

"Mrs. Blythington," Fritz said earnestly, "please
understand my reluctance to speak candidly. This is a very
sensitive matter."

"If we're to become friends," she responded, "you must
call me Annabelle. I do understand your reluctance. If you feel
it's best, I'll go and help Angelina in the kitchen."

Fritz thought for a moment. "That won't be necessary,"
he said. "I do ask that you discuss what I say with no one; not
even your husband."

"I promise to keep your secret," she responded soberly.
It excited her that he would take her into his confidence. Perhaps
they were really kindred spirits.

"Why did you ask me about Badeaux and Cormier?"
Fritz asked.

"There's something fishy going on," Robert replied.
"The last incident was the Fisk murder. There were no clues, yet
Badeaux was able to pin the murder on those two Gypsies. Judge
Cormier got them to trial in the blink of an eye and now they're
both sentenced to be hanged for the murder. I've noticed that
saddle tramps and drifters commit almost all of the major crimes
in this parish. I find that very strange."

"I've been looking into that for over a year now,"
Fritz said. "It didn't surprise me when Badeaux found the
two Gypsies. The moment the witness came forward and said
he'd seen Gypsies around Fisk's office, I knew Badeaux would
decide who he could pin this one on. We need to get some hard
evidence that would prove their innocence and take it to a U.S.
Marshal."

Annabelle was flabbergasted to even think that sort of thing could be going on in St. Landry Parish. "You think innocent people are being hanged for crimes they didn't commit?" she asked. "This is America. That sort of thing happens only in barbaric countries."

"I do suspect innocent men are being hanged for crimes they didn't commit," Fritz said firmly. "Apparently, Robert feels the same as I do."

"I grew suspicious when I learned that Badeaux has solved every murder and major crime that's been committed since he was elected sheriff," Robert said. "I went to the courthouse and looked up the trial transcripts. Cormier was the judge each and every time."

"I wondered if I was the only one who'd noticed," Fritz said. "I'm glad I'm not the only one troubled by what's going on."

"I'm sorry it took so long," Angelina said as she stepped back into the parlor. "I had to make another pot. Jeremiah looked longingly at your cup of chocolate so I gave it to him and made some more for you." She looked at the faces of the people in the room. "What have I missed?"

"We were talking about Badeaux and Cormier," Robert replied. "Fritz has been doing some investigating."

"Are you going to talk to the Gypsies?" Angelina asked. "We need to find out where they were when Fisk was murdered."

"I asked Rivette to let me write a story about them," Fritz replied. "He says there isn't enough interest in the community to waste space on them."

"That coward doesn't want to make waves," Angelina said. "He's afraid of Badeaux and Cormier."

Annabelle thought of enlisting Adam's support and then discounted the notion. "He doesn't care what happens to anyone but himself," she thought to herself. She was immediately ashamed of the disloyalty to her husband. "I couldn't speak to him anyway; I've been sworn to secrecy."

"What will you do?" Robert asked. "Someone needs to speak to them."

"Couldn't you go in as a doctor checking on their health?" Angelina asked.

"The sheriff or a judge would have to ask me first," Robert replied. "I know of no reason why a doctor would be needed."

"We can sneak a note in to them," Angelina said. "We can tell them to act sick."

"I doubt that either of them can read," Fritz said. "Getting word to them is a good idea, though. If I can get to their window, maybe that would work."

"I'm sure their window is closed today," Robert said. "Too cold to leave them open."

"I can use something to tap against the glass to get their attention," Fritz said. "Write down what you want me to tell them and I'll pass it on to them."

Robert thought a while. "The simplest thing would be for one of them to say he has a sharp pain on his right side," he said as he pointed to a spot on his abdomen. "He'd have to moan and groan and claim it hurts terribly. The sheriff would have to get a doctor to check for appendicitis."

"That oughta work," Fritz said. "Would that give you enough time to talk to them?"

"It should," Robert replied.

"We need to do it soon, maybe even today," Fritz said. "The hangings are only two weeks off. We've got to have time to check out their alibis. I can get some time off from the paper."

The men continued to discuss how they were going to set their plans in motion. Annabelle was intrigued by their concern and their daring.

Jeremiah came out of the kitchen. "It be gittin dawk, Miz Annabelle," he said. "We bess be gittin back."

Annabelle gazed out of a window and saw that dusk was falling. She was enjoying herself more than she had in months, if not years. Even though the topic was serious, she'd been enthralled by the energy and motivation of the two men. Fritz was unlike any man she had ever known. She shook her head. That wasn't true; he was like Robert. She had never seen this side of Robert before. She hated for the day to end. She rose from her chair and bent down to get Paul.

Fritz lifted Paul from the blanket where he had been sleeping on the floor. "I'll carry him for you," he said.

"You'd better wrap him up tightly," Angelina said. "It's cold out there."

Robert went to the nursery and took Charles in his arms. Charles was still sleeping soundly.

"He'll keep me up half the night," Annabelle thought to herself. She didn't mind. Trading a little sleep for time spent listening to Fritz was a bargain.

The children were bundled up and carried out to the carriage. Before Annabelle could step up into the carriage, Fritz said, "I really did enjoy meeting you, Annabelle. I hope we meet again soon." He took her hand in his own.

Annabelle felt a thrill when their hands touched. "It's been a pleasure meeting you," she said. "It's nice to put a face to a name." She hesitated. "I hope we do meet again." She chastised herself for acting so brazenly. "You're a married woman with two children," she said to herself. "Stop acting like a giddy schoolgirl." Her hand suddenly felt cold when Fritz let go of it.

Fritz watched sadly as the carriage grew smaller in the distance. "I wish I would have met her before she got married," he said softly.

"I do, too," Robert said. He turned his head to find Angelina gazing woefully at him. She nodded her head slowly.

*****

Adam was sitting in the parlor when Annabelle returned. "It is after dark," he remarked sharply as he gazed out of a window. "Do you think you acted responsibly in taking them out on such a cold day? You should have at least returned before dark. It has grown even colder with the setting of the sun."

Annabelle was in much too good a mood to let Adam spoil her day. "We were protected from the wind," she responded, "and we were bundled in several quilts. Matilda heated some bricks for us."

Adam stared down at his wife. There was something appealing about her. "She has lost weight," he said to himself. He studied her a bit longer. "There is a brightness to her eyes I have not seen in a while." He felt a stirring in his loins. He had not been in her room in weeks. "I will remedy that tonight."

She expected him to launch into one of his tirades. She was pleasantly surprised when he took up the book that lay on his lap and began to read. She took the boys to the nursery where Matilda got them ready for bed.

"We may be in for an unpleasant night," she said. "Charles slept most of the afternoon."

"It can't be as bad as it was when he was staying up every night," Matilda responded. "I don't know how we made it through that."

Annabelle shuddered when she recalled the nights with little sleep. "No," she responded, "it can't be that bad." She kissed the boys lightly and then made her way to the small dining room.

Adam said little as they ate their supper. "I'm tired," she said after she finished her meal. She rose from her chair and walked around the table to his chair. "Good night, Adam."

Adam smiled up at her when she bent down and kissed his cheek.

She thought of Fritz as she prepared for bed. "What a striking man," she thought to herself. "The woman who marries him will get a prince for a husband."

She felt herself grow jealous when she thought of him with another woman. "Stop it," she admonished herself. "What ever is wrong with me?"

The mattress and quilts were cold when she slipped into bed. After a while they warmed up and she felt snug and drowsy. As she was dozing off, Fritz's face came into her mind once more. "He has a courageous face," she said to herself.

The door opened and Adam walked in. "Is something wrong?" she asked. Her first thought was that one of the boys might be sick.

"Nothing is wrong," he replied. "Does something have to be wrong for a man to step into his wife's bedroom?"

"No," she replied softly.

Adam walked over to the bed and began to undress. When he finished, he slipped under the covers, moved beside her and took her in his arms.

She reminded herself of her wedding vows and his right to expect her to give in to him. She prayed she wouldn't get pregnant. She tried to relax and give him what he wanted. As his breathing grew heavier, a picture of Fritz came into her mind. She attempted to drive Fritz from her mind, but failed. As Adam had his way with her, her thoughts were of Fritz. She felt his arms around her. She felt him deep inside of her. Her excitement grew as she responded to Fritz.

After several minutes, Adam rolled off of her. In a short while she could tell from his breathing that he'd fallen asleep. "I've wronged you," she said under her breath as she looked at her sleeping husband.

She rolled over to her side of the bed and tried to sleep. She remembered the sound of Fritz's voice, the way he held his head when he had something important on his mind, his smile, the touch of his hand; the thoughts came to her like water cascading from a mountain top.

When she felt Adam stir, she closed her eyes. She kept them closed and pretended to sleep as he dressed himself. She got up and locked the door after he left the room. It was long into the night before she finally fell asleep.

*****

Adam considered going up to Hannah's room, but he was too tired. Amazingly, Annabelle had drained him. "She has never made love to me like that before," he thought to himself. He wondered about the change in Annabelle. "It may be that she missed me and lost weight to be more attractive to me."

As he got ready for bed, he went over the evening in his mind. Annabelle had not shown fear, as was her custom when he had reprimanded her about taking the boys out in the cold weather. She seemed untouched by the reproof. He thought about the situation a bit longer. "She seemed more self confident," he said to himself. "Joubert must have stuck his nose in my business again."

He grew angrier as he thought of Dr. Robert Joubert. "I will order Annabelle to stay away from him," he said to himself. "He is nothing but trouble. I will speak to her in the morning."

He lay back on his pillow and tried to sleep, but he was too agitated. After some time, he recalled Annabelle's fervency as they made love. "Joubert could not inspire her to make love to me like that," he said to himself. Suddenly, the answer came to him. "She did not want to argue with me because she wanted me to go to her room. That was her plan all along."

Things were going very well. The sheriff was no longer looking for Fisk's killer now that the two Gypsies were condemned to hang. Southern Kingdom was growing and he was in no danger of losing Belle Bois with Annabelle's rekindled love for him. He rolled over on his side and was soon fast asleep.

*****

The noise of the cane striking against the glass was louder than Fritz had anticipated, and he wasn't sure he had rapped against the right window. He moved quickly to a tree that stood behind the jail and waited.

Slowly the window rose in its sash. From behind the tree he could see the person who had raised the window, without being seen. A dark haired man was looking out of the window. Fritz took a chance that this was one of the Gypsies and walked closer to the back of the jail. They stared at each other for a moment.

"What do you want?" the man asked in unaccented English. "Are you another one of those who wants to see what a condemned man looks like?"

Fritz had expected to hear someone speak with a heavy accent. He was puzzled. "I'm not here out of curiosity," he finally managed to say. "I was hoping I could help you."

"If you can pull these bars out and let us escape, then you can help," the man said, "otherwise, what could you do?"

"I want to help you prove that you're innocent," Fritz

replied.

Another dark-haired man came to the window. "Nicilate, who are you talking to?" he asked.

"Who are you?" the man called Nicilate asked.

"I'm Frank Klienpeter," Fritz replied.

"Why would you want to prove we're innocent?" the second man asked.

"Because I don't want to see innocent men hang," Fritz answered flatly.

"How can you prove our innocence?" Nicilate asked.

"First, I want to know where you were and who you were with on the day Fisk was murdered," he replied. "I want to talk to those people and then go to the United States Marshal and give him the information."

"What would he do with the information?" the second man asked.

"He would get the federal authorities to look into your case," Fritz replied.

"I'm not even sure what day he was killed," Nicilate responded. "We were given no opportunity to prove our innocence."

"He was killed on June thirteenth of this year," Fritz said. "It was a Tuesday."

"June thirteenth," the second man said. Both men thought for a while. "Nicilate, weren't we camped out around Baton Rouge about that time?"

"Yes, Vasile, that's where we were," Nicilate replied in an excited voice. "We were no where near this town."

"Are there witnesses who can prove you were around Baton Rouge at that time?" Fritz asked.

"Our entire band was there," Vasile replied, "but who would believe Gypsies?"

"I would for one," Fritz replied. "There are several others who would believe you. I have to speak to your people. Do you know where they are?"

"Our uncle told us they're camped around Washington near Bayou Courtableau," Nicilate replied. "He said they'll be here until after the hanging."

"I'll need your names and your uncle's name," Fritz said. "I want to go and see him tomorrow."

"I'm Nicilate Lipatti and this is my cousin, Vasile Lipatti. My uncle's name is Theodor Lipatti."

Fritz wrote down the names of the two men and their uncle. "I'm curious about one thing," he said when he looked up from his notebook. "You speak better English than most of the people out here. I thought Gypsies were foreigners."

"Our grandfather was born in this country," Vasile said. "We grew up speaking two languages."

"Oh, I almost forgot," Fritz said as he slapped his hand against his forehead. "One of you will need to fake the pains of appendicitis. My friend, Dr. Robert Joubert, wants to have an opportunity to speak with you."

Vasile smiled. "It would have to be Nicilate," he said. "My appendix was removed three years ago."

"What does he want of us?" Nicilate asked.

"He wants to get statements," Fritz replied. "I assume both of you can read and write."

Both men nodded their heads.

Fritz removed several sheets from his notebook and handed them to the men. "Do you have a pen or something you can use to write?" he asked.

"We have nothing but the clothes on our backs," Nicilate replied.

Fritz handed the lead pencil he had been using to Nicilate. "I would like both of you to write your statements so when Robert comes to see you, he can take them out with him when he leaves."

"We can do that," Vasile agreed. "When should Nicilate have his attack?"

"Sometime around eight o'clock tomorrow morning," Fritz replied with a grin. "I wouldn't want to get Robert up too early."

"What you're doing might not work," Nicilate said gravely, "but we want you to know that no matter what happens, we appreciate your help. You won't be liked in this town once they learn you're helping us."

"I'm more interested in not having your deaths on my conscience than I am in being liked," Fritz responded. "Sometimes we have to do what's right even when it's not popular."

*****

Robert opened the door in response to Fritz's knock. "Were you able to speak with them?" he asked. "Did they understand that you wanted to help them?"

"Hold on," Fritz said, "one question at a time. I was able to speak to them and they do understand that we want to help them. I think we misjudged them."

"I don't recall that we judged them," Robert said. "As a matter of fact, we want to save them from an unfair judgment."

"Do you recall we said they probably couldn't read and write?" Fritz asked.

Robert nodded his head.

"They can read and write and they speak fluent English," Fritz continued. "I gave them paper and a pencil. They'll write statements which you'll be able to pick up when you go to see them."

"I guess I did judge them," Robert admitted. "I assumed they'd be illiterate and would speak broken English."

"Don't beat yourself too hard," Fritz said. "I did the same thing."

"I hope you have good news," Angelina said as she walked into the room. "I've been on pins and needles waiting for you to return."

"He does have good news," Robert said. "I'll pick up their statements tomorrow."

"Statements?" Angelina asked.

Robert explained to her all that Fritz had told him about the men.

"Were they around Opelousas at the time of Fisk's murder?" Robert asked.

"They were no where around here," Fritz replied. "They were around Baton Rouge and there are people who can attest to that. I'm going to speak to them tomorrow."

The three young people were up well into the night planning their strategy for the defense of the condemned men.

*****

Smoke was rising from several campfires in the near distance. Fritz had scoured the banks of the Courtableau searching for the Gypsy camp. He shivered as another gust of wind tore through his clothes. He was cold and tired. The heat of the campfires would be welcome.

He had ridden several miles in search of the Gypsies. He hoped the smoke he had seen was rising from the Gypsies' campfires. As he got closer, he could see men, women and children dressed in brightly colored clothes. There were several wagons along the perimeter of the campground. These were also brightly colored. Large beautiful horses were grazing on what little grass was still available.

When he drew near the campsite, two men separated themselves from the people standing around the campfires and walked toward him. Both men carried rifles. He pulled on his horse's reins and stopped to wait for the men.

"What do you want?" one of the men asked menacingly.

"I need to speak with Theodor Lipatti," he replied. "It's important that I speak with him."

Both men looked him up and down. "What do you want with Theodor?" One of the men asked. "He said nothing about expecting a visitor."

"He isn't expecting me," Fritz replied. "I'm trying to help Nicilate and Vasile."

"Don't you think your people have helped them enough already?" the other man spat out. "You're hanging innocent men. Doesn't your conscience bother you?"

"I'm trying to get evidence together to stop their hanging," Fritz replied in consternation. "That's why I must speak to Mr. Lipatti."

"What is it?" a third man asked as he walked toward them. "Why haven't you invited this man to warm himself by the fire? Can't you see he's cold?"

"He says he wants to talk to Theodor," one of the men said.

"Then he'll speak to Theodor," the new man said. He led the way to the nearest campfire. Fritz got down from his horse and warmed himself by the fire.

"I am Theodor," a voice from behind him said a few minutes later. "I was told you want to talk to me."

"Mr. Lipatti," Fritz said as he turned and extended his right hand to Theodor, "I'm Frank Klienpeter."

Lipatti looked Fritz over carefully. He ignored the extended hand. "Forgive me if I'm not overjoyed to meet you," he said, "but I don't feel favorably disposed toward your people at the moment. There's been a great miscarriage of justice."

"That's why I'm here," Fritz responded. "There are several of us who believe your nephews are innocent. We want to get proof of their innocence so we can go to the Federal Marshal."

"What could he do?" Lipatti asked.

"He could stop the execution and look into the case," he replied. "He could see to it that their lives are spared."

"Why did you come to me?" he asked. "What can I do?"

"Nicilate and Vasile told me they were with you near Baton Rouge on the day of the murder," he replied. "I'd like you to ride with me to the marshal's office and speak with him. A friend of mine is getting statements from Nicilate and Vasile that he'll give to the marshal."

"You have a friend who is also helping to free them?" Lipatti asked in disbelief. "Are there others?"

"There are many of us who believe your nephews are innocent," he replied. "We are as appalled as you are."

"Will your friend be there when we go to see the marshal?" Lipatti asked.

"Yes, Robert will come with us," he replied. "There is no time to waste."

Lipatti turned to a group of men standing by the fire and shouted orders in a language Fritz didn't understand. Soon two saddled horses were brought to him.

"My friend Josef is coming with me," he said. "I hope that's not a problem."

"Not at all," Fritz replied. "Was he in the camp near Baton Rouge?"

"He was there," Lipatti replied.

*****

"Do you have an appointment?" the short fat man behind the desk asked when he saw four men, two well dressed and two dressed in strange apparel, walk into the office.

"No, we do not," Robert replied. "We have an extremely urgent matter to discuss with the marshal."

It was clear the man wasn't pleased that these men had invaded his office. "I'll ask him if he wants to see you," he said. "Who should I tell him is asking?"

"I'm Dr. Robert Joubert," Robert replied.

The man walked away and was back about a minute later. "Marshal Smith says you can go on in," the man said as he wrinkled his nose at the two Gypsies.

"Please come in," Smith called when Fritz knocked at his door. Smith rose from his desk when they walked in and shook hands with Robert and Fritz. The other two men remained out of arm's length. "Please have a seat. What can I do for you?" Smith was a tall wiry man with a large black mustache. He appeared to be about forty years of age. His eyes were dark brown and intense.

Fritz and Robert sat down, but the two Gypsies remained standing.

Robert and Fritz looked at one another. "Marshal Smith, I'm Frank Klienpeter," Fritz said nervously. He tried to compose his thoughts. Two men's lives were riding on their ability to persuade Marshal Smith to look into their cases. "I've been looking into something that caught my attention over a year ago. I looked back through the records to the time Sheriff Badeaux was elected and found something very suspicious."

"What did you find?" Smith asked kindly.

"There have been no unsolved murders since Badeaux

became sheriff," Fritz continued. "Almost all of the men who were hanged for the murders were drifters and saddle bums. I found it odd that very few of the locals were even suspects in those cases. What made me even more suspicious is that Judge Cormier sat on the bench for every one of those cases."

"Are you saying innocent men were charged with those murders so Sheriff Badeaux would have a perfect record?" Smith asked.

"There are two young men who are to be hanged in less than two weeks for the murder of James Fisk," Fritz replied. He swept his arm in the direction of the two Gypsies. "These men and many others can attest to the fact that the two men weren't even in St. Landry Parish at the time Fisk was murdered."

"We were camped near Baton Rouge during the months of June and July," Theodor said.

"Marshal Smith," Josef spoke for the first time since he'd left the Gypsy camp, "We were camped on the east side of the Mississippi River for over two months. Nicilate and Vasile didn't come west of the Mississippi until August. They were with us during the months of June and July."

"Are you willing to swear to that in a court of law?" Marshal Smith asked.

"I am," Josef replied, "as are all of the adults in our band. If Nicilate and Vasile were guilty, we would have turned them over to the sheriff ourselves."

"Why didn't you testify at the trial?" Smith asked. "Surely those men were allowed to present witnesses."

"I have statements from Nicilate and Vasile," Robert said. "They weren't allowed to present witnesses at their trial. They weren't even allowed to testify of their innocence."

A vein in the middle of Marshal Smith's forehead bulged out. "I can't promise your men will be found innocent," he said, "but I do promise they'll be given a fair trial." He took a few moments to control his anger. "I want this kept quiet until I speak to a superior court judge. If Sheriff Badeaux and Judge Cormier are guilty of what you have asserted, they may try to get rid of the witnesses. I don't want a whisper of this to leave my office."

Marshal Smith walked to his door and called out, "Come in here, Dan."

The man who they had spoken to earlier entered the office. "Dan, I want you to keep quiet about these men coming here today," he said. "If word of this gets out on the street, I'll have your hide. Do you understand me?"

"Yes sir," Dan answered. Even though it was cool in the office, perspiration beaded on his forehead. "I understand."

"Make sure you do," Smith said. "If you don't, I'll see to it you're charged with malfeasance in office. That ought to get you a few years in a federal pen."

"I understand, Marshal," Dan said.

"Get some paper and pens and ink," Smith said. "Bring them in here."

"Yes, sir," Dan said. He left the office and was back shortly with the items Smith had requested.

"Gentlemen," Smith said to Josef and Theodor, "I need you to write out statements verifying that Nicilate and Vasile were with your band east of the Mississippi during the months of June and July. We can wait until the trial to get the statements from the other people in your band if we need them."

Josef and Theodor set about writing out the statements.

Dr. Joubert, Mr. Klienpeter," Smith said as he shook their hands. "It takes courage to do what you two men are doing. I hope you've thought through the consequences. Badeaux and Cormier are very popular with the people in this parish."

"We knew what we were risking," Robert said. "Had we kept quiet, two innocent men would've died."

"Is this what you wanted?" Josef asked as he handed his statement over to Smith.

"That will do very well," Smith answered after he'd read the statements. "I'll take them personally to a superior court judge this afternoon, if there's time." He looked at a clock sitting upon a shelf. "There should be plenty of time."

Josef offered his hand to Marshal Smith. "I'm at a loss for words to express my gratitude for your kindness," he said as Smith shook his hand. "I had no hope you would even listen to us."

"I'm only doing my job," Smith said. "My job is to make sure the guilty are punished and the innocent are protected." He rubbed his chin with his left hand. "If you had no hope that I would even listen to you, why did you come?"

"The two young men are Theodor's nephews," he replied. "I came to help him bear his sorrow."

"Has your experience with the law in America been that bad for you?" Smith asked.

"We are third and fourth generation Americans," Josef replied. "Most people don't trust us, but they mostly leave us alone. This was our first really bad experience."

"Why did you think I wouldn't help you?" Smith asked.

"We are different," Josef replied. "I thought you would back your own."

"My ancestors come from all over the world," Smith said. "Although we come from many places, in this country we're all Americans."

"That's what Constantin, our leader, says," Josef agreed. "He insists that we all learn to speak as Americans. He says we are Americans first and Gypsies second. We were beginning to think we couldn't be Americans."

"We'll see what we can do to restore your faith in America," Smith said. "Unfortunately, in every culture there are people like Badeaux and Cormier. We have to do our best to weed them out."

"You're right," Josef said. "We have had to punish some of our own."

Theodor handed his statement to Marshal Smith. Tears were rolling down his cheeks. "Thank God there are people like you in America," he said as he embraced Smith. "I know you'll do what's right."

He turned to Fritz and Robert. "Thank you for all you've done," he said. "You are welcome in our camp any time."

There were handshakes and backslaps all around. "I'm glad I talked to you about Badeaux," Fritz said. He put his arm around Robert's shoulders.

"We'd better get over to Angelina and tell her what's happened," Robert said. "She said to let her know the moment we knew something."

"You go on and tell her," Fritz said. "I have to get back to the paper."

*****

Judge Benjamin Bertrand was sitting at his desk looking at a plate that held a piece of boiled meat and a few leaves of lettuce. He looked impatiently at his law clerk when he entered his office. The diet Dr. Allan Joubert had him on was robbing him of his kind disposition.

"What is it, Jeffrey?" he snapped. "It had better be important to pull me away from my delicious dinner." He chuckled half-heartedly, hoping his attempt at humor would make up for his bellicosity.

"Marshal Smith is here to see you," Jeffrey replied. "He says it's very important."

"It had better be," Bertrand snarled. "Show him in." Bertrand scolded himself for his vile temper. "Some real food would cure all of this," he said to himself.

Smith walked into the office and stood before Bertrand's desk.

"Did you come to see what I was eating or do you have something on your mind?" Bertrand asked. He tried to keep his ill humor in check.

"I didn't want to interrupt you, Your Honor," Smith said.

"You're here now," Bertrand said. "Let's hear what you have to say."

Smith searched for the right words to begin. Bertrand made a come-on gesture with his hand.

"I have evidence that Sheriff Joubert and Judge Cormier are in cahoots in something that really stinks," he said.

Bertrand pushed his plate away and turned all of his attention to Smith. "What kind of evidence?" he asked. "It had better be something substantial to make that sort of accusation."

"It's substantial all right," Smith said. "They've been putting innocent men on trial and hanging them so they don't have to put up with angry citizens."

"Hanging innocent men?" Bertrand mused. "That would be hard to prove. We can't get testimonies from dead men. Is this something you're theorizing?"

"No theory," Smith stated emphatically. "Two young men are in the parish jail right now awaiting execution for a crime they didn't commit. Heck, they weren't even in the parish when the crime was committed."

"What kind of proof do you have to back up your allegations?" Bertrand asked. "That sort of thing must have been brought up at their trial."

"The men said they didn't have a chance to defend themselves or refute anything that was presented against them," Smith said. "I went to the courthouse and pulled the transcript of the trial. Cormier isn't all that bright. The transcript backed up what the men said."

"That's something," Bertrand said while scratching his temple, "but that's not enough to go after the sheriff and a district judge." Bertrand looked directly into Smith's eyes. "Anthony, we've known each other for several years. I trust you, but you'd better be sure before you go any further with this."

"I have more, Your Honor," Smith said. "I have statements from two men swearing that the young men were on the east side of the Mississippi when the murder occurred. There are many more witnesses."

"How did this come to your attention?" Bertrand asked. "Or did you discover this yourself?"

"Doctor Robert Joubert and Frank Klienpeter came to me with the information," Smith replied. "I should have noticed something, but I didn't. Klienpeter spoke to the men through their jail window and Dr. Joubert went into the jail and got their statements."

"He just walked into the jail and got their statements?" Bertrand asked in a voice of amazement.

"Not exactly," Smith replied. "One of the men was having pains the sheriff thought might have been appendicitis. He got Dr. Joubert to examine the man."

"I have an idea how that came about," Bertrand

chuckled. "I don't want to look too deeply into that."

Smith smiled. "If Dr. Joubert and Klienpeter hadn't gotten involved, two innocent men would have been killed."

Bertrand gave Smith a penetrating gaze. "You do realize the can of worms you're opening," he said. "I see you brought something with you. Let me see what you've got."

Smith placed the statements and trial transcripts on Bertrand's desk. Bertrand dropped his glasses from the top of his head to the bridge of his nose and began to read.

"These men are Gypsies," he said when he lifted his head. "How can you be sure they're not lying?"

Smith's face turned red. "They're American citizens," he replied. "I thought the law guaranteed us equal protection."

"Don't get yourself in a lather," Betrand said. "That's what a lot of people will say. I was pretty sure already, but I wanted to see where you stood. You'd better be ready to defend your convictions."

"Yes, Your Honor," Smith responded. "I already thought about that."

"You say the other transcripts are pretty much like these?" Bertrand asked.

"Yes, Your Honor," Smith replied.

"How many people know about this?" Bertrand asked.

"Nine including you," Smith replied. "I told all of the people that I don't want a word of this getting out until I say it's okay."

"Hmm," Bertrand said. "I think this does stink. Badeaux may have to find room in his jail for himself and Cormier. This is really serious."

"Are the men going to be able to get another trial?" Smith asked.

"We'll have to convince some powerful people to accept the testimony of Gypsies," Bertrand answered flatly.

"But, sir," Smith sputtered.

"Would you let me finish?" Bertrand asked. "You know I believe you and I'm inclined to believe your witnesses. There are people with strong prejudices who have to be convinced."

Smith's face grew red from the anger he felt over the

injustice.

"Getting angry won't do anything for those men," Bertrand warned.

"What should I do?" Smith asked.

"You said you can get some more statements," he replied. "Get as many of them as you can. I'll have to look into this some more. I need to bring the right people in on this." He scratched his head. "I can promise you this, though, I'll do everything I can to make sure those boys don't hang to make Badeaux and Cormier look good."

*****

Hannah was beginning to wonder if Adam had yet another mistress. He hadn't come up to her room in almost a week. Something or someone was occupying his time.

She lay her book down on her bedside table, walked over to a window and gazed at the former slave cabins on the dusty lane Adam had named Shady Lane. In the moonlight, she could see smoke rising from several chimneys. All of the cabins had been repaired and painted. "But for Adam, I'd still be living in one of those cabins," she thought to herself, "or one similar to them, and I'd still be ignorant. There is much for which I should be thankful."

She wished that Adam would come up to see her. She missed the intimacy, but she also had a nagging problem she would sooner or later have to discuss with him. She was over two months late on her cycle. Usually she was as regular as clockwork. Adam loved Martha dearly, but would he welcome another child?

There was a soft knock at her door. She hoped it was Adam. She rushed to the door and found him standing out in the hallway.

"Am I welcome?" he asked imploringly. "I am sorry I have been ignoring you."

In the light cast by the lamp on the bedside table, Hannah detected a guilty look in his eyes. "He must have another mistress," she said to herself. "This is the way he looked when he started with Giselle."

"You're always welcome," she said. "Come on in."

Adam walked over to the bed and lay down fully clothed. "I am so tired," he said.

"Are you sleeping well?" she asked.

"No," he replied. "I have had little sleep in the past few nights."

"Would you like to talk to me about what's on your mind?" she asked. "Sometimes it's not as bad as it seems after you've talked it out."

Adam lay on the bed for a while without moving or speaking. "There is something I find perplexing," he finally said. "I went to Annabelle's bedroom Saturday night." He stopped and looked into Hannah's eyes. "You may prefer that I keep this to myself."

"I really don't want to know what goes on in Annabelle's bed," she responded. "I don't even like to think of what goes on there, but something's bothering you."

"Something happened when we made love Saturday night," he said. "Annabelle was different, more passionate. I have never known her to be as responsive as she was that night." He looked up at her once again. "Do you really want to hear this?"

She looked down at him and nodded.

"I assumed she had lost weight to make herself more attractive to me," he continued. "I thought she was more impassioned because she missed me and wanted me to spend more time with her." He stopped again and looked at his hands. "I slept with her the following four nights." He shook his head. "She did nothing to dissuade me, but she was barely responsive."

Hannah sat on the bed beside him and thought over his conundrum.

"What do you think?" he asked.

"I think she's a young woman who had two children in less than two years," she replied. "I think she was glad you went to her, but she doesn't want to get pregnant again for a while. She was up almost every night with Charles. Do you really blame her for holding back?"

"I would never have thought it could be that simple," he said with relief showing on his face. "I had imagined all sorts of things. I even thought she might be having an affair."

Hannah shook her head. "Annabelle was raised by parents who believe strongly in the Ten Commandments," she said. "She's not the kind of woman who would even consider having an affair."

Adam put Annabelle out of his mind and drew Hannah into his arms and kissed her passionately. "I have missed you," he said. "It has been so long." He unbuttoned the top button of her dress and kissed her neck.

"I missed you," she said. She decided to wait until after they'd made love to tell him her news.

Roughly half an hour later, Adam awoke with a start. "How long was I asleep?" he asked.

"About five minutes," she replied. "You must really have been tired."

"I am never too tired for you," he said as he slid his fingers along her body.

"Are you sure?" she asked. "You're not growing tired of me after three and a half years?"

"I could never tire of this beautiful body," he replied emotionally.

She felt heat moving through her body as he touched her. She rolled over toward him and moved her body up against his. Adam was kissing her and caressing her gently. The flames grew higher with every touch. She was ready for him to take her but waited for him to make the move. "Now, Adam," she cried out as he sent flames throughout her body.

Sometime later, she lay exhausted in his arms. "I thought you said you were tired," she remarked. "You didn't make love like a tired man."

"I have only to see your marvelous body to feel reinvigorated," he said. "How could I even think any other woman could please me as you do?"

"I love you, Adam," she said. "Don't make me have to wait so long."

"I promise I will not make you wait again," he said. "I feel such contentment when I am with you."

Hannah started to tell Adam her news but he started talking before she could begin.

"Our dream is coming true," he said excitedly. "Did I tell you I have engaged a new land agent?"

"No," she replied, "but I had assumed you'd gone to another agent when I read that Mr. Fisk had been killed. That was terrible."

"Yes," he responded. "Thankfully, the sheriff was able to catch the murderers." "It was just as Gertzer said," he thought to himself. "Everything will be over once those two Gypsies hang."

"Did he find out why they killed Mr. Fisk?" she asked.

"I heard they tried to rob him and he fought back," he replied.

"I'm sorry I interrupted you," she said apologetically. "You were telling me about your new land agent."

"Yes, I was," he responded. "I got completely sidetracked. I am now buying land through Norman Gertzer. We were able to pick up another sixteen hundred and thirty arpents of land."

"How much does that make now?" she asked.

"We now own twenty-one thousand and ninety arpents," he replied proudly. "We are working toward connecting the two plantations."

"That's amazing," she said excitedly. "I used to think this was a huge plantation. Over twenty-one thousand arpents of land. You have to be the biggest landowner in the parish."

"No, but I will be," he said determinedly. "With the money we are making selling the crops, we will be able to purchase even more land. We are rich."

"Rich," she said the word rapturously. "From slave girl to riches." She smiled brightly at him and then cast down her eyes.

"What is wrong?" he asked.

"You're rich," she replied. "I have nothing I can call my own."

"I wanted to put Lance des Chenes in your name," he

said, "but you would not allow me."

"I still think that was best," she said. "That would have caused too much trouble for you and for me."

Adam reached for his pants and pulled them up from the floor. She wondered if he were angry and preparing to leave.

"Here," he said as he handed a paper to her.

"What's this?" she asked. She read the writing on the paper. "Oh, Adam, I am rich, but don't you need the money to run the plantations?"

"Five thousand dollars is only a beginning," he said. "I will continue to deposit money in your account. If something happens to me, I want you to live comfortably for the rest of your life. I have also opened an account for Martha. She will have the money when she turns twenty-one."

Hannah's body began to shake as she wept.

"I thought you would be pleased," he said contritely.

"I am pleased," she sobbed. "This is so thoughtful of you. You're so sweet."

"I know I have hurt you many times," he said remorsefully, "but I do love you. You mean more to me than any other person in this world."

She lay in his arms and felt safe and warm. She felt like waiting for another time to tell him her news but thought it would be best to get it out in the open.

"Adam," she said. "There's something I need to tell you."

"What is it?" he asked cautiously.

"My cycle is over two months late," she answered bleakly. "I think I'm pregnant."

Adam's mind was in a whirl. He now had his heir and another son. Martha was very dear to him, but another child with Hannah was something he had not really considered seriously. Out of the corner of his eye, he saw her waiting for his reply. "Are you sure?" he asked.

"I'm sure I'm over two months late," she replied. She was disappointed that he hadn't greeted the news more enthusiastically.

Adam saw the hurt on Hannah's face. "I hope we have

another girl and she is as pretty and delightful as Martha," he said marshaling up all the enthusiasm he could.

"I know this comes as a surprise to you," she said, "but I followed my mother's instructions. I'm just as surprised as you are."

"I am truly happy that we will have another child," he said. "It took a few moments for the news to sink in."

"Are you really happy?" she asked. "I was worried that you'd be upset."

"Why would I be upset?" he asked. "We both knew this could happen. Our child will be cherished by both of us."

They held each other closely as they thought their private thoughts.

*****

"I'm more nervous than I was when I took my final exams," Robert whispered to Fritz as they waited for the meeting to begin.

"I wish they'd hurry up and get here," Fritz said. "I've got butterflies the size of buzzards."

Marshal Anthony Smith walked in with Judge Benjamin Bertrand, District Attorney Lucian DeVille, Federal Judge Jason Anderson and another man Fritz had never seen before.

Marshal Smith signaled Robert and Fritz to come forward and join the other men at a large table.

Smith introduced Fritz and Robert to the four men who had walked in with him. Fritz learned that the other man was U.S. Attorney, Thomas Stafford.

Judge Jason Anderson cleared his throat. "I don't know what you thought we'd accomplish," he said more to Judge Bertrand than to the other men in the room.

"I don't think any of us here want to see innocent men hang," Bertrand responded.

"I don't think we have enough evidence to go against a sitting judge and a sheriff who's been duly elected by the people," U. S. Attorney Stafford said.

Fritz and Robert both took an instant dislike to Stafford.

He was a pedantic little man who spoke in a high-pitched nasal voice.

"Now, Tom, I think we have sufficient evidence to move ahead with this," Bertrand said. "You're just afraid of the bad publicity you'll get from this case."

"I don't care about the publicity," Stafford countered. The bad publicity was paramount in his mind. He was hoping to get appointed to the judicial bench. Going after a judge and a sheriff on the word of Gypsies wouldn't help his cause.

"Then what is it that can get you to overlook statements from over forty people who can prove the two men were no where near here at the time of the murder?" Bertrand asked.

"Those are statements from Gypsies," Stafford replied.

"They're American citizens," Smith said angrily. "Their testimony has the same weight as the testimony of any other American citizen."

"Are you willing to risk your career over this?" Judge Anderson asked.

"I can't believe anyone would put their career over the lives of innocent men," Smith replied. "You can have my badge if that's what it takes to open your eyes."

Judge Bertrand put his hand on his friend's shoulder to caution him. "I agree with Marshal Smith," he said evenly. "The day this job gets more important than people's lives will be the day I need to resign. I believe there were murders committed, but not by the two young Gypsies. I believe Cormier and Badeaux misused their power."

"I think we have enough to convict Cormier and Badeaux," Lucian Deville said. "I read the transcripts and the witness statements. It's clear that Nicilate and Vasile Lipatti were railroaded."

"You can't be serious," Stafford responded. "We all know Gypsies lie all the time. Do you think they wouldn't lie to protect two of their own?"

"I want to know how you arrived at that conclusion," Judge Anderson said icily.

"Well, they're notorious thieves and troublemakers," Stafford responded.

"As a respected attorney, I'm sure you're prepared to present evidence to back up your allegations," Anderson responded.

Stafford looked uncomfortable. "I don't have evidence with me, but we all know their reputation," he responded.

"That's what I feared we'd come up against," Bertrand said. "That's why it was possible for innocent men to be convicted of crimes they didn't commit. There's no outcry when saddle tramps, riffraff and Gypsies are murdered so the record can look good. Their lives aren't important."

Anderson turned to Fritz and Robert. "I understand you've met the condemned men," he said. "Would you tell us about them?"

"They're third generation Americans," Fritz replied. "I expected them to be ignorant and illiterate, but I was wrong. They speak better than most of the people in this parish and they can read and write. I also visited their encampment. The only thing I found different about them was their dress and their nomadic lifestyle. They're proud to be Americans, at least they were before all of this happened."

Judge Anderson nodded to Robert.

"I was impressed with them," he said. They seem to be good, decent, law abiding people." He stopped for a moment and scanned the faces of the men sitting at the table. "We'll all lose a piece of ourselves if we allow innocent men to die to save our reputations. I don't know why Judge Cormier and Sheriff Badeaux decided their positions were more important than people's lives. If you've got to let someone die to protect them, you can have my life."

"That's a wonderful speech," Stafford responded. "You're a doctor. You don't have to fight for your political career."

"Is that what this is all about?" Fritz asked angrily. "Saving your political career. What would you do if those two men were your nephews or your sons?"

Smith opened his mouth to reply, but Judge Anderson cut him off.

"Tom, I think you've said enough," he said. He turned to

DeVille. "Lucian, do you really think you have enough to convict Cormier and Badeaux?"

"Yes, Your Honor, I do," Deville replied.

Anderson turned to Bertrand. "Ben, I think you should release the Lipattis and have warrants issued for Cormier and Badeaux."

"I won't stand for this," Stafford cried out.

"You don't have to," Anderson responded. "As of now, you're suspended. I suggest you resign before I take further action."

Stafford stared coldly at Judge Anderson. Anderson returned his gaze calmly. Stafford clenched his jaw, but remained silent.

*****

"What's this?" Judge Roy Cormier asked when Jason Allan, a prosecutor from the district attorney's office handed him a copy of an arrest warrant. Cormier read several lines of the document. "You can't be serious."

"I have one more to deliver," Allan said. He turned and started to leave.

Cormier's eyes were filled with terror. "Another one?" he asked. "Who would that be?"

"Sheriff Badeaux," Allan said. "He'll be arrested on the spot. I almost forgot. A deputy is on his way to arrest you. I guess I should have waited for the deputy, but I don't think you can run very fast. He should be here in less than a minute."

Cormier dropped his eyes once more to the document. "Murder," he said to himself after reading a few more words. "I haven't murdered anyone. All we did is make sure the people were happy."

He rose from his chair and began to pace. "A deputy is coming to arrest me," he said. "After all I've done for this parish." He picked up the document and read a few more words. "I need a good lawyer."

He paced back and forth while deciding what he should do. He saw movement outside his window. A man was stepping down from his horse. "That's probably the deputy," he said to himself.

He moved to the window and looked out. The man wasn't in sight. "He's probably already in the building," he said out loud. "I can't go to jail."

Cormier walked back to his desk and sat in the chair. He opened a drawer and withdrew a handgun. "They're not gonna have the satisfaction of watching me hang," he said. He put the barrel of the gun to his temple and pulled the trigger.

When Deputy Alonzo Ortego walked into Cormier's office moments later, he saw the judge slumped over at his desk. Ortego felt Cormier's pulse. "He's gone," he said out loud.

*****

"Come in," Sheriff Glenn Badeaux said when he heard a knock at his door. Jason Allan walked into the office and stood in front of Badeaux's desk.

Badeaux rose from his desk and offered his hand to Allan.

"I don't think you're gonna want to shake my hand when you find out why I'm here," he said.

Two sheriff's deputies entered the office.

"What do you mean?" he asked. His hand dropped to his side as he searched the faces of the deputies.

Allan handed Badeaux a copy of his arrest warrant. "I need to have this warrant executed," he said.

Badeaux read the name on the warrant. "If this is supposed to be some kind of joke," he said in a tight voice, "it shore ain't funny."

"This is no joke," Allan responded. "If you'll read the warrant, you'll know I'm not joking."

Badeaux held the warrant up and began to read. When he read the charge on the warrant, he lifted his head and glared at Allan. "Murder!" he shouted. "I never murdered anybody. I'd like to know who's behind this."

Allan turned to the deputies. "I've shown you a copy of Sheriff Badeaux's arrest warrant," he said. "Please take him to a cell and lock him up."

"You can't do that!" Badeaux shouted. "I'm the sheriff."

"If you'll look, you'll see the warrant is signed by Judge Bertrand," Allan responded. He motioned to the deputies to approach Badeaux. "Lock him up. We'll let a jury decide whether or not he's guilty."

Deputy Alton Delafosse timidly approached Badeaux. "We probably don't like this any more than you do, Sheriff," he said, "but we got to do our jobs."

"You're fired," Badeaux cried out. "You too, Taylor. Get your stuff and get out of here."

"You've been relieved, Sheriff," Allan said. "You can't fire anyone."

"I was elected by the people," Badeaux said. "You can't come in and tell me what to do."

"I'm not going to argue with you," Allan said. "Lock him up men."

"You're gonna be in big trouble when Judge Cormier gets hold of this," Badeaux spat out. "He'll lock you up in jail." He glared at the two deputies. " That goes for you two ingrates, too."

"This'll all be cleared up after I talk to the judge," Badeaux said to the deputies and the assistant district attorney. "He'll know what to do. You men will be sorry you were ever born."

"Judge Cormier won't be of much help to you," Allan responded with a smile. "He's on his way here in handcuffs. I served the warrant on him just before coming here."

Badeaux's body sagged. "You can't arrest a judge," he sputtered. "Nobody can arrest a judge."

"No one is above the law," Allan retorted. "Not even a judge."

Delafosse took Badeaux's arm to lead him out of the office and to his cell.

"Get your hand off of me!" Badeaux shouted. "I can walk. When this is all straightened out, you'll be lucky if you can get a job cleaning out spittoons in a barroom."

"Get him to his cell," Allan said in a voice edged with

steel. "Let him walk. If he tries anything, cuff him and shackle him."

Badeaux glared once more at the deputies, then made his way out of the office. He stopped at the cell door and glared at Allan. "You made a big mistake," he said gravely. "I'll get you back for this if it's the last thing I do." He stepped into the cell and then turned and faced Allan and the two deputies. "Judge Cormier is gonna figure this out. It won't be long before I'll be looking at you in a jail cell."

Deputy Roscoe Taylor swung the cell door closed and turned the key.

Badeaux took hold of the bars on the door and pushed. "You think you did something, Taylor," he said. "I'll take care of you right after I take care of Allan."

Allan and the two deputies turned and walked away.

*****

Roughly two months later, Theodor, Nicilate and Vasile Lipatti stood on the front steps of the courthouse deeply absorbed in conversation with Robert and Fritz.

"I didn't expect him to be convicted, much less sentenced to death by hanging," Theodor said. "How many years had he been sheriff?"

"Eighteen years," Fritz replied.

"He must've been an honest sheriff at first," Robert ventured.

"He may have been," Fritz agreed, "but he wasn't sheriff more than two years when this started."

"He looked lost in there," Vasile said waving his arm toward the courthouse. "He didn't have much to say all the way through."

"Jason Allan told me Badeaux crumbled when he heard Judge Cormier had killed himself," Fritz said. "He was counting on Cormier getting him out of this."

"Are you going to be leaving now that the trial is over?" Robert asked.

"We want to watch Sheriff Badeaux get what he

intended for Nicilate and Vasile," Theodor said. "We can wait another three weeks."

"Are you going to the hanging?" Nicilate asked.

"No," Robert replied. "Badeaux is getting what he deserves, but I really don't want to watch."

"And you?" Nicilate asked as he nodded toward Fritz.

"Not unless I have to cover it for the paper," Fritz replied. "In spite of everything, I kinda feel sorry for Badeaux." He looked down at his feet and then looked into Nicilate's eyes. "He took many lives and it's just that he pays with his own life, but I feel no need to watch the spectacle."

"Well, I want to thank you again for what you did for us," Theodor said as he offered his hand. "These two would be dead by now if it wasn't for your intervention. Come to our camp before we leave. We'll have a festival."

"I'd like to do that," Fritz said.

"Would it be all right for my wife to go with me?" Robert asked.

"Sure," Theodor replied. "You can bring someone with you too," he said as he punched Fritz lightly on the shoulder."

"I don't think the woman who has his heart will be able to attend," Robert thought to himself. He felt sorry for his friend and for Annabelle.

"Dr. Joubert, Mr. Klienpeter," Nicilate said as he offered his hand. "I'll always remember what you've done for us. When I marry, I'll name my first two sons after you."

"Thank you for saving our lives," Vasile added. "We'll have two Roberts and two Franks in our band." He hugged Fritz and then Robert.

CHAPTER TWENTY-SIX

January 15, 1869 – February 15, 1869

"I find all of this very unsettling," Adam said to Norman Gertzer. "Judge Cormier committed suicide and Sheriff Badeaux was hanged on the scaffold he intended to use on the two Gypsies. How can you be so sure we have nothing to worry about?" Adam was in Gertzer's office sitting in one of the chairs facing Gertzer's desk.

"Nobody saw me in Fisk's office and you were at home when he was murdered," Gertzer explained patiently. "They could only learn about us if one of us talked, and I'm sure not about to tell anyone I killed Fisk."

"The deputy who was appointed sheriff until an election can be held, uh, what is his name?" Adam asked.

"Delafosse, Alton Delafosse," Gertzer replied.

"Yes, Delafosse," Adam agreed. "Was he not involved in the investigation of Fisk's murder?"

"He could've been involved," Gertzer replied, "but how does that matter? Badeaux had no idea who killed Fisk. There was nothing in Fisk's office that could possibly connect me or you to his murder."

"Delafosse knows Fisk was my land agent," Adam said. "That connects me to Fisk."

"Fisk was the land agent for a lot of people," Gertzer replied. "Those people are just as connected to Fisk as you are." He was trying his best to remain patient with Blythington. "He sure isn't acting like the tough fellow I thought he was," he said to himself.

"Do you think we should stop buying land for a while?"

Adam asked, "at least until the incident is forgotten?"

"No, I don't" Gertzer replied. "Delafosse would grow more suspicious if we started doing things differently." He leaned forward. "Mr. Blythington, you pay me to take the risks; I take the risks. I'm very careful. You're only buying up land as it becomes available."

"Yes, that is true," Adam agreed. "When you put it that way, I can see there is no need for worry."

"You changed your mind real quick when you realized it's my neck in the noose, didn't you?" Gertzer thought to himself. "Don't get too comfortable because I'll bring you down with me if there's a problem."

"I'm glad you understand," Gertzer said. "Now, can we get down to business?" He rose from his chair, went over to the filing cabinet, and looked through several folders. He pulled two of them out.

"What have you got for me?" Adam asked.

"There's one I've been trying to shake loose for sometime," he replied. "Belongs to one of the Negroes who was freed before the war. He's got a hundred and fifty arpents. He hasn't budged."

"What is so important about his land?" Adam asked. "It is only a small amount compared to what we want to acquire."

"You've got two hundred arpents north of his land and your land is all around the rest of his place," Gertzer replied. "He's got what amounts to an island in your plantation. By law, you have to provide him with an access road. That's land you can't plant."

"I can see that would be a problem," Adam agreed. He could tell that Gertzer was holding something back. "Is there another problem?"

"I really don't like Negroes owning land," Gertzer replied. "It just doesn't seem right."

"I have no problem with Negroes owning land," Adam said coldly, "as long as their land is not land I need."

"I've got these other two," Gertzer said as he handed Blythington two folders. He wanted to change the subject when he realized Blythington was not pleased with his opinion on

Negroes owning land.

Adam went over the information contained in the folders. "When will they be available?" he asked.

"They're available now," Gertzer replied. "I know how you emphasized you want the land before spring planting. You'll have about a month to spare."

Adam looked at the property descriptions once more. One of the farms was eleven hundred arpents and the other seventeen hundred. "These are larger farms than the ones we bought previously," he said.

"I told you we'd start with the small ones and then go on to the larger ones," Gertzer said as he smiled proudly. "In a few years, all of the land between those two plantations will be yours." He leaned back in his chair. "After Dupre' passes away, you'll have one huge plantation." He smiled again. "I can make something happen to speed up his passing if you'd like."

Adam toyed with the idea. "That would be the sure way to point the law in my direction," he said to himself. "I do not think that would be wise," he responded. "I will have the land in time."

*****

"I'm so glad you came," Angelina said as she greeted Annabelle at the door. "Where are the boys?"

"They were both asleep and Adam was out in the fields," she replied. "It's such a warm and beautiful day for the middle of February. I couldn't resist going out for a buggy ride."

"So, you escaped," Angelina laughed. "Come on in. We were just sitting down to coffee."

Annabelle removed her bonnet and the light cape she was wearing and handed them to Angelina. She then followed her friend into the parlor.

"Annabelle," Robert exclaimed, "what a pleasant surprise. I'm sure you remember Fritz." Robert hugged Annabelle.

Fritz rose from his chair and walked over to Annabelle. "This is a pleasant surprise," he said as he took her hand in his.

Annabelle felt a rush of excitement from the touch of his hand. Her heart raced as she looked into his eyes. She withdrew her hand from his reluctantly and turned toward Angelina when she heard her name called."

Angelina was smiling delightedly. She had seen the look in Annabelle's eyes. "I wish you two could be together," she said to herself. "He would be so much better for you than what you're stuck with."

"What did you say?" Annabelle asked.

"I asked you if you wanted to join us for coffee," she replied.

"Yes, thank you," Annabelle answered. "Let me help you."

"Nonsense," Angelina responded. "The coffee is already made. All I have to do is pour it into the cups. I'll only be a minute. You go on ahead and have a seat."

Annabelle sat in a stuffed chair near Fritz. "I read about Sheriff Badeaux's hanging in the *Clarion*," she said. "It's sad that he was responsible for the deaths of so many innocent men."

"I'm glad we were able to save at least two," Fritz said. "If I'd come to Robert earlier, maybe we could have saved others."

"There he goes again," Robert said. "He saved those two men and no telling how many more who would've been falsely accused and all he can do is castigate himself for not acting earlier."

"I suspected Badeaux and Cormier for over a year before I talked to you about them," Fritz said in an anguished voice. "I don't know why I kept on investigating when I already knew the truth."

"You're being too hard on yourself, Fritz," Annabelle said softly. "A lot of people should've known what they were doing. No one bothered to question their actions. We all felt safe because we had such a competent sheriff."

"That's what I've been trying to tell him," Robert said. "Maybe now it'll sink in through that thick skull."

Angelina walked back into the parlor carrying a tray that she set down on a low table.

"Where's Bertha?" Robert asked. "Why isn't she serving the coffee?"

"It's Sunday afternoon," Angelina replied. "She wanted to visit her sister. I'm not helpless."

"But we pay her to do the things you do," Robert said with exasperation. "We're also paying a maid to watch you do her work."

"Oh, Robert, they do a lot," Angelina responded. She began to pass the cups of coffee.

"I'll never win this argument," Robert said resignedly.

"Annabelle, I have to tell you about the wonderful time we had at the Gypsy encampment," Angelina said animatedly. "You wouldn't believe the food. I think all their single ladies were captivated by Fritz."

Annabelle turned her attention to Fritz. He was blushing beet red.

"One or two of them came and talked to me," Fritz said. "I wouldn't call that captivated."

"One or two, my eye," Angelina continued. "There were dozens of them hanging around you. I think the men were a bit jealous."

"Did you have fun?" Annabelle asked Fritz.

"It was interesting," Fritz replied. "The food was great and the people wore colorful clothing. Theodor got carried away and continued to make speeches thanking us. I think he was hitting the wine barrel too often."

"They were grateful for what you and Robert did," Angelina said. "I'm proud of both of you."

"I'm proud of you, too," Annabelle added. "You were willing to stick your necks out to help those men. Not many men would be willing to take those risks."

"What risks?" Fritz asked. "We weren't locked up in jail facing death by hanging. There might be some people who don't like us, but no one has threatened us."

"You may not have heard the last word on this," Annabelle said. "Judge Cormier and Sheriff Badeaux had some very powerful friends. They may be only biding their time."

"That's true," Angelina agreed. "You both need to be

careful." She sat down beside Robert and held his hand.

"Poor Fritz," Robert said. "He has no one to give him comfort." He turned and winked at Annabelle.

"I would comfort him," she said to herself, "but I'm a married woman." She blushed when she thought of her feelings for Fritz. He did nothing to provoke her, but she felt flustered when she was around him.

"I wonder where the Gypsies are now?" Fritz asked, changing the subject. "They wander all over. I don't think I'd like that kind of life. I like putting down roots."

"There is something to that," Robert agreed. "I travel more than enough as a doctor."

"Sometimes I think I'd like to see faraway places I've read about," Annabelle mused aloud.

"I didn't mean I don't want to travel, " Fritz said. "I wouldn't mind taking a trip to Europe or even Asia. I want a home to return to after the trip."

"I would travel anywhere in the world or live anywhere you wanted me to if you were with me," he said to himself.

"Are you and Adam planning to take a trip?" Angelina asked.

"No," Annabelle said shaking her head. "I don't think Adam wants to leave St. Landry Parish. He thinks of little else but his land."

"I don't see how he can think of anything besides you," Fritz blurted out. He was astonished when he heard the words he was thinking come out of his mouth. "I'm sorry, I shouldn't have said that."

Annabelle couldn't help herself. She stared at him in amazement.

"I guess I'd better be going," he said as he rose from his chair.

Annabelle reached out her hand and placed it on his arm. "Please stay," she said. "Tell me more about your visit to the Gypsy encampment."

"What's gotten into me?" she asked herself. "I'm acting like a brazen hussy."

Fritz sat back down in his chair. "The thing that

impressed me most was their music," he began. "Some of the music was vibrant. Most of the people got up and danced gaily." His face took on a sad expression as he recalled the music. "Some of the music was so sad and stirring. Even though I didn't understand the words, the meaning came through just by the sound of their voices and the instrumentation that seemed to pull at my heart. Nicilate told me they were songs of bad experiences in the old country and songs of lost love."

"That's how I felt," Robert said. "I saw Angelina crying several times."

"Me crying?" Angelina responded. "Yes, I cried, but don't think I didn't see the tears streaming down your face."

"It must have been a moving experience," Annabelle said. "I wish I could've gone with you."

"There are so many things I wish I could do," she thought to herself.

Annabelle felt herself being captivated as she listened to Fritz describe his experience with the Gypsies. When he had exhausted that subject, she asked him how he had become a newspaper reporter. From there, he told of his adventures as a reporter. She was pulled back to the present when the clock on the mantle chimed five o'clock.

"The time seems to have flown," she said as she rose from her chair. "Adam will be furious with me for being out alone after dark."

"I'll follow you back and make sure you're safe," Fritz offered.

"How sweet of you," Annabelle responded, "but it's much too far and the nights are too cold."

"I won't take no for an answer," Fritz said. "How would I live with myself if something were to happen to you."

"Let me get you a quilt," Angelina said to Annabelle. "You'll be the one getting cold in that buggy. All you brought with you is that light cape."

Robert and Angelina hugged Annabelle good-bye.

Fritz helped her up into the buggy. "I'll be right behind you," he said.

Robert followed Fritz to his horse. "There's no telling

what Adam would do if he knew you were following Annabelle home," he said. "He's a strange man. Stay close enough so you can help her if anything happens but leave enough distance so no one can tell you're with her."

"I understand," Fritz responded. "I don't want to get her in any trouble." He mounted his horse and followed behind her buggy at a distance.

*****

She turned her head around and saw Fritz behind her in the distance as she veered into the oak tree lined Southern Kingdom driveway. She stopped the buggy and waved. Fritz waved back and then headed back to town. She slapped the reins on the horse's back and set out for the house.

No one was waiting for her when she entered her home. She made her way to her bedroom, removed her cape and bonnet, folded the quilt Angelina had loaned her and went into the bathing room to freshen up for supper.

When she stepped into the informal dining room, Ruth was coming out of the kitchen. "Magret say suppah jes bout reddy," she said.

"Have you seen Mr. Adam?" Annabelle asked.

"No Mam," Ruth replied. "I ain't seed him since dinnah time."

"I wonder what's keeping Adam out this late," she pondered. "It was good luck, though, finding that he hadn't yet returned. He won't know that I came in late."

She went into the kitchen and spoke to Margaret. "I'm not very hungry," she said. She saw a pan of fresh biscuits on the table. "All I want is one of your biscuits and some fig preserves."

"How bout a big glass a moik to wash dem down?" Margaret asked.

"Thank you, that would be fine," Annabelle replied.

She returned to the informal dining room and in a matter of minutes, Mary brought her supper out.

"Thank you very much, Mary," she said.

She sat alone and ate supper. When she had eaten, she

walked over to the nursery where she found Charles and Paul sleeping peacefully.

"Charles was a handful this afternoon," Matilda said as she rocked back and forth near the sleeping boys. "Paul was an angel."

"Charles only has a strong personality," Annabelle said. "He'll settle down as he grows older."

"I hope you're right, Mum," Matilda said. "I wish he were more like Paul."

Annabelle bent down and kissed Charles lightly on his cheek. He stirred but he didn't awaken. She leaned down and kissed Paul's cheek. He opened his eyes, looked up at his mother and smiled. "My sweet little one," she said as she ran her fingers lightly through his dark wavy hair. He closed his eyes and was fast asleep once more.

"Have you seen Mr. Adam?" she asked Matilda.

"Not since this morning," Matilda replied.

"I wonder where he could be." she said to herself.

She left the nursery and returned to her room. Almost as soon as her head touched the pillow, thoughts of Fritz filled her mind. "Had I waited, there may have been a life for us," she said to herself. She thought of her two young sons just down the hallway. "No, I wouldn't change a thing. I wouldn't give up my boys."

*****

"It's been such a lovely day," Hannah said. "Martha's growing up so quickly. She'll be three in June." She held Adam's arm tightly as she sat beside him in the buggy.

"Three years old already," he said. "I will be twenty-seven in July. Time is flying by so quickly."

"And I'll be twenty-four next month," she added. "You know, in some ways it seems as though we've known each other forever, and in some ways it seems we just met."

"I never dreamed I would own so much land," he said. "I own two large mansions and countless other houses and barns. I employ scores of men and I own thousands of head of cattle and horses." He looked out into the darkness as though he were looking out over his kingdom. "By the time Charles is eighteen, I should own more than twice as much. He will take over when I am gone."

"You have many years before you need to think about your replacement," she said. "You're still young and strong." She squeezed his arm and pressed her body closer to him. "It's getting colder."

"I was having so much fun with Martha, I forgot the time," he responded. A chill ran through his body. "It is growing colder." He slapped the reins on the horse's back and sped the horse from a walk to a trot.

"What will you tell Annabelle when she asks why you're out so late?" Hannah asked. "She's probably worried about you."

"I doubt she will ask," he replied, "and if she does, I will tell her nothing. I do not answer to her." His voice took on a harsh tone as he finished the sentence.

"I'll soon have to move to the cottage," Hannah said. She felt her stomach. It wouldn't be long before it was obvious that she was pregnant. She was nearing her fifth month of pregnancy. She felt a deep foreboding about this child that she hadn't felt during her pregnancy with Martha.

"You are hardly showing," he said. "You can stay with me another month or two."

"I am showing," she countered. "It'll soon be obvious to everyone. How will we explain my pregnancy to Annabelle?"

"Why would we have to explain your pregnancy to Annabelle?" he asked.

"Because she's your wife and I'm your housekeeper," she replied. "She'll want some explanation if I stay with you."

"How will you explain your absence?" he asked. "It would be simpler to let her believe you are having a baby for a man you loved who left when he found out you were pregnant."

"First of all, Adam," Hannah said sharply, "I don't want anyone thinking I'm a big enough fool to get pregnant for a man who'd run off on me, and secondly, do you think she'd believe that story since she hasn't seen a man coming around to see me;

but to answer your question, I'm going to tell everyone I'm going to visit an aunt in New Orleans."

"I did not mean to upset you," he responded. "I do not like the thought of you being away from me."

"You're so sweet, Adam," she said. "I didn't mean to be so sharp with you. It won't be easy on me either."

"If only this pregnancy had not come up," Adam said to himself crossly. "It is not fair that I should be put through this."

When Adam remained silent, she said, "I hope you aren't angry with me. I'll be so lonesome without you."

"When do you plan to leave for the cottage?" he asked.

"I thought I would spend one more week with you and then go," she replied. "I guess I'll start packing around Wednesday and leave Saturday."

"So soon," he said.

"Annabelle may already have noticed a difference in me," she responded. "If I wait too long, she'll know I'm pregnant. We don't want her to suspect we've been intimate."

"I wish I could send her away for a few months and let you stay," Adam said. "It really is not fair that I have to go through this," he said to himself.

"It won't be all that long," she said. "Only a few months and I'll return to you. You will come and visit me, won't you?"

Adam failed to answer because he was absorbed in self-pity.

Hannah turned her head so she could see his face clearly. The look on his face made her angry. "Do you think I planned to get pregnant?" she asked harshly. "Don't you think this will be hard on me too?"

"Why are you upset with me?" he asked. "What did I do? I know you did not plan to get pregnant. I know this is not easy on you. Please do not take your frustration out on me."

"Oh, Adam," she said. "Sometimes you really do upset me."

"Why must we quarrel?" he asked. "We have only one more week together before you leave for the cottage. Must we spend the time this way?"

Hannah fought to control her temper. "I don't want to

spend our last week quarreling," she replied. "I asked you if you'd come to visit me and you didn't answer."

"I am sorry," he said contritely. "I did not hear you."

"That's because you were too busy feeling sorry for yourself," Hannah said to herself. She struggled once more to keep her temper in check.

Adam became uncomfortable when she remained silent. "I will come to visit you," he said. "You know I will visit you and Martha."

Hannah kissed his cheek. "You can't help that you're such a jackass," she said to herself. "The time will pass quickly," she said.

*****

Matilda smiled brightly when Annabelle entered the nursery. "They're both sound asleep," she whispered.

Annabelle placed her hand lightly on Matilda's shoulder. "Charles looks so innocent when he's asleep," she said.

Matilda nodded her head. She was trying her best to like the little boy, but he tried her patience sorely. Paul, on the other hand, seemed to always be in a good mood.

Annabelle bent down over Charles and kissed his cheek. Without opening his eyes or awakening, he turned away from her. She bent over Paul and kissed his cheek and patted his head softly. He remained motionless.

"You look tired, Mum," Matilda stated in a voice filled with worry. "Are you sleeping well?"

Annabelle smiled weakly. She supposed her worries were written all over her face. "I'm all right, Matilda," she replied. "Thank you for your concern."

Matilda was pretty sure she knew the source of Mrs. Blythington's sadness. Mr. Blythington seemed to go out of his way to be cross and rude to her. Her heart went out to the younger woman.

Annabelle smiled wanly and then made her way to her own room. After she had cleaned up for the night and dressed in her flannel nightgown, she knelt by her bed and recited the prayers she'd learned as a child.

Her heart was heavy. Tears slid down her cheeks as she prayed. She didn't understand what had caused Adam to distance himself from her as he had. She asked for God to intervene and soften his heart.

She lay still for several minutes, waiting for her body heat to warm her mattress and quilts. She was thankful when her eyelids grew heavy. Moments later, she was fast asleep.

As she slept, she dreamed of Fritz. He was standing in front of a white church. When he saw her, he smiled brightly and beckoned to her to come to him.

"I was beginning to think you'd changed your mind," he said when she reached him. "Everyone's waiting for us."

He took her hand and turned toward the church. She was surprised to see her family and close friends seated in the pews when she entered the church with Fritz. The people rose to their feet when she walked in on Fritz's arm. They were all smiling happily.

Her heart was gladdened. It was as though peace and serenity were soaking through her body. She turned her head and gazed into Fritz's eyes. The love she saw there made her heart skip a beat.

"I love you," Fritz said as he smiled down on her. "This is the happiest day of my life."

"I love you, Fritz," she responded.

She lifted her eyes and looked toward the altar. A man dressed in black stood there waiting for them. Her heart sang with joy.

Suddenly, the scene changed. She found herself in the Southern Kingdom parlor. Adam was shouting at her. His face was almost purple with rage. He was calling her a tramp and accusing her of adultery. She tried to open her mouth to defend herself, but not a word would come out. She bowed her head as he continued to harangue her.

She finally found her voice. "I'm sorry," she cried out, even though she knew she wasn't guilty of his accusaitions. "I'm so sorry."

Adam slapped her face and continued to hurl insults. She lifted her head in time to see him reaching for her throat. She tried to move out of his way.

She awoke with a start. Although the night was cold, her body was soaked with perspiration. She gazed around the room fearfully in the pale moonlight. Her heart was beating wildly. It took her several moments before she realized it had only been a dream.

Even though she was close to exhaustion, she kept her eyes wide open. She feared that if she fell asleep, the horrible dream would return. "Not all of it was horrible," she said to herself. She immediately felt guilty. She had no right to love any man but Adam. She vowed to try harder to overlook his shortcomings and look for his strengths.

*****

Angelina was surprised, but pleased when she saw Annabelle pull up to her home in her buggy. She went out to help Annabelle unhitch the horse from the buggy.

"I guess I'm becoming a nuisance," Annabelle stated apologetically when Angelina reached her side.

"Not at all," Angelina assured her. "We're always happy to see you." She took hold of the horse's reins and led him to the stable.

"You're just in time for coffee," Angelina said when they had finished with the horse and buggy and were entering her home. "Robert's out making rounds. We have all the time in the world to visit."

"I hope I'm not keeping you from anything," Annabelle said.

"Nonsense," Angelina responded. "It's too cold to do anything outdoors. This is the perfect day to sit and visit."

"Isn't this nice," Angelina stated after Bertha had served the coffee. "I don't think kings and queens live any better than we do."

"Probably not," Annabelle agreed.

"I can tell something's on your mind," Angelina stated

bluntly. "You may as well come out with it."

"First Matilda and then you," Annabelle responded wearily. "I must be easy to read."

"It's not hard to tell when someone is as sad as you are," Angelina stated compassionately "What has Adam done this time?"

"Nothing really," Annabelle replied. "I had a strange dream last night. Part of it was really horrible."

"Tell me about your dream," Angelina said. "Maybe I can do like those people who claim they can interpret dreams."

Annabelle shook her head. "I don't know if I want this one interpreted," she responded.

"Are you going to tell me about your dream?" Angelina asked after Annabelle had been silent for about a minute. It was as though she had gone into a trance.

Annabelle shook her head once more. "You'll probably think it's silly," she replied. She blushed when she recalled the part about Fritz and the church.

"You're beginning to get on my nerves," Angelina stated in mock anger. "Come out with it."

Annabelle told Angelina about the scene at the church.

"I know what that means," Angelina said when Annabelle had finished. "You're really in love with Fritz."

"I can't be," Annabelle protested. "I'm a married woman with two children."

Angelina didn't want to argue with her friend. She knew that sometime in the future Annabelle would have to face some facts. "What about the rest of the dream?" she asked.

"It was terrible," Annabelle replied in anguish. "Adam was shouting at me. He accused me of being an adulterer. He tried to choke me."

"That one's not hard to interpret," Angelina responded. "In your dream, Adam was scourging you because of your love for Fritz. It wasn't really Adam who was trying to punish you. You were punishing yourself because of your guilt."

Annabelle shook her head. "I'm very fond of Fritz, but I'm not in love with him," she protested. "I vowed to love Adam."

Angelina wanted to shake Annabelle until her teeth rattled. The woman was in denial. Adam was a cruel man who only loved himself. Annabelle would be miserable as long as she was with him. Fritz was a kind and gentle man. Annabelle could be happy with him, but she would never break her marriage vows.

"Are you happy with Adam?" she asked.

Annabelle lowered her eyes. "I vowed to be faithful to him as long as I live," she replied in a hollow voice. "I can't break my vows."

Angelina shook her head. It would do no good to argue with Annabelle. She said a silent prayer that her friend would find peace and joy.

*****

Norman Gertzer sat nervously as Adam looked over the land descriptions he had prepared for him. It was impossible to tell from the expression on his face whether or not Mr. Blythington was pleased with his work.

After several minutes, Adam looked up. "Are these available now?" he asked.

"No, but they can be real soon," Gertzer replied. "Just give the word and we'll get things moving."

"Will you have problems with the present owners?" Adam asked.

"Nothing we can't handle," Gertzer replied with self-assurance. He had a hard look on his face.

Adam was sure Gertzer would not like his question, but he felt compelled to ask. "What happens if someone complains to the sheriff?"

Gertzer frowned. He didn't like it when his competence was called into question. "We can make sure that doesn't happen," he replied stonily.

"I have confidence in your work," Adam assured Gertzer, "but I am sure you understand my concern. I have a long-term goal in mind. If anyone complains to the sheriff, it may be difficult to fulfill my plans."

Gertzer fought to keep his temper under control. Blythington couldn't eat his cake and have it too. There were certain risks that would have to be taken. Thus far, he was the one who was taking all the risks.

"I'm doing all I can to protect you and get you what you want," Gertzer stated with an edge to his voice. "You've made it clear to me that you want all the land between your plantations." He pointed to the folder on Adam's lap. "All of that land lies in that area. We can wait until those people want to sell, but that could take years."

Adam drew a deep breath and exhaled slowly. He had to admit that Gertzer was right, but his experience with Sheriff Badeaux had frightened him. What he really wanted was for Gertzer to acquire the land without letting him know how he was going about convincing the owners to sell. What he did not know would not worry him.

"Do you want me to get that land for you?" Gertzer asked after Adam had remained silent for over a minute.

Adam nodded his head.

"Will you be satisfied after you own Belle Bois and all the land between your plantations?" Gertzer asked.

Adam sat back in his chair and stroked his chin. He had not stopped to consider what he would do at that juncture. "Will it ever be enough?" he asked himself. "As long as someone has one more arpent of land than I do, it will never be enough."

"No, it will not be enough," he replied. "It will never be enough."

"That's just what I thought," Gertzer said to himself. "It's never enough."

*****

Hannah sat at her dresser brushing her hair. She had hoped that Adam would come to visit her, especially since this would be her last night at Southern Kingdom for some time. It was already ten o'clock and there was no sign of him. She had really wanted to spend this last night with him.

She wondered if she could wait a few more days before moving to the cabin. She left the dresser and walked over to the full-length mirror. She examined her reflection in the mirror. From the front, it was difficult to tell that she was pregnant. Most people, if they noticed anything at all, would think that she had gained a little weight. She turned to the side and shook her head. If anyone looked closely, they would know that she was pregnant. To her, it was glaringly obvious.

Her heart skipped a beat when she heard a soft knock on her door. She hurried over to the door hoping it was Adam.

"I was hoping that you were still up," he said when she opened the door.

"I was beginning to think you weren't coming," she responded. She waited for him to take her in his arms.

Instead, he walked over to the bed and sat down. "It has been a long day," he said.

"Are you still upset because I'm leaving?" she asked.

"You could wait another week or two," he responded petulantly. "It will be lonely in this house without you."

"I'm already showing," she responded. "I should have left a week ago, but I put it off because you didn't want me to leave."

He sat silently at the edge of the bed staring at the floor.

"You don't look happy," she said. "What's bothering you?"

"I went to see Gertzer today," he replied.

"Did you have an argument with him?" she asked after he had remained silent for several moments.

"No, nothing like that," he replied. He had a far away look in his eyes. "He asked me when I would have enough land."

"Did you tell him you wanted to join your two plantations?" she asked.

He shook his head. "No, I did not," he replied with a strange look on his face.

"What did you tell him?" she asked.

He turned his head and looked into her eyes. "I told him I would never own enough land," he replied. "Land is power. I do not want anyone to be richer or more powerful."

Hannah searched the face of the man she had thought she knew so well. The eyes that had always held a gentle quality when they were alone no longer seemed the same. His eyes seemed to glow, but not with warmth. His face seemed to be carved out of stone, yet she detected sadness in the set of his mouth. Despite all of his land and wealth he had found no satisfaction. A cold shiver ran down her spine. Although she would continue to love him with every fiber of her being, she knew no woman could fill the void in his heart. She realized he would always be searching for something he would never find.

Also by Aberdeen Bay

When Summer was in the Meadow

When Summer was in the Meadow records and preserves a time
that is receding all too quickly into the lost pages of the last century.
Based on actual events of the 20's and early 30's, the work is the
real-life story of Evelyn Johnson, a child who in her own voice
draws us into a magical world of backyard circuses, church picnics,
and friendly neighbors. As she matures, her narration reveals with
poignancy and humor life as it was lived by ordinary people during
a critical period in American history. The story has historical appeal
in its evocation of life in the South and in its recall of actual places,
events, and persons of the time — from the talkies and Lindbergh to
FDR and the Great Depression. In a larger sense, however, this is a
story about ourselves and the power of remembrance to shape our
lives and the lives of those who follow us.

Author: Betsy Hamlet Nichols
Publisher: Aberdeen Bay
ISBN-13: 9780981472539

Printed in the United States
220282BV00003B/1/P

9 781608 300082